Truck Stopped

SATAN'S DEVILS #11

Manda Mellett

COPYRIGHT

CAST OF CHARACTERS

Officers

Drummer – President- Old Lady – Sam
Children – Eli
Wraith – Vice President - Old Lady – Sophie
Children – Olivia
Heart – Secretary - Old Lady – Marcia
Children – Amy, Jacob, Isabel
Dollar – Treasurer
Peg – Sergeant-At-Arms - Old Lady – Darcy
Children – Noah
Blade – Enforcer - Old Lady – Tash
Joker – Road Captain
Children: Maya (niece)
Mouse – Computer Expert - Old Lady – Marianna

Patched Members

Bullet - Old Lady – Carmen
Beef
Hyde
Jekyll
Lady

Marvel
Roadrunner
Rock - Old Lady – Becca
Slick - Old Lady – Ella
Shooter
Viper Old Lady – Sandy
Drifter
Truck
Sharp

Prospects
Hound
Roadkill

Deceased Members
Adam
Buster
Tongue
Hank
Bertram

SATAN'S DEVILS MC

PROLOGUE

TWENTY YEARS IN THE FUTURE

*D*rummer...

"How you doing, Prez?"

I raise my eyebrow questioningly, then respond. "Just resting my bones, Sergeant-at-arms. Take a load off." I wave Peg to the Adirondack chair alongside mine. Two of the comfortable wooden chairs had been added to the veranda circling the clubhouse some years back, and come in useful for us old-timers. On the opposite side of the clubhouse door is a swing chair that's popular with the old ladies. It's vacant now, the light breeze making it sway gently back and forth.

Peg groans a little as he eases down, and rubs his thigh above his prosthetic leg.

"Troubling you?" I narrow my eyes.

"They might have sorted out the electronics, but even after all these years, the fundamental problem is still the stump."

Yeah, there's been many changes as the years have passed by. Some good, some not so good.

Peg catches me eyeing the bikes, parked up in a line. "Miss the thunder and roar of the old exhausts."

"Still got mine," I tell him.

He chuckles. "Me too. But most of these are electric. Fuck, who'd have thought we'd have charging points all around the club back in Bastard's day? Or that it would be easier to find electricity than be able to top up with gas?"

I have a mental image of my father turning over in his grave at how time has marched on. The bikes aren't even all Harleys. Some manufacturers were slow getting an affordable electric model to the market, and foreign bikes started to become popular.

"That fake electronic engine sound is nothing like the real thing, eh, Peg?" We both shake our heads. "But we've had some fun, over the years."

"Like that is it, old man? Reminiscing about shit in the past?"

I nod toward the mountains, golden in the late afternoon sun, and picking up my whisky tilt my glass toward the scenery. "Good to look back, Brother, and see how far we've come."

"You thinking about anything in particular?" He settles himself in, stretching out his long legs and smoothing a hand over a very grey beard.

"Yeah, I am. About the good and the bad. Currently settled on one of the darkest times for the club."

Peg gives me a 'which one?' look, then offers a few choices to choose from. "When Ella's sister was taken? Or when Sam disappeared? One of our run-ins with the Tucson crime family, the Herreras?" Peg snorts. "Or that crooked politician? About the time the wildfire nearly took out the club? Or the coup by Snake and the San Diego crew? Which particular darkest time are you thinking about?"

Again I shake my head, smirk, then frown. "Not thinking about external influences. I was thinking about the human ones. Specifically Truck and Allie. Those were dark days for the club."

He's quiet, thinking back but I don't rush him. We've got all the time in the world. I lean back my head and let the sun warm my face.

It's a few minutes before he speaks, "You're right," he eventually replies. "Showed how far a man, and a woman for that matter, can be stretched without snapping."

"You think they didn't snap?" Once more my head moves side to side. "Affected us all, Peg."

"Yeah. It did that. But you know what they say?"

Us two old-timers say it together, "What doesn't break us, makes us stronger."

It's my turn to chuckle, then my mirth fades. "Remember how it all started, Peg?"

CHAPTER ONE

SIX MONTHS AGO

_T_ruck…

"Take five."

As the captain gives us the sign to take a short break, I bend over, place my hands on my knees and draw in several deep breaths. The smoked-filled air does nothing to ease my lungs, but gradually my heart rate slows. This is my rest, my respite. It will last only a few moments before I'll return to the fray.

"Water, Truck?"

"Yeah." Gratefully I take a bottle from my teammate, Pete. Opening it, I down half the contents in one go, before taking a breath then finishing the rest. I'll sweat it out almost as fast as I can drink it.

"Got it beaten back at least." He nods toward the houses which we'd just managed to save, and to where another team is hosing them down with water, making sure the fire can't flare up and take hold once again. A few minutes ago we thought they'd been lost for certain, but fire's not only an unpredictable beast, but also ambivalent, seeming to veer between this target and that. All we can do is try to keep ahead of it, focusing on what's currently in its path, analysing wind direction and determining what type of fuel it might be able to find.

"This place is a fucking mess." Pete peers through the smoke. We might have saved this part of town, but in the direction he's looking, it's like a war zone.

Neither of us mention the bodies we've seen; some, having made unsuccessful attempts to escape, still in their burned out cars, others trapped in their homes. This is a serious fire. Some people have lost everything they've owned, while others have paid the ultimate price.

I slap his back. There's no point dwelling on the carnage we've seen. We need to focus on preventing more loss, counting every house and life plucked from the fire's grasp as a win. "We saved this part. All we can do is keep pushing it back."

We're tired, weary. The only sleep an occasional couple of hours in the truck for the past week as every effort is being put into fighting this fire. We're all exhausted, but none of us will give up. Fire isn't our enemy, it's a challenge, something to overcome. Something to try and keep at least one step ahead of.

I'm a firefighter from Arizona. Last year I was on the front line as fire roared down toward the compound of the Satan's Devils MC, the motorcycle club of which I'd been patched in as a full member shortly before joining a hotshot firefighting team and coming to California. Back in Tucson, my job involved putting out structural fires one at a time, or attending motor vehicle accidents. My twenty-four hour shifts were mostly spent keeping fit, sleeping, or sitting around bored, waiting for that call to come in. Occasionally we got fires that did try to beat us, and lasted longer than one shift, but that was, thankfully, the exception.

I'd joined the Army straight from high school, did a few tours in Afghanistan. Hated the conditions, both for us and the civilians we were half protecting, half suspecting of being insurgents, but loved the feeling of working with a team; always knowing there was always a man behind me or at my side who would never let me down.

We'd been routinely searching a village one morning when we lost a man to a sniper. A subsequent explosion didn't kill anyone but took the leg of one of the members from my unit. It wasn't the danger that made that my final tour, but the knowledge that it may not be me who could end up dead or injured, but the men who I'd become so close to. That was what I couldn't take and what had made me decide to leave.

What does a vet do when he's found a family that he then loses? He looks for another.

It hadn't taken long for me to decide to become a firefighter. I'd entered the Army not for money or prestige, nor to finance an education. I know my limits. Instead I was driven by a genuine need to serve, to protect my country. I may not have wanted to do that from a distance any longer, so joining the fire service meant I could give back at home. Not unlike serving with fellow soldiers, firefighters form a close-knit team, a brotherhood who work together, facing anything that's thrown at them.

I might not be the sharpest tool in the box, but I'm physically fit, and like most of my comrades I'd left back in Tucson, relish the opportunity to keep training and maintain my body at its peak.

Fighting the wildfire last year had been an inspiration. A challenge that made me accept the spot on a hotshot team when it opened up. That's how I've found myself in California, in one of the worst wildfires the state has ever seen.

My five minutes is almost up. My memories have reminded me of the reasons why I'm here, why I'm putting myself through this day after day. Sure, the area behind me is blackened and burned, but ahead? Well, that's our success. What we've saved. When it's safe to return, there'll be people smiling at the sight of their houses still standing. The grief of those who weren't so lucky must, for now, be put out of my mind. This fire will beat me mentally if I focus on what we were unable to save.

"Fucking hell," Pete swears beside me. "What the fuck does that asshole think they're doing?"

A four-by-four is driving along the road, where burning embers are still falling. It appears to be heading for one of the houses in front of us.

"I got this." As the car pulls up, I'm trotting over, my pace fast, my rage rising. Why the fuck do civilians think of coming back into the danger area? Can't this asshat see the fucking fire raging around them?

A loud whistle pierces my ears. "It's jumped the firebreak."

The loud, shouted warning causes me to look up, then quicken my steps until I'm running. A tree, tinder dry and a hundred foot high by my estimate, has burst into flames. Branches are already falling, firefighters redoubling their efforts to damp down, many looking up and starting to retreat. *If that tree falls it will be right on the house I'm heading to.*

"Get back!" I shout as a woman gets out of the SUV. "Get fucking back."

She looks at me, then the house, then, ignoring my frantic gesticulations, runs inside.

Shit. I have no option but to follow her in.

There's no electricity. The skies overhead are dark with smoke making it feel more like night than day—if that's indeed what it is. Like my fellow firefighters, I've lost all sense of time.

"Ma'am?" I call out as soon as I'm inside, peering through the gloom, trying to make out where she could be.

Then I hear a voice desperately calling a name.

"Smudge, Smudge. Come on, Smudge."

Following it, I come to a bedroom. I flick my flashlight around and in the light of the beam catch sight of a middle-aged woman on her knees, reaching for something under a bed.

"Ma'am, it's not safe. You've got to get out of here."

"Smudge," she calls out again, her voice now coaxing as she ignores me entirely.

I surmise it's a fucking cat or dog she's come back for.

"Ma'am," I say sternly. "Smudge can look after himself. You've got to get out of here, now."

"I'm not leaving *her*."

I'm going to pick this woman up and drag her out if she's not careful. In my mind's eye I see that burning tree outside.

"Ma'am. You have to leave, now."

"Got her!" she shouts triumphantly as she turns with a ball of grey fluff in her arms. "Need to get her travel crate—"

"Just fucking go!" From the corner of my eye, I see movement outside the window. With my hand on her back I push her so hard she stumbles, but luckily her movement takes her in the direction of the door.

That's the last of her that I see as a sound like thunder roars through my ears and I'm on the floor, a heavy weight crushing me and the smell of my burning skin reaching my nostrils.

The tree must have fallen. *I'm gone.* And all for a fucking cat.

I hope the woman got out.

I'm pinned. My arms, legs. All I can do is toss my head and try to dislodge whatever is red hot and burning my face. *My hand... what the fuck's happened to that?* My leg. I don't know which pain is more excruciating.

I hear shouts. *My team is coming for me.*

They might be too late.

$$\text{———————————}$$

CHAPTER TWO

*A*llie…

A man stops and rolls down his window. He looks clean enough, but who can tell? There's that normal flicker of concern inside me, but as usual I push it down. I've got rent to pay unless I want to be homeless. Optimistically, I tell myself, as usual, there's always a chance I could end up like Vivian in *Pretty Woman*, but my brain counters that there's fat chance tonight. Millionaires don't drive around in beat up Fords.

"Fifty dollars," I tell him in answer to his enquiry.

"Get in," he replies, his head turning to scan the area around us. Yeah, don't want any of his friends to see him picking up a prostitute off the street.

As I expected, he drives to a darkened parking lot used by nine-to-fivers during the day, and almost abandoned at night.

I get out without being told. He opens the back door.

I hold out my hand. "Money first."

He hands it over, then, as I fold it and put it in my pocket, he gestures for me to get inside. It's cramped as I expected, but just room to get enough of our clothes off for him to slide on a condom, and then I get down to giving him what he's paid for.

He grunts and thrusts and I make the sounds of encouragement I know he'll appreciate, and pretend I'm into it as much as he is. Truth is I let my mind wander.

"I found these in your room."

Shit! A box of condoms has landed in front of me. Mom should be pleased I'm practicing safe sex.

"Are these yours?"

It's a direct question, I can't lie to her. "Yes."

She carefully lays down the utensils she's holding, and focuses her stare on my face. The arrangement of her features don't give away her thoughts, but deep down I feel fear rising.

"We brought you up to be a God-fearing girl, Alison." Suddenly her mouth twists. "You go to church every Sunday, and prayer meetings during the week. How can you sit there in God's house knowing you've sinned?"

I don't see it as sinning. The boy who persuaded me to have sex was one that attends bible classes with me, in fact, he's the preacher's son. There had been no roar of thunder, no bolt of lightning had struck us. Did God really care? He'd made females one way, boys another, surely that was with a purpose?

I have no answer for her. So I stay quiet.

"Is this why you've been getting poor grades?"

No, it's not. I'm not academic in the slightest. I find reading hard, and math unintelligible.

Mom doesn't accept that, she just thinks I'm lazy. Unlike my brother, Jason, who's always top of his class and who can do no wrong in my mother's eyes, while I'm the one she's always watching to make a mistake. This time I have. I can tell by the way her face reddens that it's a big one.

"Is there a boy you're going to marry?"

"No, Mom." I gasp in surprise. I'm only sixteen. Plenty of time to think about marriage in the future, I certainly haven't looked at any of the boys I've dated in that way. For a second, I imagine a father finding

a box of condoms in his son's room. He'd probably slap him on the back and congratulate him with pride that he'd lost his virginity. A double standard for certain. Boys are supposed to have sex, but it seems everyone overlooks that in order to do that, there needs to be girls who put out for them. Unless all boys turn to rape.

The church I go to is patriarchal. Every week I listen to sermons where it's dictated women are supposed to be subservient to men. To be seen and not heard, to become good housewives, and heaven forbid that they enjoy opening their legs.

The teachings are nonsense, but my mother laps them up. Didn't stop my deadbeat father from leaving her for another woman, even though she'd had dinner on the table every night when he'd walked through the door.

"You're just like your father," Mom suddenly snarls. "I've done everything to bring you up right, yet here you are, sixteen and already a whore. You disgust me."

I should fall on my knees, beg her and God's forgiveness. Should let her drive me to church to pray away my sins. But I can't. I'm not sorry.

"I don't want you influencing Jason. I want you to go. Pack your clothes and leave this house. I can't have a sinner living here. What would Pastor Robson say if he found out?"

I've seen the way the pastor leers when he sees us young girls. He'd probably lick his lips and wish it had been him I'd lost my virginity to. But of course, my mother would never dream he'd have thoughts like that.

"Mom, you don't mean it." I heard the words, but don't believe them. "It's condoms, that's all." At least I'd listened in sex ed, brief though that lesson was. "I can't leave, I have nowhere to go."

"You should have thought of that before you started encouraging the boys."

"If you're worried about Jason, he's only eight years old for good-ness sake. I don't talk to him about my boyfriends. I'll keep it that way."

"Jason is pure, Alison. I won't have him corrupted."

I love my brother, of course I do, but I can't help being jealous he's far and away Mom's favourite.

"I mean it. I can't have you living in my house. Go now. Run off with one of those boys you've been playing around with."

"Mom…"

Suddenly she advances and slaps me across the face. Stunned at her unusual violence, I step back. "You're no daughter of mine. Go find your father, that's who you take after. You'll never amount to anything. Your whole life you've been nothing but trouble!"

I knew she preferred Jason, but I never expected she'd wash her hands of me. "Mom, let's talk about this—"

"Nothing to talk about. Now go pack."

I stand, stunned. I'd come in from school, hungry and expecting dinner. She intends to throw me out without even offering that. "Mom, please—"

"You should have thought of the implications when you went with those boys. I want you out of here before Jason comes home."

Jason is at football practice. After that, he will be having dinner with his friend. Mom chose a time when he was out of the way.

She's turned her back, and it's then it hits home that she's one hundred percent serious.

Where can I go?

Carla's house. For tonight anyway.

I'm sixteen, and homeless.

A final grunt, followed by a bark of satisfaction. I clench my muscles and issue a groan. He sits up, removes the condom and zips his pants before opening the door without thanks or conversation. When I get out, he locks the passenger door and drives off, his tyres screeching as he peels out of the parking lot.

Sometimes the johns are more accommodating and offer a lift back to where they picked me up. Others, like him, have difficulty dealing with the guilt that they've gone with a prostitute, and want nothing more than to distance themselves from the act.

At least he didn't try to kiss me. I may have watched *Pretty Woman* too many times in the past, but the idea that kissing on the lips was intimate had become my mantra as well. The connection of mouth to mouth was something reserved for my future partner. If I'm ever lucky enough to find one, that is.

Another trick turned, and then another. A hundred and fifty dollars in my pocket and it's been a good night. I make my way to my car to drive back to my shoddy apartment. I can't afford much else, some nights I make nothing at all.

As I walk the darkened streets, I consider that I've been doing this for two years. My mind drifts back in time once again.

After I'd left my mother's, I'd visited my best friend from school, and stayed there that night. But she was also from a God-fearing church-going family, and one phone call from my mother to hers meant I was out on my own the next evening. Carla was forbidden to ever speak to me again, in case having sex was contagious.

It was when my sixteen-year-old self was walking the streets the night after my mother had thrown me out, wondering where it would be safe to settle down, thinking I was going to have to learn about shelters, when a car had stopped alongside. The first of many over the next twenty-four months.

I'd had sex before, it hadn't been earth shattering. The handful of boys I'd been with had been as inexperienced as me. Truth was, it hadn't meant much to me one way or the other, and I couldn't see what all the fuss was about. But they seemed to be happy after, and I had the power to put a smile on their face.

Turns out it wasn't dissimilar with a stranger. The only difference was, I had money in my pocket after.

Of course, there were some johns rougher than others, and as I got to know the friendlier of my fellow streetwalkers, I began to appreciate the risk that the career I'd fallen into carried.

"Hey. You got money?"

Shit. I'd been thinking so hard I'd forgotten to scan my surroundings.

"No," I lie to the rough-looking man who's appeared before me.

"You've been working, slut. I saw you get into a car. So you can fucking give me your earnings."

Give him what I've worked hard for? Not freaking likely. I eye him up, regretting I left my pepper spray in my car. The vehicle I can already see, so close yet so far.

"I don't have any money. I owed it to someone." I hold up my empty hands, showing I carry no purse.

"Empty your pockets, bitch."

Placing my hand in my back pocket of my shorts, I pull out my car keys and hold them so one is facing out. I launch forward, my attack taking him by surprise. I stab at his face, then, taking advantage of his shock, lunge toward my car.

He's fast, grabbing hold of my hair, yanking me back hard and throwing me down onto the pavement. I feel hands groping my shorts and hear a triumphant shout as he finds my hard earned money.

"You cut me, bitch, you're going to pay for that."

Oh shit. I should just have given it to him in the first place.

"What's going on? Get off her or I'll call the cops."

A car has slowed down, and a woman is shouting out the window. With my money in his hands, my attacker jumps up and runs off.

The breath has been knocked out of me. Pulling myself into a sitting position, I suck air deep into my lungs, fully expecting my saviour will drive away. Instead, I hear a door slam, and high heels tapping on the pavement. Surprised, I look up.

"You hurt?"

"No. But I was robbed."

She eyes the clothes I'm wearing. No bra, a short cropped tee, and shorts which barely cover my ass. No disguising how I earned what I'd lost. I wait for a lecture about how I make a living.

"Christ, you know, I see you, and remember how lucky I am."

Yeah. She's probably got a husband and family.

I wait for her to leave, but she surprises me, reaching out her hand to help me to my feet.

"You on drugs?"

That's one thing I've never resorted to. "No. The money was for rent."

"Hmm, there are easier ways of earning it."

"Not for me," I say quickly, adding in my defence, "I never finished my education, I've got no other skills."

"Bitch, don't worry about that. What I'm thinking about, you're perfectly equipped for."

Is she a pimp or a madam recruiting? I've avoided those as well.

"I'm doing fine. Thank you for stopping." If she hadn't, I might have ended up in the emergency room.

"Listen for a moment, I think you might like my suggestion. My name's Jill." She holds out her hand.

Automatically I take it, and respond as expected. "Alison. Allie." Then shake my head, unable to imagine she could offer anything that I want.

"I live with the Satan's Devils MC. You heard of them?" I nod, no one lives in Tucson without seeing them flying around on their motorbikes. "It's a small club. A couple of the men have old ladies, but the rest are single. They provide me with room and board, and money for anything extra I want. In return, I fuck them."

My eyes open wide. I had not expected that.

She leans in and lowers her voice even though there's no one within hearing. "Have you ever been fucked by a biker?" I think for a second whether any of my customers may have looked like they could own a motorcycle, but none come to mind. My head moves side to side, so she continues, with a grin and a lick of her lips. "Then you've never been fucked. They use their cocks like they ride their bikes, hard, putting their hearts and souls into it. Mmm mmm. I'm never left unsatisfied."

I don't think I've ever been satisfied. She's piqued my curiosity. "And it's only them you fuck?"

"Mostly. Sometimes there are visiting chapters, and I have to be available, but as they're all bikers, it's all good. They can be rough, but that's their way. They take care of their women, would never hurt them or raise a hand to them. It's much safer than this." She waves her hand around. "There were two of us, but Slutty had to leave because her father was ill. They're too much for me to handle alone."

She's suggesting they have a vacancy?

"Want me to ask at the club if there's an opening for you? You may be able to come see for yourself, and, er, have an interview."

I can imagine what form that would take. From what she's said, though, I might enjoy it.

"I might be interested," I offer, cautiously.

She goes to her car and opens her purse. By the street lights I can see her writing on a piece of paper, then brings her pen and notepad back over to me. "That's me, now give me yours. I'll have a word and be in touch. Oh, and they'll want to know you're clean."

"I can get tested." I try to do that regularly anyway.

She looks at me, *really* looks at me, from my face to my breasts and then to my ass and thighs. "I reckon you'd be a good fit."

For the first time in two years, I think things may be looking up. I'd still be whoring, but to men I'd get to know. To live on a compound, and not walk the streets, to not put my life in danger every time I get into a stranger's car sounds like Utopia.

Put it this way, if the chance was offered, how could I turn it down?

CHAPTER THREE

PRESENT DAY

*A*llie…

"'Bout time Drummer let you off bartending duties, Allie. It's all you seem to do nowadays. I can think of a far better use of your time."

As Marvel winks suggestively, I shrug and smile as wide as I can. "I don't mind. The other girls are shit at this anyway. You'd only complain if Diva was here. She always gets the drinks muddled up." Glancing across the room I watch as the aforementioned whore and her friend, Paige, are enthusiastically snuggling up to Road. It won't be long before he takes them both into one of the crash rooms, which gives me an idea. "Marvel, why don't you go with Road?" They've all played together enough times before.

"Nah," he shakes his head. "I'm in the mood for something different." He turns, surveys the room, then calls out, "Pussy? Come take over for Allie."

He doesn't explain why. It's obvious.

I'm employed, if you want to call it that, as a sweet butt for the Satan's Devils MC and have been for ten years now, acting as a whore in exchange for room, board and pocket money. It was good to get off the streets, and I don't regret a minute of the time I've spent here. For the first nine years, I worked solely on my back. But the club members seem to be finding old ladies, so there's not so much demand for whores anymore. As a result the sweet butts double as bartenders to free up the prospects. I don't mind, recently, tending bar is what I enjoy most.

But it's not all sunshine and roses. Jill, the woman who'd been responsible for setting me up in this life, had made two cardinal mistakes. One was falling for a member who didn't return her affection, and the second, betraying the club. She'd been tortured and killed by a rival MC a year back.

She'd become a bitch, and I didn't regret her no longer being here, but I wouldn't have wanted her dead. She'd introduced me to this lifestyle which had been a revelation after working the streets. Johns paid to get off, not to give a good time to the woman. Bikers though, Jill had been right. While some of the time they're just users, other times they'd pride themselves on making the woman they're with come.

First orgasm I ever had had been with Adam. A complete surprise as I hadn't thought I was capable of enjoying sex. That first time was an eye opener, and was just the start of good things to come.

Of course, I'm a whore. My only value being in how well I service the men. If I ever stopped pleasing them, I'd be cast loose.

I've watched old ladies enter the club, it seems like there's a rash of them now as one by one the members have found their one, the person who completes them. I'm realistic, unlike Jill, or Chrissie for that matter who'd once set her sights on Wraith, I understand a biker *never* takes a whore as his old lady. No one wants a woman all his brothers have had.

There'll be no escape, no out for me. I'll stay what I am. A sweet butt, just another term for a whore. Am I ashamed of what

I do? Fuck no. Perhaps being constantly available to a pool of men isn't what most women would aspire to, but it's not as bad as it sounds. Sure, I have to fuck whoever wants me, but hey, I like sex, why not admit it?

What makes me any different from the men? No one bats an eye at the thought that they use a woman just to get off. Why shouldn't I do the same? I've got needs, and have no thoughts about or desire to settle down. Why tie myself to one man when I can have all the variety I want? If at times they use and discard me, the other times when they make sure I enjoy it too make up for that.

The thought of sticking to just one man? Well, that's boring, isn't it? I've heard the members here joke enough with the married men about how tedious it must be to keep to just one pussy, and have shaken my head, knowing exactly how they feel. Men's cocks, and what they do with them, are all different.

Except... I frown seeing Marvel still trying to attract Pussy's attention.

Marvel's a good man like all the men here. He doesn't treat me as a whore, but a woman he's going with for the night. He wouldn't leave me wanting. He'd take me to a crash room, make me come, probably with his tongue or just fingers if that's his preference tonight, then I'll let him fuck me however he wants, and knowing him, I'll have another orgasm.

But tonight, I'm not feeling it.

I lean over the bar and whisper into his ear. "Marvel, I can't, I'm sorry. It's the wrong time of the month."

His eyes narrow, and his lips thin, but he doesn't say a word. When Pussy, at last, comes over, he dismisses her, gets up and leaves.

"What's up with him?" Pussy's head tilts to the side as she watches him stride stiffly across the room, her brow furrowed.

"I told him I wasn't up for it." I grab a clean cloth and start wiping the bar top.

"You never are recently," she observes, shrewdly. "You keep

palming them off onto the rest of us. Not that I mind." She turns, and leans against the wood, her eyes surveying the room. "With all the men here getting ol' ladies, there's barely enough single men left to keep us occupied."

"There's Road." I nod toward the man who's walking off, as I expected, with Diva on one arm and Paige on the other. "Marvel, of course. Dollar, Shooter and Jekyll."

"You missed Drifter."

"You tried him yet?"

She winks. "Yeah, he's young, but he'll learn. I think Matt will patch in soon, which will be more fresh meat."

There's one other member, but neither of us mention him. There are six single men, if Matt patches in, seven, and four whores. "If more men catch the old lady bug, us sweet butts will soon outnumber the bachelors."

"Not enough to go around? Is that why you stay behind the bar all the time, to give us more of a chance?"

I shrug. "Does it matter?" Paige, Diva and Pussy don't like bartending so much, preferring to do the job they're supposed to. But I don't mind at all. It's become an excuse, and if I take all the shifts, none of the girls object. Or the men. I know all their drink preferences before they need to speak. I've also become adept at a cocktail or two, and have the fridge stocked with wine for the old ladies.

"Rather you than me. Hey, look who just walked in."

It's Shooter. I grin. As a prospect he was given the name Spider as he was as spindly as fuck, all long skinny arms and legs. In the past three years, he's muscled up. Like any new member brought to the table, he'd wasted no time getting to know us girls. I know only too well why Pussy's face has lit up. He might not have the biggest cock here, but he's certainly learned what he can do with it. Us sweet butts may have been responsible for that.

I'm not surprised when Pussy makes a beeline for him, her hand resting on his chest. "Want some action, big boy?"

I grin. Pussy certainly does.

"Allie? Can you come here?"

I glance around the room. There's a number of men, but with Pussy, Diva and Paige tied up at the moment, if I leave my post…

"Hound. Take over for Allie," the loud voice bellows across the room.

As one of the new prospects comes running over, eager to impress, I realise there's no way I can avoid talking to the prez.

Not that I've got anything against Drummer. He treats all of us girls with respect, always has, even when he'd have one, or more of us in his bed each night. Now what that man can do with his dick, well, it would put the Kama Sutra to shame, and I'm sure he could teach Casanova a thing or two. Yeah, being called to Drummer's room, or having him take you over the pool table, wasn't a chore at all. Even now I could get wet just thinking about it.

All that changed when he met his old lady. If anyone had asked back then, I would have said the prez was one man who'd never settle down or be faithful, but I'd have lost that bet. Since finding Sam, he's not once looked at anyone else. What he wants me for now will have nothing to do with his sexual appetite, that's reserved for his old lady.

It's only lately I had been wondering what it must be like to have such a man focused only on you.

"Prez? What can I do for you?"

As I stand nervously in the doorway to his office, I remember a few years back, the answer would have involved anatomy, pussy, ass or mouth. Now I can't predict what he's going to say.

Unless… There are too many whores here?

That's going to come. But surely, I wouldn't be the first out. I've been here the longest, and am now in charge of keeping the other girls in line. *But I'm getting older.* Not for the first time I wonder what will happen when I'm no longer attractive. At twenty-eight, I can't deny I have wrinkles where I had none before. Sweet butts don't have retirement plans, and I have no idea what I'll do when I'm no longer wanted here. It would be like being thrown out of my home all over again.

Perhaps it's that he's bringing a new girl in?

Nah, doubt it. We have enough to keep all the single men satisfied.

"Sit down, Al."

He points to the chair in front of his desk, and runs his hand over his short salt and pepper beard, while staring at me with his steel-grey eyes. My hands twist in my lap when I sit, my legs cross, then uncross. I feel like a kid back at school being summoned to see the principal.

For a moment, he lets me stew. Then he leans forward, resting his elbows on the desk. "Marvel has just been to see me."

Shit.

"You got medical problems I don't know about?"

His question brings my head up. *What does he mean?*

Oh. "No, Drummer. There's nothing wrong with me."

"Marvel said you're fuckin' bleedin' again. Same as last week and the week before that." Drummer's eyes narrow. "If that's the case, I think you need a check-up, girl."

I press my lips together, and stare down at my hands, picking at my nails.

"Look, Al. I respect you. Respect all the girls. I know you don't have a written job description, but we all know what you're supposed to do. I'm pleased with how much you work the bar, you do that like a pro, but that's not all we expect of you."

I know. I'm well aware what I should be doing, but lately, it's not what I want. I used to love being the centre of attention if only for a few hours. I loved feeling skin on skin, loved a man moving inside me, loved the power that gave me, even when the man mistakenly thought that he held all the cards. For brief moments I was in control, had him in the palm of my hand. But these last few weeks?

"You want to leave?"

What? No! But how do I get out of this. "Drummer, I… I don't know what I want to do. If I left…" *Where would I go? What would I do?*

"You were eighteen when you came here, Allie. I remember it well. Jill…" A look of pain crosses his face, it's echoed on mine too.

Jill could be a bitch, but before she'd fixated on Rock and subsequently betrayed the club, she'd been someone I called my friend, overlooking some of her bitchier moments as she'd been responsible for changing my life.

I watch as he pulls himself back from the past. "Jill recruited you. You've always been a good fit with the club, and loyal too. It's been, what, ten years now?"

I nod.

"Wouldn't think the worse of you if you wanted to leave." He stands, turns, and regards the Satan's Devils' flag hanging behind his desk. "Club's changed, Al. You've seen that. Huh," he chuckles, "all those years ago? I'd have laughed in your face if you'd suggested I'd find my old lady. Never thought Wraith would settle down. Rock, Blade, Peg, Slick… Christ, even Mouse. Dart and Beef have even left Tucson to be with their women."

"Dart and Beef are VPs now, and that's down to you, Drummer. You raise good brothers here." Credit given where credit due.

A chin lift shows his appreciation for my comment. "Fact is, Allie, the chapter now has more married men than single."

He's going to say what I'm dreading. "You think the ratio means there are too many whores here?"

His eyes widen. "Fuck, no. There'd be a riot if I got rid of you or any of the sweet butts, the club can never have too much pussy. Nah, Allie. But I do want to talk about *you.*"

My fingernails are fascinating me again. *What would I do if he ordered me to go with Marvel?* I could do it if I had to. Christ, I've had enough experience when I've not been in the mood, but somehow, the bikers have ways of turning that around. Sure, there's been times when I've felt I've been used, but mostly I end up enjoying the experience. It's just… *If he asks me to explain, how can I?*

"You're twenty-eight, Allie." He states my age.

Is he going to tell me I'm too old?

"Wouldn't surprise me if you see everyone around you hooking up, and want that for yourself. Thing is, girl, if that's what you want, you're not going to find what you're looking for here."

"I'm not looking for an old man," I lie, knowing, that's the root of my issues.

He shakes his head. "Brothers don't fall for whores, darlin'. You know that as well as I do. Problem is, we've all had you. Yeah, I'm not pretending to you, Sam or anyone else. I used to fuck you, and, with the exception of Joker and Lady almost everyone else has too."

His words are a stark reminder.

"Drummer, I'm only too well aware of that." I flash a brief smile, while simultaneously squirming.

"If you want a man of your own, Allie, maybe you should leave the club." He runs his hand over his face again. "You've given us ten years. You came here young, so you're still in your prime. Be easy for you to find someone if that's what you want."

My head shakes, it seems like it's of its own volition.

"No? Well, it has to be something else. You don't want to leave the club, but you don't want to fuck the brothers. Avoided them for weeks now, and, according to Marvel, you weren't putting your heart into it for months before that." Drummer's eyes sharpen again. "Playing the field isn't what you now want, is it, Allie?"

I feel my brow crease as I look up to meet his eyes.

"How long has it been since you fucked a brother and enjoyed it?"

I gesture dismissively as if I have no idea.

"I'll hazard a guess, shall I?"

Another rise and fall of my shoulders.

"I'd guess it's been six months."

He's right. I can pin point the day, the hour, the very minute. At first, it hadn't been a conscious decision, but since then, I've not enjoyed being with another man. When I tried, it was mechanical. Then when we got the news, I'd even felt ashamed. *Maybe if I was faithful to a dream, he'd recover and live.*

"You've been clever, Allie. Men don't gossip like women do, and, there's still the other three whores around. Your excuses worked, to a point. But Marvel has reached the end of his tether with you, and others will soon too."

It sounds like I'll be instructed to pack my bags. Pack up ten years of my life. Then what would I do? I've no skills, no education to speak of. No way of supporting myself. This time I know what would be waiting for me, so I don't want to go back to working the streets. I just couldn't. Desperate, I ask, "What if I just tended bar, Drummer? No need for pay, just somewhere to stay."

He's shaking his head. "Nah. That won't do."

"Drummer…"

His fingers rap the table. "I'm going to tell you how it is. Then I'm going to give you a job to do."

"I'll do anything Drummer."

"Except fuck," he replies, drily. He continues, "I've seen the way your eyes light up whenever his name is mentioned. Working the bar you overhear more than you should, but we trust you, even when you lean toward the speaker when we discuss how he's doing. You're that eager for news, you can't hide it." He pauses to let it sink in how I've given myself away.

An apology starts to come to my lips, but he gives me no time to speak. "The last man you willingly fucked was Truck, wasn't it?" Without waiting for confirmation, he carries on.

"Truck had just been patched in, first and only whore he ever touched was you. Then he went to California and got hurt."

He's telling me nothing new.

"We don't know much more than Truck's on the mend. That he hasn't made an appearance at the club makes me suspect he's come back a changed man." Again his fingers drum softly. "How much do you know, Allie?"

"I don't know anything, Drummer," I whisper, admitting my hopes and dreams which will never come true. "Why he affected me so much, I don't know. But since him, and then, when we thought he could die…"

"You wanted no one else to touch you."

"Stupid of a whore, right?"

Suddenly he stands and looms over the desk. "Was I stupid, Al? Wasn't I a whore? Christ, I've had more women than you've had men. Probably fucked more than you too. One, two, three or more in one night, individually or all together. But I'm a man, that's allowed. The title manwhore is worn with pride, not with shame."

His words echo the thoughts I so often have. *Why is it different for a woman?* But there's one thing he's not taking into account. "You give me a home, feed me, and enough money for me to buy the essentials. I think that counts as being paid. And that's the definition of a prostitute."

He plants that steel gaze on me, then, out of the blue, he starts to laugh. "If that's the case, I doubt there's a woman alive who hasn't been paid one way or another for her services. Bought drinks, a meal. A night out. Depending how hard to get she plays it."

"I doubt you ever had to pay." I give him an admiring glance. Drummer's in his early forties, but still looks in his prime. The grey streaks in his hair not detracting in any way. And as for that body under his clothes, well, from memory I know, Sam, his old lady, is one lucky woman.

He chuckles again. "Even a one-night hook up means

opening your wallet. Can't pick a girl up at a bar and expect her to pay."

But however he dresses it up, I'm a whore, and that's going to count against me for the rest of my life. Drummer's right. If I want to find a man of my own, I've got to look outside the club. Trouble is, the one man I want, though absent, is still a member.

"You like Truck?"

His direct question takes me by surprise. It forces the truth out of me. "God help me, but yes. I didn't expect, Drummer… I'm sorry, I didn't think it would affect what I do."

"But after you went with him, you didn't want anyone else."

That's the truth of it. I don't understand it myself. Never expected to find a cock that I thought I could settle for. *But it wasn't his cock. It was the whole package, the man himself who came along with it.* For six months I've yearned for something I can't have, and I hate myself for it.

"Okay," he leans forward. "Truck's back in Tucson, but he hasn't come back to the club."

I've got eyes and ears. "He hasn't spoken to his firefighting crew either." I'd overheard Darcy talking to Peg.

He winks. "Knew you heard a lot from behind the bar."

What can I say? People treat a bartender as if they are deaf and invisible.

"It's worrying. Accept that man went through something terrible, something that means he's turned his back on all his friends, but hell, we just want him home." Again Drummer smooths his beard. "He's still a brother, and if he's hurting, he needs his family around him." He pauses, then his eyes sharpen, and I couldn't look away even if I wanted to. "I want you to go see him. Make him see you. Bring him back to us, Allie."

I stop breathing, trying to compute his instruction. "I know Sam's tried to visit. A lot of brothers too. Peg—"

"He won't open the door to anyone," he interrupts. "Just speaks through that damn intercom he's had installed. We've all tried."

My brow furrows. "Why do you think I'll succeed when he wouldn't talk to you? Surely I'm the last person he'd want to see?"

Drummer's always been straight with me. Never straighter than now. "I'm making the assumption his cock's still in working order. You can offer something others here can't. So that's your job, Allie. See him, fuck him, and bring him back to us. I'll make it clear at church you're no longer available."

I gasp at the final sentence. It's what I wanted, but more than I expected. "Drummer, I'll do anything you want me too. Tend bar, clean—"

"Fuck, woman, we got prospects for that. And, if this goes as well as I hope, I think you'll have enough on your hands bringing Truck back into the fold."

TWENTY YEARS in the future - Drummer

"WE PATCHED TRUCK IN."

I nod. "Even though he didn't know how long he'd be away, or whether he'd ever come back. Fuckin' brave man, proud to have him as a member." I glance up at the sun, noticing the shadows from a saguaro have grown longer. "It couldn't have been more than a couple of weeks or so before we'd got the news he'd been injured saving a woman and child."

"Huh," Peg exclaims. "Even that was fuckin' shit. It was a woman, but not a child." He snorts.

"What the fuck did we know at the time? We got information second, third hand, heard nothing at all from the man. All we heard was it was touch and go for a while. I went to LA with Slade, remember him?"

"Truck's captain, wasn't he?"

"Yeah." I raise and lower my chin and resume, "All they'd tell us

was that Truck was going to stay in the land of the living, but nothing more. When he came round he refused to see us, either together or separately. Fuckin' hard leaving a brother alone, but what can you do if he refuses help?"

Peg doesn't answer the rhetorical question.

"You tried though, didn't you? May have had to wait until he came back to Tucson, but you had a fuckin' plan. Like always." He shoots me a look of admiration. "But what the fuck made you think of using a whore to get through to him?"

Reaching out my fist, I bump him on the arm. "You might not be able to remember, Brother, but most men think with their cocks."

"I remember just fine," Peg snarls. Then realises how that might sound. "And my cock's still in full working order." He winks. "Compensates for my missing leg."

Hmm. Don't think I want to think about Peg's cock, nor the Jacob's ladder piercing we've all heard about. Over the years and more than once, I've had to tell Sam that no, I'm definitely not getting my fucking cock pierced. However much Darcy seems to admire what Peg manages to do with it.

"Dad!"

Peg holds out his arms. Lisa deviates from her direct path to the clubhouse and comes over to give him a kiss. He's proud as punch of his daughter, as we all are of our kids. "I've decided what I want for my twentieth birthday."

"No motorcycle, hon, I've told you before."

She pouts at him. "Dad, please."

Peg sighs. "I'll think about it and speak to your mom."

She'll get her way, I'm sure of it. That kid has her dad wrapped around her little finger.

"I want to join Sam's club," she continues, with a wink in my direction.

As I'm thinking there used to be a time when the kids were in awe of me, Lisa blows another kiss toward her dad, straightens and continues into the clubhouse.

"*Your old lady has a lot to answer for, Drummer,*" *Peg mock chides me.*

I smile, and shake my head. Some years ago now, Sam started an old ladies' riding club. It had begun as a joke with just her and Marcia. Blade succumbed and let Tash have a motorcycle, then, surprisingly, it was Becca who persuaded Rock to get her a ride. Just as some of the other old ladies who came along later convinced their men to let them have bikes. Of course, they might think they're independent, but there's always a brother or two going along on their rides with them, and a prospect following in the crash truck. The Satan's Devils Ladies Riding Club. For a second I wonder what my father would have had to say about that. Nothing good, I imagine.

"*Anyway, back to Allie.*" *Peg reminds me what we were discussing.* "*Did you really think it would work?*"

I shrug. "*I took a gamble. Something had to give. If she hadn't been able to get through his door, I was going to break the fucker down myself.*"

"*I'd have been right behind you.*"

Peg would. He's always had my six.

CHAPTER FOUR

Allie...

Go see Truck and bring him home.

It sounded so simple when Drummer laid my task out. I'd been ecstatic. It was exactly what I wanted to do. Knowing others had been unsuccessful in their attempts to step over his threshold, I didn't dare think of visiting Truck by myself. It wasn't something a whore would do, but now I've received a direct instruction from the prez, I've got an excuse to try and see the man I haven't been able to get out of my head for six months. It's a task I'm determined I won't fail.

I know it won't be easy. *Why would he want to see me if he didn't want to talk to anyone else?*

Unless, as Drummer suspects, conversation is the last thing on his mind, and he's in need of some relief.

My issue is, I want him to see me as a woman, not a sweet butt.

I spend more time than it should take trying to get ready, veering between one outfit and another. *Do I dress like I do on the compound? Skimpy top and short skirt?* Would he be unable to resist? It would certainly advertise what I had to offer, but would signify nothing else.

In the end I settle for jeans and a new tee, even going so far as to wear a bra. I put on makeup, and then scrub it all off, staring at my reflection. I've been Allie, the sweet butt, for so long, I don't even know who the woman is underneath. Maybe now's a good time to find out.

Reapplying a little eyeliner and mascara, then dusting my face with powder, I think I've enhanced what I am naturally, without going over the top. When I've finished, I put my phone and wallet in my back pocket, then walk down to the auto-shop at the entrance to the compound. I'll be borrowing one of the club's SUVs as I normally do if I go into town. My old beater died several years back, and it wasn't worth trying to replace it.

"You look nice." Slick stands from leaning over a bike. "Different."

I blush from the compliment. Nice is the look I was going for, but it's not how I usually appear. "Can I borrow a car?"

"Sure. You know where the keys are. Going anywhere fun?"

"I hope so." My response is heartfelt. Truthfully, I have no idea what I'll be walking into.

Grabbing the first set of keys that I come to, I go to the Nissan and adjust the seat which had obviously been used last by someone much taller than me. I then take a moment to sort out the mirrors, realising I'm delaying my exit from the compound. Finally, I program the address Drummer had given me into the GPS.

Truck. *I'm going to see Truck.* While accepting he might not let me in, there's still a kernel of excitement inside.

I'd first seen Truck when he came to the compound with Peg's old lady, Darcy, and her firefighting friends. It was easy to see how the big man had gotten his name. He was tall, a fraction shorter than Peg so maybe six feet three or four, and broad. Not fat, but muscular. The first thing that had caught my attention was his easy laugh and playfulness on his face. An energy too, a buzzing excitement around him. He was totally bald with a shaved head, and having a nicely shaped skull, it had suited him.

I had been shocked when he joined the Satan's Devils as a prospect.

Being a firefighter put him on a different level than the other men the club had had prospecting for them over the years. For a start, his shift pattern had to be accommodated. Then there were some activities he was excluded from. I'm not stupid. Though whores are kept out of club business, we all knew when something was going down. Men would disappear, but Truck would be elsewhere. Due to his government job, he was kept away from the more unsavoury elements of club life. He'd have had to have been deaf and blind not to have suspicions, but seemed to accept what the club did, as long as he could turn away and have no direct involvement.

A prospect needs to put up with shit, prove over his time that he can be trusted. I'd watched Truck, knowing from early on he was going to make the grade. It was in his attitude. No task was too small to give it his whole attention. If I was asked to score his performance, I'd give him ten out of ten.

Of course, all this I saw from a distance. As a prospect, the whores were out of bounds to Truck, and would be until he was a member.

I remember the day he'd got patched in as it happened so fast and surprised even him. When I'd been with him that night, he was still hyped up and shared some of the details. He'd thought he was going to have to turn in his prospect patch as he was assigned to a hotshot team and would be away from the area for some undetermined time. But instead of letting him leave, Drummer held a vote on making him a full member, even though there was a chance it would be a very long time before he could take his seat at the table.

Truck had been humbled that night, and over the moon with the new patches on his cut, even though he was leaving his newly adorned leather vest behind. As he had an early start the next morning, he hadn't gotten as drunk as most men do when they reach the end of their prospecting time, but he had made use of his new status to go with a sweet butt. The one he chose had been me.

I was the lucky one. Truck had fucked as though his life depended on it. It was part celebration that he was now a full member, part recognition what he was heading into would be dangerous.

I'm used to being fucked by the brothers, it's been my life for ten years. Most, knowing they don't want to lead a whore on, shy away from intimacy such as the meeting of lips. That hadn't bothered me, I believed in that philosophy too. It wasn't different with Truck, the only time Truck had kissed me was when he placed his lips against my cheek when it was time for him to go.

In every respect it was exactly the same as all other encounters. Save in one way. The effect he had on me. When he had walked out that door early the next morning, I couldn't forget him.

He'd gotten to me, like no one else ever had, and like I expected no one ever would. From that point on, I didn't want anyone else to touch me. Of course I had to, it was my job, but I resented every man who came inside me. When I knew Truck had been hurt, my unease with other men got worse. I just couldn't rid myself of the feeling that they were eroding the memory of him being in me. Time passing made it harder, not easier to forget him.

Stupid, stupid whore. I bang the steering wheel in frustration.

But my honesty with myself can't subdue the burn of excitement inside me. *I'm going to see Truck again.* Does he remember that night? Or was it just one more fuck to him? *Would it be better to count my losses, tell Drummer I can't go through with this?*

Six months hasn't wiped out the memory of his touch.

Six months. Truck's had a long road to recovery.

What's happened to the man I knew for a year, and had in

my bed just one night? How badly was he injured? Why this refusal to let anyone in, or to come home to the club?

Often men joining the MC are damaged, they might come back from overseas with PTSD, but find comfort and support within the family. *Why is Truck not coming to us for help? Why is he hiding himself away?*

Am I going to get my questions answered? Or, will he just refuse to have anything to do with me. He hasn't let anyone else in, why should his first visitor be a whore?

The excitement changes increasingly to nervousness as I drive into Tucson. *What happens if I fail?*

No, not an option. Apart from my personal investment in seeing Truck, Drummer's tasked me with this because he's worried about the firefighter become club member. There are many selfish reasons why I want to see the man again, but at the bottom of it all, it's Truck who matters. Whatever's happened to him, Truck needs his friends. There's a reason he's eschewing both his families, but whatever he's dealing with, he shouldn't be doing it alone. He needs to let people in.

The GPS, as expected, leads me to the right street and I find the apartment block quite easily. After I park in the lot around the back, my hands shake as I press the button to lock the car. He'd been injured so badly it was touch and go for a while, but no one knows what really happened to him, only that it was bad enough that he's only recently returned from rehab to Tucson.

All we otherwise know, courtesy of Darcy, who's a firefighter herself, is that he was invalided out of the service. A sign he'll never regain full health.

Losing the job which he loved would have devastated him. Another reason he needs the club. *What state will he be in, mentally or physically?* No one's been able to warn me what to expect. I vow then and there, whatever his injuries, I'll accept him. It's the man inside I want, even if he now inhabits a broken body.

I straighten my back. *I can do this.* With a purposeful stride, I walk around to the front of the building.

Truck's apartment is on the first floor, his entrance direct to the street. I find the right number and knock on the door. A buzz, and then a voice through the intercom.

"What are you doing here?"

His voice. So familiar and yet so strange. Huskier, deeper than I remembered from before, and that tone of anger.

"Truck, I've come to see how you are. Can you let me in?"

After a pause, a snide voice comes, "Drummer got you making house calls now?"

He was never spiteful before. I run through everything in my head. Drummer's tried and failed to get in, and so, apparently have other brothers as well as his firefighting team and friends. If I just say I'm here to talk to him, he'll treat me the same way. What have I to offer that the others couldn't? *Sex without ties.*

I'll play on his assumption. "Yeah. Drummer thought you might be in need of a woman." Inwardly I groan. *I've told him I'm here as a whore. Way to get him to see you as anything different.* But if it gets me through the door, I'll count it as a step in the right direction.

Maybe he's not as desperate as Drummer thinks. He may have someone else. A chill settles inside me when I realise I hope he doesn't. But who knows? Good looking man like Truck could easily have a nurse who's been attracted to his fine figure, handsome face…

"I could use a fuck."

Duel emotions flood through me, elation and disgust. The crude response indicates he's going to let me inside, but for one thing only. *After all these months, is this what I want?* I could walk away, or, I could step through the door if he opens it, and let him use me. For a second, I'm torn. Then realise, whatever the reason, I'll have achieved my objective, succeeded where everyone else has failed.

My attempt at dressing like a normal woman in the hope that

he'd see me differently was all for nothing. He hasn't forgotten what I am, hasn't remembered our night together in the same way I had. Probably never thought of it again. *Stupid, stupid to hope otherwise.* It seems he's remembered all too well. I'm a sweet butt, a whore. Nothing else.

The door remains closed. I remain waiting outside. As minutes pass, thoughts continue to war in my brain. Stay? Or go? If I stay, I'm the whore he thinks I am. If I leave, I'll lose any chance I may have had to do what Drummer had asked, or the chance just to see him.

I am a *whore.* There's no escaping that. But maybe, just maybe, getting inside is worth playing the part for him once again.

I'm staying. I rap with my knuckles on the wood. "You gonna open this door, Truck? Kind of hard to give you what you want with this barrier between us."

A further delay, then I hear the sound of bolts being slid back, a key turning in the lock, and then the door opens. Truck must have stepped to the side as I don't see him. The interior is dim as he has the blinds closed. Nevertheless I walk over the threshold.

Suddenly the door swings shut, and I feel him behind me. My heart skips a beat, as I feel arms I thought would never hold me again, pulling me against his chest for a moment. Then, he walks me forward so I'm facing the back of a couch.

"Take off your jeans and bend over."

Oh no, oh shit. No finesse, no conversation. It's no different from the johns I went with in the past.

The hearts and flowers romance I'd been hoping for has been swept right away. I'm a whore, so I follow instruction.

It's Truck. This is what I want.

But not how I want him.

You got inside his apartment, other's didn't.

But at what personal cost? Christ, I tried to fight it, but I did have dreams of becoming his old lady even though I didn't admit it in those terms to myself. Old ladies don't get fucked over couches, or maybe they do, but with some romantic foreplay.

He stayed out of the light. He doesn't want me to see him.

My realisation is confirmed when he says tersely, "Stay like that. Don't look around. Whatever you do, don't turn to face me."

Why not? Is he badly scarred? It's the only reason that makes sense. *I wouldn't care.*

Hands, surprisingly gentle, caress my ass, rubbing up and down my thighs. They're rough, calloused, but the touch is slightly uncertain.

He pushes my tee up and undoes my bra, then moves his hands under my breasts and palms them.

"Soft, but firm. Just as I remember."

His voice does something to me, and when he tweaks my nipples, I feel myself getting wet, despite my misgivings about the situation.

He moves one of his hands down, palming my mound. He sighs deeply and warns gruffly, "It'll be quick, Allie. I haven't been with a woman since I last had you."

My heart leaps. I want to tell him I've not been with another man, but I can't. It would be a lie even though recently I've been backing off. What I am, what I do, that's why I got through that door. Unlike the others who have come calling, I've got something he wants. Something he *needs.* I'm just a sweet butt. He wants to get off and he knows he can use me.

"Stay there." His warmth leaves me. I see a shape which appears to be limping, but obeying him, I don't turn around or watch as he leaves the room, hearing him return quickly. A tearing sound reveals he went to get a condom.

He's back, leaning over me, his fingers probing. "Wet for me, you little whore, aren't you?"

I've longed for sweet nothings to reach my ears, his coarse words are anything but. In my dreams he'd told me he'd missed me. *Stupid. Stupid.* I put a hand to my face to stifle my sob, wondering if by coming in, staying, and allowing him to use me, I'm validating what he believes I still am. That after he's got what he wants, I'll return to the compound and make myself available to any other man. But why should he think any different? That's what he watched me do every day of that year while he was prospecting. How could he know he spoiled me?

I feel him probing at my entrance, and can't prevent myself stiffening.

"Allie?"

"I'm okay." I can do this. I've done it before with men from visiting chapters. A cock is a cock after all. I wiggle my hips and push back against him. "What are you waiting for?"

He flicks my clit, then pinches it. "You turned on, Allie?"

"Of course." I am, and I'm not. *This is for him, not for me.* For the first time I'm in this position, I wonder what the hell I'm doing.

His cock is back, pushing, easing into me. He's big. Despite my occupation, I'm tight, and it's hard for him to get all the way inside.

He's in. I breathe again, my eyes closing. *Enjoy it, Allie. This is what you dreamed of. Being back in Truck's arms, having him inside you. It's Truck. The man you wanted.*

"Fuck you feel good, Allie. Fuck, I can't last."

His hips are pumping, his cock sliding in and out of me. One hand toys with my clit.

"Fuck, so good. It's been so long," he gasps hoarsely.

"Truck," I cry out. Then purposefully tense my muscles, pushing back as he pushes in. "I'm close, Truck."

I'm not. I'm faking it. My mind's working too hard for my body to relax and enjoy it.

"You there, Allie? Cos I'm gonna, oh, fuck, I'm coming Allie."

He groans. I politely moan. Then, he pulls out, his head resting on my back for a moment.

"Got to go and get rid of the condom. You can see yourself out. Thanks, Allie, I didn't know how much I needed that. I wouldn't object to you or another sweet butt making a house call again. Oh, and tell Drummer, thanks."

He leaves me.

Jerkily, I stand, pull up my underwear and slip my jeans on, feeling like my heart is broken. All my dreams gone. I wait, but he doesn't come back, even after I hear a toilet flush. I glance at the door. He dismissed me and expects me to leave, just like the whore he knows I am. If I stay, he could be angry. He made it clear he doesn't want to talk, doesn't want me to even see him. I'm invading his space, I feel awkward just standing here.

If I just go, I've lost my chance. *He invited me back.* Maybe next time I'll achieve more? Or, he might change his mind and never let me inside again.

I don't know what to do. But as I stand hesitating, I hear a shower start.

The sound of the water running does nothing to muffle the sobbing of a man in utter distress.

CHAPTER FIVE

Allie…

I act automatically, without a second thought. Within moments I've taken off all my clothes, leaving them in a heap on the floor. I follow the sound of the shower, go uninvited into his bedroom, then into the adjacent bathroom, opening the door quietly.

I relish the sight of his naked body behind the frosted glass, the form slightly less bulky than I remembered. His head is bowed, his hands over his face, and those gut-wrenching sobs are still coming.

Allowing myself no room for doubt, I open the door and step inside, putting my arms around him.

He jumps and flails.

"It's me, Truck. It's me."

"I told you to fucking go." He sounds furious. His anger doesn't scare me, but his tears do.

The frosted glass and the water cascading over his head and down his body prevent me from getting a look at him, and soon, I've lost my chance. He's turned me so my back is against his front, and has the door open with the obvious intent of pushing me out.

I've got seconds before I lose him forever.

"Truck. Don't push me away. You're upset, let me help."

"You want to fuckin' help? Get out of here. You've had what you came here for, now fuckin' get gone."

I didn't come here for his cock, but now's not the time to tell him that. *How can I get through to him*?

"You're blocking everyone out, Truck, when you clearly need someone." Calculating fast, I remember I'm the only one he's let over his front step. "I'm a nobody, Truck. A whore as you reminded me. Use me for this. Speak to me, I'm a good listener."

Imperceptibly his arm tightens around me. For a second his chin drops and rests on the top of my head. "Just go, Allie. There's nothing for you here." His tone has gentled.

"Truck, please." I'm open to begging if it means he doesn't turn me away. Now that I have intruded, once I leave, I know he won't let me back. His sobs break my heart. Even if it's just my body he wants, if that would bring him any comfort at all, he can have it. "Truck, please. I don't care how, use me if you want to, but there must be some way I can help. You need it, Truck. You *need* someone."

"Too many fuckin' people thinking they can help. Trying to get into my business. What can you offer that they can't? Talk? I saw enough shrinks for that, not that it did any good."

"I don't know what support I can give, I just know I need to try. I wanted to come to see you today, and not because Drummer asked me. You've got a club, and your co-workers all worried sick about you. Everyone needs someone, Truck. Let me be that for you."

He's quiet for a moment. The only sound is that of the water cascading over us. I think I notice a slight drop in temperature as he replies at last. "So Drummer sends me a whore for company. A whore who wants to talk. Whatever fuckin' next?"

It's not my imagination, the shower is running cold now. I shiver, Truck swears, and reaches over me to turn the water off. His hands trace the goosebumps that have arisen on my skin. He pulls me in closer, presumably to share his body heat. *Truck is still there, the good man I remember.* I've just got to reach inside, find him and bring him back out.

"Allie, Allie. Why the fuck did you have to come here? Why didn't you leave when I asked you too?"

Somehow I know he's not expecting me to answer. What would I be able to say? *I fell for you, Truck. Just one night and you ruined me for other men.* It wasn't just his cock or what he could do with it, though that wasn't a disappointment in any way. It was far more than that. A connection which gave meaning to an otherwise meaningless act.

My body shudders again. "Can I get a towel, Truck?"

A moment of silence as he considers my reasonable request. Then a long drawn out sigh which does nothing to reduce the tension in his body, instead it has the opposite effect. His voice, which had softened, hardens as he growls, "Help yourself. But don't blame me after, I tried to save you from this."

I don't know what he means. My brow creases as he releases me from his hold, then I move to the rail and take a *thank fuck* warm towel. I wrap it around me, but keep my back to him for a moment. His words, his actions, the way he's not let me see him has me prepared for the worst. Whatever I do, I can't show any reaction. Sympathy would be wrong, pity worse. Revulsion way down at the bottom of the list.

What could be so awful?

The atmosphere is heavy with expectancy. Neither of us speak, both waiting on the inevitable. It's like a storm is about to break.

I swallow hard, then take a spare towel. Bracing myself, I turn and pass it to him. I barely have time for even the briefest glimpse before he covers his face with the towel. Instead, I view his body. He's lost muscle, its noticeable, but this is a man who prided himself on keeping fit, and would have done so even if his job hadn't demanded it. It's clear he hasn't returned to the gym since getting out of rehab.

His left arm is withered and looks twisted, and there's something wrong with his hand which is curled into a fist. Moving my eyes on a downward journey, I take in his side and leg. From under his arm pit, down to his ass, all the way down his leg, his skin is a mass of scarred tissue. His leg looks like it's had burns and massive surgery too. Then his stance gives away further injury. He's standing lopsided, his weight mostly on his right and hardly any on his left.

Nothing I see detracts from the internal beauty of the man.

Instinctively I know he's hiding the worst from me. I step closer, one hand landing on his bicep, the other giving a gentle tug on the towel that's covering his face. "Let me see."

"Allie." It's half a growl, half a plea.

I'm relentless. "Let me see."

I tug again. With a tortured sigh, he releases the hold he has on his makeshift mask, and the towel comes away in my hands.

My stomach rolls, not with disgust, but horror that he's gone through what he obviously has alone. I force myself to remain completely impassive.

One side of his face is unmarked, showing the beauty of the man I remember. It's a mocking comparison to the left side which is a mass of angry red scars presumably covered with skin grafts. The most shocking? Well, that's the empty eye socket.

Raising my hand I deliberately place it lightly on the injured side of his face.

My action astounds him. He grabs it, his fingers tightening around mine as he pulls my hand away. "Don't pretend, Al. No fuckin' pretence. I'm a fuckin' monster."

"No," I tell him sincerely, "you're Truck." Placing my free hand over his heart, I continue, "In here, where it matters."

"Am I?" he replies, cynically. "Am I really?"

I go to confirm it, but he shakes his head, saying tiredly, "Just go, Allie. I'm broken, and nothing can fix me."

If I leave now, he won't be opening that door again.

What can I do? What do I say? It's clear this man in front of me needs help. Am I qualified to give it? Who am I, but a whore, an uneducated woman who's even forgotten what street smarts I'd learned as I've lived a semi-protected life since I turned eighteen—well, protected from the citizen world that is. The life I've lived has not been without danger.

Should I be aware of the risk of my behaviour resembling that of a whore taking the chance to latch onto a member? I'm all too well aware, Jill and Chrissy died when they attempted to do exactly that.

I feel a frown playing at my lips. *Am I doing the same as them? Am I as bad as the two women I used to work beside, sharing men together?* I thought Truck and I had connected, but maybe I'd been wrong. Maybe it was all one-sided. Maybe I should step back. It never ends well if a whore gets ideas above her station.

I'm certainly not a psychologist. Even if I were, I probably wouldn't know where to start, not being aware of what Truck's issues actually are. Oh, on the outside it's only too evident he's been through a lot. I already knew he was injured to the extent he'd been medically retired from the fire service. I can't begin to imagine the mental anguish of losing a job he loved, and had been prepared to give his life for. We had suspected he would have some scars but had no idea he'd been injured as badly as he was. He's been through a worse hell than I anticipated. And to lose an eye? *Fuck.*

This is beyond me to fix.

While my thoughts have been whirling around my head, I've been automatically drying myself off. With the towel wrapped around me, suddenly aware of my nakedness in a way it hadn't bothered me before, I open the door as I hadn't brought my clothes into the bathroom.

"I'm going to get dressed."

He says nothing, but I feel his gaze burning into my back as I leave.

Retrieving my clothes from where they lie on the floor, I put them back on, finger combing my curly hair.

What do I do now?

Play this by ear. I've never been in this situation before. It strikes me that while my experience with men is vast, it's only been in one way. When was the last time I sat and had a conversation with a man? I can't remember. Exchanging polite comments and jokes when bartending doesn't count.

"You need to get back to the club, Allie. I'm sure you will be missed by now." Dressed, he's followed me out.

"Why don't you talk to me, Truck? The club doesn't need me, I've got all the time in the world for you."

"Drummer told you to give me special treatment, did he?" Glancing at him I see Truck's destroyed face attempting a smirk. "Gave me my own personal whore? Sorry, babe, I'm not feeling it now. Got better things to do."

My face glows, but I push my anger back down. I deserve his words, he's spoken nothing but the truth. Except for one thing. "It's true Drummer sent me, but it wasn't because I'm a sweet butt." I'd have come here in any event. Staying away from Truck, knowing he was so close, had been killing me.

Truck's keeping his back to me, even though I've seen him and the horror that remains of his face. I long to tell him it doesn't matter, that he's still the same man to me, but he's giving me no chance to show it.

"So why the fuck are you here, Al? I mean fuck all to you, or you to me."

That pulls me up. Damn it. My palm hits my forehead. All the time I've been thinking there was more between us than just sex that night, Truck's never given a second thought to me. Of course he wouldn't, all he did was have sex with the first available sweet butt, it wouldn't have mattered had it been me, Paige, Pussy or Diva.

There's a couch behind me. I sink into it, putting my head in my hands. No sweet butt ever makes it with a biker. What happened to Jill and Chrissy should have warned me of that. No good comes of having hopes above my station.

For the past few months, all my focus has been on Truck, and that remarkable night we spent together, while it was nothing special to him. Now I've got to make some decisions. The thought of going back to the club, going back to letting any man use me is abhorrent. It hits me as it's not hit me before, the reasons why I haven't wanted to work on my back since the day Truck left. For the first time, sex had meant something to me. It had gone beyond a physical act, had shown me what I'd been missing. Since the first boy I went with, I'd only ever experienced that with Truck.

I'm greedy.

I want it again.

But Truck doesn't want me.

I've nothing to offer but my body, and that, it appears, isn't enough.

I've been quiet too long. Truck fills the silence, every word like a nail hammered into my coffin. "Go, Allie. Look, tell Drummer thanks. Yeah, the release was great. I don't mind if he sends you or one of the other girls, at least you're paid to ignore what I look like. You can tell him why I'm staying away now."

I work hard to come up with a suitable response as Truck confirms that any of the girls would be able to see to his needs. It's hard to deal with the disappointment that's tearing me in two. Knowing I can't let Truck see how shattered I am, in the end I settle for, "I can't tell him what I don't understand, Truck. What the hell's keeping you from the club?"

"What. The. Hell?" Truck snarls. "Haven't you got fuckin' eyes in your head?" He pauses and his mouth twists as he realises what he said. "My eyesight is fucked, my leg and wrist too. I can't ride my fuckin' bike, so I can't be a member. Leaving aside who'd want someone who looks like this around."

Even as a sweet butt I know the rules. If Truck truly can't ride, then he's right, he can't be in the club. But is that the truth? Has he just not tried hard enough? Peg's got a false leg for fuck's sake, and Truck's still got one working eye. Maybe he just needs a longer recovery. As for his looks? Who'd care about that?"

"No one would give one damn about your appearance."

"Yeah? You really think they'd want me scaring the kids?"

Twenty years in the future – Drummer

Peg nods *at Alba who's just backed his bike into a vacant spot. The man shrugs as Peg points at a scrape on his bike.*

"Dropped it again?" the sergeant-at-arms snorts.

"Nah, woman backed into it at the parking lot."

Both of us wince in commiseration. Alba, short for Albatross, is always having fucking bad luck. The reason he was given that road name.

"I'll get Sharp to sort it." Alba doesn't sound particularly bothered as he passes us and goes into the clubhouse. What would be a tragedy for anyone else is almost a normal occurrence for him, and Sharp, who's taken over as manager of our auto-shop is well used to fixing his ride.

"Do you remember how it all started?" Peg asks, when Alba has disappeared inside.

"What? Truck and Allie?"

"I was thinking about how this turned into a family club. The influx of old ladies."

I frown. "You talking about Bullet?"

Peg shakes his head. "Nah. Bullet's always been with Carmen, they were together when he joined the club. And Viper and Sandy were married over forty years."

They were. We celebrated their ruby wedding a couple of years back. Just before...

Peg interrupts my chain of thought. "There was Heart and Crystal, of course, but it was Wraith who seemed to be the turning point. After that we all started falling like flies."

My eyes shutter as I think back. "Christ, you're dredging up old memories, Peg. Hadn't thought of those days in years." Gears turn in my head, synapses fire, and memories come to the fore. I think it's easier to dredge up recollections from the past these days, than to remember what I just walked into a room for. One memory in particular enters my brain as I give a short laugh. "Wheels, remember? That's what we called Sophie when she first arrived."

"She was in a fuckin' wheelchair. Never thought she'd get out of it."

You wouldn't think that now. Like Peg himself, it's hard to remember she's got a fake leg at all, unless you see her in the pool. "Down to you, Peg. All down to you that she did."

He grins. "Wasn't going to let her get away with that shit." He stares at nothing for a moment. "Seemed a strange fit. She didn't even talk our language."

Chuckling softly, I agree, "She sure expanded our vocabulary. Heard Heart call something the dog's bollocks the other day."

"Yeah, and I even asked for a cup of char." Peg's head moves side to side in disbelief. "She was a breath of fresh air coming into the club."

"Never expected Wraith to settle down, that's for certain."

"Hey, my ears are burning!"

Unbeknownst to either Peg or myself, my VP has come out of the clubhouse. "What are you two old-timers gossiping about?"

"Old times," I respond. "In particular, when you got with Wheels."

Wraith starts, then grins. "Haven't called her that in years. Fuck, that brings back memories. Good ones and bad ones." His face tightens. "I sometimes wonder what kind of member Hank would have made."

"A good one," I say, firmly. I believe it. Man had been close to being patched in when he'd been killed. Never good thinking about the people we'd lost.

"You two staying out here for a spell?"

When I nod, Wraith disappears back into the clubhouse.

"What the fuck has history got to do with Truck and Allie?" I ask. "Thought that's who we were discussing."

"Old minds ramble." Peg grins. "But I do wonder whether we started a trend that Truck thought he'd follow."

"*Not at first,*" I remind him. "*He wanted nothing to do with the club, and nothing to do with Allie.*"

CHAPTER SIX

*F*ruck…

I stand, my fists clenching and unclenching at my sides, my brain silently screaming out for her to just go. I don't even know why she's here in the first place. Despite what she says, I'm sure Drummer sent her here to fuck me. Crafty bastard, he chose a way that he thought would work, a man has needs after all. The use of a sweet butt had been welcome. But why did he have to choose *her*?

I'm a man. When I'd recovered sufficiently for nature to rear its head by the way of my natural masculine urges, I'd used my hand. From the very first time I'd seen the monster I'd become reflected in a mirror, I'd resigned myself to mine being the only touch on my cock. This was going to be my life for the rest of my days. Who'd want a man so broken and scarred?

Then she'd appeared. Not just a woman, but a sweet butt whose job it is to service the men in the club without criticism or complaint. As soon as she appeared on my doorstep, I knew what the deal was. I could fuck her and she'd walk away without looking back when I dismissed her. It's what they do, what they expect. She wouldn't, couldn't ask for more. Even if my appearance turned her stomach, she'd still open her legs.

I made it easy for her, didn't let her see the abomination that's now my face. I took her and did what other members would do, sent her packing immediately.

Only, she hadn't left. Had instead witnessed my breakdown. I'd been disgusted with myself for using her, and it had hit me hard, the knowledge of what I've turned into. Forced me to look into my future, where it will only be whores who will accept my attentions for the rest of my life. Someone who's paid to provide their services. Better than my hand? Not with the self-recrimination that comes after.

It's going to be hard to come to terms with that's the best I'm going to get. What woman would want someone like me stepping out with her? The act which should have provided a physical release, had instead opened the floodgates on everything that's wrong.

I've lost my job and the camaraderie of being on a team. I've lost my family in the club. I've lost the ability to do what I love, and those dreams of a future wife and kids? Blown to the wind.

There's nothing left.

I'm bitter as hell as well as angry. I've lost everything that mattered to me in my life.

My eyes flick to the drawer where I keep the letter I received while in the hospital. It's a fucking joke, a thank you from the woman who'd run back into that house, causing me to chase after her to save her. She offered no apology for her impulsive actions, only gratitude for mine. Because to her, all that mattered at the end of the day was that her cat was alive.

Do I fucking give a damn? I'd rather have my mobility, my unfettered sight, my job, my club, my old life. All for the sake of a bundle of fur whose time on earth is limited. It will die a natural death before I've lived out a fraction of the sentence handed to me.

It's not that I don't like animals, but fuck, from now on, I think I'll always hate cats.

I want Allie to go. I want to be alone. Alone I can work out what to do with my life now that everything's been taken away.

No, that's not the truth, there's nothing I can work out or resolve. Alone I can mourn what I've lost.

She's sitting on my couch, seems to have put down roots. If she doesn't go soon, I'll have to physically evict her. Her presence is making the air difficult to breathe, shrinking my home to impossible proportions.

Why did Drummer have to send *her?* Out of the four sweet butts, she's the one I wanted to see least.

Prospecting was hard, I don't deny it, even though the club was easier on me because of the respect they have for my job, and because I started already possessing much of the trust other prospects have to earn from scratch.

All those months I split giving my all to my job as a firefighter and then, after my shifts, to the club. It had been a hectic time. Matt and I were run off our feet with the different duties and jumping to all the members demands, but we'd done it.

My love for the club warred with my love for my job, my duty, as I saw it, to protect and serve. What firefighter could sit back, seeing the wildfires getting worse: bigger and seemingly more malicious? Anyone's house could be lost, whether they were a prince or a pauper. Fire, the great equaliser, taking from rich and poor alike. Like a recidivist, it was getting worse. Now it was intent on not just taking possessions, but lives.

I could help, it was where I was needed.

I took the decision to leave the club, but instead of feeling let down, they honoured me by patching me in as a full member. That had been one of the proudest, most amazing experiences of my life. To be given my full patch that night before I'd left for California.

The high that I'd felt could never be equalled.

I was leaving early, so I couldn't drink, but I was still encouraged to take advantage of my new status in other ways. Sweet butts.

I'd always been fascinated by these women who were very much part of the club, but also distant from it in many ways. I'd picked up that before the men started settling down with their old ladies, the sweet butts held more sway. Gradually the pendulum swung in the opposite direction, particularly when Drummer, the president, took an old lady. The sweet butts who used to have free run of the club were banished when old ladies and kids were around.

But still, they had their time, and their uses.

The sweet butts were provided for by the club, in exchange they'd make themselves available to any and every one of the men. A crooked finger, a knowing wink, and the sweet butt would understand exactly what was expected of them, and went off to do their job with a smile. It had occurred to me that these women must like sex. They never showed the slightest hesitation, whether it was one man or more.

Though other clubs may be different, the Satan's Devils sweet butts were never forced. If they weren't feeling up to it, they wouldn't be dragged out of their beds. They weren't hurt, and like anything else belonging to the club, were fiercely protected.

Although society might look on them as scum, I learned a certain respect for them. Why should a man receive a slap on his back for the number and variety of women he goes with, and a woman not afforded any admiration at all? It's a strange social dynamic.

There's a general belief that sweet butts are all looking for that one special member, the brother who'd take them on the back of his bike and make them his old lady. I know a couple of our sweet butts had met their sorry end as they'd set their sights on men who were unobtainable. But I couldn't have said any relationship between a club girl and a member would ever work. These girls like sex and lots of it. It would be hard for them to settle down and only ride one cock for the rest of their lives, just as I couldn't understand the men who were addicted to one pussy.

That night I was patched in, I only had a few hours before I would leave. Never one to turn down an opportunity, I looked around for an available sweet butt and spied Allie. I already knew she was friendly and fun, loyal to the club and the men in it. It didn't hurt she's also pretty, with ample tits and a perfect heart-shaped ass. Well, you couldn't miss her attributes with the skimpy clothes which appeared to be her uniform, screaming availability and fuck me.

I led her into the crash room with no expectations other than getting my rocks off before heading out into a dangerous situation. Like any soldier about to resume active duty, the idea of my mortality had been close to the forefront of my mind, and fucking a good way to deal with it, to scream to the world that for that moment, I was alive.

Whether it was that I was still on a high from the euphoria of the change in my fortunes, being made a full member instead of leaving the club, or whether it was the thought of the inherent danger of the situation I was heading into, I'm not sure, but the sex with Allie was out of this world. So much so, I stayed with her until I had to leave, fucking her every which way to Sunday, knowing I could grab a nap on the plane.

Her responses seemed genuine, her enjoyment undeniable—unlike earlier—when I knew she was faking it.

But then she's a seasoned whore, no need to read any more into it. Her experience showed as she gave me everything exactly how I liked it, and let me take from her what I wanted.

That night had been so good. It must have been that it was the last act I'd taken before leaving the clubhouse, but when I'd gone away, the memory kept returning to me. Her scent, her touch, the feeling of being inside her. When I had a break from firefighting and got the opportunity to lay down my head to rest, as I closed my eyes it was her face I saw, smiling above me. When I had the chance to use my hand on myself, it was my memory of her that fuelled the cum spurting from my balls.

I had planned to seek her out when I returned from California, if only to repeat that mind-blowing experience. She was a good fuck, that's how I remember her.

Now she's here, in my house, and I want nothing to do with her. The juxtaposition of my past and my future jarring, my hopes and expectations lost. She's nothing special, being here she's only proved what I knew all along. Women like her will fuck anything. Even someone who looks like a freak.

If Drummer had sent someone else, maybe I'd have been better able to deal with it. But her? It's liked he's stripped me of my manhood, taunting me with a life I've lost.

Because of a fucking cat.

I've been so lost in my own head, worrying about myself, I hadn't stopped to think about the girl on the couch or her feelings. The girl who'd given me the best fuck of my life that last night I was in Tucson. I notice her now, she's still got her head bowed in her hands, she's unmoving, apart from her fingers which are tangled in her still-damp curly hair, tightening and loosening as if she's purposefully tugging at the roots to cause a sting of pain.

Why doesn't she just go? She's done what she came for.

She'd changed when I said Drummer should send somebody else. Someone with the same experience who could equal that performance I remember. These girls know how bikers like to fuck, they're probably all pretty much similar.

Could she be upset that I basically told her I didn't want her? For the first time in months, I feel something other than self-pity and anger. A brief flicker of guilt. My lips press together, the action still pulling at my left cheek which hasn't the movement it had before. *She's a sweet butt.* She provided what she'd been asked to do. No more, no less.

But she had done more. She'd tried to comfort me, and hadn't run screaming when I let her see exactly what I am now.

Truth is, except for the heavenly feeling of being in her cunt, I don't know much about her. Strange thing to say about someone whose path crossed with mine for a year. Fact is, though, there's a hierarchy in the club. Officers and members at the top, then come the prospects. Old ladies, well, sometimes I wonder exactly where they fit in, but they sure are important. Just one rung off the bottom of the ladder are the hangarounds trying to get patched in. And right at the end, seen as a necessary evil, are the whores.

I don't think I've really thought of Allie as a woman before, just a combination of tits and ass there for my use. I'm not proud, it's just the way it's always been. I've taken my steer from the other members.

I'd expected her to run crying when she'd seen my face, not as much from pity, as disgust.

She hadn't.

I've been lost in my thoughts too long, virtually ignoring her, though that hadn't been my intent. It's been a long time since I thought about anything other than what I'd lost. Her presence has brought back memories of the club, and why I'd originally joined it.

Seeing movement out of the corner of my eye, I watch her stand up. She's moving stiffly like a marionette being jerked by strings. I'd have had to have lost my other eye too to be blind to the fact she's hurt.

What do I care? I've got enough to worry about with myself.

But I do. Maybe my humanity isn't completely lost.

"I'll tell Drummer you'd prefer one of the other girls next time." The words seem difficult for her to get out as she pats her back pockets, as though checking she hasn't dropped her phone or wallet. "I'll see myself out."

"My left side took the brunt of my injuries. They bolted my arm and leg back together, but I'll never have full movement or strength back, my ankle is fixed in place, and I've lost two fingers on my left hand. I'm a mess of scars as you can see. Some from the burns, some from skin grafts." As words I hadn't intended speaking spill out of my mouth, I can't tell who's more shocked, her or I.

She winces, but it's on my behalf. "Are you in pain?"

I nod, while acknowledging that part of my anger comes from feeling like an injured bear most of the time. "Mostly headaches. That's from trying to adjust to using one eye."

"Your eye," she begins to ask in a matter of fact tone, "don't they do fake ones?"

I see red. "Yes," I spit out. "They offered me a prosthetic eye, but why the hell should I bother? Of course I wear a fucking patch when I go out, don't want to upset people's sensibilities."

She looks at me assessing, not at all upset from my sudden burst of rage. "It's not just for other people, Truck. It's for you. Okay, it wouldn't be real, but a prosthetic eye would give you more confidence to be with people."

She's wrong. In the mass of scar tissue covering my face, even a fake eye wouldn't make me look normal.

I bang my hand on the back of the couch. "I don't want to see anyone, Al. I… can't. I can't deal, not right now. I need time to process. There's no point trying to do the impossible, make me look normal. I just need to be alone."

I wait for her to tell me what therapists have already tried, that I should reach out and talk. But I can't. It's too soon. After six months, I've started to believe the time will never come. I need to come to terms with and accept my limitations now. Seeing people living the life that I'd thought was mine would be too fucking hard.

Again, she surprises me by not continuing to argue. "Okay, I'll leave you alone. I'll explain to Drummer. I'll ask—"

I interrupt, "I don't want another sweet butt to come around, Allie."

A flicker of something crosses her face. I can't read what it is, but it forces me to take a step back and think for a moment. Fuck, I shouldn't be taking all my frustration out on her. I resent that she came visiting in the first place, but there's part of me that's found solace in her being around. I don't mean just physically either. But her sacrifice, letting me have my release without getting hers, her no nonsense approach to my looks and my injuries, forces me to add, "Allie, I appreciate that you didn't run off screaming when you saw me. If… If you want to come back, you can. I can't promise what mood I'll be in."

She nods, but that expression crosses her face again. She's giving an interpretation to my words which I hadn't meant to imply, that another sweet butt may have a different reaction. *Fuck, I'm hurting her without meaning to.* I've evaded human company so long, I don't know how to speak to people. Then, again, I don't want to encourage her.

I wait for her to go, but she turns to me instead, her eyes examining my face but with no hint of unease. "I think you ought to consider the prosthetic, Truck. Not for others, but for you."

I shrug. "It would only be cosmetic. Whether I had one or not, doesn't make any difference. Not to me."

She wants to improve my appearance. I wait for her to try to persuade me, but surprisingly, she says no more on the subject.

Instead, she asks, "Can you drive yet, Truck?"

I don't tell her that the doctors have cleared me, but my one try had been a failure and I hadn't even gotten out of the parking lot. My brain needs to get used to receiving signals from just one eye, and as yet I don't quite trust myself. I've attended enough motor vehicle accidents, MVAs as we call them, to know someone who has difficulty with their sight shouldn't be behind a wheel. Instead I wear a patch and take an Uber. "No, I can't drive."

"Let me know if you want a lift or anything. Or just a friend to keep you company if you have an appointment to go to."

A friend? Is that how she sees herself. *Do I need one? Nah, I've gotten by alright up to now.* I pause too long in my reply.

Without waiting for me to reject her final offer, she takes the hint, walks to the door and, at last, leaves.

TWENTY YEARS IN THE FUTURE – Drummer

"OF COURSE *I didn't know if it would work," I tell Peg. Watching the light play on the mountains, thinking yet again how amazing this place is, and how lucky we are to have our compound here. I doubt I'll ever get tired of it. Well, I haven't yet, and we've been here getting on forty years.*

"It could have ended like Jill or Chrissy. You took a risk, Drum."

I did. I shift my old bones, trying to get into a more comfortable position. "Chrissy. Christ, that seems so long ago, Peg."

"Sweet butts had gotten used to men being as available to them as they were to us, they saw things changing and didn't like it. Wraith was the catalyst, when he decided to make Sophie his old lady." Peg chuckles. "When the VP found his one, seemed almost all of us followed."

"Our need for sweet butts certainly decreased," I agree with a grin, then frown as the memories come back. "Chrissy was mad that Wraith had set his sights on the Englishwoman, and hadn't a use for her anymore."

Peg's eyes crease, as though he's trying to remember. "Yeah, didn't she give details of the ride he was going on to the wrong people?"

"She did. Almost got him killed."

"What I remember, Drummer, is you taking her out mercifully. She didn't see it comin', and you didn't make me, or anyone else do it."

"I killed a woman." My mouth twists in distaste. "First time and last, Peg."

"Had to be done. She knew too many secrets and we wouldn't have been able to trust her. She hadn't seen it coming, at least you don't have to live with that."

I'd walked behind her while she'd been sitting at our table in church, and fired that bullet into her brain when she least expected it. Didn't want to place that burden on any of my brothers. I'd had no choice, didn't mean I'd enjoyed it. Took a long time for me to be able to view that seat without imagining her in it. By the grace of the devil,

Wraith hadn't ended up dead. I've no doubt in my mind, she deserved it.

"Wraith got his ol' lady though." Peg suddenly snorts a loud laugh. "And his four fuckin' daughters. He kept tryin' for a fuckin' son, never got one."

"He stopped after Hilda."

"Yeah, that name."

"Sophie's great-grandmother, I think." I'm chuckling too. Not so much at the old-fashioned name we've now become used to, but that Wraith had indeed kept trying for a son.

"He spoils those girls rotten though. Loves them to pieces. You never wanted another kid, Drum? You stopped after Eli and Zane.

I nudge him and wink. "Didn't want to risk not being able to yank his chain." It had been a standing joke for years that I, as prez, produced male sperm, my VP only female.

"I like having one of each, balances us out." Peg contemplates, looking out over the scenery. "We've been lucky with our kids, Drummer."

That we have.

As if summoned by our thoughts, Noah, Peg's son and Jacob, one of Heart's twins, approach, their worn Satan's Devils cuts on their shoulders. Two chin lifts in greeting, then they walk past us into the clubhouse.

We're quiet for a moment, then Peg picks up the threads of our conversation again, returning to the subject of the sweet butts.

"Jill, now she tried to get her claws into a member. She didn't succeed, just got herself killed."

Instead of going into the circumstances of Jill's betrayal, Peg circles back to the original subject. "So, even after that, you thought Allie could get through to Truck? And survive it? He might not have wanted anything to do with her."

CHAPTER SEVEN

Allie…

I close the front door behind me, then walk around the back to the parking lot where I'd left the borrowed car. I lean against it, cradling my head in my hands, before getting in.

It's only now I allow my feelings for the destroyed man in the apartment behind me to come out.

I'd known he'd been hurt, knew he could no longer do his job, but I hadn't realised how badly. It's obvious the mental scars are as bad, if not worse than the physical ones I could see clearly. He's changed so much from the prospect I knew before, the jovial, happy man who'd do anything for anybody.

I feel so damn useless. He needs help, I don't know what I can do to provide it.

I've watched prospects come and go. Secretly grinning at the way the members make their lives hard for them while knowing it's a game with a serious outcome. I've been around ten years, I know what goes on in the club, I even have a pretty good idea where some of the bodies are buried. Brothers need to trust any man brought to the table with their lives and freedom. Bring the wrong man in, and the whole club could go down.

So prospects are tested. Their role is to willingly do everything asked of them. They'll clean bikes, mop up puke, keep brothers stocked with condoms and dispose of used ones. No task would be considered unreasonable, and a shout of 'Hey, Prospect' will bring any of them running with no questions asked.

Truck, older than most of our recent prospects, never complained whatever he'd been asked to do. Heart had him cleaning up after Grunt when the dog's stomach was upset, and he did that willingly without even a comment about the smell. He didn't wait to be asked when he saw something that needed to be done, just slipped in and got it resolved. It was obvious he'd do anything for anyone, and not just because he wanted his patch, but from a genuine desire to help.

I never saw him get angry, unless it was justified on someone else's behalf. I can't remember a time he hadn't been smiling or laughing.

To see him like he was today? That was hard. He is a changed man. He's broken. However much I'd like to fix him, I'm not sure that I can.

I shudder, and a sob escapes. Not for me, but for the man I'm leaving hurting and alone. *Can't do more here, girl.*

No, I can't. I get in the car and drive back to the compound, thoughts whizzing around my head of how I can help. Each one dismissed as I'm sure each is a non-starter. Truck doesn't seem to want help. How can you provide aid to a man who doesn't admit he needs assistance?

I park the car at the auto-shop, return the keys, then, as I'm passing the clubhouse to go up to the residence the sweet butts share at the top of the compound, Drummer's walking down toward me.

"Allie," he acknowledges.

I hadn't specifically told him where I was going, that it was today I was going to follow his instruction, so I enlighten him. "I've been to see Truck."

"Yeah? You talk to him?" His eyes narrow, then when I indicate, yes, he issues an invitation by pointing to the clubhouse.

My shoulders rise and fall and I give a loud sigh as I follow him inside, knowing he's not going to like what I have to tell him.

I was right. After I've catalogued Truck's injuries, he's quiet, and there's a frown on his face.

Then he looks up and nods approvingly. "You did well, Allie. More than anyone else. You got to talk with him, and now we know what we're dealing with."

"He thinks he'll have to leave the club, Drummer. His left side, his leg, his hand." I might not ride a bike myself, but I've been around them long enough to understand how they work. "The clutch, the gears, he'd have difficulty with them. He seems to think where he's got to now is the best he can be, and that he'll never be able to ride."

He looks thoughtful. "Ways around anything if you put your mind to it. Sam's Vincent Black Shadow has the gears on the right, same as my Norton. Clutch though, nah, that's still on the left. But maybe we could build something custom."

"Then there's his eye," I remind him.

"Wouldn't say I'm an ophthalmologist, but I'm sure the brain adapts when someone's lost an eye. I suppose it depends on the vision of his remaining one."

"I'm no eye doctor either, but I suspect it's something he'll learn to adjust to in time. Then don't forget, he's worried about what he looks like."

"His appearance put you off?"

I sit forward, the words coming out almost as a snarl. "I didn't give a fucking damn." Then correct, "Apart from seeing the effect it has on him. He calls himself a monster and believes it."

Drummer takes that in, his face hardening. "Wouldn't affect what we think of him, he's still the same man. Well done, Allie. You've taken the first step. You've just got to keep working on him. I'm not saying it's not going to be difficult, but I want him back in the club. First step is to get him to see me."

"Not sure he'll agree to that." I'm one-hundred-percent certain he won't, but don't want to appear negative.

"I appreciate what you're doing, Al. I know this can't be easy."

"I'd do it, Drummer, whether you asked me or not."

He sits back in his chair, linking his hands behind his head. "Told you, I'm going to bring this to the table. For now, you'll officially be relieved of all other duties but tending bar. Your one focus is to make sure we bring Truck back into the fold. I'll make sure everyone knows that."

What happens if I fail? What happens if Truck comes back and wants nothing to do with me?

The questions must show on my face.

"Girl, you've given ten years to this club. We won't turn you out on your ear."

"I don't think I can be a sweet butt anymore," I all but whisper.

Drummer sighs. "I can't offer you anything without discussing it with the members first. Should the time come, I'll bring it up then. I'm not going to make promises I can't keep."

I can't expect him too. But it puts more pressure on me. If things don't work out with Truck, I may well lose my home. *What would it be like, to see Truck around the club going off with another sweet butt?* I could stay, hope that I have a few nights with him, that's better than nothing, isn't it? Better than him never returning to the club and me losing touch with him completely. I could handle watching him walk off with Diva and Paige, couldn't I? If the alternative is never seeing him again. *Could I do that?*

"Allie," he draws my attention again. "We've got four sweet butts and seven single men. Fuck, I remember the time it was just you and Jill. Fuckin' glad she found you and brought you to us. I think she was too."

She had been, I remember as I think back. The club was only around twelve men or so then, but as the sole sweet butt, she'd been kept busy.

"Wasn't long after me that Pussy came. And then there was Chrissy." I notice his face twists at my words.

"Sweet butts are important to the club. It keeps everything tight. Men don't have to go searching for pussy, they've got it here on tap. And secrets can be contained on the compound. Sweet butts are club property, but a woman who isn't a sweet butt or old lady? Not had to deal with that before, unless they were here temporarily under our protection."

That's how Sophie ended up with Wraith. She came here, found her man, and stayed. But I'm certainly not in that category. "I know Drummer. I'll have to do some thinking."

"That you will, Allie. That you will."

I try to convince myself that nothing has to change, but leaving Drummer's office, I realise the truth of two things. One, I already know I don't have it in me to be a sweet butt anymore, but the other is, it would kill me inside to watch Truck with another woman.

I've got to convince Truck he wants me.

I've taken the first step, and should be proud that I've managed to succeed in seeing him while everyone else has failed.

But I can't be. It probably wasn't me. If one of the other girls had gone, would they have had the same result? He saw me as someone available for a quick fuck when he was feeling horny. *He said I could go back. Not anyone else.*

Leaving the clubhouse, I walk to the top of the compound. As I approach the small two-storey house where I live, I take a moment to appreciate my home. This house hadn't always been here. At first I, and the other sweet butts, used to live in what are now the crash rooms in the clubhouse. Then, when Drummer's house was being built, Viper and Bullet's crew built two more, one for visiting officers to use, and one for us girls. It was nice to have somewhere to ourselves, somewhere we could kick back and relax, or, after a long night, be able to sleep well into the day without being woken by the noise in the clubroom.

As more and more old ladies join the club, we've been spending less time at the clubhouse. The women tolerate but don't like us, I don't blame them, they all know we've slept with their men. Although they've given up trying now, it was hard for Pussy, Diva or Paige to believe the brothers would settle down. Me, too, if I'm honest. Who would have expected the brothers to keep to one pussy, when they'd been used to variety? I'm ashamed now to admit, we'd all tried it, tested them in little ways, draped arms around them, rubbed breasts against arms, all in the presence of the old ladies. We had an excuse, we *knew* these men, knew what we were going to be missing, so yeah, we didn't want to give them up. Seems it was the best of the men who were being taken, first Wraith, then Drummer, then others falling like flies. The old ladies had stolen our men. It's no wonder there's no love lost between the two groups of women, and that we're discouraged to mingle.

Our house is now one of a collection, besides Drummer, Wraith and Heart have had theirs built up here too. Construction is well underway on Rock and Becca's as they're expecting their second baby.

I pause as I pass the kids' playground, shaking my head. It's something I never expected to see all those years ago when I'd first joined the MC. This place has changed beyond all recognition.

Sophie and Sam are sitting in the sun, watching their four kids play together. As I walk by, I don't take it as an insult that they don't turn to greet me, I'm used to it. I spare a quick smile as I see Eli's head bent next to Olivia's. Those two are insepara-ble, and have been since they were born, just a few weeks apart.

But what happens? What exactly is my status if I'm neither sweet butt nor old lady? Shunned by the women with old men, and possibly by the whores who I'll be walking away from.

Where would I fit in? It's a question I don't want to think about now.

I don't need to take out a key, no one locks their doors. Who'd come onto a biker compound? Stealing from the club would be a good way to commit suicide.

As I walk into the kitchen, the welcome aroma of coffee greets me. Paige, Diva and Pussy are sitting around the table with cups in their hands. As I gesture to the pot, Pussy nods.

Filling a cup, I go to join them.

"You had business in town?" Diva asks.

"Yeah." I don't feel inclined to fill them in on where I've been and why.

"We were just talking." Pussy focuses her blue eyes on me.

I shrug. I expect they were. Gossiping, probably.

"Who do you think has the biggest cock in the club?"

I grin, it's a topic we visit from time to time. "Size. What does it matter? It's what they can do with it that counts."

"Have you ever gone with Peg? I hear he's got a Jacob's ladder." Pussy licks her lips.

My head shakes. "He didn't go with the girls, even before he married Darcy."

"Same with Mouse," Paige pouts.

"I miss Tongue," Pussy's face tightens. "The things that man could do with his tongue…"

"Yes! He had a stud in it, didn't he?" I join in the reminiscing.

"We," Diva points to Paige and herself, "never met him."

"It's a shame Adam's gone too." I recall another member we lost. "He was a quiet one, but boy, did he give you a good time." I remember he'd been my first biker, and my first orgasm. He'd made me realise coming to the club had not been a mistake.

"What I regret most is Wraith taking an old lady," Pussy observes. "I keep waiting for him to get fed up with just Sophie, but so far no chance. Even when she was pregnant I couldn't tempt him away."

I've noticed her still flirting with him, but didn't realise it was with actual intent. No wonder the old ladies hate us. They have an argument with their men? We're all available to provide comfort of the physical kind.

"You have a hankering for him to be your old man?"

"Fuck no!" she exclaims. "I wouldn't mind sharing him. Just want a ride on his cock every now and again."

Diva and Paige sigh together. "Never taken him for a spin. He had his old lady before we arrived."

I sit back in my chair, my hands around my cup of coffee, content to listen. Not that I hadn't heard it all before.

"If you could become an old lady, who would you want?"

"Available men, or taken?" Paige's eyes gleam.

Pussy shrugs. "Doesn't matter."

"Well, I'd like Beef if he was still here. Fucking shame he had to go." Diva pouts. "He had stamina. Could satisfy both of us. Can't believe he's got a woman now."

"Won't last." Paige shakes her head at Diva. "One won't be enough for him."

"They've got sweet butts in the Colorado chapter," Pussy observes. "He's probably making use of them."

"No," I re-enter the conversation. "Beef's a good man. He won't step out on his woman. Didn't go with any of us after he got with Sally, did he?"

"Sally! Pah! Now there's a woman who'd never satisfy a man."

"What about you, Al?" Diva asks. "Who would you want as your old man?"

I shrug. I know the answer, but it's someone who's even more unattainable than one of the men who's got an old lady.

"Has Viper had a blow job from anyone lately?"

Pussy's question makes me think. He's got Sandy as his old lady, but never used to turn a blow job down. "You know," I answer her, thoughtfully, "once Sam came on the scene, that was the end of that."

"Fucking old ladies. Taking our men."

"Could you do that?" asks Pussy, addressing no one in particular. "Settle down with one man?"

Diva's shoulders rise and fall. "I'd like the security more than the man, I think. As long as the sex was good, I could do it."

"Hey," Paige leans in conspiratorially, "I took Drifter for a test drive the other day."

"Yeah, I've been with him too."

"What do you think?" Paige asks Diva.

"Think he needs teaching a thing or two. He's got the basics down right, though."

"The only man I'm not keen on is Dollar." Pussy frowns. "He treats me a bit like a whore on the streets. I keep thinking he'll get out his wallet at the end of it."

"A hundred times better than being a streetwalker." I shudder.

Paige and Diva understand. "A thousand times," Paige continues my train of thought. "On the streets you were always taking chances. Most johns were okay, grateful. Some were rough and wanted it how they couldn't get it at home."

"Some you'd have an argument with about using a condom," Diva takes over with a shudder. "You always went out worried you wouldn't come home."

"Hygiene could be an issue." Paige's nose wrinkles. "I hated the old men in particular. They used to smell of body odour and cabbage."

"Cabbage?" I snort. Diva shrugs. I don't know whether I'd describe it as that, but she's right, they did have a particular smell about them.

Whatever my future will be, I need to avoid going back on the streets. Cocooned here, I'd almost forgotten how bad it could be. Nope. Never doing that again.

Diva brightens. "But here it's a lot better. None of the brothers would go without a condom, they're too worried about having kids. And, except for when there are visiting chapters, we know everyone too. They wouldn't hurt us, Drummer wouldn't let them. And they're bikers." She says the last as though it sums them up.

And it does. They ride and live fast, fuck hard too. If a woman couldn't take their style of loving, she shouldn't be around them.

"Dollar's a strange one." Paige returns to Pussy's comment. "He's polite. Never fucks in the clubroom, always in private. I see what you mean about him behaving like a john."

"He done that thing with you?"

"Yeah," we all agree and share a moment of laughter.

When that dies down, Diva looks concerned. "Do you think they'll get rid of us? If they all find women."

"They won't. Look at who's left. Dollar, Shooter, Drifter, Marvel, Road and Jekyll. With the exception of Road, I can't see any of them settling down."

"And Truck," Pussy says, "if he ever comes back."

I don't comment, instead I change the subject. "Look at the time." I point to the clock on the wall. "I need to get ready to go to the bar, and you three need to get dressed," *or undressed rather,* "and get to work." Since Jill's death, I've been put in charge of them.

"I'm bleeding," says Diva.

Pussy and Paige groan.

"When are you going to start pulling your weight?" Pussy asks me directly.

What do I say? It's one thing to evade a question, another to outright lie. Taking a breath, I tell them, "I'm permanently on bartending duties. I've spoken to Drummer. Now, don't pout, Diva. You hate tending bar."

"True, that. Rather ride a cock any day."

Pussy gives me a strange look. "You going through a dry spell? Voluntarily, or have there been complaints?"

I look at her sharply. "No fucking complaints. I'm just not feeling it right now."

She's been here almost as long as I have. As she returns my gaze shrewdly, I hope she'll let the subject drop.

She does, well, until Diva and Paige go to get ready, then she leans in. "You've got your sights on someone."

I gaze back impassively.

"If it's someone in the club, it won't work, girl. We all know that. If it's someone outside, you'll have to live a lie. What man wants a woman who's been selling herself? Think of Chrissy and Jill, look what happened to them. You're setting yourself up for heartbreak. I like you, Allie, always have. Don't want to see you get hurt. Hankering after a member never ends well."

As she stands, her hand squeezes my shoulder. As I watch her walk off toward her bedroom, her final words echo in my head.

It never ends well.

She could be right.

It's too late.

~

TWENTY YEARS IN THE FUTURE – Drummer

"ALLIE NEEDED *a push in the right direction," Peg observes.*

"She had no faith in herself. Her bitch of a mother kicked her out of her home at sixteen. Fuckin' sixteen, Peg."

We're both quiet. All our kids, even those studying away at college, still regard the compound as their home. I can't imagine what one would need to do to be turned away. If they committed a crime, we'd probably hide them.

"She'd never known what it was like to be wanted," I continue. "Her mom never did, and she never really had friends she had chosen, or a man who'd made her feel special."

"Some did, but only for an hour or so at a time." Peg nods over at

me. "It was easier for her to believe Truck wouldn't want her even as a friend, let alone anything else."

"You told her in no uncertain terms to get her ass back round there, if I remember correctly."

"Me, Road and Marvel. Girl had guts. That I do remember. Unsure of her welcome, but still she put herself on the front line. Think it helped that we believed in her."

"She never believed in herself. So she needed a boot up the ass to get her moving in the right direction."

"It worked."

"Sure did." I raise my arm and rap on the window behind me. Within moments a prospect arrives with the whisky bottle in one hand for me, and a fresh beer for Peg in his other.

"The brothers didn't like Allie being taken off the rotation as I recall."

They hadn't. It had been hard for us all to get our heads around having a woman on the compound who was neither whore nor old lady. It wasn't the way we rolled.

The respect they had for Truck had allowed me to offer a compromise. Allie's sole role would be getting Truck back to the club.

Once he was there... It had been anyone's guess what would happen.

CHAPTER EIGHT

*F*ruck…

Reaching out for my cup of coffee, I misjudge its position and knock it over.

Fuck this!

Getting a cloth I wipe the floor—yet again—angrily throwing the filthy rag into the laundry basket in the bathroom. *Thank fuck the spilled drink missed the rug.*

Going back into the kitchen, I place both hands on the counter and bow my head. *I feel so fucking useless.* It's one thing having an arm and leg with no strength, but the loss of my eye is even harder. I used to have 20/20 vision.

The doctors made it sound so easy. *Your other eye will compensate in time.*

What they hadn't said is that judging something as simple as picking up a cup can go wrong. I jump at shadows, anything I can't see properly to that side of me. Day by day I'm discovering more of what I've lost, rather than learning how to cope.

Anger continually burns inside of me. It seems I can't do anything anymore. Not my job, not ride with my club, or even, pick up a fucking cup of coffee.

Is it worth carrying on? When I've lost so much? For the first time since I returned to Arizona, I half turn toward the bedroom where my weapon is stored in the gun safe. *A bullet could end everything.*

I snort. Knowing my luck, I wouldn't aim it right.

But there are other methods. I eye the painkillers wondering if I took them all at once, whether I'd go to sleep and not wake up. But I'm a big man, maybe the amount I have left wouldn't be enough. Best get a new prescription filled to make sure.

What the fuck am I thinking?

My dire thoughts disturb me. I have never contemplated ending my own life, nor considered for one moment I'd get so low. Never. I've seen enough of the horror caused by it. Even attended incidents where people had taken themselves out in various ways. The man who'd wrapped his car around a tree had been one of the worst, I was on the team of firefighters who had to cut the body out.

I remember thinking, how could you reach such a level of desperation that you just couldn't go on?

Damn. That's not me. I fight. Wars, fires, you name it, I'm there in the thick of it. That's who I am.

That's who I was.

The question is, have I got the strength to fight for a life that I don't feel is worth living?

Raising my head, I stare around my apartment, my gaze landing on the possessions I've collected over the years, including medals proudly displayed. Well, I certainly won't be adding to their collection. Sure, I understood my job was risky, but I expected to return from California the same as I was, or in a wooden box. I had had no idea I'd be returning as such a broken man.

Pushing on my arms I pull myself upright, realising I've got two choices here. I can rebuild my life, perhaps not as it was, but see where it takes me, or, give up.

I thought I'd reached rock bottom when I'd woken in that hospital with the doctor cataloguing my injuries. Now, it seems, I hadn't. For those first few weeks then the months in rehab I was concentrating on making the fullest recovery I could, still optimistic that I could get back to some semblance of the man I had been.

It's now, month's later, when I realise that none of my efforts will restore my lost sight, nor will they restore me to full mobility. I've reached my lowest point.

I'm tired. I thought time alone would help me come to terms with everything, now I realise, solitude only has me feeling lost and lonely with only the belief that I've nothing left to live for.

I was always a gregarious man, I need people. Need to feel useful. But how can I now? I can't face anyone. Previously, being a big scary man wearing a leather cut had been enough for mothers to turn their children's faces away. Looking like I do now? It would take a far stronger man than me to show my face in public.

I never thought of myself as weak.

Thoughts of ending it all is because I'm going stir crazy.

Six months ago, I thought I had it all. A job I loved, teammates and brothers. *The people are still there.* A voice in my head reminds me, followed by my mantra, *I don't need or want anyone.*

Fucking liar.

I'm a coward. There, I've admitted it. Taking the easy way out would work for me, I wouldn't need to struggle anymore. But what would be the effect on those I left behind? They'd be filled with guilt they hadn't done more to help me, when it was I who kept them out. They'd be the ones to feel the loss.

I owe it to them to come through.

But, how? With sudden resolve I walk to the bathroom and force myself to look into the mirror. The gap where my eye should be, which I cover with a patch on the rare occasions I leave the house, taunts me.

Would I have more confidence, less fear, if I gave in and did what I'd been advised to do when I was in the hospital?

What I have now isn't enough, the terror that if I simply go on as I am, I might eventually find myself eating that bullet, has hit me hard. I might not want to see my crew, nor see my brothers in the MC, but to do that to them? They're my friends, even though I'm not strong enough to have contact with them, taking my life would cause them to hurt.

I look at my hair. I used to shave my head regularly, now I've let it grow, and it's not flattering. It's come back sparsely. I started going bald when I was still in my teens, and having a shaven head was my way of disguising it. *Would I feel more like me, if I started my old regime?*

Taking my electric razor, I apply it to my skull. Soon, clumps of hair are falling into the basin, and minutes later I'm able to trace my hands over my smooth skull. Better? More like the old me, that's all I can say. But it's a positive step forward. *Be strong. You can do this.*

Before I can weaken, I go to my wallet, take out a card and dial the number on it.

Then, when that call is done, place another.

All brothers and prospects at the club have everyone's numbers stored in their phones, and that includes the sweet butts. Well, why not? They're on call, at any time. As a prospect, I'd never had reason to use any of their contact details. But now?

I tap on Allie's number.

When she answers, she sounds out of breath. *Have I interrupted her with one of my brothers?* My first impulse is to hang up. Then I reason, what else would I have expected her to be doing?

"It's Truck. Sorry to interrupt."

"No, you're not interrupting anything. I left my phone to charge upstairs, I had to run to answer it. What can I do for you?"

I limp to the couch and sit down, considering my response. Ask her to come around for me to sink my cock into her? To be honest, that time last week hadn't been memorable, I got off, sure, but for the first time in my life, a woman I was with had to fake it. Whore or not, that had hurt my pride. "You offered to give me a ride if I needed it."

"I did. When and where? Tell me and I'll be there."

"Whoa, slow down. You sure, Allie? I know you've got commitments." I'm surprised how much it disturbs me to think about the services she provides to the club.

"I'll make time."

"Next Tuesday. I need to be there early…"

"I'll be around your place first thing." She doesn't ask where or what for. Just implies she'll drop everything to be there for me.

"Thanks, Allie." My gratitude comes from the heart. Her response, her willingness, her having no second thoughts about her offer to help makes me realise that's what friends are for. What I've been turning away all these weeks I've been back.

I know it's not just her. If I emerge out of my self-pity, I would see I have a whole bunch of people who would drop everything if there was something I needed.

I was called Truck as I was built like one. Tall, muscular, strong, the last both physically and mentally. I've been the man others lean on. Now that I've been brought to a shadow of my former self. I need assistance, but it irks me. I've always been the one needed, not the one doing the needing. The reversal of our positions means I feel weak. The last thing I want is for anyone to feel sorry for me.

Allie, though, didn't imply that at all.

I can deal with her. She's already seen me at my worst, seen me giving into my pain. For some reason I don't object to *her* seeing me weak. Must be because she's a woman who whores for a living, so she's a nothing. I remember as I come back to myself, she's still on the line.

"Truck… how are you? Is the pain getting any easier?"

If she was anyone else, I'd tell her I'm fine. Somehow instead, I give her a glimpse of the truth. "Readjusting is hard, Al."

She's quiet for a moment. I suppose there's nothing to say.

I'm grateful she's not coming up with platitudes, telling me that things will get better with time. Sure, they'll change, but they won't improve. There's no magic spell that can fix me.

"I'll be there on Tuesday, Truck. If you want anything in the meantime, *anything*, just give me a call."

Anything. Politely I end the call, placing the phone down on the table and massaging my left wrist. I know what she was offering, but I won't be taking her up on it again.

Sure, I like fucking. I'm a man. When I prospected I wasn't blind to how men use the women in the clubhouse, fuck, they used to do it in the open when the old ladies had retired for the night. The sweet butts seemed to enjoy it, and I couldn't deny I was looking forward to that part of the benefits of being a member.

That night with Allie, she'd been into it as much as me. Last week? She was simply a whore performing a service. I'd been a john, using her like anyone else. Meaningless sex? All I'm going to get now looking like this, I realise, I don't want it.

No, I won't be calling her for those services again.

For the next few days, I eat mechanically, sleep erratically, watch TV and breathe air. The basics to keep me alive. Each day is a repeat of the last. Nothing satisfies me. I order groceries online, open the door when the bags are set down outside and the delivery person gone.

This is my life now. Perhaps in time I'll get used to it.

Enough times I pick up the phone to cancel the arrangements, but something stops me. A knowledge deep inside that I have to do something.

At last Tuesday dawns, and true to her word, there's a knock on the door.

Like the last time she came to my apartment, Allie is dressed like a woman, not a whore. It still seems strange to see her wearing clothes that leave everything to the imagination. Sure, her tight fitting jeans hug her ass, and her tee shirt clings to her bra, but the flesh itself is hidden from sight, perversely making me want to see more. I like her like this. Less makeup than I'd seen her wearing in the clubhouse. It makes her prettier to my mind, more attractive.

No. Don't go there. If I asked, she'd have no hesitation bending over the couch for me. *Because that's her job.*

"So," she walks in with no knowledge of the thoughts in my head and asks casually, "what's happening today, then?"

Her business-like approach pushes my carnal thoughts aside and I respond in the same way. "I've decided to go ahead with the prosthetic eye."

I hold my breath, waiting for her to gloat. Waiting for her to acknowledge she may have had a part to play in my decision.

"What's involved?"

No reference to it being her that had encouraged me, it makes it easier to explain. "When I had my eye removed, they put a cup inside, like a placeholder to stop the socket closing up. So I had the option of a prothesis when I was ready."

"You're ready now?"

I have to do something. I indicate my body. "With everything else going on, it wasn't a priority. A fake eye doesn't give me my vision back, but just makes it easier for others to look at me." I touch the scarred skin on my face, and snort a mirthless laugh. "Not that I think it would make much difference."

She's quiet, thoughtful, and I wonder what she's going to say. When she speaks, she surprises me. "Your friends, Truck, they just want you back. They wouldn't care what you look like. You're still the same man where it counts."

I go to tell her she's wrong. I'm not the same person anymore, when she continues.

"Strangers, yeah, they may judge you on looks, only because they don't know the man inside."

She doesn't sugar-coat it, just tells me how it is. Her forthrightness is refreshing.

I glance at the clock. "Better get going."

I've been recommended to go to an ophthalmologist who has

an office in Tucson. Allie drives what I recognise as one of the club's SUVs competently. As we travel along familiar streets, I feel panic inside me, knowing my vision has been affected more than most people would believe. The thought of never driving myself again is crippling. Losing my independence is hard, and relying on other people worse. But if I can't even pick up a coffee cup, how can I judge driving distances accurately? I can't. That limitation is hard to accept.

We arrive well in time.

"We're here, Truck."

"I just need a minute." *To brace myself for the reaction of strangers.*

I'd never have described myself as a handsome man, but I hoped I came close to it. Children had never run from me screaming, and I'd never had trouble attracting women. Now? My face draws attention for different reasons. Even in rehab I'd seen the expressions on various faces which went one of two ways, horror or pity. Only a few doctors and nurses were impassive to it. Until Allie. I eye the woman beside me, noting she takes it all in her stride. Shame I can't do that, but hey, she doesn't have to live with it.

"Truck," Allie starts, in a patient tone I hadn't expected from her. "This doctor deals with prosthetic eyes, doesn't she?"

Of course. My one eye rolls.

"What you look like won't come as a surprise to anyone. Your patch, your scarring. They'll be used to it here."

"Am I vain?" I ask her suddenly, wondering myself whether that's at the root of everything. Such a shallow reason to hide away.

"No," she replies emphatically. "You've had life changing injuries, there's no two ways about that. It's knocked you off kilter. I can't even pretend to know how you're thinking, but I know it's not vanity lying beneath. If anything, you're still trying to protect others, this time, from yourself."

I'm fucked up in the head is what she's politely saying. But she has said one thing that's right. This doctor's office is the one place where they'll know about my type of injury.

Taking a breath, I slide myself out of the car, using a second to balance myself. Then, with my new rolling gait, I walk across the parking lot toward the entrance. Behind me I hear the beep of the SUV locking, then Allie's footsteps as she catches up to me.

I give my name at the reception desk, then take a seat in the waiting room. I've an early appointment so there's only one other person sitting down. They take a look, then move their gaze away politely.

"So, Mr Allen. What's your first name?" Allie asks, conversationally, having overhead me speak to the receptionist.

I shrug. "Not that anyone uses it anymore, but it's Greg."

Still wondering why I'm putting myself through this, when it's for others not for myself, I pick up a magazine and start thumbing through it. It's about cages, not bikes, so it doesn't hold my interest.

Luckily, I don't have long to wait.

"Mr Allen?"

Nodding that's me, I stand. Allie gets to her feet as well. I glance at her questioningly, my eyebrow raised in challenge.

"I know what these appointments are like. You're given tons of information which you can't remember later. It's good to have someone there to take it all in."

A whore? Coming to a doctor's appointment with me? I'm just about to turn her down with a scoff, when her words sink in. Yeah, all the info the doctors in California had hurled at me, well, some of it hadn't stuck. And it's not like I'm going to be stripping my clothes off. Even that wouldn't reveal anything she hasn't seen already.

With a disbelieving shake of my head, I give in.

CHAPTER NINE

Allie...

I don't know why I felt so driven to hear what the eye doctor was going to say to Truck, but I'm desperate to help him. I want to understand what's driving him, or more accurately, what's not. I need to have some clues of how best to help him. Though he hasn't said much, he acts like a man who's had enough. That scares me. Truck needs something to live for, and he's not going to find that hiding away.

"I'm Dr Austin." A pleasant middle-aged woman reaches out her hand to Truck, then glances at me with her chin raised.

"I'm a friend," I exaggerate to explain my presence.

Her face widens as she smiles and nods. "It's good to have support at times like these. Please sit." As we do, she consults some notes in front of her.

"Right, Mr Allen, or can I call you Greg?"

"Truck's what everyone calls me."

She glances at him, and smiles again. "Okay, Truck it is. How are you doing?"

Truck glances my way, then responds, "I'm doing fine. Thought it was time to improve my appearance."

Her sharp eyes land on him. Removing her glasses, polishing

them, then replacing them on her face, she points to her screen. "Says you lost your eye about six months ago. That's not a lot of time to adjust. I suspect you're still having problems."

Truck looks at her curiously. "What do you mean?"

"Before you lost your eye you had 20/20 binocular vision, didn't you?" She waits for the chin lift of confirmation. "You know how two eyes work together?" Without waiting for a response, she goes into her spiel, seeming not to care if he does or does not. It's all new to me, so I listen intently. "Two eyes allow you to see in 3D. When you look at an object, both eyes focus on it. This means you get information from two points of view that the brain then combines and analyses. This not only allows you to see where the object is, but also its shape, size, and if it's not fixed, how fast and what direction it's moving in. When you lose an eye, you revert to a 2D view of the world. Those cues you had before, well, they're now missing. With the loss of three dimensional sight, you can easily get confused."

Truck remains silent.

"You have to relearn how you see the world. You may misjudge where objects are, how far they are away and their speed of movement. Your depth perception will be different. You may misinterpret what you're seeing as your brain fails to come up with the right explanation. A shape may not be what you believe it to be."

"I'm here to get a prosthetic eye," Truck suddenly snaps. "I'm well aware I can't see properly."

"That's not how I work, Truck. Yes, we'll sort out a prosthesis but you already know that won't give you your vision back. We also need to train your brain to accept signals from just one eye instead of the two it's been used to."

I sit forward. "Will Truck be able to drive again? Or ride his bike?"

"Yes, there is no reason why not. Some people use an additional interior mirror to compensate for the lack of peripheral vision on that side. It's a case of learning to use monocular cues, and turning your head side to side. If you're interested, Truck, I'm friends with a driving instructor who can talk you through techniques for driving safely after the loss of an eye. I'm well aware from your line of work you know the importance of that."

I find that interesting, but I want to know Truck's reaction. She's offered him both help and hope. *Is he going to accept?* I notice Dr Austin is sitting back, giving him time to process the information.

"What you say makes a lot of sense," he says at last. "No one has explained it like that before. I did try to drive, got out of the parking lot outside my apartment. I felt… dizzy is the word for it. Drove straight back, and hit the wall when I reversed. Only gently, thank fuck—God—I was going a snail's pace, but, well, lost my confidence then. I couldn't judge the distance."

"I'll book you in for some sessions. It will be hand and eye coordination, techniques to learn to scan for people and objects around you. It's not normally covered in rehab as they concentrate on getting you mobile again, and doctors in the hospital just want to make sure your injury healed correctly. People tend to forget how two eyes work, and what's lost when you lose one."

Again Truck takes a moment to take that in. Then, for the first time I've seen him since before he went to California, a genuine smile curves Truck's mouth, and his chin rises and falls. "I didn't know how much it would help to know what I'm going through is normal."

"People underestimate the impact of losing an eye. It's an uphill struggle to learn to cope. Unfortunately the mental adjustments necessary aren't always discussed after an enucleation." She glances at me, then adds, "That's the operation to remove an eye."

"It was all done so fast. The surgeons were trying to save my arm, my leg. Fuck, my life."

"Exactly," Dr Austin agrees. "But we'll help you make the most of the vision you have left. Now, let's talk about what you came here for. You have an ocular implant which was put in at the time of your operation, so all we need to do is make the prosthetic and fit it.

"Is it glass?"

"Not nowadays, no, though people still refer to it as that. It's made of acrylic, and is coloured to match your remaining one. While the pupil won't react to light, the prosthetic will move with the other eye."

"Do I… take it out at night?" I notice Truck seems to view that distastefully.

"No. Once a month you'll need to clean it, but you'll sleep with it in with no problem. Have you any other questions? I've arranged a consultation with the ocularist, he's waiting for you now. And I'll be in touch about the therapy sessions."

Truck has nothing else he needs to ask, she seems to have given him enough to think about for now.

There's more of a spring in his step, an optimism, as I tag along with Truck. I'm with him while the ocularist talks him through the ins and outs of making the prosthetic. It's a detailed process and will take several visits, from making a cast of his eye socket to trying their best to match the colours and paint his new eye to match his existing iris, even down to using shredded red cotton to mimic the veins. I'm impressed at the lengths they will go to when matching his fake eye to his existing one. From very close up, it's explained, the eye will look fake as the pupil size won't match the other as it changes. But the muscles in his socket will make it move in co-ordination with his remaining eye.

On the drive home, he's quiet, thoughtful. By the time we arrive, I look across to the passenger seat and notice he seems exhausted, as if the appointments had taken their toll on him.

"Next week you start your sessions. Let me know and I'll drive you."

"Allie, no. You've got—work—to do at the club. I can't monopolise your time."

I go to correct him, but he doesn't give me a chance.

"I'm not an invalid. Don't treat me like one. I can get an Uber like everyone else."

I wish he'd let me help, but what can I do if he refuses my offer? "Let me drive you, Truck. It's no bother."

"You've been a great support today, but let me do this, my way."

It's the dismissive tone of his voice that stops me from pressing my case. *He doesn't want my assistance.* Is it a good sign he wants to take these next steps by himself?

My problem is, I don't know him at all. Even if I'd become close to him before he left for California, he's come back different.

I settle for, "If you change your mind, you know where I am."

"I'd ask you to come in…" His words sound awkward, as if he doesn't seem to know how we should part.

Neither do I. What are we? Friends? Friends with benefits that he knows are there if he asks for them? *How does he see me?*

I make it easy for him. "Sure, you've got a lot to think on. That doctor seemed to know what she was talking about."

He remains seated next to me. "I haven't been to therapy," he admits. "Not since rehab."

He should be talking to someone about how to get on with his life. Those understanding words he heard today helped a lot. I'm reminded of Drummer's suggestions of ways he could get back on a modified bike. Truck needs to think forward, and in my view, therapy would help. "Don't you think you ought to? You've lost a lot, but like Dr Austin, there are people who understand and can suggest how you can adjust."

"I'll think about it."

Drummer wanted me to ask him to come to the club, but I don't think he's in the right headspace yet. I do, however, take the liberty of reaching over and putting my hand on his and squeezing gently.

"You need someone, Truck? You call me."

He gets out of the passenger door, and I watch this strong

man who'd been brought so low shuffle toward his front door wishing there was more I could do to help him.

I drive away thinking today has been a success. For him, and for me. *He let me in.* A small step, but surely it's positive?

But as the days pass and he doesn't contact me again, I start to wonder whether he ever will. Whether he's relearning to see the world, coming to grips with driving and becoming independent again, and starting to live life in a world that doesn't include a whore in it. That's the basis of everything. Even if Truck wanted a friend, he wouldn't choose one like me. Best I stop dreaming.

"You okay, Allie? You've just polished the same glass a dozen times."

That Sam is speaking to me is surprising.

I place the glass with the others, and turn back around. "Just thinking, Sam."

"About Truck?"

My mouth gapes. "You know?" Rapidly I wonder what I could have said to give that impression. Certainly I haven't spoken to her. Whores don't go out of their way to speak to old ladies. And vice versa. I wonder why she's approached me.

Sam looks around, but apart from Tommy who's sweeping up over by the pool table, we're the only two in the clubroom. "Drummer told me. I'd noticed you weren't going with the men, so I asked him." Her mouth narrows. "You like Truck, don't you, Allie?"

I stare at her suspiciously. Is she going to tell me sweet butts should steer clear of members? But the expression on her face is sympathetic, so I decide not to deny my feelings for the scarred man.

"I do Sam, more than I should. Pretty stupid of me, huh?" I've come to the realisation that Truck would never dream of making me his old lady. He wouldn't even date me. Dating is what you do with a woman you want to get to know, not one you can take without any pretence at the social niceties. There's no mystery to me.

Sam looks at me sharply. "You've spoken to him, Allie. He let you inside his apartment. Don't you think Drummer's tried? I went too, with Darcy. He wouldn't open the door, even to someone on his firefighting team."

"I'm a whore, Sam." I shrug. "That's the only reason he let me in. You know men, they get fed up with their hands after a while."

"Don't forget Truck was a prospect. He couldn't go with a sweet butt for almost a year. He'll be well used to servicing himself."

"Doesn't mean he wasn't getting it elsewhere."

"True, but doubtful. He was here every minute he wasn't on his firefighting shift," she surmises. Her head tilts slightly. "What are you going to do?"

Again my shoulders rise and fall. "It's been two weeks, Sam. I don't know what to do. He knows I'm here if he wants me. I just don't feel I can intrude, don't feel I can go around again unless I get an invite."

"Does he know?" she asks quickly. Then clarifies, "That you haven't been working?"

"No." I think that would be the worst thing for him to know. Thinking I'm still a whore means he'll feel entitled to use me. If he called me around for a booty call I wouldn't refuse. I'll take him any way that I can.

"Tell him. It might make a difference," she stresses.

I'm saved from answering when the door opens and Road and Marvel walk in. Sam nods at the men, then tells me, "Zane and Eli will probably be driving Sophie mad by now. I better go and rescue her."

"Beer?" I'm already grabbing bottles and opening them.

"Thanks, Allie." Road leans his elbows on the bar. "Have you heard from Truck?"

"No." It seems they dragged the truth out of Drummer when

he introduced the change in my role at church. I suppose he had to say something. They're still providing my keep and a roof over my head after all, I have to do something in return.

"Rather than waiting for him to contact you, why don't you dress pretty and go to see him?" Marvel suggests. I'm well aware the suggestion isn't for me, but because Truck's brothers are impatient to have him back.

"I'm not going to tart myself…"

"Not dress as a sweet butt," the man originally from California interrupts. "Wear something conservative, but pretty. How about a nice dress?"

I'm getting fashion advice from a biker? The absurdness of it makes me crack a smile.

"Marvel's got a point. Truck knows you as a sweet butt, he knows you're a biker girl. But what if you showed him something different? The woman you really are?"

I stare at Road, thoughts whirring in my head. What type of woman am I? I've been a whore all my adult life, and a couple of years before that. What am I underneath? I don't even own a dress or feminine clothes. All my skirts are on the point of indecent. When I go off the compound I usually wear jeans or shorts.

"Hey, Al," a booming voice interrupts. Caught up with Marvel's suggestion, I hadn't noticed Peg walk in. "Drummer said Truck's pretty weak on his left side. Need to get him here and to the gym where I can start to work with him."

I sigh loudly. "If it was as easy as that, Peg, he'd be here now. He won't come to the club and won't see any of you. I don't even know if he wants to see me again."

"Then go to him. Thought you wouldn't give up so easily, girl." Peg fixes me with a glare.

I purse my lips, thinking. I could pop into Tucson, buy some nice clothes. Doesn't have to be expensive, just something that doesn't make me look like a whore. First time for everything, I suppose. I can't remember a time when I wore a dress, not since I left home.

"I'll go into town tomorrow," I decide out loud. "I need to go shopping…"

"No time like the present, girl. We'll get one of the others to tend bar. You go and do your thing, and make sure you get in that door."

Peg's the sergeant-at-arms. When he says snap to it, you do.

With only a short detour to grab my purse, I'm yet again taking the keys to the SUV, and heading off into Tucson, taking myself to the nearest Walmart where I look at racks of clothes I normally ignore. I'm taken by a retro fifties dress, yes, that looks a style that might suit me. I even team it with a linen jacket. I hardly recognise myself when I look in the mirror. Making a sudden decision I remove the labels, then still wearing my new clothes, take the tags to the till and pay for them and go out into the autumn day feeling like a different woman.

Bolstered by presenting a new persona to the world, I go to Truck's apartment. My hand is shaking as I place my finger to the bell.

I hear the footsteps, then a pause as presumably he's checking who's calling.

Twenty years in the future - Drummer

I sip my whisky once again, musing on the past. "I'd known Allie a long time, watched her. She wasn't like Chrissy or Jill. Peg, you know what they were like. If it hadn't been Wraith or Rock, it would have been someone else. It wasn't the men themselves, but the desire to be anyone's old lady. From what I saw, Allie's feelings for Truck took her by surprise as much as anyone else. It was him, the man, not just that he was a club member. It might have been easier for her if he hadn't been patched."

Peg's head dips up and down slowly. "Truck had some shit to work through in his head, and not just about his injuries."

"He had. But I hoped Allie would be able to get through to him. She liked him, a lot. I could tell. It was something about the way she spoke about him, or rather, what she left unsaid. It was like you finding Darcy, or me finding Sam. Someone snuck in and got under your skin without you noticing."

Peg takes the opportunity to settle himself too, bending his leg before straightening it again, obviously relieving an ache.

"You know," I tell him as I watch his prosthetic ankle flex, "that looks like a real limb."

"They can do amazing things with electronics nowadays. If it wasn't for the stump, I could imagine I had my leg back."

It's his imagination working that thing, sending nerve impulses to fake muscles that make it act like flesh and blood. Twenty years ago, his prosthesis wasn't anywhere near so technically advanced. In fact it works better than Truck's real leg.

"I knew Allie's feelings, of course. I didn't know his. Yeah, it was a risk. But if he rejected her, I was going to help her get away from the club, set her up somewhere. Wasn't going to abandon someone who'd given us the best years of her life."

"Know that, Drum. Would have voted aye on it. You must have been thinking though, she could have gotten hurt." He pauses and shakes his head. "If you were right and she felt a fraction of what I did when I first met Darcy—let alone how much I feel for her today—she'd have been devastated to be rejected."

I know what he means. I fell for Sam hard and my love has only grown over the years.

"Truck saw her as a sweet butt, Drum. What if he'd never moved on from that? She'd been trying so hard to leave that in her rearview, yet you sent her there knowing he might use her for sex and nothing else."

"As things turned out, it might have been the wrong step." Leaning over, I place my empty glass down. "Might have been better to

have sent her away when Marvel made his first complaint. Would have saved a lot of pain."

"Nah," Peg objects. "Wouldn't have saved her any. Her feelings would still have been there. What you might have done wrong, what we all did, was give her hope." He too, puts his beer bottle on the floor beside the chairs.

Would I do the same again, if I could go back in time? I'm a MC prez, I make decisions and don't have regrets. The older me can only look back and agree with the actions I'd taken, knowing I'd take them again.

I'd taken a risk, toyed with a sweet butt's feelings because I wanted a brother back at the club.

Mentally I shrug. Just one more stain on my blackened soul.

CHAPTER TEN

Fuck…

These last two weeks have been trying. Multiple times it's been on the tip of my tongue to tell the ocularist not to bother. I've attended regular appointments from having the initial wax cast of my eye socket taken to the actual prosthetic being finished, and I've been on the verge of backing out numerous times. Why do I want the bother of a fake eye? It won't replace what I lost.

Two days ago was the final fitting.

The ocularist had held up a mirror. My intake of breath had been sharp. I'd taken the mirror from his hand, and held it myself, looking first from a distance, then moving it closer. I felt tears prick behind my eyes as I couldn't believe what I saw. Unless you look very carefully, I've got two eyes. The transformation was remarkable. Doesn't do anything to hide or minimise the scarring, but I don't look like such a freak. When I kept watching, I saw a tear roll down the left side of my face. I laughed out loud. Of course, my tear ducts remain, but I never expected to see myself crying out of two eyes again.

Not that I often cry, but that it appears that I can, seems another positive step.

After feeling that it was all a waste of time, I suddenly realised this had been the right thing to do. No more patches, no more visual reminders of what I'd lost.

I'd got into the Uber with a new confidence. Unless they got right up into my face, no one would know I'd lost an eye, and even then, the ocularist had done such a good job, it would fool most.

At first, my eye was constantly watering as my body needed to adjust to the alien object, but this morning I'd woken up, and as predicted, it seems I no longer treat the prosthetic as if it's something that shouldn't be there.

I'll have a few more appointments to make sure it's settling well, then all I need to do is take it out once a month to clean it, and have it professionally cleaned once a year. Most of the time I'll be able to forget it's not part of me. This morning, as I had shaved my head, I'd looked into the mirror, turning my head this way and that, admiring the new part of me. Then, I watched myself smile.

Allie had been right.

I still look like a monster, but not so much.

I feel… different. Not normal, I'll never feel that. But maybe there's a kernel starting to sprout inside me that wants to do more than simply exist. Problem is, I've no idea what I'm capable of doing.

For now, I just continue going through the motions, my normal daily existence. My boring routine broken mid-afternoon by the doorbell ringing.

Knowing I'll be sending anyone who's come calling away, I walk to it, my hand inching toward the intercom, until I look through the peephole.

Suddenly, I'm nervous. *What's she going to say?* I hesitate for a moment, then shrug. Why should I be worried about the reaction of one of the club girls. Doesn't matter what they think, if I wanted a fuck, they'd do anything I ask anyway.

I open the door.

It's Allie. But, it's not.

I've seen her naked, seen her in sexy barely-there clothes. I've seen her in jeans and a tee. But never have I seen her wearing a pretty dress. She looks like she's arrived to be taken out on a date.

For a moment I'm taken aback, for a second wishing that was the case. But this is Allie, a sweet butt, not the type of woman you have to make any effort to get into her panties.

I haven't said anything. Neither has she. She's staring at my face, and slowly, a huge smile spreads across hers.

"Truck. You look, great! It worked. You can't tell it's fake. Oh my God. What a transformation! It's amazing."

Her pleasure is infectious, I find myself grinning back. "You like it?"

"I love it!"

She's so genuinely pleased for me, I find myself stepping back from the door, my action being an invite for her to come inside.

Once over the threshold, she turns and looks around the room. Unlike the previous time she was here, the blinds are up, and natural daylight floods the room.

"You're feeling a bit better about things, aren't you, Truck?"

She's right. I am. I'm still mourning everything I've lost, still wondering about the man I now am, but at least I'm keeping my more dire thoughts at bay.

As she surveys my domain, I watch her. She's beautiful, it's easy to tell why she's one of the most popular whores in the club. Dressed as she is? She could go anywhere. Suddenly I wonder why she's here, and all dolled up. *Is she on her way to meet someone?* Lucky man, if she is. *Would she be allowed to have a relationship outside the club?* Hmm, not sure Drummer would like that. Perhaps he doesn't know.

"Why are you here, Allie?"

She spins back around, giving me another pointed look as though checking my eye is still there. "I came to see how you were doing, Truck. I never expected…" She waves a hand at my face.

"I nearly backed out," I admit. "But I'm glad I didn't."

"Do you want to go out?" she asks, suddenly.

Of course I don't. "Allie, no. I don't want to go anywhere." My mantra for the past few months.

"Not to meet people, you're not ready for that. How about a drive? It's a nice evening."

The thought suddenly comes into my head that it would be a great evening for riding my bike. I don't even know what's happened to it now. Still in storage at the club I expect. I'll have to get around to selling it soon, not that it's worth much, but the money would be useful. I'll never be able to ride it again. Some of the pleasure I'd felt when seeing Allie's reaction to my eye disappears.

"Nah." I shake my head.

But she's not going to give up. "Oh, come on. What else have you got to do?"

I open my mouth then shut it again. Anything I say would be an excuse. I've got nothing planned. *What would it hurt?*

Suddenly I'm suspicious. "I'm not going to the club."

Her eyes narrow. "Don't trust me much, do you?"

Trust her? Suddenly, I realise, I do. "I trust you Allie, just want you to understand. If we go anywhere, I don't want you to make any detours I'm not ready for."

"Well, you drive then."

Wait. What? I throw up my hands in exasperation. "I can't drive, Al. I'm not ready for that."

"You can. I'll be there to warn you if I see something you don't. You know what the problems are, let's try and compensate."

While I'm scared to get behind the wheel of a car again, having someone with me, someone I already know keeps their eyes on the road and drives competently, might just give me the confidence to try. As my injuries are on the left side, as long as I don't drive a stick-shift and need to use a clutch, I'd be okay to drive.

Suddenly I make up my mind. "Okay. But not far. And we'll take my car." It's about time to give it a run.

But we don't take mine in the end as the battery is dead from being unused for so long. Allie stands and stares at it. "I'll get Blade—"

"No, not giving you an excuse to bring a Satan's Devil to my home," I tell her, sharply.

"I was going to say, to lend me his lithium battery to jump start it with." She rolls her eyes in frustration. "Trust me, Truck. I'm not going to push you to do more than you're ready for."

"I think we're going for a drive because you pushed me," I tell her, wryly.

Half an hour later, I'm glad that she did. The SUV's got large wing mirrors which compensates for my lack of peripheral vision on my left side. It's also got a blind spot warning light, being a newer model. I start thinking about trading in my own car for something equipped with that, and realise I'm beginning to think of tools I could use to help in my life, rather than hiding away and avoiding facing my problems head on.

We don't talk, she just lets me take a route I want, up toward Pima Canyon.

"Hey, Truck. Pull over."

There's a parking spot, I use it. When I get out, I realise why she stopped us. The sun is just setting over the mountains, flooding the area with a golden light. I stand behind her, enjoying the moment, relishing her obvious delight in such an everyday sight, and to my surprise, find I'm sharing it. Simple pleasures, something I haven't appreciated in a while.

The light makes her hair gleam. Standing close, I can smell a faint perfume, light, and slightly musky. She's entranced with the sight in front of her, I'm enjoying the view from behind, my eyes rising from her slender feet encased in gold coloured sandals, rising to her shapely calves, then, having to leave her thighs to my imagination as they are hidden under her dress. A gentle breeze blows, her dress swirls gently, the material framing her ass.

My cock twitches as I wonder what she's wearing beneath. *Pretty panties, perhaps? A lacy bra?* My fingers itch to take her home, explore and find out.

"Peg wants to talk to you." She spoils the moment.

"I don't want to talk to him. I can't be a member, Allie. I'm nothing to the club. I've accepted it, they have to too."

"Peg wants to work with you in the gym." She ignores me. "Says you need to strengthen your leg, build your muscles back up."

"You betrayed my confidence." My voice snaps. The only way the sergeant-at-arms could know my condition is if she's been gossiping.

"They're worried about you. They asked how you were, I told them is all."

Why it's annoyed me so much, I don't know. But it has. Angrily I toss the keys at her. She easily plucks them out of the air whereas with my new lack of hand and eye coordination, I'd have dropped them. "Let's get back. You drive. It's getting dark and I don't see so well then."

For a moment I'd forgotten. For a moment I'd felt like a man out with his girl. Her reminder of the club made me remember what her role in it is. She's not a girl you take out, she's a whore you fuck.

"Truck…"

"I want to go home," I say petulantly, and turning, walk back to the SUV and get into the passenger side.

I was thinking about seducing a whore for fuck's sake. She's probably already been in at least one bed today, or over the pool table.

Opening the passenger side door, I sit on the seat then pull my body around, cursing again the weakness on my left. If I'm honest it's not improving since I stopped physical therapy, so

Peg's offer makes sense. But that would mean going to the club, which I'm not prepared to do. Sympathy for my injuries would be one thing, but to hear it confirmed, that I can't be a member anymore, would really hurt.

As would seeing men paw over Allie.

"Truck," Allie starts as she adjusts the seat.

"No, Allie. This was a mistake." She turns up at my apartment looking like the girl next door, the one everyone would be proud to go out with, but her clothes just hide what she is beneath that fancy dress. She's been with the club such a long time, it's all she's ever been and all she will ever be. She'd never be able to be faithful to a man. I've seen her at work, and experienced it for myself. This is a woman who loves sex, and lots of it.

So do I.

Fuck, I'm a man. I can do who I want.

I'm not saying I wouldn't fuck Allie again, I would, and I'd probably enjoy it. She'd make sure I had a good time. Then she'd go off and do one of my brothers.

"Please, Truck, let me explain something."

But whatever she wants to say will go unheard. Fuck it. The club's pulling out all the stops to get me back there. To see for themselves what a mess I've become. I can't be fixed, this is beyond anyone.

It dawns on me I'm only putting off the inevitable. I'm hiding away, refusing to open my door, resenting them trying to make contact with me. The easiest way to sort this is to face it head on. Get it over and done with, prepare myself to hear the finality in Drummer's voice when he acknowledges the truth, I can't be a Satan's Devil any longer.

"Tell Drummer I'll be there at the next church." Yes, that's what I'll do. Then he can officially cut those brand new patches off the cut he's keeping safe for me. I can't ride, so I don't fulfil that part of the club's regulations. He can revoke my membership, then they can wash their hands of me and I'll be left alone.

No more attempts to get me to the club, no more sending whores to make house visits.

I'll go to that driving instructor that Dr Austin recommended, learn techniques to cope when I drive. Then, I'll be independent, and decide what my future will be.

She pulls up outside my apartment. "Truck," she tries once again.

"This is goodbye, Allie. Don't come here anymore." She twists me in knots. *I want her.* But I don't want a whore.

"Please, Truck."

"Look, you haven't failed, Allie. You've done what you set out to do. I'll come to the club. Drummer can see me for himself."

"You'll really come back?"

No, I won't. But they're not going to leave me alone until I show my face. After that, I won't be a member any longer.

"I'll be there, as I said. At the next church."

TWENTY YEARS IN THE FUTURE – Drummer

"NEVER EXPECTED YOU TO BE NEXT."

"Huh?"

"After Wraith. I'd have laid money on any of the others, or no one at all."

When I catch up with his line of thought, I shrug. "Didn't go looking for it, it just happened. Best thing I've ever done was stop when I saw Sam at the side of the road." Half of me is wondering how he got to that when we'd been talking about Truck and Allie.

Now he guffaws. "Do you remember Viper's reaction when he found out he had an adult daughter?"

"He wasn't impressed." Which is an understatement.

Peg suddenly doubles over. For a moment I'm concerned, until I see his shoulders shaking with mirth. "That night..." he gasps out. "That night..." then stops again. He makes an effort as my teeth clench, believing I know where he's going with this. My fears realised when he pulls himself together enough to say, "Outside the clubhouse. We all found out you'd fucked her..."

Viper hadn't been discreet, choosing that moment to start caring about the daughter he'd never known he had, and yeah, he'd been right. I had fucked her. Wasn't my proudest moment, and I had deserved the punch to my jaw. Problem was, he'd been shouting, and everyone had heard.

Peg starts to sober up. "Bad business with the slave traffickers though, thought we'd lost Sam for a moment there."

So had I. Just when I was pulling my head out of my ass to admit how much I wanted her, she'd been taken from me. It might be more than twenty years in the past, but my gut clenches when I think how I could have lost her.

"She's the best thing that ever happened to me, Peg. Can't imagine what my life would have been like without her in it. We've ridden side by side for years now." In a couple of years I'll be celebrating my silver wedding. Me, who got my name for banging everything in sight, has remained faithful to one woman. My younger self would never have believed it.

"We've done good, Drummer."

He's right. We have.

"Sam's like the missing piece of me that I never realised wasn't there." I sound sappy, even to my own ears, but Peg simply raises his chin to show he knows exactly what I mean.

"I always wanted an old lady. I'd already been married, you know that. Got burned pretty badly, but before it had all gone wrong, I knew what it was like to have someone to come home to. You, though, you were the confirmed bachelor if ever there was one. Surprised the fuck out of us when you settled with Sam. Never had a doubt you'd make it, though. Anyone could see she'd changed you, Drum. You're a better man since she came along."

I don't question it. Sam has balanced me. Having her beside me hasn't made me soft, but has made me more protective, more aware of what I had to lose, and possibly, more cautious.

"Huh. That was the time we had twenty bodies to get rid of."

I smile. "It was you, wasn't it, Peg, who came up with the answer?"

His shoulders rise and drop. "Maybe it was. But Road got a practice race track out of it up in the forest."

"And had it extended from time to time." Over the years there may have been a few other bodies.

"I wonder how Road's doing now? Have you heard from him recently?"

"Nah." Road had transferred out years back. "Last I heard he'd given up trial-bike racing, he was getting too old."

"Couldn't keep up with the youngsters, I suspect."

"Years pass, take their toll, Peg."

"That they do, Prez. That they do."

CHAPTER ELEVEN

Truck…

The Uber drops me off at the gates of the compound, then does one of the quickest three point turns I've ever seen, before tearing back down the track with dust billowing after it. He's got extra in his pocket for his bravery in bringing me right to the front of the lion's den.

Watching, I shake my head. *What did he expect? Bikers to swarm out and rob him?* Probably.

The gate is opened by a man wearing a prospect cut. For a second I can't place whether he's Hound or Roadkill. Doesn't matter, Prospect will do in any event.

I feel eyes on me as I drag my way up the incline to the clubhouse. It reminds me I don't do enough walking, and even the short stretch has made my ankle ache.

As I approach I see all the bikes parked outside and recognise every one, even noticing Beef's Fat Bob is missing. I wonder why he's not at church.

I'm slightly apprehensive as I draw closer. Allie will have told them I'm returning today. *Please God don't let them have arranged a celebration.* I'm not a returning triumphant hero, I'm a broken man who can no longer use the moniker, biker.

I'm also late. The Uber took longer turning up than I hoped, so I'm not surprised to find the clubroom empty. I do hear female voices from the kitchen, so quicken my step, hoping my luck continues and I'll see no one before I'm in the meeting room. I'd prepared to meet my brothers for the first time since I was injured in the fire, but somehow had overlooked I'd see women and children too. Fuck, I hope my face doesn't scar them for life.

I hesitate at the meeting room door. For almost a year I worked my butt off, my only aim to sit around this table. I never expected my first time would be when it came to say goodbye. I swallow down the lump that's risen to my throat, harden my resolve, and push down on the handle.

"So do we need to increase the dues this year?" Prez asks Dollar, not pausing when I step inside the door.

With only a brief look to see who's interrupted, Dollar replies, "No, I propose we leave them as they are."

"Seconded," Rock shouts.

Slick points to an empty seat by his side. I may not have been in church much before, but when I have, I'm certain that was Beef's. *Where is he?* As well as the absence, I notice additions. Fergus had been patched in the same night that I had, and it seems Matt has as well now. I lift my chin toward the men I best remember as prospects.

"Truck," Drum asks me directly as I move around brothers to get to the chair, "you okay with keeping the dues at the same level?"

"As if anyone would object," Joker scoffs.

This is my first and last time at church. I just wave my hand to show I agree, then get my left leg comfortable under the table.

"Viper. You had something to say about progress at the mall."

I raise my hand. I don't want to sit here and pretend, I want to get this over with.

"Truck, we'll come to you later." Prez nods at Viper who starts giving his report.

I let his words float over my head. What do I care how their businesses are doing, or anything else? I stare down at my fingers, or to be accurate, where I'm missing two on my left hand. Part of me itches to hide it, but I force myself to leave my ruined appendage in sight. So it won't come as any surprise when I make the confession that's so hard to voice. *I can't ride anymore.*

"Prez, I want to ask. What are we going to do about Allie? You said we'd revisit it once Truck takes up his seat around the table."

"I did," Prez responds to Marvel.

I'm just about to refute that I've returned to the club, when Prez stares so hard, I slam shut my mouth.

"You thinking of claimin' her, Truck?"

What? "What the fuck, Drummer?" What on earth have they been reading into the fact she's been visiting me? "I don't know what the fuck she's been saying, Prez. But no, I won't be claiming her. She's a whore."

Another hard stare from Drummer, then he sighs. "Then, we have something to discuss."

Peg leans forward. "I'm concerned about sending her away, Prez. She's got a lot of info in that head of hers, even if she doesn't think she does. If she falls into the wrong hands, she could bring us down."

Blade spins his knife. "I like Allie. Known her a long time."

"Think all of us *know* her, Brother," quips Rock.

The enforcer glares at Rock. "As I was saying, I've known her a long time. I like the bitch. But the only option that I see if we don't trust her to keep her mouth shut, is to take her out."

What the fuck is he saying?

The conversation gets my thoughts away from my own predicament and onto hers. "What the hell are you lot talking about? What's Allie done?" What could be so serious they're talking about sending her away or heaven forbid, ending her life?

"It's more what she hasn't done, I think you'll find," Lady quips, seeming less concerned about the conversation than I'd have thought.

"She doesn't fuck anymore," Road puts in helpfully. "Can't keep a sweet butt who keeps her legs closed."

She doesn't? I frown. "Since when?" She opened her legs for me, just as I had instructed.

"A good few months," Wraith supplies.

"At first she made half-hearted attempts," Marvel takes over, "but she wasn't feeling it. Then she made every excuse under the sun to get out of it."

"Coincided with you leaving for California." It's Drummer who gives it to me straight.

I'm faced with raised eyebrows as my brain tries to process the information it's just heard.

"She's a whore," I repeat. "Once one, always one. Even if I had those thoughts about her, I wouldn't claim her."

"Fuckin' lucky Sophie didn't think the same thing about me," Wraith snarls. "Only difference there is that I didn't get paid."

Drummer's eyebrows are raised, making me remember his name. He got his handle by banging everything in sight.

"You a fuckin' virgin?" Lady asks.

"Of course I'm fuckin' not."

"How many women have you had?" Shooter asks as if he genuinely wants to know.

"Two, three?" Rock helpfully supplies.

Hey, before I was a biker I was a firefighter. "I've had my fair share."

"More than, I suspect," remarks Drummer.

I shrug. "It's different for women. And especially for her. Like it's been mentioned, everyone here has been in her cunt."

"Not me," snarls Peg.

Mouse too is shaking his head.

"Certainly not us," Joker raises his eyebrow at Lady who gives a sharp nod of agreement.

"Well, most," I amend.

"Which will make me jealous as fuck of the man who gets her heart." Road's eyes narrow. "Allie's a good woman."

Remembering that one night I had with her, I can certainly see why. The thought that they'd be envious is something I hadn't expected. But even if I looked at her that way, she wouldn't want to be claimed. Not now.

"Allie doesn't want me," I tell them, my head moving from side to side. "Maybe the man I was before…"

"Who you still fuckin' are, Brother," Rock snarls.

This seems as good a time as any. I take a deep breath. "No easy way to tell you this, but I shouldn't be sitting around this table." My voice breaks. "I can't ride. Won't ever be able to. Only thing I can do is leave the club."

"Could get fuckin' painful," Joker warns.

Painful?

"I can attest to that." Heart shudders.

"Hey, we pulled our punches with you because you were fucked in the head." Blade spins his knife and stops it pointing at Heart.

"He's still fucked in the head. He's repopulating the club all by himself."

For that, Mouse gets a punch in the arm from the man sitting beside him.

Showing no animosity, Heart explains, "With Marcia's help." He adds in my direction, "She's pregnant again."

Prez has been focused on me, ignoring the banal conversation. Suddenly he pushes back his chair and half stands, then leans forward with his weight on his hands and spits out, "That what you want, Truck? For your brothers to give you the beating you'll remember for the rest of your fuckin' life? 'Cause that's the only way you're walking out on this club."

"I'm not walking out. I haven't got a fuckin' choice," I shout, all my emotions rising to the fore. "I've got a bike sitting here somewhere which I'd give all that I have to ride again. *I can't!*"

Drummer sits back down, shaking his head. "Never took you for a fuckin' coward."

Now I see red. "I'm no fuckin' coward." I've medals on my wall to prove that.

"Coward from where I'm sitting," observes Peg.

The VP joins in too. "From my seat as well."

I bang my left arm down on the table, palms up, showing my withered wrist and ruined hand. "This says you're wrong. My leg's fucked as well, I've got so many pins in my ankle it won't flex properly. I can't see as well as I used to. I can't use a clutch or kick through the gears…"

"So we build a custom bike. Electric shift with take care of the gear changes, we can modify the clutch."

"Sam will help, she's got some ideas," Drummer offers to Blade.

"Get you into the gym, build your strength up. I know your leg's been shattered, your arm too, but your muscles will be able to compensate, as long as you put the work in." My mouth drops open as Peg seems to make it sound easy.

Prez glances at me, but I keep my mouth shut. My immediate impulse to reject help swallowed back down. They're thinking of workarounds, searching for ways to make the most of what I've got left. *Is there really a possibility I'll ride with the club?* A dream I'd worked so hard for and thought had disappeared, now seems to be a glimmer of hope once again.

"So there's your choices," Drummer sums up. "You choose which one you want. A beatdown—which won't be gentle as you'll have pissed all of us off—or you work with Peg to get fit, and with Blade to get a bike you can fuckin' ride."

Choice? I choke up, and just about manage to get out the words. "I don't think I'll choose the beatdown."

Joker snorts. Heart nods as though I've made the right choice. A slow raise and lower of his chin from Prez. A hand clap from Wraith. Words of relief from around the table. Then Drummer stands, reaches behind him, and comes down the table toward me with something held behind his back.

"I've given you one pass today, *Brother*. The next time you appear underdressed around this table, it's the beatdown for certain." He hands me my cut.

Immediately I slip it on, feeling the weight I'd carried for those twelve hard prospecting months settling comfortably on my shoulders. Knowing it no longer carries the prospect patch, but the Tucson rocker.

I sob, then lean my head into my hands, trying to pull myself together.

They give me a moment, but no more before Road states from the other side of the table, "I can't tell which is the fake one."

"Yeah, they move together. Matched the colour well."

"Truck, look at me."

Turning my head, I look at Rock who's leaning across the table.

"Fuckin' good job, close up, if you're looking for it, you can see."

"Can you take it out whenever you want? Great fuckin' party trick at Halloween if you can."

Joker bangs his hand down on the table. "Can you imagine tricking the kids?"

Drummer's eyes open wide then he starts shaking his head. "For fuck's sake don't give Eli ideas. He'll have Truck popping it out on purpose to scare his friends."

He needn't worry. I won't be popping it out, as they put it, for anyone. But as the comments keep coming, I start to chuckle. An alien sound I haven't heard from myself for seven months. Then my shoulders start shaking and laughter comes out, and tears are running down my face.

"Fuckin' assholes," I tell them, noting not one has commented on my scarring, or treated me any differently than before. My disability? Something to cope with and work around. *Why did I stay away from the club?* I have no fucking idea.

"Move here. Live on the compound," Peg says suddenly. "You've been on your own too fuckin' long, Brother. Stay here. It will be easier to get to the gym."

"Spare suite now that Beef's gone," Viper offers.

Beef's gone? "Beef, he's not…" A chill goes through me.

"Nah, he's not dead. He's got himself the VP spot up in Colorado."

"Got a blind bitch for an ol' lady, too."

"Yeah, she's hot. Lucky that she can't see what an ugly fucker her ol' man is."

Information is being fired at me from all sides. Beef gone? I hadn't expected that. But good on him for making VP. Seems there's been a few changes since I'd been gone.

Running my hands down my face, I come to a decision. "I'll consider moving here. You're right, it does make sense. Only kept the apartment in town as it was close to the station." *A station I'm going to have to visit soon. I've been a fool keeping my distance from people who love me. I've neglected my firefighting team as well as the club.* "But I've got a condition."

"What?" Drummer's face hardens, and I know I'm in no position to make threats.

"Nothing happens to Allie."

"Think that brings us back around to the question I originally posed." Drummer tugs at his beard. "She's not a sweet butt anymore, but do we still let her keep a roof over her head?"

"Never had a woman like that here before, or not one that we haven't offered our protection too."

"She makes a good fuckin' bartender." Road, who seems to be on Allie's side, puts in. Makes me wonder whether he'd like to claim her for himself.

"Not saying there's anything wrong with it," Prez says. "Just that we could be starting a precedent. What if Pussy begins to have ideas in her head? Wants to shut up shop, but stay?"

"Can't see that," says Rock. "They enjoy providing their

services too much. Anyway, if, for example, Pussy did, she'd have to offer something else instead, like Allie's already doing."

Peg clears his throat. "They're all going to get old. We going to throw them out then, after years of service?"

Viper, quiet up to now, speaks up. "I say, let Allie stay on her terms. We'll play it by ear if the others follow suit. As Rock says, those girls are as hungry for sex as we are."

He's right. Which is what I thought about Allie. Which is what has me wondering about why she stopped.

Our one night together? That's all we had. Apparently it had been enough to get her to rethink her lifestyle.

What the fuck is going on in her head? Does she have ideas about becoming my old lady? Only one way to find out. I'm going to have to ask her.

But what will I do with her answer?

"Okay. We happy to vote? Make it official?"

They vote. Heart records it.

CHAPTER TWELVE

Allie…

Knowing Truck was coming to the compound today, I made myself scarce.

Leaving by the gate at the rear, I walk across the firebreak that's now well maintained, and carry on up into the forest. It's not long before I come to the dirt track that Road uses to practice his off-road riding. I smile to myself. They think I don't know, but I do. Where else would they have buried twenty bodies? It's disguised well, no one would guess our enemies lie beneath. The area should feel haunted by ghosts, but it doesn't, not to me. No one lies dead here who doesn't deserve it.

There's a tree trunk, and I sit, worrying at my fingernails. I look up as I hear a sound. That's not particularly concerning, there's unlikely to be someone straying so far off the beaten track and so close to an outlaw biker compound. So it's with curiosity that I wait to see who appears, more annoyed that my solitude will be interrupted.

"Hey, Allie. You okay?"

It's Sam. It could have been worse.

"I'm fine, Sam."

"No you're not. Shift your ass along. Let me sit down."

I do. She takes a backpack off her shoulder. "Saw you head out so grabbed some provisions and followed you. Thought you'd be off by yourself."

Drummer and her house, like that of the sweet butts', is at the top of the compound. She must have seen me pass by out of the window.

She rummages inside her pack, and brings out two glasses, and a bottle of margarita.

I was going to tell her I wanted some alone time, but suddenly what she's brought looks damn attractive. She pours two glasses, hands me one, then, when she holds up hers in invitation, I automatically clink mine against it in a toast.

"What are we drinking to?"

She presses her lips together, then says seriously, "That Truck makes good choices."

"I've lost my chance with him, Sam. Sure, he's come to the club. but I think it's just to show them why he can't stay."

Which puts my future in doubt. I've examined my feelings and know I could never go back to servicing all the men again, because they wouldn't be Truck. Sure, I don't see a future with no sex in it, but I wouldn't be able to return to the life I lived before.

"Drummer won't send you away. Whatever the outcome, Al."

"You can't say that, Sam. I don't want to be a sweet butt, and sweet butts and old ladies are the only women here."

"Drink up," she instructs. Then pours two more glasses. "I can't say I know what you mean, I was always more interested in bikes than men. I was a virgin when I met Drummer."

It must be the drink, but I giggle. "Everyone knows that."

"Yeah, neither Viper nor Drummer were discreet, were they? I heard all about their altercation. Unfortunately, so did everyone else."

Altercation. That's one way of describing it. Viper, Sam's father who'd only just discovered he had a daughter, had decided to throw a few punches and then get into a very public screaming match with Drummer when he knew that he'd fucked her. I doubt there was anyone not aware of what had gone down. It's another reason Drummer did well in his choice of old lady, Sam's not fazed about it.

The prez's old lady sips her drink, then chuckles. "Do you remember that day when this track was first completed?"

"I remember it had been hell. All those poor women."

"We'd rescued them from the slave traffickers. That's right, you and the other sweet butts stayed with them, but the rest of us came up here." Her eyes glaze slightly. "Peg started it, he rode Road's dirt bike. Looked so much fun, so everyone else took a turn."

"But you got the fastest time." I'd heard all about it. It had been the main topic of conversation that night.

"I did," she confirms with a grin.

That's something I'd missed. Club members and old ladies having fun, sweet butts not included. I wonder where I'd stand now. Forgotten or invited? Who knows?

"That was when Diva and Paige decided to join us." Sam remembers the enjoyment, the celebration that the club had overcome the great odds they'd been facing. I remember the trauma and pain of the women who'd been rescued. But then, she'd been kidnapped and tortured. Like for the men, the task of making the dirt track look well used which had turned into a competition, was probably a much needed release.

We're quiet for a moment, lost in memories.

Until Sam brings us back to the present. "What was it like, with Truck? Why was it different with him than the other men?"

Another drink poured and drunk, and I'm already feeling tipsy. "It was more than sex, Sam. The job of a whore is to make the man enjoy it. It isn't so much getting pleasure yourself, but knowing you've given him something. Knowing, for those moments, the power is all in your hands."

"Or your pussy," she giggles, suggesting the drink is having an effect on her as well.

"That too," I agree with a laugh. "The sweet butts all try to be the best. To be the one the men want most. That's actually impossible, men have different wants and desires, and one prefers one, another another. But you get to learn what they like best, and do what you can to give it to them."

"So, what happened with Truck?"

"It's hard to explain. I obviously knew nothing about him. It was my first time with him, and his with a whore. But it was different. Oh, at first it started off the way I expected, but that changed. Suddenly I wanted to give him everything, that part of me I'd kept hidden." I think back and admit to myself, *I'd wanted to kiss him.* "I didn't want it to be about me having power, having a big strong man under my control. When he, when he…"

"Made you come."

"Yeah." I grin. "Well, it wasn't anything I'd ever felt before. It was more than just a physical release."

"What would have happened if he hadn't left?" she muses.

"I'd have made a fool of myself," I respond. "Yearning for something I couldn't have."

"Perhaps all things happen for a reason. I came to find my dad, and met Drummer."

"I wouldn't have wanted Truck to get hurt."

"You're coping so well, Allie. I know your heart must be bleeding for him, but you don't show it. I think that's probably exactly what he needs and wants. Someone to be there for him and support him, while keeping their own shit to themselves."

That's what I've tried to do.

"If Truck…" I break off. Truck's made it clear he doesn't want me. To him I'm just a whore. I've stopped going with other men, and when he knows, if that doesn't change his mind, there's nothing more I can do.

"If Truck doesn't know a good thing when he sees it; if he

doesn't claim you as his old lady, Drummer will make sure you're okay. I know my man, Allie."

I sigh. "If Truck stays with the club, I don't think I'll be able to, Sam." Even just the thought of seeing Truck take advantage of Diva and Paige hurts.

"Then Drummer will set you up somewhere else. Don't worry about your future. You've given ten years of your life to the club. I know the men appreciate it."

It hasn't exactly been a sacrifice.

"What if…" and the idea's so ludicrous I accompany it with a laugh. "What if I did become his old lady? How would you and the others feel about that?"

Her arm loops around my shoulder. "We'd welcome you with open arms."

Would they? Or is that the drink talking. Somehow I don't think it would be as easy as she suggests. She's accepted Drummer's past, that she's certain he'll remain faithful is all she needs going forward. But Sam's special, she's got the right attitude to be a prez's old lady. Not everyone is like her.

"You'd rather leave the club than watch Truck with the sweet butts. You'd give up everyone else, and the life you've known since you were a teenager. That's what would earn you the respect of the old ladies."

We drink some more, but in silence. Knowing how Eli and Zane run her ragged, I reckon Sam's enjoying some peace and quiet. Drummer's kids, not surprisingly, are a bit of a handful. I've never thought of having children of my own, and it crosses my mind whether Truck might want them or not.

Why am I torturing myself? Even if he does, he made it plain it wouldn't be with me.

"Come on." Eventually Sam stands and holds out her hand to help me up. "I've got to go and see what those monsters of mine are up to."

The sun's going down fast. I hadn't realised how long we'd been out here.

At her reference to her children, I comment, "I bet you miss Jayden's help."

"Like hell I do. But Jayden seems so happy now she and Paladin are together."

"Yeah, what is that with everyone moving to Colorado?"

We're still gossiping about Beef and Pal's transfers away from the club when we reach the compound. As we go through the gate and prepare to separate to go to our houses, I see the last person I expected, leaning against my front door.

By the light spilling out through the windows, the first thing I notice is that he's wearing his cut. The sight of this tall, still handsome to my eyes biker, makes my stomach clench. So close, but so unobtainable.

Why's he here? To tell me he's come back to the club? *And how, if he can't ride a bike?*

Is he looking for a sweet butt to use?

Oh, God, don't let him ask me to find one for him, or worse, ask for me to service him. I'll happily let him fuck me, but not with the knowledge he'd then leave me, and move on to the next sweet butt's bed.

I don't want to fuck. I want to do something I've only ever done with Truck. I want to make love.

His eyes fix on me as I draw closer. I notice how good he looks with the prosthetic, you'd be hard pressed to know it's not real. Though I can tell as the gap closes between us, there's an emotion shining from one and not the other.

I stop, a foot away from him, my heart ceases beating as I wait to find out what he wants.

He keeps staring, unnerved, I return his gaze.

Suddenly he snarls, "Why the fuck didn't you tell me? Why the fuck did you let me carry on believing you were a whore? Why the fuck, Allie?"

I don't know what to say. Should I tell him it's because that's what he'd assumed when he used me and I didn't want him to feel guilty?

His eyes don't move from my face, I look away and down at my feet.

"Allie," he says in a warning tone.

When I still don't respond, he takes the initiative. The hardness in his face falls away, and his expression becomes softer, almost sympathetic. "Allie. There's nothing between us, never can be."

Each word feels like a nail being hammered into my coffin.

"I'm going to be living here, at the compound. Need to get this straight. I don't know what's in your head, but if it includes a house, picket fence and you and me, you've got to lose that image now."

I go to tell him a lie, that I never think of him like that at all. Instead when I open my mouth, out comes the truth. "I thought we connected. That night before you left for California."

"We fucked, Allie. It was good, yeah. But that's all it was."

I stare into his eyes, hoping to see a sign that he doesn't truly believe that, but it's clear that he does.

"Club voted to let you stay on, even if you're not a sweet butt anymore. So you're free to do what you want to, Al."

The news that I'm not losing my home should make my heart dance. But how can I stay? With him living here, seeing him every day? How could I stand it? *What else can I do?*

Pulling myself together, I try to hide what I'm feeling. "I'm glad you're staying, Truck." I point to his cut. "It's good to see you wearing that again. You made a good decision today." *For you.* Not so much for me.

"Allie…"

"I hear what you say," I croak out the words. "I'll keep out of your way."

"No need for that. Just wanted to clear matters up so you know how things stand. I won't be claimin' you Allie."

He couldn't make it any clearer. But best rip that band aid right off. No more hoping or dreaming of what could be.

"I hear you, Truck," I repeat. *Stupid, stupid whore, to ever think it could have been different.*

He stays still, unmoving, staring again at my face. Behind me the door opens.

"Truck! You're back!" a delighted voice says. Then, "Oh my God!"

I turn to see Pussy standing with a hand over her mouth, and her face I swear is turning green. "Your face!"

If she'd punched Truck he couldn't have reeled more. He steps backward fast, then, without a word, spins and limps back down the track toward the clubhouse.

"What the hell?" I round on her. "Why did you have to say anything?"

Her eyes widen. "Allie, did you not see? That scarring? Fuck. And watch how he's walking…"

My hand comes up of its own volition and slaps her around the face. "That man is a fucking hero. He knows what he looks like and he's the one who has to live with it."

"Well, shit. You might be able to ignore it, but if I ever have to do him, it will be with the lights off."

Still rubbing her cheek, she steps around me and strides off in the same direction Truck had taken.

Now it's my turn to feel sick as her suggestion rings in my ears. *Truck can do anything. Fuck anyone.* And I won't be able to raise a single objection.

Twenty years in the future – *Drummer*

My attention is caught by a hawk flying overhead, the bird with sharp eyes, majestic and cunning. That it's the road name of my oldest son is not a coincidence.

Peg breaks the silence. "She got him back to the club, though."

I glance over toward him.

"Allie."

Ah, we're back to that now. "She did."

Peg grins. "We gave him a hard time around that table when he finally turned up."

"Couldn't have given him that beatdown," I admit. "Though he'd have taken it if that was the choice he'd have chosen."

"Man was fuckin' lost. Christ, he really believed he'd never be able to ride a bike. That day might be in our future, Drum, but we're old, our bodies are wearing down, we know it's just over the horizon, but we've had time to get used to the idea. To have it suddenly slammed on you? Fuck, I can understand how he was feelin'."

"Who's getting old? Speak for your fuckin' self, Brother."

Peg raises an eyebrow, his way of telling me I'm older than him. Yet the four year age difference seems to be nothing at all now. As I've discovered, bodies all age differently. In ways he tries to hide, Peg's now the older man. We both wear glasses now, mine just for close work, Peg needs his all the time. I'm also sitting to his right as he's deaf in his left ear. Yet, mostly, the passing years have been kind. As Peg points out, one day we'll be hanging up our riding boots, but I'm hopeful we've still got years left in us yet.

"Truck—that first church with him in attendance. Showed what this brotherhood stands for Peg. I didn't need to say a word, uttered no warning. No one mentioned how his face had been ravaged."

"It's got better over the years. Still scarred, but not so noticeable. I agree, that first day, it looked fuckin' terrible. But we had the man there, didn't give a damn about the body he was in."

"You worked him hard, as I remember."

"Nah. I just gave him some pointers. Once he decided he was going to help himself, he put the work in. Couldn't do anything about his ankle, but he learned how to compensate. Been a fuckin' good brother over the years."

"I don't think he'd have coped if he hadn't come back to the club. That man is a team player, Peg, if ever there was one."

CHAPTER THIRTEEN

*T*ruck…

After sitting through that bizarre church, I had two things on my mind. One was pleasurable, the thought my brothers had forced me back to the fold. The other more unpleasant. If they had expectations about me and Allie, they had to have come from the woman herself. I had to knock any ideas she might have had on the head quickly. If I'm moving to the compound, she needed to know her place which most certainly isn't beside me.

I decided to take care of unpleasant business first, so had gone straight up to the sweet butts' house to find her. I didn't have to wait long.

It had been a difficult conversation. My head said the right words, but inside I found myself wishing it could be different. If I hadn't known anything about her, who she is and why she's here, I might have wanted to explore what we had found that night and taken things further.

She said we'd connected. We had. It was the best sex I'd ever experienced. More than that, it was fun, we'd laughed and clowned around as well as fucked. But the thought was there in the back of my head that all she was giving me was the same as she gave to everyone. That it just showed how good she was to make me feel so special. That she'd been giving it her all as her way of providing me with a good send off.

She hasn't been with anyone else for months. Well, that's on her. She'll have to end her dry spell with somebody else. That's what I'll be doing.

Not with that bitch, Pussy though. A grimace covers my face as I walk back to the clubhouse, while I think to myself, I really fucking hate cats.

None of my brothers had commented on my appearance, for which I'd been grateful. They had just concentrated on the things that could be improved, my leg and my arm. I wince as I wonder what Peg's got in store for me. I've no doubt he'll be working me to the limit of my endurance, and beyond.

I pause for a moment by the railing, looking out across the compound and over to the desert beyond, lit by the light of a full moon. I can just make out the saguaro.

This is such an amazing location for the Satan's Devils' compound, no wonder it's the envy of other chapters. I'm surprised Beef wanted to leave it. Still, kudos to him for becoming VP, I'd always been impressed by the man, even though he didn't go easy on prospects.

I remember the summer before last when the view hadn't been as good as it is now. Wildfire had swept down from the mountains. Luckily it had looped around the compound, but it had been a worrying time. It's how I'd first come to meet the Devils. I'd been impressed by the men and intrigued by their way of life.

I'd ridden a motorcycle back before I joined the Army, and had a yearning to ride again. That became a hunger once I spent time among these men. As my firefighting crew member, Darcy, hooked up with Peg and became his old lady, after the fire Slade, my captain, me, and Hammer, my other teammate, had come to the clubhouse a few times. I'd watched, learned and asked questions. I saw the camaraderie and wanted to be a part of it.

I didn't go into it blind. At the time I was still a probationer at the fire service, and knew all about having to prove myself. It was part of what attracted me to the club, that they didn't take just anyone. So I became a prospect, and had no regrets.

"You doing okay, Truck?"

Drummer comes to join me as I stand leaning on the railing. "I think so, Prez. I'm grateful for in there." I indicate the club-house with a backward jerk of my head. "I know that you must have warned people not to make a big thing of my scars."

His steel grey eyes narrow. "I didn't say a fuckin' word. Didn't bother anyone enough to comment on it. It's you we wanted to see sat around the table. Don't give a damn about what you look like."

"Can't really miss it, though." I indicate the left side of my face.

"Probably looks and feels worse to you, Truck. Not minimising what you've gone through, but hey, you've got a few scars. Think most of us have, though they're not as visible as yours." He too, stares out into the distance. Then having dismissed the subject as though it's of no importance, moves on. "Thought you could move into one of the suites that Viper and Bullet's crew have just done up."

The suites here are permanent accommodations for the single brothers. Men with old ladies are occupying the houses at the top of the compound, except for the few who live in town. "One of the crash rooms would be fine for me, Drummer. I don't need much, just somewhere to lay my head while I'm working with Peg to get some strength back on my left side." *If that's even possible.*

"Nah. Still enough single men around who want to party, you wouldn't get much sleep in the clubhouse, Truck. Take the suite. It's unfurnished so you can move in whatever you want to bring with you."

The suites are nice. Fuck, I've been in enough of them before stocking up bedside tables with condoms and cleaning up after the brothers. There are two to each bloc, and they all come with ensuite bathrooms. Not much smaller than my apartment, except I wouldn't have a kitchen. But there's a big enough one here, and meals are cooked for everyone. The concoctions the women come up with copying Ma's recipes are tasty. Sandy gets them to try out new meals before she puts them on the menu at the Wheel Inn. On those nights what's dished up isn't far off gourmet food. My stomach rumbles at the thought.

"Okay, Drummer. I'll take a suite. It will only be temporary, mind you. I'll get some of my shit together and arrange to have it brought here tomorrow." I pause, then bring the elephant up. "We have to accept I might not be able to ride again, even with a modified bike."

"You will." There's no room for doubt in his voice. It also sounds so much like an order, it makes me smile.

I better get back home. Today's been a lot for someone who's done nothing for months, and my leg in particular is starting to ache. Taking my phone out of my cut, I hold it up. "Going to try to persuade an Uber to come here and drive me back into Tucson." *Allie would have given me a lift had I asked her.* I shake my head. Can't ask her for anything now. Not even a favour.

"Fuck that. You're a member. Get one of the prospects to take you tonight, and collect you and bring you back tomorrow."

I hadn't thought of that. I give a wide grin at the reminder I'm on the other side of the shit now. It feels good. Of course I can order them to do anything I like. Clean my fucking apartment while they're at it. Maybe not that, but they can certainly carry the heavy shit out in the morning.

"I should have come back earlier." I was a fool to keep away.

"Nah, don't second guess yourself like that, Brother. You needed time to get things straight in your head. You're here now, and that's all that matters."

"So what have I missed since I've been away? Club seems quiet." By that I mean there was nothing raised at church which suggested trouble was on the horizon. "I notice Fergus seems pretty comfortable sat around the table now, and Matt's been given his patch as well."

"Fergus is now Drifter, and Matt seems to have picked up the handle Sharp, he was only patched in a week or so back. As for quiet? That's the way I like it. But there'll be something around the corner. Always is. So, what have you missed? You already know Mouse found himself a woman. Remember you looking out for Drew her teenage brother." He snorts. "Kid wants to prospect for us, Mariana isn't having it."

My eyebrows rise. It had been strange when Mouse found someone, the computer guru always seemed more interested in computers than women. Drew though, well, I suppose I didn't know him long enough to realise he was that enamoured of the club. Maybe I could support Mariana's cause by explaining a few facts of the prospecting life. "Anyone else got an ol' lady?"

"Blade."

"*Blade*?" I'm stunned.

"Yeah. He's with Tash. Oh, and have you met Tommy?"

"Yeah, he's another of our prospects. Not that he'll ever get patched in."

I turn quickly, expecting to see a look of disgust on the Prez's face that a new prospect is clearly failing to make the grade so soon.

But Drummer is grinning. "Tommy is special." He taps his head. "Blade found him on the streets along with his old lady. He's an overgrown kid, but we've all taken to him. Does the grunt work without complaining."

Hmm. I'll be interested to meet him. I suddenly grin. "Another reject from society?"

Prez knows exactly what I mean as he chuckles. "Yeah, he fits right in." He thinks for a moment. "I think that's all that's happened, apart from Beef, but you just heard all about him."

Mouse, Blade and Beef, all found old ladies while I've been gone. Is there some sort of disease going around?

But *Blade*? Never thought I'd see the day when he was

brought to his knees by a woman. I'm quite looking forward to meeting her. As well as this strange Tommy.

"Marcia's pregnant, again. They're not sayin', but I reckon it might be another set of twins."

I bark a laugh. "Place is getting overrun with ol' ladies and children."

Drummer gives me an unreadable look. "Nothing wrong with that. Nothing like settling down to steady a man and give him reasons to live for."

Is that what's missing in my life? Someone to come home to. Someone waiting for me, and only me. Do I ever want children? I'm thirty now, maybe I should think of settling down. With a good woman. But even if I had such yearnings, where would I find one? Anyone worth their salt would take one look at my face and run a mile. The only type of woman who'd want me is one who was desperate, maybe not so hot in the looks department herself. No beauty would want to tie herself to a beast like me, nah, I'm part of society's rejects, my only potential partner would probably be one as well.

The picture of Allie, looking so beautiful wearing that dress and watching the sunset comes to my mind. Another image quickly chases it out. That of Road pounding into her as she lay sprawled over the pool table.

"I'm going up to the house. Go find one of the prospects and tell them what you need."

I jerk my chin as Drummer walks off, and turn to go into the clubhouse. Hound—I've got which prospect is which sorted out in my head now—is picking up empty glasses, but Roadkill seems to be just hanging around. As I cross the room to him, I think how glad I am that Matt's been patched in. It seemed so unfair I got my Satan's Devils insignia prior to him.

Matt had already been prospecting when I first came to the club. We'd worked well together, always rushed off our feet but still sparing time to joke while we were doing the shitiest jobs. He'd done his time and more and deserved to be recognised.

Fergus, well he'd prospected nearly a year and then had to leave the club to look after his dying mother. He'd been patched in a short time after he came back. It's my fault I know none of the changes, I was the one who'd kept my distance. *Drifter and Sharp, not Fergus and Matt,* I remind myself. I'll have to do my best to remember.

Roadkill stands at my approach. "You need something, Truck?"

"Lift back to Tucson. Tomorrow you'll come back and pack up my stuff." I think what I'll need to take. "Bring Hound too."

He agrees without comment, already having learned not to question a member.

As I follow him down to where the cars are parked, shrugging off my cut ready to get into a cage, I realise this was not what I was expecting a few short hours ago. I'm filled with warmth at the thought of being a Satan's Devil again. I'm almost giddy at being accepted as a full member, never having expected to take a seat around the table.

The vacant seat. It's hard to get my head around that Beef's gone. Still, good for him to get that promotion. And that news about Mouse and Blade? While I've been wallowing by myself, seems I've missed one fuck of a lot happening in the club.

Roadkill doesn't drive as cautiously as Allie, and I find myself reaching for the oh-shit handle a couple of times. I don't want to distract him, not at the speed he's driving. But when we enter the city and he slows down, I at last ask the question that's been niggling at me.

"Roadkill?"

He doesn't pretend not to understand. "I got pretty hammered one night. Next morning I was puking my guts up. My roommates said I looked like something that had been run over by a truck. Started calling me Roadkill, and it kind of stuck." He grins, showing he doesn't mind. Then, explains why, "Better than some of the shit my other friends got stuck with.

Rather be Roadkill than Shitface. And please do not ask how he got landed with that."

Grinning I heed his warning, though can't stop my mind thinking about the possibilities. None of them good.

"See you tomorrow. Ten sharp." We've just pulled up outside my apartment.

"We'll be here." He waits for me to clamber out, and then drives away.

It's strange, opening the door to an apartment I'm about to leave. For good? I've no way of knowing. I'll continue paying rent until I know whether I can ride or not, but if I can, I wouldn't mind a permanent move to the club. My home, which had felt a refuge since I left rehab, suddenly seems silent and empty. Today has shown I'm a person who likes people around me. Well, those who don't make a show of looking at my face.

What's not to like about living at the compound? It's rent free, there's an onsite gym and swimming pool, sluts on call whenever I want them. Not Allie, though. She's not a working girl anymore.

Which could be a problem, I muse, frowning. My cock jerks at the thought of sinking into her tight cunt again, and doesn't twitch when I think of any of the other three.

I shake my head. It's probably that I had to face her today that has her on my mind. That extraordinary revelation earlier means that I can't think of fucking her again. She's not a sweet butt any longer, so going back for another go around might give her ideas, like the shit Drummer voiced about me claiming her. It's a shame, as I like her. She's kind, supportive… but she's been fucked by all of my brothers. Whores do not become old ladies.

I set down my keys and wallet, and reverently place my cut over the back of a chair, staring at it in wonder. *Never thought I'd feel the weight of that leather again.* Soon, maybe, I'll feel the vibration of an engine under my ass, and see the pavement whizzing past beneath my wheels. Something flickers in my chest, and I realise what it is. My heart, beating with hope and optimism.

I feel hyped up. *Should have stayed at the clubhouse.* But habit brought me back to seek the isolation I'd come to want. Suddenly I want someone to share my good news with. Someone who would be as happy for me as I am for myself. Someone to blow away the doubts that I won't succeed.

Damn it. I want Allie. Not just for sex, for her company.

CHAPTER FOURTEEN

*A*llie…

"Truck's come back. He's going to be moving his stuff into one of the suites. Maybe Beef's? Well, not the one next to Rock's, Becca and Rock are using that for Hope until their own house is finished. I wonder which they'll be putting him in…"

I tune out Diva's voice. I thought nothing could be worse than Truck flat out saying we had no future together, but I'd been wrong. I thought I could forget him, get over him, but not only has he returned to the club as a full member, he's going to be living on the compound as well.

"You went with him, didn't you, Allie? What's he like? Big man like that has got to have a big cock. He know what to do with it?"

I want to punch her in the face for even talking about him. Everything she's saying strikes me like daggers straight to my heart. *What's it going to be like to watch him going with any of the whores?* Or, late at night when the old ladies have gone and I'm still minding the bar, will I see him fucking in the open?

Why is it when you've lost something, you realise how much it meant? I knew I liked Truck, but now that there's not even the slightest hope lingering, I know I was already in love. *Am* in love, I correct. And there's nothing at all I can do about it. Watching him with the other girls, that's going to be enough to kill me.

"Well?" Diva prompts, in a tone that makes it sound like she's asking a very reasonable question.

It's not that she's not. Any other man, any previous time, we'd be sharing experiences. Maybe a warning that someone likes something in particular, so it doesn't come as a surprise. Laughing with the comparisons of who dresses to the right and who to the left, who's pierced or circumcised. But this is Truck she wants to know about, nobody else.

I grit my teeth and tell her, "It was so long ago I've forgotten. You'll probably find out for yourself."

"I'm sure I will. It will make a change to have someone new. Maybe Paige and I will try to tempt him tonight."

I can't bring myself to tell her to go for it, so I turn and walk out, not having the faintest idea what I'm going to do, but I just want to get out.

I close the front door behind me, then just stand with my hand over my mouth, feeling physically ill at the memory of the conversation I've just had. I've no doubt Truck will find his night sorted, only too well aware that in the past I, like the others, had targeted the men we wanted for the night. Going with someone you preferred was one way of avoiding those you didn't enjoy so much. Blade, now, for instance. He used to frighten me when he got out his knives.

"Allie? Have you got a moment?"

I've got hundreds of them. "Sure, Prez. What can I do for you?"

"Follow me."

Without checking I am, he strides off. He walks past his house, past Wraith's, and down past the first couple of blocs containing the brothers' suites. He stops at the third which houses the one Beef had moved into allowing Rock and Becca more space. I know it well, having been here in my professional capacity a time or two before, until Beef met Sally and got involved. When he walks up to the main door, I see him bouncing keys in his hand.

"Shouldn't be in too bad a state. Viper's been doing the suites up as brothers have moved out. But still, it hasn't been used for a while. Not sure what a mess it will be inside."

I'm not a sweet butt anymore. *Is he going to ask me to do some cleaning instead?* I suppose he's in his right to ask, I've still got a club-provided roof over my head after all.

The thought hits me making me smother a gasp. *Is he going to ask me to get it ready for Truck?* If he did, would I mind? I decide not. Why should I resent doing something for the man, even though he'd rejected me?

He opens the door, then stands back and waves me on inside the small hallway. There are two doors leading to two suites. One to the left, one to the right. It smells of fresh paint. He turns a key in the lock of the one on the right, and then waves me on inside. It's got basic furniture, a bed, small table, desk and wardrobe. The floor is tiled, and there's a gentle whirr of an air conditioner. It hasn't been used for a while, and everything is covered with a layer of dust.

Drummer glances around and frowns. "Well, what do you think? Of course I'll get the prospects to clean it."

If he's going to ask the prospects to make it presentable and not me, why has he brought me here?

My brow creases. "Drummer, you've lost me. What do you want me to do?"

He turns and those steel-grey eyes settle on me, they look softer than normal. "You're not a sweet butt anymore. Thought you might want to get away from the whores. This suite is empty, we've got to the point where we've got plenty spare." He pauses and shrugs. "You've heard Truck's moving back to the compound?"

I nod.

"Yeah. Word travels fast." His expression doesn't show whether he's pleased or worried by that. "Thought you might like your own space while Truck gets himself sorted."

The thought of not being faced with Diva, Paige and Pussy, or having to deal with their questions about Truck is welcoming. More than that, I no longer feel inclined to take part in the type of conversations which often arise, such as Dollar's particular partiality.

But I have to come clean. "You know I had personal reasons for trying to get Truck back to the club, Drummer." Part of me wonders if I hadn't encouraged him, would I have been able to develop our friendship without him being reminded every day what my prior occupation had been. If Truck had never returned, would there have been a better chance of a future for him and me?"

I look down for a second, admitting a man like Truck needs something more than a woman beside him, he needs his team. If I'm brutally honest with myself, I could never have been enough. Shit is what shit is, and I've just got to deal with it.

Drummer's been waiting patiently for me to verbalise my thinking.

"Truck doesn't want me, Prez." At last I explain and shrug. "I've got to make plans to leave the compound. So is it worthwhile moving? And anyway, this is a member's suite."

Of course, the alternative to living with the sweet butts is to take over one of the crash rooms, but I'd rather not have to do that. Don't want to hear Truck getting his needs seen to next door.

"Allie," he sighs, waving me toward a bare but new looking mattress. I sit. He props his foot on a chair and leans his hand on his knee. "Suites are standing empty, you, I suspect, would like to get away from the sweet butts while you get your head straight about what you want for your future. I know this isn't much and you'll need some shit. I'll give you a small budget and you can sort it how you want."

A tempting idea, but I have to tell him, "I wouldn't be here long. I can't stay. But I would appreciate some space to decide what I'm going to do. I don't want to walk out of here homeless and without a job, else…"

"Else you'd end up doing what you did before."

Yes. That's the problem.

"You might find he just needs time, Al. Laid a lot on the man yesterday."

I'd like to think that, but I need to be sensible. "I can't change the one thing that needs changing. My past."

"Time," Drummer repeats. "Truck's got to rediscover himself as a man, got to build himself back up the same way Blade and Sam are going to build him a bike. His life's changed completely. You need time as well. Time to find out who you really are, and what you want to be."

I look up at him. "I can't see I can be anything else other than what I am. Else why would I have chosen the life I've lived for the past dozen years?"

A sharp look. "I doubt very much that this would have been your preferred career path. What choice did you have?"

He knows my history, knew I was thrown out of home when my mother thought I was promiscuous at sixteen. I don't try to sugarcoat my past. "My brother, he might have been much younger, but he already showed he'd gotten the brains in the family. Lessons went right over my head in school. I'm no good at math, Drummer. I don't even write very well. Reading a book is beyond me."

"I didn't know," he admits.

My shoulders rise and lower. "A teacher suggested there might be a reason for it and suggested I get tested, but Mom said I was just lazy. I don't know, perhaps I was. I found everything too hard. Much easier to look out the window and daydream. Yeah, I was the stupid one in the family."

"You're not stupid," he says with a bite in his voice. "Far from it. Don't talk about yourself, that way, Allie. Okay, so schooling and you didn't get on, but that's nothing to measure common sense by. You've got a stack load of that. Don't put yourself down."

My lips press together. "Even you have to admit, my options are limited, Drummer."

Suddenly he barks a laugh. "Never had to be an occupational advisor before. But take some time, you think about what you'd like to do, and I'll put my thinking hat on too. What do you like, Allie?"

Again, I shrug. I don't know. Maybe he's right, I do need some space and time to think about what I can do with the rest of my life.

"Tell you what, I'll see how Satan's Angels is fixed. Might be able to get you behind the bar."

Glancing up again, I crease my eyes, wondering if he's serious. "Behind the bar here, I don't need to know how much shit costs or take money and give change."

"Told you before, don't put yourself down. That might not be as hard as you think."

"Waitressing I could do." I'm thinking about the Wheel Inn, the restaurant the club owns.

"That's a thought, too. In the meantime, I know we expect you to tend bar here, but the rest of the time use as you want. It's your future we're talking about."

"I don't want to be here long, Drummer. I couldn't stand—"

"Want my view?" Again he interrupts, and continues without waiting for my nod. "Don't give up. Truck's got a lot on his plate. Seems to me both of you need some thinking time. While you're doing that, make this place your home. As I said, I'll give you a small budget to get any furnishings you might need."

"What's the point, Drummer? If I'm not going to stay here long enough to make use of them?"

"Who knows what's going to happen Allie?" He says it with a hint of finality. "Anyway, I'll leave you to sort yourself out. Oh, this is yours." He presses the suite key into my hand, then takes out an envelope from his cut and hands it to me. Then, he leaves.

Bemused, I stand then turn around. The first thing I notice is how quiet it is, and it strikes me I've never been alone in my life. First I lived with my mom and brother, then shared a room with another streetwalker. When I came to the club, I shared with Jill, then Chrissy and the other girls.

This suite is my own home, my sanctuary. As far as I know, the adjacent one is empty. It might only be temporary, but at least Drummer's given me a refuge all to myself.

I look down at the envelope he's handed to me, and tear it open automatically. A pile of dollars flutter to the floor. Scooping them up, I count them. *Five hundred dollars?*

Stunned at his generosity, I put the money in the bedside table drawer, not sure what to do with it, wondering why he'd given me so much money I hadn't earned. *Ask him?* That might look like I was throwing his gift back in his face. Drummer's a man who knows what he's doing. Maybe the right thing is just to thank him.

Opening cupboards and drawers, in the closet I find some plain sheets and a comforter, so I make the bed first, then consider going up to the sweet butts house to grab my clothes and toiletries, but I'm not eager to go into explanations which I don't understand myself. Bewildered at the change in my circumstances, I slide open the door and look out over the balcony.

My own suite. I never expected this.

A new start. A new me.

Suddenly I don't want to collect my clothing that barely deserves that name. Instead, I grab the bills Drummer had given me, stuff them into my wallet and put that in my purse. Then, with determination, I exit the suite and go down to borrow a car once again.

I've got shopping to do.

CHAPTER FIFTEEN

*T*ruck…

Peg had allowed just sufficient time to get the furniture I'd decided to bring with me installed in my suite, before he came to collect me.

"This is how it's going to work, Truck," he tells me as we're walking down toward the clubhouse. "Today we'll assess what muscles we need to work on, and I'll draw up a plan of how we'll be doing this. I'll give you daily exercises. You'll be answering to me if you don't follow through."

Answering to the sergeant-at-arms is what I don't want to end up doing. *Before* I'd have been able to take him on, though bets would have been laid as to which of us would have come out the winner. In the state I am now, the man who wears a prothesis could take me on without his prosthetic leg, and with one hand tied behind him. I grin at his warning, but by the stern expression on his face, realise he's not joking.

"I'm going to work you hard, Truck, and you're going to fuckin' hate me. But I'm determined to get you riding again."

"You forget, I'm used to hard physical work. Running up multiple flights of stairs with a full firefighter's pack was something I did regularly." As a firefighter, during our twenty-four hour shifts, much of the time was spent hanging around for a call out. We used that downtime for working out and training.

"I'm well aware of that."

Yeah, Peg would be. He's married to a firefighter after all.

"Do you mind, that Darcy's gone back to work?" Their son, Noah, is a few months old now.

"Mind?" Peg rounds on me, his face going red. "Of course I fuckin' mind. Don't want Darcy putting herself in danger. You…" He breaks off without completing his thought. I guess he's saying I'm an example of what can happen.

"But," he leans in, conspiratorially, "no one else knows this. She's pregnant again. This time I'm hoping she'll give up work and look after the kids."

He might be right. But I know how a firefighter feels. It's in the blood, that desire to serve, to protect and save. To fight fire, that one unpredictable enemy. I say nothing, which is probably for the best. Whether or not she keeps working is between husband and wife.

"Congratulations," I say, belatedly. "You going to tell everyone else?"

"Yeah. Darcy and I agreed last night. She's reached the twelve week mark, so we're going to go public."

Good. I don't like holding onto a secret I might let slip accidentally.

This morning doesn't sound like it will be too much effort. Peg will just be drawing up a program and seeing where I'm up to, I think, as I follow the sergeant-at-arms into his second home. The gym.

Originally most of the equipment had been installed for him when he'd come back from his service missing half a leg. He's added to it over the years, and it was here he'd got Sophie, the VP's old lady, back on her feet. Well, one flesh and blood leg, and the other a fake one. You'd never know when she'd arrived here she had been confined to a wheelchair. Of course, I hadn't known her then, but had heard the story.

"Hey, Tommy. Come here and meet Truck."

A man who'd been wiping down the parallel bars walks across, his gait a rolling one. He's big, tall and broad, and has a big smile on his face which fades when he looks from Peg to me. He doesn't say anything at first, just moves his hand to his face as if suddenly worried his own might be scarred.

Then, he says, quietly and concerned, "Oh, man. Does it hurt?"

I'd tensed. I'd expected people to show disgust or horror, but Tommy is only worried about me. "Nah, not so much now."

Tommy's face goes blank for a moment, then he brightens. "You're the fireman."

He must have heard the talk in the clubhouse. "I am," I confirm.

"You finished now, Prospect?" Peg asks.

Tommy nods, puts down his rag, and leaves us alone.

The sergeant-at-arms stares after him. "He's good people, Truck."

"He was on the streets?"

"Yeah. Street smart, though otherwise slow. What could we do? Couldn't throw him back out there, so he's staying. Won't ever be able to ride a bike, but as long as he's wearing his prospect cut, I don't think he cares." He turns back to me. "Right, let's see where you're up to."

I hastily revise my thought that this morning is going to be easy. Christ, I thought my captain had been a hard enough taskmaster, he doesn't come close to Peg. I lift weights, then he adds to them. I reach what I think is my limit, he shows me I haven't. Even rehab starts to become a pleasant memory, and those training days at the firehouse? I start looking back on them fondly as a walk in the park.

Peg isn't satisfied until I'm struggling to breathe and sweat's pouring off of me.

"That hand." He doesn't stop, but lets my legs take a break. "Squeeze this."

I squeeze the squidgy ball he's handed to me.

"Again."

I do.

"Again."

And again, and again.

My hand hurts, my arm aches, my legs have lost all feeling. At last I collapse on the mat with him standing over me.

"Okay," he waves a chart at me, "we'll increase the weights daily. Go take a shower and rest now. Be back here first thing tomorrow."

I doubt I'll be able to move in the morning.

At last, released, I go to my suite and wash the sweat off me, standing under the hot water letting the heat seep into my sore muscles. Then, I dry off, spy the bed Roadkill and Hound had transported and set up for me, and crash onto it.

Before my tiredness wins out, I smile. I'm a man used to physical activity. I'm used to being pushed to my limits and beyond. While every part of me is screaming, I relish the pain that comes from well worked muscles. It's been too long since I've felt this way. Exhausted and worn out, the last thing I hear before I lose the battle to keep my eyes open is the banging shut of a door from the suite opposite mine.

I'd thought it was unoccupied.

A moment wondering who's living next to me, then sleep takes me under.

My forty winks turns into a much higher number and when I wake, a few hours have passed. Stretching, an ouch comes from my mouth, and I doubt there's a part of me which doesn't protest, but it's a good ache, different from the pain of my injuries. Gingerly I stand, dress, put on the cut which still feels so good to wear and make my way down to the clubhouse.

Entering, I notice it's full.

Babies are being nursed, toddlers played with, and Sophie, Sam, Marcia looking on fondly. Becca is cuddling Darcy so I reckon her news has, by now, been shared. Over by the bar, their old men are looking fondly on.

Avoiding the happy families, I make my way over to Road and Marvel standing at the end, hopefully discussing something that doesn't involve procreation or diapers.

"Hey, Truck." Road stands aside so I can make my way to the bar. His eyes examine me for a moment, then he chuckles. "I can see Peg's put you through your paces."

"You can tell?"

"Yeah, unless you're sporting one fuck of a boner." Marvel laughs. "You looked a bit stiff as you walked in."

"That would be Peg's work," I agree. Then hurriedly add so there's no miscomprehension, "Not a boner, but yeah, my muscles are fucking sore."

I turn to get a beer. Peg might not have made my cock stand to attention, the sight before me, however, risks me embarrassing myself. Allie is patiently waiting for whoever needs serving to step up. She's wearing another of those fifties' style dresses, this time in a black and white pattern. It's nipped at the waist emphasising how slim she is, and reaches down to her knees. Her hair is pulled back into a messy bun, and she looks absolutely adorable.

Her eyes widen when she sees me, then, without me having to put my request in, anticipating my needs, she hands me a beer having popped the top off.

I barely have time to thank her before she's called to serve at the other end of the bar, and can't stop myself watching her ass as she walks away. A memory of how good it felt to be inside her comes back to me, then Road asks something, and, as I turn to answer, I remember that he, and his companion, also know that feeling.

Why did she have to be a whore?

"A fully electric bike would be the last resort," I answer him, when I've composed myself. "I'd be back on two wheels, but it's that vibration, the roar from the exhaust, that's part of the exhilaration."

"Agreed. And safety's a consideration." Joker interrupts our conversation. "A loud exhaust warns you're coming."

"I groan, myself," Marvel chirps.

Road slaps him around the head. "We're having a serious discussion here. Don't want to know about the sounds you make when you fuck."

"Hey, Al. Who's the loudest when they come?" Marvel yells at the woman behind the bar.

Her eyes meet mine. For a moment they widen in horror, then become resigned as she manages to choke back, "A lady never tells."

"You'll be asking her who's got the biggest cock next." Road shakes his head.

"What?" Marvel doesn't look contrite. "You think they never talk about us? We discuss *them*. Now Allie there," he points his beer bottle toward her, "she's got this way of…"

Abruptly I push away from the bar, not wanting to hear details of any of their encounters with the woman I'd otherwise want. Can't deny it. One look from her and I'm ready to go. Trouble is, I may have been one of the last to fuck her, but I was at the end of a very long line.

As I turn, I catch sight of her and the expression of loss and resignation on her face. Something twists in my gut. Instead of moving away as I'd intended, I swing back.

"Allie's not a whore any longer," I snarl at them. "Show her some respect. She's heard every word you're saying."

Marvel looks stunned, and his mouth snaps shut. It opens, then closes. He resembles a gaping fish, but I have the sense not to point that out.

Road casts a look toward Allie, then back at me. His eyebrows rise. "Suppose you've got a point there, Brother." He slaps Marvel on the back. "She's off the market now, man. Reminiscing about how good she was in the sack won't be bringing her back."

"You sure about that?" Marvel asks, unaware how close he is to getting punched. "She might well reconsider when she realises what she's missin'." He rubs his crotch.

The hand that I can use forms a fist. I'm just about to use it to plant in Marvel's face, when Allie steps up.

"Sorry boys, but I've been there, done that. Nothing so spectacular that I want to go back."

Her eyes meet mine as she speaks, and there's a message there. *She doesn't mean me.* I turn away before I can see the hurt in her eyes.

"Fuckin' bitch," Marvel states. His glare toward her back as she walks off after her parting shot worries me.

But Road gets in before me. "She's not a sweet butt now, Marvel. As Truck said, show her some fuckin' respect."

"No, she's not," Marvel responds, still looking unhappy. "But if she's not, and she's not an old lady… What the fuck is she still doing here? What's she doing to earn her keep if she's not working on her back?"

"You got a beer in your hand?" Road asks, reasonably.

"Hey, Marvel, Road. Want some company tonight?"

Pussy, I sigh with relief, has excellent timing. With her breasts, barely contained in her top, rubbing against Marvel's arm, it doesn't take long for him to be distracted.

His arm snakes around her. "Yeah babe." His eyes flick to the centre of the room where the old ladies are gathering up the kids, then back to Road. "Better use a crash room. You coming?"

But Road shakes his head. "Nah. Maybe later, Marvel."

Hmm. As I watch them walk off, I wonder how gratifying it really is to be a member and now able to go with sweet butts. To be honest, I'd prefer a woman to myself, not one to use after one of my brothers has had her that same night.

But each to their own. Left with Road, I remember I have a question. "Who's in the room next to mine?"

His eyes crease. "You're in Beef's old suite, aren't you?" At my nod, he continues, "No fuckin' idea. But hey, let's go ask Rock. He might know."

I follow Road over to where Rock is holding his baby, Rose. He's a big tattooed biker. Against his chest, his daughter looks tiny, but the love on his face is shining through. Something clenches inside me. *I thought I could have that.* Before that fucking cat took everything from me.

Nah, life has worked against me. What woman would want me now, looking like this, and so damaged? A man who can't even ride a bike.

Unaware of my thoughts, Road asks, "Rock, who's in the suite next to Beef's old one?"

Rock looks a bit surprised by the question. "No idea. Don't think anyone is. No one's moved in from what I've heard."

They both look at me.

"Thought I heard the door open and shut," I explain.

"Probably a prospect checking it out," Road offers as a reasonable explanation.

That must be it. I nod.

∿

Twenty years in the future – Drummer

"Once Truck had come back to the club, you didn't stop trying to get them together."

Peg's right. "She'd been good for him. Gave him what he needed, even if he thought he didn't want it." *As I think back, I remember how sneaky I'd been.*

"Would you have still tried to push them together? If you'd been able to see into the future?"

I take a moment to consider the question. At the time I had seen nothing beyond two people who had a need for each other. Truck needed someone to lean on, a friend, a companion and a lover. Someone who'd have his back and always be there for him. Allie, with her compassionate spirit and common sense approach to life which had been gained from experience not read in books, was just right for him.

She needed an escape from the life she'd fallen into. I'd had no doubts had her family been supportive, she'd never have ended up living the way she had. Oh, she liked sex, I knew that from experience, but hopping from one bed to another out of duty, that wasn't the woman she was underneath.

Peg's right, I had pushed them together, thinking I was doing right at the time. But the suffering that followed was something I'd never expected. There were no signs, nothing had served as a warning.

"We all suffered, Peg." I take another sip of my whisky. "Christ, that year, fifteen months. Some of the worst trauma I'd ever seen in the club."

"It was longer than that. Took years for them to fully recover."

He's right. None of us were unaffected. We'd faced up to our enemies, I'd killed men with my bare hands, but none of us had had the skills to fight what was coming.

"I don't know," I answer him at last. "If a crystal ball had warned me what was on the horizon, maybe I'd have done something different. Sent Allie away, kept them apart…"

"Two souls may still have gravitated together," he observes in his wise way. "Not saying you did wrong, Drummer. But you're right, those were dark days."

CHAPTER SIXTEEN

*A*llie...

I want to kill Marvel.

As I stand, wishing the ground would open up and swallow me, I wonder, what else did I expect? Men here are never going to see me any differently. Angry at myself, I wipe a useless tear from my eye.

I'd gone shopping as I'd planned, spent some of Drummer's money buying some more of the fifties' style clothes I've fallen in love with, thinking I'm finding my style which isn't wearing hooker clothes. Buying cosmetics, and perfume that wasn't heavy with musk. As I'd put on my new clothes and lightly covered my face with the minimum of makeup, I'd been filled with confidence. I'm becoming a new woman, perhaps discovering the me that had been underneath the whole time.

I'd started my shift playing bartender, and all went well. Sam had actually remarked how much the dress suited me. While Sophie and Becca had given me shrewd looks, I brushed off the thought that they may think this was just another attempt to steal their men. I knew it would take a long time to convince them I wasn't a threat anymore.

Sure, I'd had admiring glances, but not the lewd ones I used to get. Even Tommy had noticed.

"Allie!"

"Hi Tommy." I smiled at him. "Want a soda?" At his eager nod, I found the cola that he loves and I kept a special stock of just for him, and passed the can over the bar.

He'd stared, then said shyly, "You look pretty."

"Aw, Tommy. Thank you." It's odd that his compliment made me blush. "That's sweet of you."

"Tommy sweet," he grinned back, nodding vigorously.

"Whatcha up to?"

"Washing bikes."

With that explanation which seems to remind him what he's supposed to be doing, he wandered off.

Hound had caught my eye and winked. Tommy's care when he cleans the machines he's so in awe of means he's trusted to do the job he loves, and which the other prospects find tedious.

After Tommy left, I continued to enjoy myself until Truck came in. I noticed he looked like he was hurting, but it was understandable after overhearing he'd been working out with Peg. I hoped the sergeant-at-arms wasn't being too hard on him.

Seeing him had been difficult, but I forced myself to politely hand over a beer to him, and then take myself elsewhere. But a summons for another drink had me back in his direction in time for Marvel to try and draw me into their conversation. A few well-placed sentences which reminded me I could change how I look, but never the way these men saw me.

I'm a whore. In their eyes, I always will be. No wonder Truck said what he did. A sweet butt never becomes an old lady.

"Where did you disappear to?" Pussy, looking flushed, reappears from the direction of the crash rooms, and beckons to a bottle behind me.

I pour her a vodka. "Drummer's given me one of the suites."

"Wow." Her eyes open wide. "You too good for us now?"

I shrug. "He offered, I accepted."

She barks a laugh. "You're leaving me with the terrible twosome?"

I hadn't thought about that. Diva and Paige came here at the same time, and had been working the streets together long before that. I open my mouth to apologise, when Pussy stops me.

"I don't blame you. You've got a chance to get out of this life. Me? I'm stuck with it for as long as they want me."

"You ever think about doing something else?"

She considers my question seriously. "I enjoy biker cock too much. I worry about getting old, but, hey. I've got a few years left in me yet. They," she throws her head back, "are getting older as well."

Doesn't mean they won't prefer someone younger.

"Watch Marvel," she leans in and warns. "He was pretty angry. Said something about whores who don't know their place."

I had wondered about her sudden appearance. She'd taken the heat off me by attracting Marvel's attention. *He isn't going to cause trouble for me, is he?* I nod my thanks for her warning, while worrying what would happen if he complains to Drummer. Would the Prez have my back? *Probably not if the men start questioning why I'm still here.* I am not an old lady, I'm under no one's protection. *Maybe I'll need to get on with making those plans for my future, sooner rather than later.*

At least Truck's having fun, I notice as my eyes catch sight of him.

He hasn't come back to the bar, but Road's kept him supplied with beer. Marvel, his appetite having been satisfied by Pussy, is sitting with them, and they've been joined by Shooter and Drifter. Someone's got out a deck of cards, and by the groans, Truck seems to be winning.

"You look tired, Al. Want me to take over for a while? Close down for you?"

The prospect, Hound, has appeared in front of me.

I am tired. "You sure you don't mind?"

"Nah. Not many left here now. They'll all be gone soon. I'll need to be tidying up anyway, might as well serve a few beers. Ain't no hardship, Al."

I take him up on his offer. I am tired, but before I go to bed, I'll have to think about jobs that don't need skills or education. Now I've realised the Satan's Devils will never change their view of me, I know I'll have to move on. And soon, before Marvel complains about me and tries to pressure me to return to my previous line of work.

I leave via the kitchen, stopping to make myself a sandwich, then carry it up to my suite. I'm putting the key into my door, when the main one opens behind me. Like any female would, I turn to check who it is.

It's the last man I expected to see.

Truck.

"What are *you* doing here?" we both ask simultaneously,

He waves to indicate I should answer first.

"Drummer's given me this suite."

His eyebrows turn down and meet in a V. "He's given me that one." He indicates the opposite door.

Well. This is awkward.

"I'm going to bed."

I turn the key in the lock. Suddenly a hand comes down and covers mine, preventing me from pushing on the handle.

"Al, look. I'm sorry for what Marvel said. But…"

"But it's what everyone's thinking, Truck. What *you're* thinking," I huff. "A leopard can't change its spots."

He looks down to where his hand covers mine, then sighs. "I'm sorry, Allie."

Yes. He's sorry that he can only see me that way too.

"I'm going to leave."

"Leave?" his eyes sharpen.

"It's the only thing I can do." Drummer may have suggested that I give him time, that he'll come to see me as something else, but he won't. Not when his brothers are comparing stories about what I used to do. If he ever dared show he was interested in me as a woman, they'd never let him forget my past. Probably ask him if I still use my tongue a certain way, whether I deep throat him how I used to do them. I can't move on and leave my past behind me, not while I'm still here.

I might be uneducated, but I'm not stupid. Truck isn't going to come around given time, and I'm not leaving in the hopes that he'd follow me, even if I was able to land a job which didn't involve working on my back. My past will always be there, always be between us.

A look of anguish comes over his face, and he pulls his hand back, allowing me to go into my room. But as it no longer feels like the sanctuary I thought Drummer had been offering me, not when Truck's staying next door, I hesitate before stepping inside.

What if he brought Diva, Paige or Pussy back to his room?

I can't stand even thinking about his cock being near anyone else.

If I was still a sweet butt, I'd have an excuse to try to get into his bed.

But even as the thought comes to me, I know I've moved on. If the only way to have Truck is to pretend to be something deep down, I'm not, I won't go there. Suddenly I know, when I find a man, I don't want to share.

Would I ever find someone?

Not while I can't get a scarred biker out of my head.

He turns to go into his room, stumbling when he puts his weight on his left leg, and swearing quietly.

"Peg went hard on you, didn't he?"

"You could say that," he replies through gritted teeth, putting his hand down to rub his sore muscles.

I hate seeing him in pain. "I could massage that for you."

His face hardens. "Massage," he repeats. Then growls, "Not having you anywhere near my dick, Allie. Don't even think about it."

I open my mouth, then shut it. I wasn't offering anything other than to ease his pain, but I doubt he'll believe that.

It's at that point I realise the futility of getting him to see me as anything different. *He doesn't, and will never, trust me.*

And he's never going to trust I can leave my past behind.

Without saying anything else, I push down on the handle, open my door, step inside and close it without waiting to see him disappear into his.

I could let the events of this evening overwhelm me, or I could use them as a kick up my ass to get on with my life which won't involve anything connected with the Satan's Devils.

The next morning I go down to the clubhouse, and knock on the office door next to Drummer's.

As I expected, Mouse is where he normally is, half hidden behind his banks of computers and screens. The thick air also comes as no surprise, tinged as it is by the strong smell of cannabis.

Mouse looks up, eyes me, then nods toward the seat opposite as he lights up a joint.

"Allie, what can I do for you?"

Mouse, like Peg, was one of the brothers who never used a whore's services. Now he's got his own old lady, he'll never have need to. It's refreshing to speak to a man who has no carnal knowledge of me, or expectations in that direction.

I stare down at my hands. This is embarrassing, the resolve I'd had when I left my suite begins to disappear now that I'm faced with one of the most intelligent men on the compound.

He gives me the time to gather my thoughts. Before the silence grows too awkward, I break it.

"I need to look for a job, Mouse. I know it's a lot to ask, but I'd appreciate some help."

He digests that. "You want a laptop so you can put in some applications?"

I could nod, get out of here with a borrowed device, and

then… be no further forward than I am now. "I can't read, or spell," I admit, my voice deathly quiet.

A stare, but it's not critical.

"What sort of things are you looking for, Allie?"

I shrug. "Waitressing, bartending. Something like that."

"What about the Wheel Inn?"

"I sort of wanted to get away from the Satan's Devils." I bite my lip, hoping he doesn't question why.

He's still staring. "Sandy would be a good boss, Allie. And it caters to anyone, not just bikers."

I'm not so sure about Sandy. Until Sam, Viper's daughter, arrived on the compound, her old man used to get blow jobs from the whores. In his eyes, he wasn't cheating on her, just getting what he didn't get at home. None of us ever knew what she thought about that, but expected he was doing it with her full knowledge. And none of us ever turned him down because he had an old lady. Not that we had the choice. A member asked, and we complied. It was what we were there for after all.

"You find a job you want to apply for, I'll help you. But talk to Sandy, Allie. You might find she has something for you. Have you thought about going into town and approaching likely establishments?"

I prefer his second idea to his first. I haven't. I've no clue how you go about finding work except for standing on street corners. "That's a good idea, Mouse. Thank you. I'll do that."

As I go to leave, Mouse stubs out his joint in the ashtray, and stands, leaning over the table. "I admire you, Allie. Not many girls try to get out of the life, at least not before it's eaten them up and spat them out."

He might admire me, but I certainly don't feel very admirable.

CHAPTER SEVENTEEN

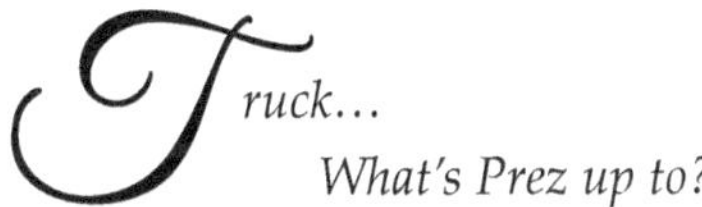

ruck…

What's Prez up to?

Why the fuck has he given Allie the suite next to mine? He's cramped my style, that's for certain. I can't bring anyone back to my room, can't rub her face in someone else having what I've made quite plain she can't have.

If I want to go with a sweet butt, I'll have to take her to a crash room. Even then I'd be followed by Allie's puppy dog eyes watching me from the bar.

Well, that would emphasize it's not her I want, just a cunt to sink my cock into.

But I'd be lying.

I don't think she'd been offering the massage I immediately saw in my head. I think Allie was offering comfort and a release from pain. But my brain immediately went there, and I was probably far too harsh, but how else could I push her away? It wasn't her I couldn't trust to keep her hands to herself, but me.

The thought of her innocent touch trying to ease the kinks from the muscles in my leg would have made me hard in seconds. I couldn't have hidden how much I wanted her touch to rise higher.

Fuck. I walk into my room and into the shower. Sure, the hot water will do wonders for my sore limbs, and my undamaged *thank fuck* right hand can relieve my aching dick.

My thoughts about staying in the clubhouse are sorely challenged. If it wasn't for the fact I had the prospect transport my heavy bed and wardrobe from my apartment, I'd have walked out and gone back home.

Which is stupid. I give myself a pep talk, weighing up the pros and cons. Here I have a gym, a taskmaster who's proved he's going to push me, brothers to drink with, and should I want them, women to fuck. I'm not lonely, my scar isn't stared at or criticised, and apart from Eli begging to let him see me take out my fake eye—which I hadn't—no one mentions my injuries at all. To them, it appears, it doesn't matter.

Even the babies hadn't started screaming. When six-year-old Amy had seen me, she offered me a band aid, then wasn't bothered and lost interest when I said it wasn't hurting, and covering the angry red lines on my face wouldn't help. Then she'd become fascinated with my missing fingers, feeling the stumps that remain with no sign of disgust, just interest.

The old ladies didn't give me fake sympathy. Darcy, obviously, wanted the details of precisely what had happened from a purely professional interest, but no one else seemed to want to know the minutiae of what had gone down.

Here, I can breathe. I can become whatever I'm able to. With these men beside me, having my back, I can do the best with what nature's left me.

The pros of staying here form a very long list.

The cons? Well, there's only one entry on that side. Allie.

Slamming my fist to my brow, I wonder why I'm letting her presence here unnerve me.

As the days pass, I find myself doing some stupid half-hearted attempts to avoid her. If I hear her door open at the same time as I'm going out, I wait until she leaves, watching her stride down the track from my balcony. Only to make sure she's gone of course, *though why, in that case, are my eyes fixed to her ass?*

When I've been in the clubroom I've asked a prospect to bring me my beers, rather than getting them myself. Of course, I feel her eyes burning into me, but refuse even to look her way.

"I was like that," observes Jekyll one night.

"Like what?" Hyde asks, looking at his watch, then nodding to have another hand of cards dealt to him.

"Soon as I was patched in. Getting the prospects to do everything for me."

"I remember," Hyde observes, drily.

Yeah, I'd heard the story. Hyde was patched in six months later than Jekyll. Must have been annoying to be at the beck and call of a man he prospected with.

I open my mouth to say that's not why I'm getting them to leap to my every whim, but what other explanation can I offer? *I don't want to speak to the woman at the bar,* sounds lame, even to me. So I grin. "What can I say? I was at the shit end long enough."

I notice Road's thoughtful eyes on me, but look quickly away.

Marvel throws down his hand. "Fuck this."

"Thought you'd rather be fuckin' that," Hyde jokes, as Pussy walks into the room.

"There's not enough variety nowadays. Get fed up with the same cunt every time. When I came here there were five sweet butts. Now we're down to three."

"I hear you, man. Might as well have an old lady," Shooter, overhearing, complains.

"Here, Shoot. Want to take my place? Talking about old ladies, I've got to get back to mine."

As Hyde stands, Shooter takes his place.

"How is Sarah?" Jekyll asks. "Haven't seen her for ages."

"Yeah, I'll have to bring her around. She's so busy getting the place decorated."

"You're not helping her?" I remember they built a new house on the plot that Ma's home had occupied before the wildfire had taken it the summer the year before.

Hyde gives me a look. "She wants things done just how, and me out of her hair while she does it. I do the heavy lifting and shit, but she's into painting."

"You officially claiming her, Brother?"

Hyde nods. "Yeah. Some time."

When he walks off, Jekyll stares after him. "Some time. Never?"

I take a bill out of my wallet. "Some time," I say firmly, laying the money down.

There's a flutter of notes landing on top of it, and I jot down what estimates people are giving. I take a gamble and say within the next month, others are much longer. Well, the couple has been together eighteen months. I have no idea what's holding them up. When they are together, they seem very much in love.

Christ, I sound sappy. Or could it be, I'm jealous?

Nah. Of course not.

We play another round, which Marvel again loses. He throws his cards down, and places his hands behind his head. "Nah," he says to Road who's offering to deal him in. "I'll sit out this time. Luck's not running my way tonight."

"You're lucky Rock's off fuckin' Becca. Else no one would have a chance."

Yeah, our resident card shark somehow thinks being with his old lady is better than spending his nights with his brothers. I have no idea why. Except, yeah, perhaps I have. I'd prefer giving my cock a workout too, if I had the chance.

As if she could read my mind, Diva comes over. She kneels by the side of my chair, puts her lips against the uninjured side of my face, and her hand blatantly on my flaccid cock. "Hear you've been working out with the sergeant-at-arms, Truck. Want me to take some of your aches away?"

I remove her hand. "Thank you, sweetheart, but no. But Marvel here, he's out of the game."

Marvel grimaces, then stands. "Okay. You reckon you can show me something different?"

"Big boy." Diva stands and grins. "What have you got in mind?" She takes hold of his hand and leads him off.

"Your cock in working order? Or is it broke?" Shooter asks conversationally.

"My cock works fine," I growl.

He shrugs. "Haven't seen you going with the sweet butts. However much Diva tries to get your attention."

I don't go with them as I don't want to upset Allie. Fuck, but that woman's cramping my style. *You don't want to go with them because they aren't Allie.* Oh for fuck's sake. I'm arguing with myself now.

"Truck here doesn't know the girls. Only Allie, and she's sweet." Jekyll sits forward as my gut cramps with the thought that he's another one who's obviously had her. "Not much she won't do."

"I wouldn't say that," butts in Shooter. "Diva though, she's got a thing about her ass. If you like going in the backdoor, she's the one for you."

"Paige," Road gets in on the act. "Now the way she gives head. Mmm mmm." He looks around as though trying to see where she is. "I could have some of that tonight."

I force myself to join in. "What's Pussy got going for her?"

"Man, she's a bit overused, if you know what I mean." Drifter grimaces. "Not as tight as she could be."

"You're not wrong there," Matt, no, Sharp now, overhears and comments, proving he, unlike myself, hasn't wasted time since he's been patched in.

Allie had been tight. Even though... I slap myself mentally around the head. *Don't go there.*

Road half-turns, and I think he's looking again for the clearly talented Paige, but his eyes have landed on Allie, then his attention returns to the table. "Didn't you feel that Allie's heart wasn't in it, though? She'd do anything you wanted, but it was like she was doing her job. There to get you off."

"Isn't that what she's supposed to do?" Shooter's eyes have widened. "I didn't have any complaints. Who wants a clingy female in bed? In, out, get the job done. Job finished."

It hadn't been like that with me and Allie. I hadn't wanted to get up and leave that morning I'd left. Seemed like she hadn't wanted me to go either. In fact, I'd been late, as we'd had a round four.

"I suppose you're right," Road submits. "Sometimes with Diva or Paige I get worried they're trying to get their hooks into me. Never the case with Allie. No connection."

We'd connected.

"She's a whore," I say, bluntly. My vehemence makes Road stare at me.

The card game is over. Road's eyes fall on Shooter, then on Jekyll, then he jerks his head toward Drifter and Sharp. "Give us a moment, will you?"

They look curious, but get up and go.

"What's up with you, Brother?"

"What do you mean?"

"Whenever Allie is mentioned, you get this weird look on your face. If I didn't know better, I'd think you wanted to kill someone." He shakes his head. "Though when Drummer mentioned you claiming her, you said there was nothing between you. I think you may be protesting too much. The way you've been reacting here says something different."

"I don't want to claim her, Road," I spit out through gritted teeth.

He ignores me. "What was it like? That night? When you were patched in and you got together?"

I offer my answer with a dismissive shrug. "Much like going with any whore, I suspect. We got together, fucked, then I left." *We fucked,* I tell myself. *That's all it was.*

"Fucked? So you know what we mean then. Allie was just going through the motions."

Though it would be better to lie, I don't. I stay silent.

"You didn't fuck?"

"Where are you going with this, Road?" I want the whole conversation to be over.

Suddenly he leans forward. "You think I don't know why you don't get your own beer? It's not because you want the fuckin' prospects to jump to your tune. It's because you don't want to face her. You won't go with the whores because you don't want to. There's only one woman you want, the one you don't think you can have."

"Oh I can have her," I refute. "I just don't want her. You heard yourself, Marvel and Shooter. Allie's been here so fuckin' long there's not a man here who hasn't had her."

"Wrong, there. Peg and Mouse for a start. And Bullet—he's never stepped out on Carmen. But yeah, most of us have fucked her. But that's all we've done. You and her, Truck? Well I can read your face when you look at her, and her feelings for you are written all over hers. You didn't just fuck that night, did you? She gave you something she's never given anyone before. Look me in the eye and tell me the two of you didn't make love."

Whoa. I hold my palms up, uncaring my mangled hand is held high. "Stop right there. Whores don't make love."

"Exactly." He sits back in triumph. Then yells, "Prospect?" When Roadkill appears at a run, he instructs, "Two whiskeys. Doubles."

The drink arrives and is set down in front of me. I stare into the amber liquid when I automatically pick it up.

Had she been different with me? Was the Allie I'd seen not the whore, but the person? If so, what's stopping me looking at her that way now? I sneak a glance from my glass to the woman standing behind the bar, laughing at something Wraith has just said. *Perhaps he can't tell, but I can. She might be smiling, but her heart's not in it.* She looks beautiful though, in yet another of those fifties' style dresses.

How come I can read her, but no one else can?

Perhaps she shows me herself.

"You know Mouse is helping her apply for jobs?"

My eyes meet Road's over the top of our filled shot glasses.

"Yeah, she can't read or write well. She tell you that? She's embarrassed about it, but Mouse is pretty certain there's a reason, apparently Drummer does as well. They think she might be dyslexic. Her mom had thought she was lazy, didn't get her help."

I take a sip of my whiskey, while considering no one has ever had Allie's back or supported her. Memories of what she's done for me come back into my head. I've taken from her, accepted her assistance, offered nothing back. And nothing she'd done had suggested she wanted it. Because in all of her life, no one's been there for her.

"She's planning on visiting bars on her own to try and get a job away from the compound. Hear she's got tomorrow night off to go try and find herself work." Road's casually spoken words rebound like bullets fired in my head.

I emit a low growl. "Who's going with her?"

He acts surprised at my question, and shrugs as if it's of no importance. "She's going by herself."

His words confirm once again, Allie's never had anyone on her side.

My woman is not going to be walking the streets of Tucson. My woman? What the fuck? But as my subconscious claims her, somehow the possessive feels right. As if I've admitted something that's been lurking at the back of my mind for a while.

Road continues, "She's asked Mouse to help her look for an apartment that she can afford on minimum wage. Of course, she'll end up in a shithole…"

"You'll end up in a fuckin' hole in the ground if you don't

shut up," I snarl, slamming my glass so hard on the table Hound comes running over.

Road sits forward again. "You don't like hearing her plans? That she's planning on leaving the Satan's Devils? That she won't be on the compound at all? You don't like hearing that? Well, fuckin' get off your ass and do something about it."

I stand, waving Hound's attention off.

CHAPTER EIGHTEEN

*A*llie...

I can't help my eyes going to Truck whenever I can sneak a look without him knowing. He never comes up to the bar for himself, always sends a prospect to get him a beer. It's not hard to fathom why, he doesn't want to face me.

That should make it easier for me to keep my distance, but something keeps drawing my attention back to him. I noted he seemed relaxed playing cards, then assumed he was winning by the smile on his face.

I'd seen Diva approach him, and held my breath until she walked off with Marvel instead.

The game seemed to come to a close, and I saw Truck's body stiffen, as though the conversation had turned to something unpleasant. A topic that had upset him, but not the others. *Had they been asking about how he got hurt?* I hope they're not pushing him to speak about things he'd rather not remember.

Now the others leave the table, only Road and Truck remain.

"What's that about?"

I don't normally eavesdrop on the brothers' conversations. Obviously I hear bits and pieces, but don't hang near. I now make an exception as I'm certain Shooter's asking Drifter about Truck.

"No fuckin' idea, Brother. But something we said has got Truck riled." His eyes flick to me, and hastily I look away.

I bend down as though checking stock under the bar. *Out of sight, out of mind.* It works. I strain my ears, and hear Shooter reply in a voice that has deepened over the last couple of years.

"He was adamant she meant nothing to him and that he wasn't going to claim her. Don't know what made him lose his fuckin' mind."

It was something to do with me. I'm certain of that.

Their voices start to fade. *Guess they've walked off.* I stand. Yeah. Shooter and Drifter are now by the pool table, if they're continuing their conversation I won't be able to hear.

My eyes flick to the object of my fixation again. Only to find him staring right at me.

Oh shit.

Truck looks extremely pissed off.

Double shit.

He stands. He takes one step my way. Then another. Then a third. There's no doubt about it, he's heading toward me.

"Prospect," he yells. "Man the bar. Allie's finished."

I'm finished? What? For tonight? For good?

"Truck," I start to stammer out.

He reaches over the bar and the fingers of his right hand curl around my arm. His hold is firm, not enough to hurt, but tight so I can't get away. He guides me to the end of the bar and lifts the hatch so I can get out.

"Truck?"

But he doesn't explain. Just leads me out of the clubhouse. Intrigued men silently parting to let us through.

Once outside, he backs me against the wall, and emotion flares in his right eye, staring intently into mine.

"Do you like cats?" he snarls out in a gravelly voice.

Of all the things I expected he might say, that was at the far bottom of the list, if even on it in the first place.

"Well?" he pushes when I don't respond to his totally out of the blue question.

I swallow, hard, then proudly manage to get out without stuttering, "I always wanted a kitten. Was never allowed one."

"Well you're not having a fuckin' cat. You got me?"

I may have got his words, but I don't understand him at all. But as he stares clearly waiting for a response, I reply, "I got you."

He pushes in closer, getting right up into my face. Suddenly his hand sweeps around my head, grasping my hair and pulling so I'm forced to look at him again. "You let me use you, Allie. You made no protest. That time you came to my apartment. You didn't say anything."

I go to speak.

"You weren't my Allie then, were you? I used you, like the whore I thought you were."

He had. I'd done nothing to stop him.

"It was different. I knew it then. Took me far too long to fuckin' see it."

I don't know where he's going with this. Every word out of his mouth is not what I expected. I don't know what he's going to say or do next.

"*My* Allie is the one who gave me her all the night before I went away. *My* Allie is the woman who came to the ophthalmologist with me. *My* Allie is the woman who encouraged me to come back to the club. *My* Allie is the woman who never asks anything for herself. *My* Allie. *Mine.*"

The last thing I anticipated would happen next was that his lips would come down on mine.

Not hard, but gentle. Almost as though he's uncertain of his welcome. I move my mouth against his, rising on tiptoe. My arms go around his back, half to balance myself and half to pull him closer as I experience my first ever proper kiss.

As if my body knows what to do without my brain issuing instructions, my mouth opens, allowing his tongue to sweep inside.

I don't know how to do this, so I let him lead as he firms the kiss, grinding our mouths together. He tastes of beer and whiskey and something else, something uniquely his. It's a flavour I could get drunk on, addicted to. I groan as I push myself harder against him, ignoring the hard bulge in the front of his jeans pushing into me. My stomach is fluttering with arousal, but right now, it's the feeling of lips against lips, tongue against tongue, which I can't get enough of.

He backs off, my tongue follows his into his mouth, a growl sounds in his throat as he takes control again, my arms tighten around him, my hands fisting the back of his cut, holding him as tightly as possible.

One of his hands is twisted in my hair, his other comes around my waist, pulling me hard against him.

I moan, he groans, and still we kiss.

I don't want this to end.

But like anything good, it does.

Eventually, he pulls back, releasing my hair, and sliding his hand down under my chin. When I try to turn away, he pulls my face back, tilting it so he can stare down into my eyes.

"You are mine." His words are forceful, a declaration of intent. "I'm fuckin' claimin' you Allie."

It takes a moment for me to process his words. One moment he's making it plain he wants nothing to do with me, and the next, this? I don't understand what's happened to change his mind. I feel as anxious as a child given a favourite toy, but scared it's going to be snatched away. It's probably not the right thing to say, but I do it, anyway. Reaching up I trace my hand gently over the left, scarred side of his face, feeling the uneven surface that doesn't detract from him at all. "Why Truck, why?"

"Why?" He cradles my head, and pulls me in gently, so my cheek rests on his cut. "Why? Because I realised you've given me part of you which no man here as ever had, even though they thought you'd given them all of you. We didn't fuck, Allie. We made love. I don't want you to leave, can't abide the thought of never seeing you again. Because you belong to me, Allie, as I belong to you. If you'll have me, that is."

I'm scared, terrified. Unable to believe my ears are correctly interpreting the words coming out of his mouth. Frightened I'm hearing what I want to and missing his underlying reasons of why we can't be together once more.

So I put it plainly myself. "I'm sorry," I start.

He rears away, then looks down with a 'what the fuck' look on his face.

But we've got to get this out into the open or else I'll always be waiting for my demons to raise their heads. "No, I'm sorry I'm not the right woman for you. Truck, I don't know what's happened, but you've been right all along. I can't change my past…" Comments when I've been tending bar have shown me that. Men here will never forget, will always be a reminder for him.

"I'm not asking you too. I was blind, stupid, stuck in my own head. You weren't a whore with me, Allie. It just took me too long to see it. That time, in my apartment, I should have known. Should have realised the difference. But even then, when I treated you so badly, you stayed. I'd trampled over your feelings, but you wouldn't go until I took what I allowed you to give, your comfort."

Slowly I shake my head and lower my face.

His fingers raise my chin once again. "After that first night, I couldn't stop thinking about you. Even lying in that hospital bed, not sure I was going to get out of it, the only woman I saw in my head, was you."

"But…"

"When I came back, I thought I'd been a fool, fallin' for a whore. My heart wanted you, my head said you'd given me nothing more than anyone else. I tried to convince myself I didn't want you, but I do, Al. I want a chance to prove it to you. I've said things, I know. Hurtful things. Have a lot to make up for." A pained look crosses his face. "If I'm not what you want, Allie, tell me now. I'll leave the compound, not you."

He'll go?

The shock of what he'd be giving up must show on my face, as he continues, "I know you won't jump back into someone else's bed, but this is your home."

"I love you," I suddenly blurt out, then bite my tongue. *Stupid. Stupid. I should have kept my mouth shut.*

He's quiet for a moment, then he forces me to look at him. Emotion blazes from his one expressive eye as he states, "Took me too long to accept I had feelings for you. Allie, my Allie."

He didn't reciprocate, but at least he hadn't run screaming away. Any response I might have made is swallowed by his mouth covering mine once again. Another kiss. More tender, shorter.

"I'd never made love before." When he goes to speak, I put my hand over his mouth, caressing his lips with my fingers. He kisses them gently, making me smile. "You've had another first too. No man has ever kissed me before. I never let them. Well, except for a couple of boys in school, but they don't count."

His breathing stills, then he sighs. The motion pushes his cock against me, and I suspect that it was intentional. *I know what he wants. What all men do.*

He's hard as rock. I move my hand down and cover his cock, then say, brazenly, "Do you want me to take care of that for you?"

But he moves my hand away. "Nah, babe. That's not how this is going to go." Before he continues, he places his hands on my upper arms, and steps back until there's a foot of distance between us. His gaze roams from my toes all the way back up to my face. "You have no fuckin' idea what these new dresses of yours do to me. Much sexier, sweetheart, than those clothes you used to wear. Tonight we're going back to our suites, our own suites. You to yours, me to mine. I hear you've got tomorrow night off?"

I'm trying to follow his side of the conversation, but it's hard. A question though, I can answer. "Yes, I was going…"

"No more looking for jobs."

My eyes crease. "But I've got to…"

"Whatever's in that head of yours, put it out. You've got bartending work here on the compound. I know why you wanted to leave, to put distance between us. But now it's not distance either of us want. So, you put your plans on hold. Indefinitely, you hear me? I told you, I claimed you."

It's all happening so fast, it's taking time for my brain to catch up. As he seems to want some sign of agreement, I nod.

"As we've established you're not working tomorrow and you've got nothing else to do…" he raises an eyebrow, but I keep my mouth shut. "Here's what's going to happen. You make yourself pretty in your new clothes." He raises one hand and strokes my hair. "Leave this loose. And I'm going to take you out on a date."

No sex tonight. A date tomorrow?

"Um, you don't need to…"

"Yes, I do, Allie. We'll go out, talk a bit. Find out about each other. Do what normal folks do. Try and upright this topsy-turvy relationship of ours."

It hits me what he's attempting. Jumping into bed together now would be nothing more than me proving all he needs to do is crook his finger and I'll go to him. This is about him working for it, as normal people do when they date. I just hope he's not going to make me wait too long. For months I've been dreaming of repeating that night.

I squirm, my arousal making me uncomfortable. "Er, if I play my cards right, might I get lucky tomorrow?"

He throws back his head and laughs, a genuine mirth. "You never know, sweetheart. We both just might."

Then he takes my hand, and starts leading me up the track

toward the bloc which houses both our suites, but he stops about halfway, pointing up. We're far enough out of the city that no light from the streetlamps obscures the stars overhead. It's a sight I've seen, but am mostly immune to after all the years I've lived on the compound. But when he tilts up my head, I look and see too.

"It's beautiful," I tell him.

"Not as beautiful as you," he replies gruffly.

I don't know how to respond, so I don't. Genuine compliments about anything other than my prowess in bed is not something I'm used to.

It's hard parting at the entrance to our suites. Our kiss so full of joint need and emotion, it seems wrong not to end up in bed together. I've no doubts he'll soon have his hand on his cock, and I aim to pleasure myself too while visions of him circle my head. It takes all that I am to stop from begging him to take me into his bed tonight, or hell, for him to join me in mine.

I even go to open my mouth to plead, when he stops me with a shake of his head.

"Don't make this any harder than it already is."

I glance down, and giggle. "Is that possible?"

"Fuck, Allie. I'm going to have my hands full with you."

I take pity on him. "Another kiss?"

"Yeah. Another kiss I can do."

It's not enough, but with the promise and hope of what's happening tomorrow, it will have to do.

I hear Truck's door open and close first thing in the morning. He'll be off to the gym to work out with Peg. After a sleepless night of tossing and turning, I've woken a bag of nerves, already hoping I don't fuck up our date tonight. While I appreciate what he's trying to do, to put our relationship on a normal footing, I wish we could just get to the main event where I'd be confident I'd know what I'm doing.

What if I open my mouth and the wrong thing comes out? Truck said he wanted to get to know me. What if he doesn't like the person I really am? What have I got to offer a firefighter?

Lack of sleep and a lot of second guessing myself has made me grumpy. When I drag myself out of bed and get down to the clubhouse, I'm not in the best of moods. I occupy myself checking the bar stock and compiling a list of things that I'll need the prospects to pick up. Running low on beer is an absolute no-no in a club full of thirsty bikers.

"Allie."

Drummer's sharp voice has me standing so fast I bang my head on the underside of the bar. *Like that's put me in a better mood.*

Rubbing my skull vigorously, I snap, "What?"

"Whoa!" He steps back, holding his hands up in surrender. "You get out of the wrong side of the bed? Or," he chuckles, "the wrong bed?"

I simply stare.

"Al. You and Truck can't stand outside the clubhouse eating each other's faces and expect to keep it quiet." He lets that sink in, and my face blushes bright red, before he continues, "Told you he'd come around, didn't I?"

I'd have said Drummer was the last man I'd ever want to confide in, but I find myself glancing around to make sure no one else is in earshot, then confess, "He's taking me on a date tonight, and I'm freaking out."

"You think you might say the wrong thing? Use the wrong knife and fork? Hey, Al. You'll be fine." His eyes narrow. "I'd say I'm a pretty good judge of character, and I wouldn't have given you both a nudge in the right direction if I didn't think you were a good fit. You realise how big a step Truck's taking tonight?"

My head tilts as my brow furrows.

"And that's the reason you're perfect for him. You have no fuckin' idea as it doesn't bother you. This will be the first time Truck has voluntarily appeared in public since he got those scars.

That he feels confident enough to do that with you, Al, well, that speaks fuckin' volumes."

My hand covers my mouth. "I never thought, I didn't think. Drummer, I don't see his scars, I see the man underneath. I completely forgot." *What does that say about me?* I've been worrying my head about myself, never thinking what a toll going out could take on my man.

"Fuckin' perfect for him, Al. Perfect."

That's all the prez says. He walks off chuckling and shaking his head.

Mid-afternoon and I'm already in the shower, doing something I haven't done for a very long time. Preparing for a date. The last time doesn't really count, I was getting ready to sneak out of the house for a secret rendezvous with a kid from school.

I'm only half enjoying the experience. Oh, Truck told me to wear a dress and keep my hair down, but make up? How much is enough, and what's too much? I put it on, take it off, then redo it again. My hands are shaking and I end up poking myself in my eye when I put on mascara. Then have to start all over again once I've washed the black smudge off my face.

A little light foundation, a dusting of face powder. Muted pink lipstick, and I'm ready to go.

Two freaking hours early.

CHAPTER NINETEEN

*T*ruck...

Although the door to her suite is opposite mine, it seems symbolic when I raise my hand to knock. I'm as nervous as I was in my teens, waiting for my prom date to open her door.

Back then I'd been a lanky youth, but while I'd never have taken a stroll down the catwalk, I was confident when I looked in a mirror that my face wouldn't disappoint. Now I'm standing here, clean shaven as I'm worried a beard might not grow properly over my scars, and very conscious of my fake eye, and my lopsided gait.

With my hand hovering in mid-air, I give myself a pep talk. *This is Allie. She's already proven she sees beyond the scars.*

I'd suggested this. It was all my fault. Give us a chance to get to know each other, I'd told her. But what if she's turned off by the shit that may come out of my mouth? Perhaps this is one big mistake.

I'd been so determined not to treat her like a whore, not to take advantage of her, to start wherever this was heading on the right foot, I'd overlooked what that implied. Right now I'd prefer to speak to her using my cock rather than my brain and mouth, not so sure they will comply.

My nervousness increases when I find the fortitude to knock, and she opens her door. *She looks amazing.* So far removed from the sweet butt that used to work in the club, my hands shake.

"Ready?" *Does she look as shell shocked as I? Or am I imagining things? What has she got to worry about? She's a gorgeous woman. Looking like that, she could have any man on the planet. Will she realise, wake up, and run a mile?*

"Are we going or what?"

"Hmm. Rethinking this for a moment there."

She's on my wavelength. "You want to go straight to dessert?" she says with a smile.

"Very tempting." I don't hide the sweep of my gaze from her head to her feet. "But I promised you a date."

I hold out my hand. She takes it.

Despite the work I'm doing with Peg, and continuing my brain training exercises to be able to rely on one eye, while I've taken to the wheel of a car during the day, I don't like to drive at night, finding lights coming toward me disorientating. Wanting her to enjoy the hours ahead, I don't want Allie to drive either, so have enlisted a prospect's help. Hound will be taking us into Tucson tonight, and will be on standby to collect us at the end of our evening.

"Where are we going, Truck?" she asks, as we walk down through the compound.

I hesitate before I respond, "I've made reservations at the Wheel Inn." I hold my breath, waiting for her to reply.

"I've never been."

I can't tell anything from her words, whether she's pleased or dismayed I'm taking her to the restaurant the Satan's Devils own.

This is the first time I'm going out in public for anything other than a hospital appointment or the like. Tonight I'm voluntarily putting myself out there for people to gawk at. At the Wheel Inn there's usually a brother or two around, and I know they'll have my back. I've not yet experimented with people's reaction to the scarring on my face, or that I've got a fake eye.

As we reach the SUV and Hound insists on opening the doors for us, I muse if it weren't for Allie by my side, I wouldn't feel ready to take this step. But her easy acceptance of the way I look gives me a new confidence to face the world.

"How was your day?" she asks, as we start the short drive into town.

I grimace. "Challenging. Peg's a fuckin' hard taskmaster. I thought Captain Slade was bad enough, but Peg? Nah, he's got him well beat."

"Is it helping?"

"A lot." I can feel muscles starting to get back to where they once were on my right side, and improving on my left. How far I'll get, I still don't know, my left ankle won't bend, however much I strengthen up. All I can do is learn to compensate.

"How's your bike coming along?"

It's obvious what she's doing. Polite conversation to take my mind off the ordeal ahead. Squeezing her hand, I respond, "Blade's got an electric gear shift on its way. It's a push button affair, and from what I've seen, he should be able to fix it fairly easily."

"Will he put that on the right hand side?"

I shake my head. "No, but on the left should be okay, that way we don't need to move the brake which would be a lot of work. It's operated with the thumb. Peg's helped me strengthen my grip, and Blade's going to do what he can to lighten the touch to what I need."

"So you'll definitely be able to ride?"

Her question pulls me up. Somehow over the past few days I've gone from never expecting to feel a bike under me again, to thinking about when. As I reply, "I think so," she places her hand on my leg, then quickly lifts it away.

Good move. It was hard to resist nudging her hand further up my thigh. I do not want to walk into a restaurant sporting a raging hard-on.

Once again Hound opens the door for us when we arrive, I hide a grin at the full chauffeur treatment, then frown and take a deep breath as we walk through the entrance.

Sandy herself comes over to greet us. "Truck, Allie. Got you a nice table in the corner."

I lift my chin toward Rock and Shooter standing by the bar, in return they raise their drinks back at me. Free drinks on the house for basically acting as bouncers in case any trouble goes down.

The Satan's Devils run a successful business here, but half the time we're not sure whether it's the excellent menu we have on offer, or the fact that it enables citizens to walk on the wild side. Whatever, having a couple of brothers here wearing cuts doesn't hurt the dollars coming in at all, and, if it helps, it's all to the good.

Allie takes her seat, and Sandy hands first her, then me, a menu.

"Can I get you some drinks?"

We order beer and wine, then are left alone.

Reaching my undamaged hand over the table, I take hold of hers. "Relax. We're here to have some great food and have a good time."

Her eyes meet mine. "I don't know how to do this," she says, hesitantly. "I've never been on a date before." She bites her lip, "Are there some rules I should follow?"

"Allie, you'll be fine. You look amazing, by the way. Should have told you earlier." I feel like hitting my head that I hadn't. "Seems I'm out of practice with dating etiquette as well."

I notice Allie's squinting at the menu, and Road's comment about her lack of reading skills comes back to me.

"What do you fancy?" I ask her casually. "The Chicken Supreme sounds good." I continue running down the menu, "Or would you prefer the steak?" I notice her concentrating on me as I vocalise every item.

Allie stops me a couple of times, pointing out there're a few dishes we've already had tasters of in the clubhouse.

"Ma certainly did the club a solid leaving that recipe book behind," I observe.

"She did. I don't know how, but a different spice here, a new herb there. It makes all the difference."

Having eventually decided and placed our orders, silence descends. When I notice her fidgeting, I go to break it. "Tell me something about yourself."

"There's not much to tell."

"How did you end up with the Satan's Devils?"

She's brief, frank. Her story utterly heart-breaking. As she glosses over details from her past, I get the image of a young girl who was ignored in preference to her younger, and in Allie's eyes, more intelligent brother. A burden to her mom who couldn't be bothered to give her the help she needed. That she survived at such a young age on the streets was a miracle. I begin to be convinced joining the Satan's Devils probably saved her life, or at least prevented her being snatched and made into a sex slave.

As she talks, it just confirms what I already know. She's about as far from stupid as you can get. Even at sixteen she knew enough to steer clear of pimps, and keep independent.

"It wasn't always easy." Seeing my interest, she gives me more details, not realising every word she speaks makes me wish it was possible to turn back time and be there to save her. "Big Mac, well, his name was Mac, and he was big, so though it was tempting to laugh at his name, once you met him, well..." her shiver completes her thoughts. "I was young, too young. I looked it too. He kept offering to take care of me. But I'd met some of the girls he had in his stable, they were dependant on drugs which he provided. I used to hide whenever I saw his car.

I had to move more than once when he found out where I was staying."

"You didn't try drugs?"

"No. Being clean kept me sharp. Kept me from making bad decisions. I saw the results of what happened when you let your guard down."

"When you joined the Devils your life must have changed dramatically." Now I know her background, I can understand it much better. What choice did she have?

"It did. I could relax. Sleep with both eyes shut." She gazes at me intently. "This wasn't the life I hoped for, Truck. In my mind, growing up, I had the expectations most young girls do, that eventually I'd get married and have a husband and kids. But I don't have many regrets, it turned out the best that it could. I like sex, why not admit it? And the Devils are mainly good men."

"Any of the Devils ever hurt you?" I ask casually, but my hand clenches under the table.

"Not for a long time. Buster, he patched over from San Diego. When he tried to rape Sophie, I wasn't surprised. He preferred women to be less willing. None of us liked him, he was too rough. But, hey, that was just one man."

Buster's not around any longer. Thank fuck Wraith had taken care of him long before I'd come on the scene, because after hearing Allie mention him, I'd have had to step up myself. I hate the thought of any man hurting her. Hate that she was ever in a position of being unable to turn a man down. My fist uncurls and again I reach over the table. "We do this, Al? We get together? You've always got the choice, sweetheart. You're not in the mood? All you have to do is tell me."

A quick grin comes onto her face. "Think I'll always be in the mood with you, Truck."

"I lost my family in a house fire. Damn smoke alarms didn't work. Both my parents died of smoke inhalation." She's given me her worst, I'll share mine too. My history that I usually keep to myself.

"Truck, that's awful." Her compassion is obvious.

I shrug. "Long time ago now. Shouldn't have happened. I'd been out for the night, staying with a school friend. That's part of the reason I became a firefighter when I left the Army. We spend time educating people on the importance of checking that their alarms are working." Grimacing, I continue. "The loss of my parents will always be an open wound. I'd bunked at friends' houses for the few months before I could join up. Seemed the best option I had at the time, and I don't regret it. The Army hadn't been easy on me, and at that time, I needed the discipline filled with anger as I was, due to the loss of my family."

I don't like talking about myself. What man does? So I turn it back to her. "Mouse believes you're dyslexic."

Her eyes open wide.

"He hasn't been spilling your secrets. I was just asking him why he was helping you with the applications. It sort of came up."

She shifts in embarrassment. "That's why you read the menu?" she observes, but not accusingly. She looks sad, my gut twists.

"Darlin', whether you can read or not, doesn't matter a damn."

"Mouse thinks that I am dyslexic. He was doing some stuff with his screen, changing colours of the font and backgrounds. Interesting stuff. Words jumped out of the page when he hit a good combination."

Yeah, that's what Mouse had told me. Apparently tinted glasses in the right colour can be a great help if you're dyslexic. Something I'd like to investigate further, if she'll let me in to help.

"We'll look into it, babe. If you want to read, we'll find a way that you can do it." Time for me to step up and do something for her, rather than the other way around. I'm certain it's not lack of ability, but something needs to help her brain click. It might be I'm more sympathetic now that I've learned how mental exercises and little adjustments can help me see with just the one eye.

Our appetisers arrive, we dig into the delicious food and eat. When both plates are clean, I move onto a different subject.

"You used to dream of having a family. You still want that?"

After giving it a moment of thought, she offers, "I don't know, Truck. I sort of got used to the idea I wouldn't be in that position." Her mouth turns up at the corners. "I've seen that babies are hard work." Her smile disappears. "I'm not certain I'd want a baby, Truck. It's not just raising a child and looking after them, think of what I'd be bringing a kid into. This world is fucked up, just look at what happened to me. Life is hard work, and I'm not sure I'd want to impose it one anyone else."

I can sympathise with her view.

"What about you?"

"Wife, maybe a kid or two in the mix." I add quickly, "But it's not a deal breaker." I raise my eyebrows at her. "Maybe a dog instead."

"No cat?"

I shudder as I realise she wants an explanation for my strange announcement last night. "Definitely not. Sorry, Al. I'll give you everything you want, but no cat."

"Why do you hate them so much?"

As I explain, a shadow comes over her face, pain, for me. This time it's her reaching for my hand, my left, not my right, her fingers gently stroking the stubby remainder of my missing digits. "To some people pets are like their children. Mean just as much. The woman who ran to save her cat put her life on the line for it. Oh, I know she put yours on it too, but she was driven to try to rescue it. I can't imagine how she'd have felt if she knew she'd left it to burn to death."

"Lots of people lost their pets in that fire, Al. We had to concentrate on saving human life."

If someone had their beloved pet with them, we did what we

could to keep them together, would never force them to leave it behind.

But I can't forget or forgive, that woman's impulsive action had ruined my life.

If she hadn't, would I have ever seen Allie as a person, or always just as a sweet butt?

"Okay," she says seriously. "No cat. I can live with that."

I go for broke. "Can you live with me?"

"You asking?" Her eyes widen.

"Told you I want to claim you. Guess I'm asking if you want to be claimed."

Her voice goes low, husky. "If I say yes?"

"Then I'll take it to the table next time we have church. When I get my bike, want you on the back."

She's quiet for so long, I start to doubt her answer is going to be to my liking. I'm thinking of arguments of how to convince her when, finally, she responds.

"If I say yes, I want to make this clear. That night I felt something I've never felt before. Never felt for anyone else I'd been with, and never expected to find it again. It was special because if was you, Truck. That's the reason I'll claim you." A wicked type of grin crosses her face, showing me this isn't going to be a one-way relationship. I'm fine with that. "It's not because I'm tired of being a sweet butt and want a way out. It's you I want. I said I love you, and I mean that." She pauses. "Total honesty?"

I nod.

"Being with the Satan's Devils as a sweet butt wasn't a chore. In fact, it was freaking amazing. I like sex, and plenty of it. I liked the variety. Never thought I'd find a man who could satisfy me all by himself, until you and I got together. Then I knew sex like that was all I wanted for the rest of my life. Because it wasn't just a cock, it was you attached to it.

"I kept working, I had to. But no one satisfied me like you had. It made me realise what I'd been missing all my life. That elusive emotion that comes with love making." Another break, then her eyes fix on mine. "That's the reason I'm saying yes. Because it's you, no one else. I've no yearning to ride on anyone else's bike."

Her honesty demands mine. "Darlin', I've been around the block. I'm a firefighter. The uniform itself makes me everyone's hero. Wearing a cut and riding a bike makes me a bad boy everyone wants. Never been hard for me to get panties dropping. Since you? I've not thought of anyone else. Sweet butts in the club do not get my motor revving. That's only you. Guess we're both ready to commit to each other."

"I think I'd like to be claimed," she whispers.

I grin back. "I would too."

CHAPTER TWENTY

*A*llie...

The meal, was delicious, I think, but couldn't tell you what I ate. After our intense conversation, the heated expression on Truck's face which I'm sure was reflected in mine, made it obvious that now we'd claimed each other verbally, the next step was to stake our physical claims too.

That first night together before Truck had left for California, emotion had entered into a whore/biker union which had come as a surprise. Something I'd recognised even then, but tried at the time to keep hidden, bikers didn't want sweet butts sinking their claws into them. One whiff that a girl had developed feelings, and it would result in the biker never coming back for a repeat. That's what had been in my head the next morning.

Until, as days passed, I realised what had been turned on, couldn't be turned off.

I'd been the first sweet butt Truck had gone with. He hadn't known what to expect, whether the all that I'd given to him, was what I'd given to everybody. But with all the rest, I'd kept that part of me to myself.

Tonight there's no need to hide our feelings.

I giggle as he places his key in his door. "Was that Hound or Roadkill that drove us back from Tucson?"

His dark eye flares. "No fuckin' idea babe. Could have been Drummer himself for all the notice I took of who was driving. Now come here." He kicks the door shut behind him, and wastes no time pulling me into his arms. "Been too fuckin' long since I've held you."

I know the men here. Know the ones who want me to get naked immediately. Know those who prefer to undress me themselves. Know how to put on an act and pretend I'm into it.

Now I'm as nervous as a virgin, not knowing what to do with my hands, whether his urgent desire means he wants me to strip so he can sink into me.

"Relax, babe," he repeats the words he used to calm me at the start of our date. "We'll find our way, together." His hands are rubbing up and down my arms, a gentle touch which is soothing. "Right now, I just want to feel that mouth."

Yes! The act which makes this so different. As I raise my face and our lips meet, despite we're both already turned on and anticipating the main event, I notice how soft his mouth feels against mine, and how careful he's being to make this sensual, not demanding.

I trace his outline with my tongue, taking the time to learn him, knowing that our declarations of claiming mean, unless I fuck this up, I'll have a whole lifetime with my man. Neither of us are virgins, both have a large body count behind us, but now we've left that all behind and have chosen each other.

We don't need to run through our whole repertoire in one night. We don't have to repeat the past, together we'll discover new ways of love making.

His mouth continues to press against mine, our tongues meet and slide gently together. He raises one hand, brushing his fingers lightly against my cheek, that simple touch sending shivers down my whole body, making every nerve ending come alive. I'm breathing him in, his essence of biker, but it's different. The bodywash, after shave, I don't know what it is, but it mingles with the leather of his cut and makes it unique.

Raising my hand, I touch his smooth, bald head, freshly shaved tonight. As if my slight touch affects him in the same way, I feel him shudder, and hear the groan which comes from his throat.

Slowly, very slowly, his tongue retreats from my mouth, and then our lips part. Raising his head slightly, he plants a soft kiss on each of my temples, then moves his lips down my cheek. As my head falls back, an unsummoned moan leaves my mouth as his mouth meets the pulse point on the side of my neck.

The effect isn't lost on him, he sucks gently. *Mark me, Truck. Make me yours.*

As if he's heard my unspoken request, he sucks sharply, enough of a bite to make me gasp, then his tongue soothes the spot. He'll have left evidence to be seen in the morning.

"Gonna mark you all over," he rasps directly against my ear, making my body tremble again. "Everywhere."

His promise sends a zing of electricity right down my body, and my clit starts to throb with need.

His hands move around me, a slight touch on my back, and my dress falls open, and down around my hips.

"Step out of it, Allie. Let me see you."

I do, then see that flare of desire in his eyes as he stares at my matching red underwear set.

"Fuckin' beautiful Allie. You're fuckin' gorgeous."

Men have complimented me before, but never have I wanted to believe it so intently as I do this moment. But one look at his face and all doubts flee.

"My turn," I tell him, my hands going to his cut. He leaves me as he stands and allows me to remove the leather off his shoulders.

A biker's cut comes second only to his bike, so I treat it carefully, folding it, then stepping away to place it over a chair. While I've been gone, he hasn't wasted a second, stripping off his tee and leaving his chest bare.

His eye are closed, his head back, and his fists are clenched at his sides.

That day in the shower I hadn't catalogued all his injuries, my aim then only to show those on his face and his missing eye weren't going to deter me. Now I see the scars in all their horrific glory, and my heart bleeds for him.

Less reddened than when I'd last seem them, but still looking angry. I move closer, and put my mouth on the first one, tracing it down from his shoulder to his hip.

"I'm not pretty," he tells me, his voice gruff and strained.

I take my mouth off him, but leave my hand touching his skin. "No wonder you hate cats."

I glance up, and see his mouth twitching. Then, suddenly, I'm hauled to my feet and thrown onto the bed.

"Only you, Al. Only you."

I take it he means no one else would have mentioned the cat at that moment, or maybe be brave enough to remind him how he got hurt. But whether it was animal or human he saved, I know I've got a hero with me in the room tonight.

He stands, staring at me. "How did I get so goddamn lucky?" A rhetorical question.

"I think you're overdressed."

"Huh?" A sheepish grin, then he undoes his zip taking his time and circling his hips. I realise he's doing his best at a sexy striptease.

It's working. A grin covers my face in appreciation, and my tongue licks my lips. Christ, I like what I see.

He takes his time, bending to take off his boots, then sliding his jeans down slowly.

Boxer briefs. Tight fitting. I like.

In a sudden movement he has his briefs off, and is twirling

them around on one finger. As I laugh, he makes his now exposed and very impressive cock circle by another rotation of his hips.

"You were wasted as a firefighter," I tell him, chuckling. "Ever thought of auditioning at the Angels?" As I mention the strip club owned by the Satan's Devils, he barks a laugh. I have a fit of giggles at the expression on his face.

"You think my cock's a laughing matter?" He growls warningly as he takes the one step needed to bring him to the end of the bed. "I'm going to wipe that smile right off your face, babe. Soon you're going to be screaming for mercy instead."

I wave my hand dismissively as though bored. "You think, big man?"

As he roars, "I don't think, I fuckin' know," he launches himself onto the bed.

In a move I didn't expect, his large hands tug into the sides of my flimsy panties and he rips them right off. "I'll buy you another pair," he tells me, completely unapologetically. "I'll get a dozen. They won't last very long."

The threat does nothing to worry me.

He takes total control of my body, and I make no move to stop him as he bends my legs at the knees, and in one motion pushes my feet towards my ass and pulls my thighs apart. Then he sits back, his eyes open wide.

"Fuckin' beautiful."

"You gonna just look, or what?"

I feel a sting on my ass cheek. The light smack doing nothing but make me giggle again. *What would it be like to be laid over his lap and those big hands spanking me?* While I've never been into that before, the thought of letting Truck manhandle me makes me wetter than I already was.

"Love you bare. You gonna keep it that way for me?"

"Uh huh." He's already lowered his head while he was speaking, and the anticipation is making it hard to think of words.

"Fuck, I'm hungry. I'm ready for another dessert."

Oh. My. God. Truck's got such a talented tongue. He uses hands, mouth and even his teeth as he starts to devour me. Now I'm not giggling, I'm writhing, screaming, clutching the sheet either side with both hands. I'm a mass of sensation and feeling, unable to do anything but hang on for the ride.

His tongue thrusts inside me, then he licks up to my clit, and circles it lightly making me push my hips up into his face. His fingers fill the vacancy inside me, curling around to find the spot that has me tensing and reaching, reaching for something that I can't quite get. He's playing with me, taking his time for his own enjoyment, getting me so close then backing off. When he eventually decides to have mercy on me, I'm not sure I'll survive reaching the peak.

He's learning my body, learning which touch has me crying out and tensing.

Now he's at the point where he's had enough, and it's all business as he unerringly returns to the places I most want him, a double assault on my g-spot and clit.

"God! God! Godgodgodgodgodgod!" I scream as I go over, my torso coming up off the bed as he relentlessly draws out my orgasm, then I crash back down again, utterly spent.

Never, not even during that night I had with him before have I come so hard.

When at last I come back to my senses I raise my head and see him grinning at me, wiping me off his face with the back of his hand, and then licking that clean as though he doesn't want to miss a drop.

"You've killed me."

"What, me? I think you said I was a god?"

I smile, relaxed, sated and happy. Then I see the size of his cock, the purplish head, bulging and ready. The thought of having that monster inside me arouses me once again. Holding out my arms I reach for him.

"You protected?"

Dejectedly, I shake my head. "I had the implant but that's gone past its sell by date. As I wasn't… well, it didn't seem worth getting one again."

He's moved so he's kneeling over me, now he places a finger on my lips. "I'll take care of things, no worry, Allie. We probably need to get tested…"

"I'm clean. I did that when I stopped…" I abruptly cease talking. Fucking his brothers isn't something I want to bring into his bed.

"I was tested in the hospital. Only person I've been with is you, Allie. I haven't forgotten I owe you an orgasm for that day. And don't tell me you had one, I know you faked it."

"Oh?" I say, impudently. "You couldn't tell just now."

His eyes open so wide for a second I'm worried his prosthetic is going to fall out. I'm laughing again at his look of confusion.

Then, an insolent grin spreads. "If that's the case I better try again."

Instead of going for a condom, he returns to what he was doing a moment ago. This time he zeros straight in on his targets and it's moments before I'm tensing and screaming all over again.

While I'm recovering, he opens the drawer and takes out a box of condoms the prospects had probably placed there, one of their duties to keep the brothers' rooms stocked. I'm transfixed as he expertly rolls it on, his lack of fingers on his left hand doing nothing to hinder his precision.

He pulls me to him, placing himself at my entrance, then starts pushing inside. "Fuck, Allie. You're so tight."

Because he's so big, like the rest of him. I make an effort to relax and stop myself from tensing, instead enjoying the feeling of my man inside me. I almost sob with pleasure at the realisation this is Truck, and he feels every bit as good as I remembered.

"Going to be hard and quick, Al. I'm not going to last long. You feel too fuckin' amazing."

I contract my vaginal muscles.

"Shit. Do that again."

I do. It encourages him to start thrusting. Slowly at first, deep pushes in until he touches my cervix, making sure he locates the spot that makes me cry out. Even when he's chasing his own pleasure he's making sure I'm getting mine too. His pace quickens, and so does the force, soon he starts hammering, the headboard thumping against the wall until it sounds like constant thunder—or is that the blood rushing in my ears?

"God, Truck."

"Can't hold it, are you there yet?"

I wasn't quite, but when he presses on my clit it's like a magic button and I'm screaming out names of the deity again.

"Fuck! Fuck! Fuck! Fuck!" His words are a chant accompanying his final erratic pumping. "Oh God, Allie! Allie!"

He rears back, still inside me, his face contorted, as if he's in pain. Then he opens his eyes and stares down at me. "You're a fuckin' goddess, Al."

He lowers his body, taking my mouth with his. I can still taste me on him, a slight saltiness on my tongue. It's a tender kiss full of passion, spent desire and possessiveness, on both our sides. My arms go around him hugging him to me, my heart bursting with the love I feel for this man.

"I love you," I breathlessly tell him.

The sides of his mouth turn up in an enormous curve. "I fuckin' hope so. I claimed you."

It's the cockiness in his tone which makes me bat his arm. Then, his mouth turns down and he becomes serious. "I love you too, Al. Think I fell that first night. Just didn't admit it. Heck, how could I recognise love when I'd never felt it before? What I do know is I had feelin's for you, you stayed in my head. Hated what you did, but not you, never you, Al. Now I've got shit straight in my mind, it feels right to admit the words."

My man has just told me he loves me. As I stare at him in

wonder, for the moment, totally lost for words, I realise all the good and bad up to now in my life have led to this point and us being together.

Life surely can't get any better.

TWENTY YEARS IN THE FUTURE – Drummer

THE SUN ISN'T *a perfect circle anymore. The bottom of it is now hidden beneath the mountain. Whether psychological or real, the warmth seems to seep away from the air.*

"Dad!" A voice snaps my head around.

"Zane," I greet my younger son. "How did you do today?"

"Straight As."

I nod, having expected nothing less. Zane isn't more intelligent than his older brother, Eli, it's just that he expresses it in different ways. He had gotten into college studying civil engineering of all things. Stayed close though, he's at the University of Arizona in Tucson. Unlike his brother or either of his parents, he even prefers a cage to a bike. Still, love him for all of that, proud as punch of him too.

Zane doesn't know it, but once he's qualified, Bullet and Shooter are thinking of taking him on, and once he's got some experience under his belt, making him a partner. Will keep SD Construction in the family that way. Shooter and Zane will run things when Bullet retires, which probably won't be too far away.

Eli, though, he's club through and through.

Two boys, brought up together. Two very different personalities and outlooks on life.

Zane nods and continues up to the house.

"Good boys, you've got there, Drummer."

"Yeah," I agree.

"Wasn't always like that."

It wasn't. Eli and Peg's lad, Noah, had got into some scrapes over the years. Hot wiring a car just to prove they could do it. Unfortunately, not one of ours. Peg and I bailing them out at the police station had led to a few firm lectures about citizen ways, and how not to bring them into our business. A lesson, luckily they learned. Of course, it wasn't so much what they'd done which was the issue, but that they'd been stupid enough to get caught.

Peg chuckles. "Not that it's been plain sailing with the girls, either. My kid, Lisa, and Rock's girl, Rose. Remember the time they had their first dates?"

Do I. I grin. "Think taking half the club along with them as escorts may have cramped their style."

"You see, Zane or Eli come home looking like they've been fucked, you'd just check they wrapped their shit up and slap them on the back."

"Peg, if Lisa came back like that, you'd search out and kill the fucker."

"Yeah, I would." Like me, he's staring straight ahead. "She's going to remain a virgin all her life."

"And you wonder why I didn't want a daughter?"

Peg shifts his legs again. "At least I wasn't as bad as Wraith. Remember when Lisa brought her friends to the barbeque last year? One of the guys tried to say hi to Hilda, Wraith got out his gun, threatened to kill him, and bury his body where he'd never be found."

"Bit over the top I agree," I snort. "Kid wet himself from what I remember. But she is only a child, Peg."

"Yeah? She's sixteen. And how old was your first girl?"

I don't tell him she was a bit younger than that.

But he admits his. "Mine was sixteen." He turns to me. "Sixteen. Same age as Allie when she first started getting paid for opening her legs. At least I was the same age. Can you imagine any of our girls having no option but to do that?"

I shake my head. It doesn't bear thinking about. It puts what she went through into perspective.

"I think her background, her ability to deal with whatever life threw *at her, helped her to survive what she had coming after she got together with Truck."*

"Yeah. I think you're right." Peg chuckles softly. "Remember him coming to the table saying he was claimin' her?"

I do. Only too well. Perhaps it would have been better had we voted no.

CHAPTER TWENTY-ONE

*T*ruck…

"From the way our brother there keeps fidgeting, I think he's got something to say." Drummer's mouth twitches as he looks down the table. "Truck?"

I've sat through church trying to concentrate, but it's hard when cries of 'God' are echoing in my head. I can't keep away from her, love the sounds she makes when she's coming. Had another round before coming into church. We're fucking like motherfucking rabbits, can't keep our hands off each other. But it's not sex, it's making love. Never felt anything like this for a woman before.

I notice everyone staring at me, and know they all know what I'm going to say. This is just making it official.

"Yeah, I'm claimin' Allie."

This is just a formality, isn't it?

"Proposal's on the table, Brothers. Before we vote on it, anyone got any comments?"

Blade spins his knife, stopping it when it points toward me. "Think it needs to be pointed out, it's never happened in this chapter before, a brother claimin' a sweet butt."

"Not a sweet butt any longer," I remind him, my jaw clenching.

"Blade's right to bring it up." I thought at least Peg would support me. It appears not. "We've had problems before when sweet butts get too close to a brother. As Rock knows only too well."

Rock doesn't seem to appreciate the reminder. Jill had tried to sink her claws into him. Her selfishness was the reason his original tat was flayed off his back. I've seen the new one, a job well done, but you can still see the uneven scarred skin if you see him close up. He grimaces and shudders. Then shrugs.

"A precedent has already been set. Sweet butt tries to lay claim on a brother and ends up dead. Okay, so Allie managed to snag Truck, doesn't mean the others will try their hand. I don't see a problem with it, as long as Truck can see past her history."

I nod at Rock, at least he sounds like he'll be a yes.

"Allie stepped away from that role some months ago." Road is definitely on my side. After all, he was the one who practically told me to go for it. "Allie's a good woman. Always was. Knows the club inside out," he pauses to glare at the couple of men who've laughed. "As I was saying, if it wasn't for her history, we'd all be agreeing she'd make a fuckin' good ol' lady."

"VP?" Drummer indicates the man to his left.

Wraith looks thoughtful as he runs his hands down his face. "I didn't expect my ol' lady to come onto the compound in a wheelchair—"

"Not even speaking the same language," Blade interrupts.

"Thank you," Wraith replies sarcastically. "As I was saying, all of our ol' ladies turned up unexpectedly. In Truck's case, she was always there, just waiting for the right man to cross her path. You can't plan how you're going to find your perfect woman, the one who's the other part of your soul. If Truck thinks he's found her, all that matters to us is whether she's a fit for the club. I vote she is. We'll just have to watch the others carefully."

"If she hadn't gotten Truck, she was going to leave the club," Mouse states. "She's not a sweet butt hankering after any biker. There's only one man she wants."

Jesus. Can we just vote on it? I'm starting to sweat. Is someone going to come up with a valid objection? I had no idea it was going to be this difficult.

Drummer raps the table to get everyone's attention. My worried eyes land on his face. His view will count for everything. "Sam likes her. But I don't want any problem with the other ol' ladies. We're a family now, and I don't want to bring discord into it."

"Good point," Wraith agrees. "Sophie will be fine with it. We've both got pasts, and agreed to put them behind us."

"Yeah, but her past isn't right in front of your face. It's the other side of the Atlantic, not strutting around the club," Dollar reminds him.

Wraith grimaces as if he hadn't thought of that.

"I didn't go with the whores, Mariana won't give a damn."

"Neither did I." Peg nods at Mouse. "Darcy will accept her."

"Huh. I've been married so long, can't remember what another cunt feels like. Carmen will probably just be pleased to get her hands on her hair." The taken men all nod knowingly. Carmen has her own hairdressing business but does the old ladies' for free.

I start to keep tally of who's for and against. In my estimate, it sounds like the majority are easy with Allie being my old lady, but I'm still tense.

"Blade?"

"Tash will be cool. She's still finding her own place here."

Slick raises his hand. "Allie's caused no problems for Ella."

"Heart?"

"Hey, it's so long in my rearview and before I met Marc or even Crystal. No problem there."

Rock scowls. "Not so far back for me, I'll talk to Becca, but you know what she's like."

Yeah, Becca's getting over having a controlling bastard of a husband as her ex. She's still learning to make decisions for herself, in this she'll probably be guided by Rock and the other old ladies.

"I'm cool," Lady waves his hand.

Then lurches as Joker sticks his fist in his side. "It's me who'd be worried if you'd fucked a whore," his partner growls.

Most brothers are looking at them in wide-eyed amusement.

Trust Shooter to remark on it. "Thought Joker was the ol' lady."

"Nah. We take turns. Joker's on top one day…"

Collective groans go around, with Blade putting his fingers in his ears and singing, "Nah, nah, nah, nah, nah."

Drummer bangs the gavel.

"Er, Sandy."

My eyes narrow. Sandy seemed fine when we were at the Wheel Inn. I raise my eyebrow toward the man who'd spoken.

"She doesn't like the whores," he says glumly. "Though I haven't been with them for some time. Doesn't seem right with my daughter around, and you being my son-in-law, Prez." Drummer's not strictly, they haven't got married. But they're together in the eyes of the biker world, and have cemented their relationship with two kids.

"Though it's been a long time since I last saw you getting a blow job," Rock remarks. "Sandy learn how to do it?"

As Viper's face glows red, Rock makes a show of sliding under the table.

While I hate the thought that Allie's been with all the men here, I have to move past that, or else we won't have a chance. I do find myself smiling at the thought I would now be getting exclusively what Viper used to experience, Allie's amazing and very talented mouth on my cock. I almost feel sorry for him if he doesn't get even an approximation at home.

As though he can feel my eyes on him, he shrugs apologetically, and adds fast, "She never swallowed."

She does, for me.

"Nah, most of them don't." The sentiment is agreed by all the men who've ever used a sweet butt for their release.

I just nod and say nothing. *No need to make them jealous.*

"So," Drummer cuts through the crap. "Sandy going to have a problem?"

I hope not. She's Sam's stepmother after all. And Sam, as the Prez's wife, is Queen Bee."

Viper thinks for a moment. "She'll be polite if I tell her, and she'll come around eventually. Just want Allie to perhaps keep out of her way until she does."

"Allie's going to have enough difficulty adjusting. She's not the kind of person to push in where she's not wanted or tout her changed status," I step up to defend my old lady. "It's going to be hard for her to find her place, the last thing she'll want to do is rock the boat."

"We won't have a problem with Allie," Prez backs me up, his eyes scanning the table. "I'm looking to everyone to keep their ol' ladies in line. Might be worth reminding you all we're a fuckin' brotherhood. A club for men which isn't run by women." He wipes his hand down his beard, and chuckles, "However much it might seem that way at times."

"We lay down the law." Peg's hand bangs heavily on the table. "Anyone needing a reminder, it's the brothers who run this club."

"Have you told that to Darcy?" Mouse calls out, a twinkle in his eye. Low chortles sound from all directions. We all know Peg's old lady continues to put her life at risk fighting fires, whatever he has to say about it.

Peg stares at Mouse, then his face cracks and he gives a rare smile. "I wouldn't dare."

"Amen to that," agrees Slick.

"Alright you bunch of motherfuckin' pussies. You ready to vote on this, or shall we bring the women in to give you the answer?"

"Ready Prez."

Thank fuck. And thank fuck again when it's an aye from everyone. Especially as Sam's arranged to have patches sewn on the woman's leather vest I picked up in town yesterday. Wouldn't have wanted that to go to waste.

I'd have left the club if the answer had been no.

Yeah, that's how serious I feel about her.

Drummer bangs the gavel. "Allie's an ol' lady."

"Already recorded." Heart, our secretary waves his hand.

"You got something to say, brother?" The prez throws at Road who's shaking his head.

Road looks up. "More ol' ladies and probably kids on the compound. Sure has changed."

"For the better," Peg snarls.

Road holds up his hands. "Not saying otherwise. Just observing."

Kids. Don't see any in our future. Allie's not particularly inclined to have them and I don't care strongly one way or the other. But our intentions in that direction are not something I feel I should share. Don't want any negative thoughts about bringing more babies into this fucked up world to be misinterpreted. Especially by Heart who seems intent on repopulating the planet all by himself. Well, with the help of his supposedly barren wife that is.

"This club is a family." Drummer's eyes sharpen. "Never thought it would turn out this way, but I can't feel the change is anything but for the better. Anyone having a problem with it can put in for a transfer."

There's silence around the table, then, surprisingly, it's Drifter who speaks up. "I, for one, like the atmosphere here. I've no other family."

The nods confirm that's the way everyone's thinking.

"Any other business? No? Then let's get out of here." Drummer bangs the gavel for the last time.

Brothers might have collected old ladies, but that doesn't

stop them heading for the bar after church lets out. The only noticeable change is that many of their old ladies are waiting for them, some cradling babies in their arms, others have toddlers hanging onto their hands.

Drummer picks Eli up and swings him around, then settles him on his hip as he asks Allie for a whiskey. His three-year-old son who's already showing he's bright as a button, and takes after his dad rather than his mom, catches sight of me and stares, then his forefinger points my way.

Drummer catches hold of it and turning to see what he's indicated, barks a laugh. *Yeah, that kid is fascinated with my fake eye.* Doubt he'd be too upset if I removed it. I wink toward the prez to show him I really don't mind.

I glance around the room, trying to spot the prez's old lady. *Ah, there she is.* She's got Zane balanced on one arm, and in the other, something she's holding discreetly. I beam and nod.

Drummer turns as she makes her way over, as if he's sensed her entering the room. Even with both carrying one of their kids, they still manage to give each other an X-rated kiss, though the only part of their bodies touching is their mouths. I notice Allie watching me from behind the bar, and we share a secret smile. I know what she's thinking as we've discussed it. Kids have their place, though they must put a damper on some activities.

When she finally breaks away from her man, Sam hands me the bag with a big smile.

Prez hollers, his loud voice from close by making me jump, the thunderous shout managing to get everyone's attention.

Tommy, standing by Tash, puts his hands over his ears, but looks interested rather than upset.

Once there's quiet, Prez starts, "Don't usually need much encouragement to have a celebration, but today I think definitely counts. First, Truck's been back a week, and it seems that he's here for good."

I am, though I haven't formally said it. But having been enfolded back into my brother's arms, this is definitely where

I'm staying. Riding a bike? Well, I'm determined I'm going to be able to do it.

"And the second thing is we've just taken a vote in church, and it's up to Truck to tell you the consequences."

At any other time I'd hate all the attention on me, everyone staring at my scarred face. But apart from Eli who's still fixated on my left eye, all the expressions are of expectation. Road gives me a thumbs up.

I clear my throat, then make my announcement. "I'm claiming Allie as my old lady." When I stretch out my hand, she takes her cue and steps from behind the bar.

I hand the bag to her, she opens it and looks inside. Her face, well, it's hard to describe which emotion is foremost. Her eyes leak tears, though she's trying hard not to cry. Her head is shaking but her mouth is turned up in a huge smile.

There's a tremor in her hands as she removes the vest, turning it over reverently in her hands as though to check the words are there, "Property of Truck."

"Hey congratulations, Brother!"

"Yay!" yells Tommy, though I wonder if he realises what the fuss is about.

As shouts of goodwill sound around us, I only have eyes for the woman I've just made mine. For a moment wondering whether now it's public, she's having second thoughts. She's gone still, like a statue. When she does move, it's to throw herself into my arms, tears winning out as she sobs against my chest.

"Hey, darlin', I thought you'd be happy."

"I, I," she sobs. "I am. I'm the happiest woman alive."

As conversations start around me, I raise her chin with my fingertips. "So why the tears?"

Flicking her eyes around the clubroom, she enlightens me, "I prepared myself that they wouldn't vote yes. I'm…"

"Whatever you were," I say, almost harshly, "doesn't matter.

You're mine, now. I'm never going to let anything hurt you, Al. Never, I swear. You come first in my life."

She wipes her hand over her eyes, trying to dry them. She takes a few deep breaths to bring herself under control, then, when she can speak evenly once again, a grin rearranges her features.

"I come first? After the club, your bike and your cut, you mean."

I toss my head back and roar with laughter, getting a few curious glances thrown our way. "See," I bend down to tell her, "you're the perfect ol' lady. Even got my priorities right."

CHAPTER TWENTY-TWO

*A*llie...

Truck takes my soft leather vest out of my hands and holds it while I put it on. The enormity of this moment is what had had me in tears, not any doubts about my man.

I'd been a sweet butt for ten years. I know how unlikely it is for a whore to become an old lady. For the vast majority of the time I was a working girl, I couldn't see myself settling down with just one man. Sure, a couple of the men I didn't take to as much as the others, and while Dollar is a good man outside the bedroom, I never enjoyed catering to his specific needs, but in general, I enjoyed having sex with them.

For certain there were times when I was used and pleasure wasn't reciprocated, but on sufficient occasions I enjoyed the experience enough to carry on.

It wasn't until Truck spoiled me for other men, that I found no one else could hold a candle to him.

To be standing here wearing his property cut is something I never thought would happen. Never dreamed of being a biker's one and only.

"Can't wait to see you with only that on."

In his hoarse whisper I hear a tone of possessiveness deeper than I'd heard before. It sends tingles down my spine as I imagine that very thing.

"Want to get out of here?"

I do, but, "Think this is a party in our honour," I point out.

"Well we won't be stayin' fuckin' long."

We won't, if I have my way, but as Sam puts her hand on my arm and tugs me away from my man, I know I've got to be sociable.

"Welcome to the old lady club," Sam hugs me tight. "Come on. Everyone wants to talk to you."

Releasing me, she pulls me away from my man, who lets me leave with a lingering look that offers a guarantee that I won't be left wanting very long.

"So." As I approach the group of old ladies, Sandy gets to her feet and puts herself in front of me, her eyes sharp. "Congratulations. You've done what no one else has been successful in doing," she sneers.

There's no need for an explanation, I know exactly what she means. Realising I've got to start as I mean to go on, I don't offer an apology or defence for my former actions. Instead, I ignore the underlying scorn.

"Thank you, Sandy."

"Hey. Good on ya, mate! You're bloody one of us now." Sophie, like Sam, gives me a hug. *Am I over wary, or does the expression in her eyes belie her welcoming words?*

Becca approaches looking tired, Rose asleep in her arms. "Welcome to the old ladies' club, Allie."

I beckon her closer. "I'm sorry, Becca."

"Hey, I heard that bitch Jill. I was there, remember? She lied to get the information out of you. Sure, it led her to Rock and betraying him, but she's gone, Allie. No need to feel guilty."

But I still feel responsible for her man being hurt. Even though Rock's healed now, and she's holding their young baby.

Marcia waves from her position on the couch. She's keeping a close watch on her two toddlers who now, having learned to walk, are becoming a handful, she's also resting her arms over her just visibly rounded stomach. Her new pregnancy starting to show now. I walk over to her to save her getting up, having to edge around Grunt who's lying beside his young charges keeping his watchful wolfhound eyes on them.

"You're going to be fine, Allie." The ex-cop takes my hand. "You're good for Truck, anyone can see that."

"I hope so," I respond.

"Amy, go see where Jacob thinks he's going." Her six-year-old stepdaughter immediately obeys with a sigh that I think imitates that of her biological mother, Crystal, who's been dead more than three years now. Amy wouldn't remember her true mom, but I often see glimpses of Crystal in her.

"Sorry," Marcia says with a grin. "Need eyes in the back of my head nowadays."

"And you're having another one."

"Yup." She grins tiredly. "Not trusting the doctors next time. Heart's getting the snip."

She wasn't supposed to be able to have children, now she's incubating her third. Or is there more than one? Neither of them are telling, and I wouldn't be surprised if the brothers had started a book.

I spare a glance back to my man at the bar, he's accepting congratulations from the men. Tash, I see, isn't here with the old ladies, but is deep in conversation with Blade, with Tommy hovering close by. I hope she's just busy and hasn't got a beef with me. Blade, well, he used to be one of my regulars.

"You planning on having kids, Allie?"

I hadn't heard Darcy approach. "No," I tell her grinning. "Think there's more than enough of them around."

She sighs, and nods over to Peg who's cradling Noah in his arms. "The great thing about living on the compound is there are so many people around, it's like every kid's got loads of brothers and sisters, and there's always a mom around to help out."

But not me. I'm still an outsider in this group. Unless I do my part in adding to the next generation, seems I'll stay that way.

"That's true." Sophie overhears and plops herself down next to Marcia. Then she adds something that makes me think I might have a use. "If Allie's not looking to add to the number herself, maybe we can rely on her for some adult conversation, not just nappies and schools all the time."

"Diapers, woman, diapers," Sam corrects. "And what adult conversation do you want? Comparisons of vibrators?"

I snort. Then double up as Eli approaches his mom. "What's a 'brator?"

But Sam isn't fazed. "Adult toys," she tells her son. "Nothing to do with little ears."

"You corrupting my son already, Al?" Prez's voice booms in my ear.

"What?" I spin around, my eyes wide.

Lightly he bumps his fist to my arm. "Only joking. I know who's to blame. And that's the last time I'm buying you *toys*, Sam."

"Ooooh. Drummer bought you a new… toy," Sophie's eyes gleam. "Which one?"

"Time to go." Truck's by my side. "I've got something for you far more satisfying than any vibrator."

I'm sure he has.

Truck more than proves it that night. And over and over again as the days pass. If I'd ever thought limiting myself to one man would decrease the number of times I had sex, I would have been proven wrong. My initial experience with Truck has meant I've had more. As for variety, well, I can't complain about that. Shower sex, up against the wall sex, even the darn back of his truck that he's now driven to the compound. Wherever we are, Truck's proved he's a very talented man with an incredible imagination.

"You too good for us now?" Diva's voice startles me. Placing the clean glass back in its place on the shelf behind the bar, I turn around.

"I'm still the same person."

"You could still come to the house, visit with us."

"Truck keeps me pretty busy, Div." To be honest, I haven't much inclination to visit with the sweet butts, as I'm not one of them any longer. I bear them no ill will, just that I've moved on.

"Well, don't forget where we are." Her eyes twinkle. "You can tell us what it's like to ride Truck's cock."

Now that is something I'm not going to share.

"Pass me a soda. Thanks." Holding the can, she walks off.

Yes, it's strange. I'm not one of the sweet butts, and not completely accepted by the old ladies. Oh, they're polite enough. I'm not sure whether it's me holding back as I'm not certain of my reception, or whether there is some lingering animosity from them. Sandy, well, apart from that night when I'd been given my property patch, she hasn't spoken to me. Seems she can't forget I used to give blow jobs to her old man.

The old ladies fall into two groups, those whose men never went with whores, who are friendlier, and those who have to try to forget I know their old men intimately.

As I get the bar prepped, directing Tommy to carry in the heavy crates of beer, then I stack the bottles ready to meet the demand when the men exit from church, I put myself in their shoes. *Would I be jealous to meet an old conquest of Truck's? How would I feel if he'd been with the other sweet butts here?*

I have to say, I wouldn't like it at all.

Hmm. I do have some sympathy for their feelings.

A stampede of feet announces my thinking time is over. For the next few hours I replenish glasses and open bottles, rushed off my feet at times. Truck takes a seat at the end of the bar, every time I get a moment, I go to stand by him.

At one point he's talking to Blade.

After I've given a tray of fresh beers to a prospect, as no one else wants a glass refilled at the moment, I go back to steal a moment with my man.

"Allie, give your old man a boot up the backside, will ya?" The enforcer's talking to me, but his eyes are on Truck.

"I don't know," Truck complains.

"Peg?" Blade shouts.

Having been given a request I don't understand, thus included in their conversation, I don't make myself scarce as I normally would concluding this doesn't come under the heading of *club business.*

Peg ambles over. "Whatcha want?"

"Truck's bike's ready. Want him to give it a try tomorrow."

"So?" Peg looks from Blade to Truck.

Immediately I understand the problem. Truck's desperate to get back on a bike, but is frightened of failure.

"Isn't anything stopping him," Peg confirms.

"Why not try?" I rest my hand on Truck's arm. "Peg and Blade will be there to help. See if your leg is strong enough to hold it up for a start. Baby steps, Truck. You don't have to go on a hundred-mile ride tomorrow. Just get the feeling of it and find out how the electronic gear shift works."

Blade looks like a light bulb has switched on in his head. "Allie's right. You won't drop it. Peg and I will both be there."

Peg nods. "You've got more strength than you had. You can at least check whether Blade's made enough adjustment to the shift." He barks a laugh. "You might end up riding it down the track and back, or you might not. If you feel any weakness I can identify what we still need to work on."

"Truck," I say softly to get his attention back. "It's progress, however small or big."

Truck looks at Blade, then Peg, and finally to me. He leans over and kisses me. "Fuckin' perfect, Allie. Fuckin' perfect."

Later that night I distract Truck, but even after we're both tired out, he's still restless. It's not hard to know the reason.

Riding a bike is everything to a biker, he's worried the morning might prove that he can't.

"No one's judging you, Truck," I remind him the next morning as he slides on his cut. "If it's not today, nothing changes. You'll continue getting stronger, and Peg and Blade will think of other ways to help."

He stares down at his foot. He should appreciate he does well to have his leg and his ankle, even though it's not dextrous enough to operate the gears. As he clenches and unclenches his injured hand, I know he's doubting whether he'll be able to work the new shift. His arm's not perfectly straight either, but I can tell the difference since he started working with Peg, and if the sergeant-at-arms is confident he'll be able to balance the bike and steer it right, I believe it. But I can understand Truck's misgivings.

He stares at me, then his hand strokes my face. "You don't give a damn, do you? Whether I can ride or not?"

"I give more than a damn as it matters so much to you, Truck," I correct him, then reassure him. "I'll love you no matter what."

For a moment his forehead rests against mine, then he straightens and pulls back his shoulders.

"Let's go see if I can do this then."

I wish he wasn't so frightened of failure. But Peg and Blade wouldn't be encouraging him to try if he didn't have at least a chance of success.

When we arrive at the auto-shop, Blade's got the bike wheeled out and ready. The chrome sparkles and gleams in the sunlight. I choke back a laugh as the hungry look on Truck's face is similar to that when we're about to make love. *Bikers and bikes.* I reckon I was spot on when I listed his priorities. But hey, I've been around the club long enough to know what I'm getting into.

I hadn't really examined his bike before, but I'm pleased to see he has a pillion seat and a sissy bar. While I haven't ridden much before—there are only a few men here who'll take a woman behind them who's not their old lady—the times I have, I've loved it. In my head I imagine riding off, with my arms hugging Truck's waist, feeling that vibration between my thighs and knowing how the ride will probably end.

"Going to try then?"

Blade's suggestion snaps me out of my reverie. *Guess it's not just Truck who's entranced by the bike.* Hmm.

I notice Peg and Blade are standing close, Slick's wheeled another bike out, but is giving the others some space.

Truck limps forward, his shorter leg holding him back, and pauses when he gets to the enforcer and the sergeant-at-arms.

"I've got the bike, Truck. Try getting on from the right if you're worried about taking your weight on your left."

Peg's smart.

Nodding, Truck awkwardly throws his left leg over the saddle, and then stands astride. "Keep hold of it, Peg. Let me see if I can get the stand up."

Peg nods and places both his hands firmly on the handlebars.

The stand's on the left, so Truck can use his good leg to support him.

He needn't have worried. He's now upright, and so is the heavy Harley. Peg raises his hands, but doesn't move away.

"Kick the stand up?" Blade suggests.

"Don't hurry me," snaps Truck. No one takes umbrage, they just let him get in the right mental space.

"Your ankle can't take it? You might need a brace. We can sort something out," Peg suggests.

Truck's grateful eyes meet those of the sergeant-at-arms and he gives a sharp nod.

Then, with full responsibility for the big heavy motorcycle, he raises his left leg and uses the calf to kick the stand up.

I swear Eli looks the same when he opens a present. Truck's eyes gleam. Then he reverses the process and the bike's resting on the stand once again.

"I made the spring as light as I could, same with the clutch."

Truck nods to acknowledge Blade's effort. "Talk me through the gears then."

I zone out as Blade complies, my attention caught by some birds in the distance. But I turn back when the engine starts with a roar, then settles down to a burbling rumble. I'm in time to see Peg handing Truck his safety glasses. I'm glad he didn't forget, having only one eye now, it's not only a legal requirement, but vital to wear protection.

Another bike starts. It's Slick, and I realise he intends to follow Truck to make sure nothing happens. Some of my own nervousness eases.

"Prospect!" Peg yells. "Open the gate!"

There's intense concentration on Truck's face, his jaw looks locked. Tension creases his forehead as once again he raises the stand. His left hand clenches as he pulls in the clutch, then, thumbs a switch.

I hold my breath as the bike starts to move.

It seems to gather speed all too fast. As I gasp, Blade leans in. "Bikes are more unstable at low speed. Truck's right to open the throttle. That gear changer works well." The last is addressed to Peg.

"You tried it out?"

Blade's eyes look over accusingly. "Of course I did."

"Hey!"

The last is shouted at me as I race to the weeds growing by the fence and am violently sick.

CHAPTER TWENTY-THREE

*T*ruck…
I'm riding my bike.

I feel like a kid the first time he has the training wheels taken off. It's like every good thing that's happened to me in my life is represented in this one moment, as I zoom out of the gate and down the track leading to the main road. I'd love to open the throttle and go on for miles, but know that isn't the sensible thing to do. Already I can feel my left ankle protesting at having to hold the unfamiliar position on the foot peg. It goes through my mind that some sort of stirrup could hold it in place and might help, especially on a long journey. I'd just have to be able to easily slip my foot in and out of it, but that shouldn't be an issue.

Indicating my intention to Slick, I sweep around wide at the end of the track, and all too soon am heading up the other way. I feel as triumphant as though I've conquered the world. The horror of my accident, the image of my death hovering in front of me, the fear of being disabled, the dread of living with my scars, all fades.

I'm riding my bike.

What more could I want?

I've got Allie, my vision is improving every day, and now, to top it all, I can ride again. I practice the gear changes. They seem smooth as silk, and not as hard to get used to as I feared. No extra strain on my left arm at all.

The open gate is in front of me. I ride straight through, stopping next to Blade and Peg, then throw a nod of appreciation to Slick who's already wheeling his bike back into the shop.

Where's Allie?

I kick down the stand and leave my bike where it is, not wanting to try to manoeuvre it around just yet, knowing Blade will take care of parking it for me, then scan, trying to find the one person I want to share my triumph with.

"Allie's not well," Blade explains. "She's sick. Over there." He points to a hunched over figure. "I did try and help, but I think the poor girl's embarrassed and wants to be left alone."

Sick?

Blade raises his chin and jerks his head. I leave my bike in his hands, and go over to see her.

She jumps as my hand lands gently on her back.

"I don't know what's wrong with me, Truck. Must be something I ate."

"Let's get you back to the suite."

I can't remember seeing Allie poorly before, but I suspect she's right. Something she's consumed has disagreed with her. Have to admit I'm still on a high from being back on my bike, and most of my mind is on that and not her.

We just about make it back to the suite when she disappears into the bathroom again. I try to tune out the retching sounds— who likes to hear someone else being sick?—and go back over the short ride in my head.

I hadn't gone far, but my eyesight hadn't given me any problems at all. In fact, I'd found it easier than being in a car. The mirrors helped me see to each side, and I'm used to doing life-savers, turning my head to the side to check before pulling out or in. Yeah, it might only have been Slick in my rear view, but I'd used the brief time not just to feel how I was able to cope with the gear changes, but checking my ability to see.

I can't stop myself grinning widely. Sure, I still need time to adjust, but I think I'm going to crack it.

Reaching down I rub my ankle. Have to sort out that stirrup contraption, that would definitely help.

"Did you overdo it, Truck?"

Allie's leaning against the bathroom door.

"Nah. I did good babe." I take in the paleness of her face. "You alright now, hon?"

Her hand covers her stomach. "I'm not sure."

"Want me to get you anything?"

Grimacing, she shakes her head. "No, nothing. I just want to lie down and try and sleep whatever this is, off. Why don't you go down to the clubhouse? You could make my excuses for me, somehow I don't think I'll be minding the bar later."

"You want to be alone?"

Her sad nod says yes. I don't blame her. I don't particularly want company when I'm spewing my guts up either.

"Come, let's get you settled."

I take her hand and lead her to the bed. I pull her tee over her head and remove her bra, for the first time ever, allowing only my gaze to feast on what I'm revealing, ignoring the urge to touch. Even though my head's not in the game, my cock twitches. *Soon, boy. Soon.* Got to get Allie feeling better first.

I pull back the sheet and she slides under it. I notice how small she looks lying on her own in my big bed which we've shared since the night of our date at the Wheel Inn, and feel a moment of guilt for my intention to leave her. But that's what she wants, and I'm sure rest will help. As for me, I can use the time to celebrate my ride with my brothers who'll understand my excitement. Still, should she be left alone?

She anticipates my protest. "Go Truck, I'd rather just sleep."

"Call me if you need anything. Anything at all, Al." I find her phone and place it next to the bed.

When she gives a feeble nod, I pull the curtains to shade the room, then, with a kiss to her forehead, leave her in peace.

"How's Allie?" Blade tosses me a look of concern as I walk into the clubhouse.

"Sick," I respond. "But I think she'll live. Just fuckin' miserable puking all the time."

"Yeah," he agrees with feeling.

"Allie not well?" Sam overhears.

"Upset stomach," I explain.

Like Blade, her face fills with sympathy. "She want anything, Truck?"

"Nah, she's trying to sleep it off. I'll check in on her later."

The girls have made sandwiches for lunch. Grabbing a beer to go with mine, I sit at a table with Blade and Peg, and dissect my ride. A stirrup contraption would be fairly easy to apply, Blade promises to sort something out. I leave it to him. He's the expert with motorcycles.

I have a chat with the prospects, tell them to make sure one of the sweet butts takes Allie's shift at the bar, then, go back to check on my woman.

When I return to the suite, Allie is dozing, so I leave her to it. I'm no doctor but know enough to believe, if she's unwell, that will do her the most good.

"Hey, Truck," Drummer booms as I re-enter the clubhouse. "Hear you're back on your fuckin' bike, man. It went well?"

Seeing Blade standing behind him, he already knows that it did. "Fuckin' great, Prez."

"Told you you'd be riding again," he says with a smirk.

"That you did." I grin back, unconcerned he's gloating.

It seems everyone wants to be told individually how I found and coped with my short ride out this morning. You'd think I'd been on a marathon journey with the interest each of them showed. I'm glowing with pleasure and pride in myself, not at all put out repeating how it went time after time. These are my brothers and each understands exactly how I'm feeling, having never expected to watch the pavement whirling past under my wheels ever again.

Allie's awake next time I return, she's got a half-drunk bottle of water beside her.

"How are you feeling?" I go to sit next to her on the bed.

She's not one to complain, so when she does, I know it must be bad. "Awful, Truck. I can't even keep water down."

"Does your head hurt? Are you just sick, or…"?

"Just sick, Truck. I haven't got diarrhoea."

Her voice sounds weak, and slightly hoarse as if it belongs to someone else. I place my hand on her forehead, it's clammy, but not hot. When I pull it away, she takes it in hers.

"I'm sorry, Truck. Didn't mean to put a damper on your success today. I was so proud of you riding that bike, then this came over me."

"Hey, darlin'. You can't help being ill. I've asked around, everyone else is alright. Perhaps you ate something you're allergic to."

Her brow creases, then she replies, "Can't think what. I didn't have anything different than normal. Look Truck," she adds, "I'm going to sleep in my own room tonight."

What? I rear back, her suggestion taking me by surprise. She'd basically moved into mine since the night we'd returned from the Wheel Inn, moving not only herself but her clothes in. Have to admit I get a certain satisfaction seeing her dresses hanging next to my shirts. My first impulse is to tell her sick or well, I want her by my side, then I realise it's her comfort that's important.

"Al, if you're doing it for you, go ahead. But I'm in this, the good and the bad. I'd rather you were here with me so I can get you anything you need. But if I'm going to disturb you, then do what you think is best."

"I'll only be next door, Truck."

Sure. I only have to open my door, take one step over to hers, and she'll be there. But as I lay awake and restless alone in my bed later that night, she could be a whole continent away and I couldn't miss her more. I've gotten so used to her warmth by my side, her arms and legs draped over me, those sweet little snuffles that come from her during the night, not full on snores, but a sort of feminine version.

It doesn't help that I can't switch my brain off. I'm convinced nothing's seriously wrong with Allie, so part of my head is reliving this morning's ride. Alone in my bed I grin like a loon, then frown. I'd wanted to celebrate with her. Something hits me in the dead of the night, I want, *need* to share everything with my old lady. Our successes, our failures, and everything in between.

I'm woken by my door opening. Wiping sleep from my eyes, I prop myself up on my elbows.

"You good?"

"I'm good." Her voice has more strength to it. "Starving though."

"Wanna go get breakfast?"

She nods so eagerly I chuckle. "Okay. Give me five minutes to run through the shower and dress."

"Make it quick, Truck."

She looks so adorable, if it wasn't for the fact I can hear her stomach rumble, I'd ask her to join me in the shower. But time enough for that later, after she's been fed.

Sophie's in the kitchen. She's plating up bacon and eggs for her man. Olly is also sitting at the table with scrambled eggs in front of her, Wraith's got Zoey on his lap. A content family scene if ever I saw one. For a second, I'm disappointed that won't be in my future, until the baby starts screaming. Then I decide I'm quite happy with things as they are.

Glancing up when we walk in, Sophie throws Allie a look of sympathy.

"Heard you were ill. Are you feeling better?"

"I'm good, Soph. I'm hungry now." But she eyes the eggs and bacon warily. "I think I'll just have some toast to start with."

"You sit down," Soph interrupts as Allie goes toward the

bread. "I'll do it for you. I suppose you want the full deal, Truck?"

"Yeah, babe. Thanks."

"Don't you 'babe' my old lady," Wraith warns, pointing a fork my way.

I laugh, as I'm intended to.

"Coffee?" Sophie waves the pot toward me.

I nod, Allie shudders. "I think I'll stick to orange juice today."

"I'll get it." I stand, go to the fridge and get some out for her.

As she starts to drink it and Sophie puts some buttered toast in front of her, I ask, "What do you feel up to doing today?"

But I've barely got the question out when she gets up and flees the room with her hand over her mouth.

"She's not better," Sophie observes.

"Maybe it's the flu?" suggests Wraith.

Maybe.

I hate seeing Allie ill. I know she hates being sick, who doesn't? One minute she feels okay, the next she's heaving over a toilet bowl. I'm unable to help. It's frustrating to be faced with a problem I can't deal with.

That first day I just gave her time to herself, to rest and get well. By the second I start to get more concerned. She still can't keep anything down, not even water. As soon as she puts something in her mouth, she brings it back up. In between, she's sick for no reason.

"Is she any better?"

"No, Sam. She's not. She's worse. She hasn't eaten or drank anything for three days now. She's feeling like death. I don't understand it. She's got no other symptoms and no temperature that I can tell."

"Truck," Sam eases herself onto the stool beside me. "Could she be pregnant?"

Pregnant? Her stark question pulls me up. "Were you like this?"

"Not this bad. I was just sick in the evenings. Huh. Morning sickness is a misnomer. But I just wondered." She bumps my arm. "You have been going at it. I hear you when I'm walking up to the house."

Should I be embarrassed? It's probably not just her who's heard me fucking my old lady. Am I? *Uh uh.* Not fucking likely.

"I always glove up, Sam. It's impossible."

"If it goes on, you'll need to take her to see a doctor. A body can't survive without sustenance of some sort. Have you thought about those nourishment drinks?"

"I have, and dismissed it. If she can't even drink water…"

Sam shakes her head sadly, then says, "Wouldn't hurt for her to do a pregnancy test. I've got a spare one if you want."

Pregnant? No, definitely not. We've both been so careful as we'd agreed not to have kids.

"No, Sam. That's okay. She's not."

CHAPTER TWENTY-FOUR

_A_llie…

If I were to make a list of my least favourite things to do, vomiting would be close to, if not at, the very top.

My stomach feels empty, but that doesn't stop it from trying to get rid of what it thinks is in it. I've lost count of the times I've had to run to the bathroom today. I don't know what's worse, dry heaving as there's nothing more to bring up, or spewing out the little sips of water I've been brave enough to sample.

I hate the constant taste of bile in my mouth, the dryness around my lips, and the rawness of my throat. Already, I feel dehydrated.

How long is this going to go on for?

One minute I feel right as rain and hungry, the next, whether I eat or not, I'm bowing my head over the toilet bowl once again.

My best decision had been to move back into my suite. Truck has no idea how often I'm being ill, he'd only worry more if he did.

I didn't go down to the clubhouse at all yesterday, not that it helped much. I've become hyper-sensitive to smells around me. A whiff of coffee is guaranteed to make me immediately throw up, and just breathing in stale beer and whiskey is almost as bad.

Even if I could stay the few minutes to pour a drink, I wouldn't be able to stand the smell anyway, which means I can't do my job.

As for sex? In the moments in between, I want to feel the arms of my man around me and his cock inside me. But what man wants a woman to run off in the middle of making love?

I must get better soon.

This is driving me crazy.

I can't remember ever being ill like this.

There's a knock at my door. Truck would just come right in after alerting me he was there. That the door doesn't open suggests it's not him. I reach out for my robe and put it on before going to see who it is.

"Hey."

"Sam, hi."

"Mind if I come in?"

"If you don't mind the sound of someone being sick."

"Been there, done that," she grins. Then the smile slips off her face. "Truck's told me how sick you are."

I sigh as I go over to the bed and sit. "I've never had anything like this before, Sam. Just wish I could shake it off."

"Can I ask you a question?"

Shrugging, I tell her, "Go ahead."

"When was your last period?"

What? I stare at her. Then the penny drops. "No." I give a short laugh. "I'm not. I can't be. I had the implant which wore off a while ago, but my periods were irregular on that and haven't sorted themselves out as yet. It's not unusual for me to miss one or two. Besides, Truck and I have been very careful. Neither of us want kids."

Am I sure about that? Truck says the right words, but sometimes his gaze lingers on the kids in the clubhouse. Deep down, does he want one of his own? Well, if so, he won't have them with me. I'm determined not to add more life to this fucked up world. Hell, I hope this isn't a deal breaker, how could I give up my man? I realise I've zoned out when Sam speaks again.

"Wouldn't hurt to rule it out." She produces a packet that I hadn't noticed her carrying.

I see immediately what it is. A pregnancy test.

"I'm not." I'm adamant. "I'm too ill for it to be that. I know you get sick in the early stages of pregnancy, but I've seen enough of you women when you're pregnant, and no one's come close to being like this. I'm ill, not expecting."

"Humour me?"

It's not often the president's old lady asks for anything.

I give a short laugh. "Right now I'm not sure I've any pee inside me but let me have it and I'll give it a shot."

It takes me a while as I haven't managed to keep water down for days, but eventually my body cooperates. Then, unsurprisingly, I'm sick once again. When I return with the test in my hand, expecting her to have become fed up and left, I see she's still waiting patiently.

I put it down on the bedside table. I already know it's going to be negative, so I am not concerned at all.

"So, what have I been missing?" I try to act like the prez's old lady hasn't just heard me puking up my guts.

She thinks for a moment, her eyes flicking toward the test as though she's more invested in the result than I am. "Oh, same old stuff. Amy's lost another tooth and is trying to persuade Heart that the going rate is five dollars." When I look a little bemused, she adds, "You know, the Tooth Fairy."

Oh. As my mom had never bothered with stuff like that, I hadn't realised it was something people actually did. "Sounds like Amy's onto a good thing."

"Or it's a plot cooked up by her and her classmates. Honestly, I wouldn't put it past them. Get the whole class to agree and tell the same story to their parents. Go on then." At her swift change of subject, she points to the stick.

Shaking my head at her impatience, I lean over and pick it

up. "Yeah, it's…" My eyes sharpen. Then blur. I pass it over to her, as another wave of sickness comes over me and I run back into the bathroom.

I'm pregnant. I can't be.

Sam's come in behind me, her hand is rubbing up and down my back. I'm embarrassed as hell that she's seeing me like this, but don't have the energy to tell her to leave. She passes me a damp washcloth.

"At least we know what we're dealing with, Allie. You're not ill, you're pregnant. There are things that can help. Ginger biscuits and saltines. I'll bring you some. Number of pregnancies here, the kitchens are always stocked with them."

"Being pregnant is worse than being ill, Sam. You can recover when you're sick."

She laughs softly. "You better?"

Yeah, the nausea's gone. For now.

"Let's talk in your room." It's her who flushes the toilet for me.

I walk back and sit down, thoughts going through my head so fast it's hard to settle on one to deal with. "Don't tell anyone, Sam, please?"

"Of course not. You'll want to tell Truck first."

How will he take it? Will he be horrified or delighted? Even if we had planned a family, it's far too early to bring a child into the mix. Do I even want to keep it?

"You've obviously got morning sickness bad. But it does wear off."

"When?"

"Around twelve weeks or so. If you haven't had a period, you don't know how far along you are. You've been with Truck, what, over a month?"

It's been six weeks since we had our date.

"I don't understand how, Sam."

She grins. "Well, the woman produces an egg, the man produces…" My glare stops her. "Too soon?"

"Too late." *We should have been more careful.*

We were.

"Can you leave me alone, Sam? I need some time alone to think."

"Okay. But I'm here if you want to talk. I'll get Truck to bring some ginger biscuits up."

"No," I grab at her hand and stop her. "Don't say anything to Truck, not yet. Please."

A thoughtful glance, then a nod of her head. "Way I read Truck, Al, is he'll support you. Whatever you want to do. You may not have been together long, but it's plain to see, all that man wants is for you to be happy."

He does. And I want to make him happy in return. I'm just not sure what it will take to do that, and whether I can do it.

When I'm left alone with my thoughts, I put my head in my hands and let the tears fall. It doesn't help I'm feeling as sick as I am, and lightheaded as I haven't eaten for days. According to Sam, I've got another six to eight weeks of this. *But it will go.* Then, six months after that, I'll be holding a baby in my arms. The thought brings me no pleasure.

But it might please Truck.

I could get rid of it without him knowing.

This early it would be a simple procedure, he wouldn't need to know. I'd go to the doctor, come back having taken the medication and feeling better. No one, apart from Sam, needs to know a thing.

I'm pregnant.

My mom never wanted me. She wanted my brother.

What was it about me that she'd disliked from the start?

I'd been eight when my brother was born, and from the first moment, he'd been the favourite.

Hey, Bean, I wouldn't do that to you. No, if I had a baby I'd do my best to love it. But would it be possible, considering the example I had? *Learn from the women in the clubhouse.* There's enough of them with babies or pregnant. The other clubs joke about the water in Tucson. I sob. They must be right. Truck and I had done all that we could to prevent this.

Oh fuck no. I cover my mouth and reach the bathroom just in time. Even the thought of water is making me puke now.

Can I do this for another two months?

If I keep the baby, looks like I'm going to have to.

When I leave the small bathroom which seems to be the place I spend most of my time now, I find Truck lying on the bed waiting for me. His hands are propping up his head. "How are you feeling? I take it no better." His gaze flicks behind me, then back. His brow carries crease lines of worry.

Suddenly I know I can't make the decision on my own. It's not right to exclude him.

"I'm pregnant," I blurt out.

His eyes narrow.

"Sam brought me a test."

"What the fuck?" He throws himself off the bed and stalks toward me. "You're fuckin' pregnant?"

Well, so much for thinking he might be pleased. He's angry. *Which is good, isn't it?*

"How?" he snaps.

I'm sick, tired. My temper rises. "Do you really need me to explain the mechanics of it, Truck?"

"Is. It. Mine?"

What the hell?

I can't believe he asked me that. Until this weekend when I got ill, we'd spent every spare moment together in bed. When would I have had time to fit someone else in? If I hadn't been a sweet butt in the past, would he still have asked me? Does he have that little trust in me?

Better to find what he thinks I'm capable of now, rather than later. His question has shown, one misstep and he'll immediately be throwing accusations at me.

Does he think so little of his brothers that they would go behind his back?

I advance toward him, then step past and open the door. "Get out, Truck. Just, get out. Oh, wait a moment. You can take this with you."

I bend toward the chair, pick up my property cut and throw it at him.

With a look of surprise and, showing improvement in his hand to eye coordination, he catches it, then, walks out.

CHAPTER TWENTY-FIVE

ruck…

I handled that well.

But heck, I've been careful every time we fucked. Held the fucking condom as I pulled out, never put my dick near her uncovered. It's a fucking impossibility. Only explanation I can think of is that she went with somebody else behind my back.

When?

How the fuck should I know? It's not like we're joined at the hip.

Yes, you are.

When would she have had a chance to step out on me? Perhaps with someone just before we got together? She'd told me there had been no one, but maybe the truth is, there had.

"Uh oh. Who we gotta kill?" Drummer gets in to step beside me. "Your face, Brother."

"Allie's pregnant."

The prez's hand shoots out and grabs my arm, effectively stopping me. His eyes examine my face. "I take it you're not too happy about it?" he asks through gritted teeth.

"One way of putting it, Prez. The only thing I'm sure of is she has to have been lying to me all this time."

His voice becomes icy. "Not sure I understand what you're saying here, *Brother*. Only one way that happened, and you were part of it," he snarls. "Never took you for an asshole who blamed the woman."

He's impugning me for something that wasn't my fault. "I gloved up. Every fuckin' time."

"So?"

"So it can't be mine."

His eyes widen, then narrow, and that deadly stare fixes on my face. It belies the deadly calm of his voice. "Come with me."

As he marches off, I've no option but to follow him. He goes into his office, opens a drawer and chucks a box at me.

I look down, then up. "Too late now, Prez. As I said, I used one every time."

"Read what's written on it." He pauses. "How many times have you fucked Allie, Truck?"

I shrug.

"Let me see. Three times a day for what, six weeks?"

He's a bit short on some days, but as an average it would work.

"So over a hundred and twenty times, yeah? Read that box and tell me the odds."

I read it, then refute. "But I haven't been careless." Ninety-eight percent effective. "Never had a problem before." I may not have fucked another girl as much, but I've been with plenty.

"Then your luck just ran out." He brushes back his hair. "You really think Allie's been unfaithful? Really? And who would you name as the father? One of your fuckin' brothers? Which one, Truck? Which one? Cause if you name someone, I'll have to strip his patch and watch while you kill him. You claimed her!"

I remain silent, thinking that's wise. I hadn't thought as far as who would betray me. Doing so now, I can't come up with a single name.

"You're thinking you can't trust her because she was a sweet butt." His head moves side to side. "Shame on you, man." Disappointment shines from his face.

"I've known Allie ten years now, you what, eighteen months? Patched you in as you'd proven yourself. Must have fuckin' missed you were a damn stupid motherfucker."

When Drummer gives it to you, he gives it to you straight.

I bow my head into my hands, then wipe them over my bare skull.

Drummer reaches behind him, picks up a bottle of whiskey and two shot glasses. I shake my head when he offers me one.

"Smell of whiskey makes Allie sick," I tell him automatically, then realise what I've said. "Oh shit."

"Shit indeed, Truck. I think you're looking for reasons which don't exist because you don't want to deal with what's happening."

Is he right? Am I looking for an excuse so I don't need to step up and accept my culpability? Christ, now he's pointed it out, I know he's correct. Allie's so sick and ill, and now I have to face that I'm responsible. There's been no one else, no one I can blame. Only me. And Allie, of course, but shit, I told her I'd protect her, and I failed.

Now I've left her alone to come to terms with something she didn't ever want; the knowledge there's a baby growing inside her.

"I want to make her happy, Prez." All my anger has fled.

"Man would have to be blind not to see you want that for each other. Now that you've knocked her up, deal with it." He gives a quick grin. "Happened to me fast too. Eli wasn't planned, but hell, never regretted it."

"Al's adamant she doesn't want kids. I accepted that. Now I've given her the one thing she's no desire for. Think that's why I almost hoped it wasn't me. That there was someone else to blame, other than myself."

He sips his whiskey. "You and she got some talking to do, but I'll tell you this, Truck. You did your best to prevent it. Allie was obviously happy to trust condoms as well. Neither of you, or both of you, are to blame. Whatever path you take to your future, you're in it together. That's what claimin' a woman means, can't just step away when the going isn't easy."

Drummer can be a hard prez. But I've heard others discuss he speaks a lot of sense and can help you get your head on straight when you can't see the wood for the trees yourself.

"Sam suffered sickness until she got to three months both times, Truck. Luckily it didn't incapacitate her as much as Allie, but hopefully she'll be getting a second wind in a few weeks."

"This thing Allie's got. That's not going to just switch off." I frown, wondering if that had also been at the back of my mind. "You say a few weeks, but hell, the way she's suffering right now... I fuckin' hate seeing her like this. How can I watch her slowly fade in front of my eyes?"

"Look, everyone needs to do what they have to. I think you need to get Allie to a doctor, see what they can do to help. If she can't eat or drink, she won't be fit enough to grow a baby."

"Surely it must ease up?" *What do I know about pregnancy?* "If she goes on like she is, she won't survive until three months. She brings everything up, Drummer. Her body's getting no nutrition." I shake my head, unable to imagine it. "Surely Mother Nature kicks in, knows she needs vitamins, protein and shit?"

"I'm no medical man, Truck. It's possible it's not meant to be. She doesn't improve? She might miscarry."

Right now I hope she does. And soon, before she gets too weak. "I just want Allie fit and well, Drummer." I stand. "I need to get back to her. Allie and I need to talk. After I've done some grovelling."

His voice stops me before I get to the door. "Been there, done that Truck. Taking an ol' lady isn't always the rosy picture you keep in your head. I might be the tough, scary MC Prez, but I'm also a man and I fuck up. Can assure you this won't be the last fuckin' time you'll be grovelling."

I suspect that he's right.

I'm sorry. I rehearse in my head as I make my way back up the track, knowing that's completely inadequate. I did the worst thing I could ever accuse someone with Allie's past of, and made the mistake of allowing her to think I don't trust her.

To be honest, I don't know how to make this right. I just know I have no alternative. Life without Allie in it? Already know that wouldn't be worth living.

I've got to convince her this shit will never happen again. Sure, I'll fuck up, but can't ever let her believe I have no faith in her. *But what are the words to make her not doubt that?* As I near the suite, I still haven't found them.

I turn the door handle half expecting it to be locked. It isn't, and turns easily. What is far more difficult to deal with is the sight of my woman lying on her bed, curled up in a foetal position, her hand stuffed into her mouth, her eyes reddened, and hearing the sounds of weeping.

It breaks my fucking heart. It took two of us, so I might not have full responsibility for her condition, but my stupid reaction? Yeah, I own that.

Her eyes widen, but I don't give her the chance to say anything. Instead I go over, and sweep her up into my arms, ignoring the pain shooting down my left leg.

She squeals as I lift her, and automatically hangs onto my cut. *She's lost so much weight.*

"Truck..."

"Shush." Gritting my teeth and trying not to stumble, I carefully carry her into my room, and place her in the middle of my bed. Immediately after I release her, she scrambles up to the top, and sits against the pillows drawing up her knees and cradling her arms around them.

"That's your place and where you'll fuckin' stay," I say quickly before giving her a chance to protest. "Don't give a fuckin' damn if you wake me up every ten minutes every night, that's where you'll be sleeping. Don't care if you're well or sick, pregnant or fuckin' not, you're my old lady, and your place is by my side."

"You hurt me."

She's wasted no time getting to the heart of the matter. "I know. And I'm sorry. Allie, sweetheart. I never wanted to do that. My aim was to give you everything in life it was possible to give you, and nothing that you didn't want. I couldn't handle the guilt…"

"You?" Her brow furrows. "You're not guilty…"

"Yeah," I interrupt. "Prez showed me that."

Her eyes close and her head droops. "You told Drummer? Anyone else?"

"Just him." I move closer. "He won't tell anyone."

"Sam knows."

I indicate the bed, a silent request for permission to sit.

She nods, then mumbles hesitantly, "I've been thinking about abortion."

"Me too." I take the risk of reaching for her hand, letting out an internal sigh of relief as she lets me hold it.

"You? You don't want a baby with me?"

I roll my eyes, well, the real one at least. "Why is it women always twist what a man says? Cards on the table, hon, okay?" Hoping I'm not going to be putting my foot further in the shit, I take a deep breath and try for a better explanation. "You and me? Riding through life together? Fuckin' perfect. You by my side, can't see anything else I need or want. You, me and a kid? Well, that's perfect too. Can't say I need it to make me happy though."

"What about, want?"

"Want." I ponder the word. "Used to think it was probably in my future, but only as a vague idea that finding my perfect woman would lead to having a kid in the mix. Wasn't something I yearned for in particular, just thought it would come as a package. What I want is you, and you don't want kids. I can appreciate that, same way as I don't want a cat." I wink, and luckily, she answers with a weak grin.

"But now I'm pregnant."

"Yes." Again I try to summon the right words.

She gets in first. "But I don't need to stay that way."

"You don't. If that's what you want, I'll be right beside you."

Her eyes widen at my quick agreement. "You wouldn't mind?"

I hope I'm saying this right. "Who doesn't examine their feelings on this when it's been all over the news? When I was sitting alone in my apartment, Al, news and talk shows were the only company I had before you came along. Came to the conclusion that it's the woman's body, and no business of the man's. He's not the one who has to rent out his uterus for nine months."

"The father, though, what if he wants the baby and she doesn't?"

"Ideally they should already know where they stand. But, as we now know, contraception isn't reliable. Let me continue?" I tell her as she goes to interrupt. She raises her chin. "So, darlin', normally I'd back away and say do whatever you want. You want the baby? I'll support you and it. Would know I was in for a lifetime commitment, and would love the little shit. As no doubt a baby of ours would turn out to be."

I've made her smile at least. Which is good. Because now, I add, "Under the circumstances, though, I'd lean toward abortion."

"What?"

I've shocked her, so I explain. "We need to see a doctor, find out the facts and options. But Al, you can't go through the next few weeks like this. You might do permanent damage to yourself. A body can't exist without food."

"Sam's going to give me some stuff which helped her and the other girls. Ginger biscuits. Apparently they help."

"What I'm saying, darlin', is whatever you want to do, I'll be one-hundred-percent behind you. But I'm not doing it from a distance. That's why you'll be staying in my bed."

"Doctors cost money, Truck." She shrugs. "I've no savings, nothing behind me. Didn't exactly get paid a wage."

"Don't worry," I say fast. "Solution's easy, babe. We'll get married and you'll go on my insurance. Still on my firefighter one as I'm pensioned off."

"Are you asking me to marry you?" Her hand covers her mouth in shock.

"Not very romantically, but I've already claimed you. Already got you wearing your property cut." I nod over to the chair where hers and mine both hang. "Putting a ring on your finger seems insignificant in relation to that, and hopefully it will pay for any treatment you need."

"I'll see if Sam can recommend an obstetrician."

That's my Allie. Practical.

And, unfortunately, that's also my Allie. Bringing our discussion to an abrupt end by rushing to the bathroom to be sick.

CHAPTER TWENTY-SIX

*A*llie…

It's not just being sick that I hate. It's constantly feeling nauseous, something I can't escape from. I tried the ginger snaps prescribed by Sam, but they barely got down before they made a reappearance. Saltines were the same, no help at all.

One by one the old ladies have offered remedies to help me, but nothing has worked. I've got an appointment next week, and can't wait for that to come around. Doctors have pills and potions for everything, don't they? Surely, they'll give me something that will stop me from being ill.

I haven't told anyone Truck intends to marry me, or that, to save me having to drag myself down to Tucson twice, we'll be going to city hall just the two of us to get it done before we go to the doctor's. One thing's for certain, I'm not going to want any photographs to celebrate the day, my face is pinched and already my clothes look loose on me.

Truck tells me I look beautiful every day, but I tell him that must be because he's using his fake eye when he looks at me.

"Do you still want to keep it quiet, Al?"

"Yes." I can see he doesn't like my answer.

"The old ladies will feel excluded. They like throwing parties when someone gets hitched."

I just give him a look. One that clearly asks, *are you really that stupid?*

But when he looks at me sadly and shakes his head I know he's realised, unless the doctor works that miracle I'm hoping for, going down to the clubhouse for even a small reception is the last thing I want. Also, he thinks they would, but there's a doubt in my mind that says they wouldn't want to arrange a celebration where I'm involved, and I don't want to be proven right, that even with Truck beside me, I'm still on the outside, a club whore turned wife. Part of me is grateful I've a good excuse not to put it to the test and find out.

Two weeks I've been like this, that's all. Not long in anyone else's eyes, but I'm starting to have difficulty remembering what it was like to be able to eat, or drink.

"I'm sorry," Truck glances over at me as I sit beside him in the truck. "We would have gotten married eventually, but I'd have gone down on one knee, done it all properly."

"I've spoiled everything." My eyes close briefly as I imagine it. I would have liked that.

"Not you, not me. Not either of our faults that something went wrong, Al, and we weren't as careful as we thought. Or the goddamn latex was faulty. Not down to one of us more than the other. As for your sickness? Christ woman, just the fuckin' luck of the draw. You pulled the short straw, I'm afraid. I wanted to make you happy, and now, you're not. Not down to you at all, you haven't spoiled a fuckin' thing."

The motion of the truck has the predictable effect, luckily it was foreseen and I lean over the bowl in my lap. My stomach's so empty it feels like I'm turning myself inside out.

"Fuck!" When Truck's hand hits the steering wheel, I know he's not angry with me, but with the situation we're in. It might be me that's suffering, but it's hurting him just as much. My man is a good one, I know if he could, he'd rather it was him than me.

I brace myself entering city hall, looking around as I walk in.

"Over there," Truck says quietly, pointing out the lady's bathroom to me. I have time to give him a grateful nod before running off.

We're on time and the judge doesn't keep us waiting. Truck wears his cut, but the judge's eyes focus on me, and soften when she sees my pallor. A couple of government staff are called in to witness our signatures, and then it's done. The only surprising thing is that Truck has bought rings, for him and me. His he has sized for his smallest digit, his ring finger being one that he lost. But it's the thoughtful gesture that, if it were possible, makes me love him more.

As we leave the office and walk through the corridors to the front door, my head starts to swim. The next thing I know, I'm on the floor with a concerned Truck leaning over me, and bystanders gawking on.

"You fainted." His lips press together. "Fuck, Allie. I caught you before you went down. They're getting a first responder…"

"No need, Truck. Just help me up." I feel so embarrassed with all the concerned and interested faces around. "Just help me out, we're going to see the obstetrician anyway."

He looks undecided, but then nods. "We're on our way to the doctor," he offers by way of explanation to the people standing around. Then, helps me to my feet.

"Wish I could fuckin' carry you," he says tersely as he supports me with his stronger right arm.

"I'm alright," I lie, not wanting him to feel guilty that his left leg isn't strong enough to bear my weight for more than a few steps. He had managed my room to his, but even that short distance had clearly taxed him.

It's this outing that's taken the last of my energy, I surmise, as I use him as a prop in the doctor's waiting room.

Truck seems to be thinking that way too. "We had to get married, darlin'. Now I know you'll have insurance. Didn't have a choice. Fuck, babe. This is all too much, isn't it?"

"We're seeing the doctor in a minute. There must be something he or she can do." I'm just banking that he has a magic wand to wave over me.

"Mrs Allen?"

Truck nudges me. "That's you now, babe."

My eyes widen as I realise he made the appointment in my married name.

"Got to get the paperwork straight from the start," he reminds me.

I hadn't considered I'd have a new legal name. *Stupid.* But it's not surprising, I haven't been able to think straight for days.

We go into a room, and take the chairs there. I eye the bed wondering if I should be lying on it. But before I can make a decision, the door opens and the doctor walks in.

"Mr and Mrs Allen, I'm Doctor Webster."

The doctor isn't what I expected. He's older for a start.

"She's pregnant and sick, Doc." Truck leans forward and starts speaking for me. "She can't keep food or drink down, and she fainted just now." Truck's concerned eyes flick to mine. "I'm really worried about her."

"Morning sickness is quite normal in the first trimester."

"Not like this. I've known enough pregnant women to know that."

"Oh, you have other children?"

Truck's eyes go wide. "No, but my brothers have lots of kids. My biker brothers that is."

Instead of focusing on me, the doctor's eyes disdainfully stare at Truck's cut. Only after he's taken it in, does he turn to me. "It's probably the lifestyle you live that's not helping. We'll talk about a proper diet which will show an improvement. No smoking or alcohol of course."

"Jesus, man. What the fuck are you talking about?" Truck leans forward, his cheeks darkening. "Did you not hear what I said? She can't keep anything down, not even water. Booze?

Fuck, she can't stand the smell of that let alone be crazy enough to drink it."

"If you can't mind your language you'll have to leave," Doctor Webster snaps. "I know your type." He waves at Truck's face. "I don't think I want to know how you got those scars. Arson, was it?"

I open my mouth to protest, but Truck gets there before me.

"Have another guess, doc. I was invalided out of the fire service having lost my eye and mobility fighting a wildfire in California. I'm also a vet. That I ride with the Satan's Devils has fuck all to do with the reason we're here today." The doctor looks taken aback, as if he's hastily revising his opinion of the man sitting in front of him. "We're wasting time. If you don't want to treat my wife, perhaps we should find someone else to see instead."

"I didn't say anything about not treating your wife..."

"It's me you're objecting to, but I'm not leaving Allie. I want to know what we're dealing with, and what our options are."

Now the doctor's eyes land on me. "Options? I take it we're discussing termination? You don't want the baby?" There's a sneer as he's clearly thinking it may interfere with the lifestyle he assumes we have.

"No," I say at the same time as Truck says, "Yes."

We look at each other. I give my old man a warning look, and continue, hating that even my voice sounds weak. "I'll admit this wasn't planned, and yes, we were careful, but it's happened. I have considered what I want to do, and I want to carry this baby to term."

"Doc, she's been so fuckin' ill. I'm worried about her, and what it will do to her, if it continues."

The doctor looks to him first, then back to me. It's me he addresses, as if deciding I'm the more reasonable person to deal with. "I'm glad that's your decision. We'll do an ultrasound, find out where things stand. Then I'll give you some advice about handling your discomfort."

Discomfort?

Truck gets in first. "Doc," he says patiently, as if he was explaining something to Amy, "she's not uncomfortable, she's sick. She's lost weight."

"I was about to go into those details." He begins asking how far along I think I am, or could be, *no idea,* my normal weight, *one hundred and twenty five pounds I think,* my diet, *nothing I can keep down.* Family history during pregnancy? *No idea.* Apart from sickness, what symptoms do I have?

Then I'm weighed and measured. Truck's worried that my weight's down by eight pounds, but the doctor doesn't seem concerned as I couldn't be definite about my weight pre-pregnancy.

He's business like when he stops tapping on a tablet at last, and directing me to the bed, instructs me to lie down and to bare my stomach.

"We'll try and see it with an abdominal scan at first. If I can't find anything, I'll have to do an internal."

He presses a button on the desk, and a nurse walks in. "This is the ultrasound technician."

The technician covers my stomach in liquid that's so cold it makes me jump, then, starts waving a wand over my stomach. The doctor is intent on the screen.

"Ah, yes. Look there."

I look but don't see anything. But there is sound, a fast paced whooshing. Truck's eyes go wide. "Sounds like my engine ticking over."

"Or a washing machine that's hyper."

"Is it supposed to be that fast?" Truck addresses the doctor.

"It sounds perfectly normal," Dr Webster replies.

"Where is it?" I ask, curious to see what's responsible for making me so ill.

The technician points out the smallest blob, not even an inch long. They take some measurements.

"I'd put you at about eight weeks. The good news is, you'll probably be feeling better after another month."

The shit is wiped off, and I get dressed, then go back to sit in front of the doctor.

"What can you do to help Allie, Doc?"

Disinterestedly, he starts to go on to list things I've already tried. A dry biscuit before getting out of bed, chewing ginger or mints. Sipping water, not downing it.

As Truck listens, I notice his jaw is tight, though when he speaks, his voice sounds patient enough. "As I said, a lot of my brothers have babies or are expecting. Every fuckin' thing you've mentioned, we've tried. Even got our computer guy googling for suggestions." His fists hit his knees. "I'm watching my wife get weaker by the day."

"She'll be fine when she gets to the end of the first trimester…"

"That's four weeks away. She won't survive! She needs something to stop this sickness."

"Mr Allen," Doctor Webster stands, "I've been an obstetrician a very long time. Your wife isn't presenting any symptoms I haven't seen before. I am averse to providing any medical intervention at this stage in the pregnancy. All I'm going to prescribe is rest, and that you revisit my suggestions and try them again." At Truck's glare, he adds, "You can get an oral solution that will keep her electrolytes at the right level. You can buy it at any pharmacy."

"Truck," I stand as well, weaving slightly as another wave of faintness threatens. Closing my eyes momentarily, I breathe deeply, fighting it off. "Let's go home."

The doctor is clearly waiting for us to leave. Our appointment is over. I hold it together just long enough to get into the truck, then the tears come. Truck pulls me to him and just holds me.

"When is enough, enough, Allie?"

"What do you mean?" I sob.

"When will the fuckin' doctor see you need help? Or when should we do something else? You can't go on like this."

I know what he's suggesting. He wants me to end this. Not because he doesn't want a baby, but because of the toll it's taking on me. Whereas I, perversely the woman who never wanted children, can't think of making that call. "You heard it, saw it, Truck. It's alive."

"So's a parasitic worm," he replies roughly. "It's leeching the life out of you, Allie. It's so fuckin' hard to see you like this."

"If I can bear it, so can you. We've both got to be strong, Truck."

"For something we agreed neither of us wanted," he growls.

"Is that true, Truck? If everything was good, would you still not want a family? Even if we hadn't planned it?"

He goes still, staring out over the parking lot. Finally, his eyes come back to me. "I see what my brothers have. What man wouldn't want that? Sons who will more than likely follow in their footsteps, girls who'll cause more than enough worry when the time comes. A legacy to leave behind them. Fuck, those men love their kids, and in my eyes, they complete them."

So he does want children. I nod.

"But Al," he continues. "What we don't see is what goes on behind the scenes. The worry of there being someone else you're responsible for twenty-four hours of every fuckin' day. The stress and strain on a marriage. Kids are fuckin' hard work. Yeah, it's a nice idea to have a family, but it's not all rainbows and sunshine. I'd be happy either way. If it's going to harm you to carry this baby, I'm happy enough to not have kids. I'll even get a vasectomy. Will do, anyway. Not going through this again."

"But…"

"No, Al. I *want* you. I'll be quite happy with just you by my side for the rest of my days. The thought of losing you? Well, that kills me. Promise me, Allie. If this gets too much, you'll tell me? Promise me. Don't put your life in danger."

He's deadly serious. There's only one reply I can make. "I promise, Truck."

But I wonder where that point would be, and whether I'd know it when it came.

~

Twenty years in the future - Drummer

"Ahoy there, Admiral!" comes a loud shout.

It can only be one person. Peg and I exchange amused glances as Tommy comes slowly down the track, carefully parking his mobility scooter at the end of the line of bikes. As adeptly as any of the brothers, the quiet beep beeping shows he's put it into reverse so it's just like the motorcycles are situated, facing out.

"You remember when we got him that?"

The corners of my mouth rise. "Sure do."

We'd always thought Tommy was around thirty when he'd arrived, but no one knew for certain, certainly not the man himself. Maybe he was older, who knows? But the years have taken their toll on him. Always a big man, his weight kept piling on, despite Peg getting him onto an exercise regime and the women trying to watch his calorie intake and limiting it where they could.

The man became slower and slower, soon getting out of breath when he walked up the incline. But he never complained, and continued doing whatever he could, and always with a smile on his face. None of us liked to see him struggling, and it was Sam who'd suggested the solution.

Some had doubts and were concerned that even on a machine that couldn't go any faster than eight miles an hour that he would be a danger to himself and to us. Blade said he'd have nightmares of him riding into the bikes. But Sam was insistent, and as in many things, I've learned it's easier to just go along with her suggestions.

But we didn't get any old mobility scooter, oh no, we got the one with the front end which resembles a Harley.

Fuck, his face. I chuckle to myself as I remember it. "He couldn't have been happier if we'd bought him his own motorcycle," I remind Peg. "The man broke down and cried."

"He fuckin' hugged it," Peg replies. "To him it was his own bike. Learned to ride it fuckin' quickly as well."

I glance over to where Tommy is standing, a rag in his hand as he wipes some almost invisible dust from the handlebars. He loves that scooter as much as I love any of my bikes.

"It had been worth it, just to see his face, Brother."

"That it was, Drum. Man might be suffering though he'd never tell us, but the joy he gets from that machine, well, that gives us all pleasure."

Peg's right, it does. The sight of a beaming Tommy coming down the track on his 'Harley' puts a smile on anyone's face.

He's now carefully attaching it to one of the charging points outside the clubhouse. After having cared for his most precious possession, slowly he walks over to us, his hand clutching at the railing as he takes the two steps to reach the veranda, then he takes a couple of deep lungfuls of air as he regains his breath.

"Admiral," he says, again in greeting. Then adds respectfully, "Peg."

Admiral. I choke back a laugh. Soon after he got here he'd been watching some film or other and decided I was like the man leading a fleet. He'd decided to give me the title, much to everyone's amusement, and nothing I could say could alter his mind. No one else dared use it, well, the couple who tried caught the wrong end of my fist.

"You doing okay, Tommy?"

"Tommy's good. Tommy's hungry."

"Got fried chicken inside," Peg notes.

His eyes brighten and he rubs his stomach. "Fried chicken for Tommy. Mmm mmm."

I'm shaking my damn head as he walks into the clubroom. "Dysfunctional family, that's what you've always called us Peg."

"*Stand by it, too,*" *he states firmly.* "*Everyone's got their place here, Drummer. All we ask is loyalty.*"

He's right. And strange as Tommy might be, he's got that in spades.

"*Life went on, didn't it? Through all the shit Truck and Allie had coming.*" *I jerk my head behind me.* "*Tommy, the kids… We had to keep putting one foot in front of the other despite everything.*"

"*Only one direction to go in,*" *Peg agrees.*

"*But sometimes we don't have where we're going mapped out.*"

"*Truck and Allie didn't. They were caught blindsided by everything.*"

CHAPTER TWENTY-SEVEN

*T*ruck…

I walk into our regular church with my head bowed, the weight of the world on my shoulders.

"You look like shit," Rock observes.

Shrugging, I simply turn my head toward Drummer, waiting for him to start the meeting, prepared to sit through reports from Dollar which won't hold my interest at all. But for once, the Prez's eyes are surprisingly soft when they return my gaze.

"Truck, time for a discussion. I hope you won't take it the wrong way when I say that we all hold Allie in high regard. She's been part of this club for as long as many people sat around this table can remember, and it's fuckin' hard to see both you and her struggling. What can we do to help?"

"She's pregnant," I state the obvious. It's not a secret, everyone now knows. "Her body's just not coping. I married her so…"

"You what?" Joker looks stunned.

"Why did we not know this?" Peg snarls.

"When?" Road's eyes narrow. "Didn't see you sneaking off."

I realise they wouldn't have seen Allie's ring on her finger, she never comes out of our suite. And as for mine, well, as I no longer have the proper digit they wouldn't have realised the implication. Now, I hold up my little finger bearing my wedding band. "That day when we went to see the doctor. Didn't want to make a fuss. Of course, eventually, I would have asked her, done it properly and told everyone in advance. I had to do it fast to get her on my insurance."

"I'd say congratulations, but I don't think you're in the right place to receive them," Drummer observes. "I would have liked to have been told, but I can see why you treated it as a formality. Good thinkin', Brother."

"I'll record it," Heart says practically.

"I'll update your records," says Mouse. "Anything I can help with, just let me know."

I thank them both, glad they're not making a big thing of it.

"So you went to the doctor, what can he do?"

"Nothing, Prez. He thinks it will sort itself out at the end of the third month."

Slick is shaking his head. "Ella had morning sickness, but it wasn't anything compared to what Allie's going through. What did you think of the doctor you saw, Truck?"

My teeth clench. "Not a fuckin' lot. Had a discussion about the drunken lifestyle he thought we were living. Old fashioned as fuck. Bet it's been some time since he last saw a textbook."

Peg looks confused. "Where the fuck did you find this asshole?"

"I spoke to my surgeon asking for recommendations, and this is who he suggested."

Heart frowns. "Why don't you go see Dr Cassidy? That's the woman Marc uses. She's excellent. Oversaw Marc and the twins, and is looking after her this time as well."

That's an idea. "Think we might do that, Heart." Anything is worth a try at this point, and it would be good to get a second opinion.

"I think you should." Prez raises his chin. "In the meantime, can we do anything to make Allie more comfortable? She must be bored out of her head sitting up in your suite the whole time."

"She's weak, liable to faint. She needs to constantly be near a toilet or bowl, she's sick at least twice every hour, day or night. She gets terrible headaches too."

"Not surprised. She hasn't eaten in weeks." Even Blade looks concerned.

"Or drank anything. She must be getting dehydrated."

"What about Doc? Can he set her up with a saline drip or something?" Rock suggests.

Mouse looks doubtful. "Doc's just a paramedic. I don't know if he'd like interfering with a woman who's pregnant."

It comes out before I can stop it. "I fuckin' wish she wasn't."

"What are you saying, Truck?"

I might as well lay it on the line. "I wish she'd get rid of it. I hate it, you know? Hate what it's doing to the woman I love."

"If that doctor is right, you've just got to get past these next few weeks. Take it a day at a time and hope for improvement. How about we set up a rotation of old ladies to go keep her company, try to keep her spirits up?"

I nod at Prez's suggestion.

Then frown when Joker opens his mouth. "Yeah, no wonder she's miserable, if all she's seeing is your ugly mug all the time." My lips actually twitch. I know it's something he'd say to anyone, and not a reference to the scars on my face.

Lady slaps him around the head for me.

I answer the prez. "Company would be good, as long as they don't overtire her."

"I'll speak to Sam. I'm sure everyone will want to be in on it."

Viper raises his hand, and offers in an apologetic tone, "May need to leave Sandy out of it. She's still not come around."

"She's an old lady and should listen to her old man," Drummer snarls. "But if she can't be pleasant, I doubt Allie would want to see her anyway."

Neither do I want Allie faced with any more unpleasantness. She's got enough to cope with as it is.

"I think the other old ladies, with the exception of yours Mouse, and Bullet, know what she's going through to some extent. But Sandy? She'd have given her right arm to be pregnant, and never experienced it. She's jealous, and hell, suspicious as Allie seems worse than anyone else and is getting the attention for being that way."

"She thinks Allie's making it up?" I glare at Viper. "What? She's exaggerating to get sympathy?"

Viper shrugs. "Got to be honest with you, so yeah. Part of it is her thinking she's playing on it."

"You nip that shit in the bud," Prez roars. His hands rake back through his hair as he glares at Viper, clearly upset with him.

Good. I don't even like someone thinking something bad about Allie. She doesn't deserve it.

That's the end of the discussion about my wife. We spend the next couple of hours discussing club business which I pay some attention to. Knowing my brothers are there to support me and my old lady has helped.

Afterward, Prez follows through, not that I expected anything else. Sam gets straight on it. Allie even seems to brighten when she's not alone for much of the time. Sophie and Marcia seem to be welcomed the most.

But despite her spirits being lifted a little, Allie gets no better. To my dismay, she keeps getting worse.

I'd made the appointment to see Dr Cassidy as Heart had suggested, but it's another week before she can fit her in. The day of our visit, I drive the truck up as close as I can get it to our suite, as she's far too weak to walk.

On the way Allie's quiet, as though conserving her energy, her silence only broken by retches as she uses the bucket too many times.

Breaks my fucking heart.

The difference in doctors is striking, and is there from the moment we walk into her office.

"I've got the notes from your last doctor," she starts. "You saw him, what two weeks ago? I don't need to go over the basics. I'll weigh you again, and we'll check how baby's doing on the ultrasound."

"Allie's really sick." I can't keep quiet. "I'm worried she's harming herself and the baby."

Dr Cassidy examines Allie with her eyes, then notes, "Well, that's what we're checking today."

Allie's watching the screen, seeing the lump of cells that's causing all her problems. I'm watching the doctor's face.

"Okay, clean up. Then we'll have a discussion."

When we're once again sitting in front of her desk, Dr Cassidy's face is serious. "You've lost a total of ten pounds if your pre-pregnancy weight was correct. We normally get concerned if you drop significantly, and five percent would be worrying. Your loss is more than that. We cannot let this go on."

"The baby?" Allie's concerned.

"The measurements are what I would expect. Baby is growing."

Because it's leeching the life out of her. Parasite is how I'd referred to it, and I think I could be right.

"Should she have an abortion?" I ask.

I don't see shock that I've raised the word. Instead I see sympathy.

"How do you feel about that, Allie?"

"Doctor, I never wanted a baby. But now I'm pregnant, I don't want to give this up. And it's just a case of getting through the next couple of weeks, isn't it?"

"Yes, and no. You don't have morning sickness, Allie. You've told me none of the normal remedies work, and with the symptoms you're presenting, I'm pretty confident in a diagnosis of Hyperemesis Gravidarum. HG, as we call it, is severe sickness experienced during pregnancy. It's not that common, but can be traumatic for a sufferer. It is more serious and debilitating than normal morning sickness. At the moment there's no actual treatment or cure, all we can do is mitigate the symptoms."

"Does it stop, like morning sickness?"

"Morning sickness lasts typically for the first trimester. With HG, the majority of patients will see improvements after week twenty, but in extreme cases, it can continue for the whole of the pregnancy and only stop at the birth of the baby."

"No way," I say quickly. "Allie will be dead in another ten weeks. Allie, you must consider…"

"No," she says firmly. "If you can put a name to it, can you treat it?"

Doctor Cassidy nods. "There are some things we can try. A process of elimination to see what might work. But I can understand your husband's concern, Allie. This is going to put a toll on your body, mentally and physically. A number of sufferers with this condition do consider termination."

"My body might be weak, but my mind's strong," Allie insists.

All Allie's stubbornness is coming to the fore. Tell her she can't have something and it makes her more determined. I'm wishing I didn't have such a fighter as my wife. I wish she would take the easy way out. Though I admit, nothing about this would be easy, whether she decides to continue the pregnancy or not. Part of the reason I didn't want to look at the ultrasound, didn't want to view that clump of cells as anything other than something slowly killing my old lady.

"You still have time to think about what you want to do. But for now, we need to take care of you, Allie. I'm going to admit you. You are badly dehydrated, so you'll be given fluids intravenously."

Allie's eyes flick to me in horror.

I won't be taking my old lady home? But I don't let my own worry show. Something needs to be done, and I'm filled with relief that this doctor recognises it. "It's the best thing for you, Allie."

"It is," the doctor confirms. "We'll try various anti-nausea remedies as well. See if we can make you more comfortable."

"For how long?"

"That's difficult to say, Allie. But you'll be in the right place. If you're continuing this pregnancy, it's what you've got to do for both your health, and the baby's."

The doctor makes a call and finds a bed for Allie at the hospital next door. I can see her fighting tears as I walk her over. *There's an easy way out,* I want to tell her. *Just stop this now.* But she won't. As if she can read the thoughts in my head, her mouth fixes into a stubborn line.

She's checked in, then settled. She might not like the idea, but she's so weak, she doesn't make much protest and soon she's in bed wearing a hospital gown, and a promise from me that I'll get one of the women to buy her some proper nightwear. She's got none of her own, she's never bothered to wear it.

I'm chased from the room while they put in a line, and return to the doctor's office in the adjacent building on the off chance that Doctor Cassidy is free to talk to me.

"I thought you'd have questions," she says, as her receptionist shows me in. "I had a patient cancel so I have some time."

"She wants to keep the baby," I start with a frown. "But won't her condition harm its chances?"

"The baby could be born underweight or premature, but we'll be monitoring him or her very carefully."

"What about Allie? I've served, Doctor Cassidy. I've seen people die from starvation. I can see the signs with Allie. I can't lose my wife.

"I understand that, which is why I'm keeping her in the hospital for now."

"I'm worried about organ failure."

"Again, we'll be running tests and making sure everything's functioning." She draws in air, then breathes it out slowly. "At the end of the day, it's her decision and we'll support whatever she decides. It's true, ten percent of people with this condition have a termination, but others are determined to continue."

She waves me to a seat.

"Does it happen to many women? I've never heard of it before."

"Morning sickness varies from person to person, and pregnancy to pregnancy. This isn't morning sickness per se, but something more serious. It affects about one in a thousand people, but Allie's case is certainly among the worst ones I've seen. Tell me, she says she doesn't know her family history. Why is that?"

"She never got on with her mom. Was thrown out of her home when she was sixteen. Would it be helpful to know more about her past?"

"It would be interesting. The condition does seem to run in families, and particularly if the baby is a girl."

"You're saying it's likely we could be having a daughter?" I frown. The thought of a little girl looking like Allie flits across my mind. I suppress the burst of elation as I wouldn't want her if it meant risking the health of my wife.

"Odds higher than fifty percent in this case, yes. Unfortunately there's also a likelihood of it reoccurring in future pregnancies."

"Won't be any chance of that," I tell her. "I'll be taking steps."

"She definitely needs a good man like you beside her, Truck."

I start at the use of my name, then query. "You know my handle?"

She smiles. "You forget. My miracle patient is married to one of your brothers. I saw Marcia the other day at her regular appointment. She told me you'd be dropping in. I know from Heart that you bikers prefer to use your biker names. Oh, and she might have let drop you were a firefighter."

"She warned you what to expect?" My hand touches my left cheek.

"I didn't need any warning. I see all sorts in here. I don't care what you look like, all I care about is whether my patients have the best support they can. And in this case, both mother and baby have."

Of course I'll be there for Allie, but I have no idea what to do for the best. "What can I do to help her?"

"It's common for HG sufferers to get anxious and depressed. Not going to lie to you Truck, she might become bedridden unless we can get the sickness under control. No one likes lying around in bed all the time."

"There's Marcia and all the other women at the clubhouse. They're already keeping her company and trying to help."

She nods.

"Long term? If she continues the pregnancy, what's the prognosis?"

"The strange thing about this condition is that it can disappear or lessen as the months go on. The worst case scenario is if it continues to the end. Then, as soon as she starts to give birth it will stop. She'll need to regain her strength, which could take time, but there shouldn't be any long-term physical complications."

If I hadn't been a soldier I might not have noticed, but the effects of injury come in many forms. I address what she hasn't said, "Physical? What about mental?"

Another up and down of her head. "You've served. You understand PTSD."

Only too well. I know a lot of my mood swings are down to not only my service, but what happened in the California fire.

"It might not appear to be the same thing, but what Allie is going through is traumatic."

It is. I just had it at the back of my mind, if she went the whole nine months and delivered a healthy baby, that would be the end of it. Especially if I made sure it couldn't happen again. Now she's warning me Allie might live with the results for the rest of her life.

"Therapy, support. There are ways to help. You'll just need to be aware of it."

"Is there a higher risk of post-partum depression?"

She sighs. "I won't lie to you, some people believe there's a link. Truck, I'm being straight with you here as I think you're a man who can cope if you know what you're dealing with. The best you can do for Allie is be by her side and support her whatever her particular needs turn out to be."

I can certainly do that.

CHAPTER TWENTY-EIGHT

---

*T*ruck…

I drive back to the compound hating that there's an empty seat beside me. Once I've parked, I have no inclination to go up to my suite alone.

A fucking drink. That's what I need.

Of course, I don't get to the bar unmolested.

"Hey, Truck. What did you think of Dr Cassidy?"

"She's good. Very good," I say absentmindedly.

"Did Allie get on with her?"

"I think so, yes."

Heart looks at me oddly. "She back in her suite?"

Sadly, I move my head side to side. "They're keeping her in." I describe how I last saw her, with a cannula in the back of her too thin hand. "Saline, and they're giving her a blood transfusion as she's badly anaemic."

Heart's hand lands on my back. "Allie's in the right place, Truck. Know you'll have hated leaving her, but hey, they know how to look after her. Hopefully it will only be for a day or two."

He's right, and that's what I'm holding onto, and hoping it won't be too long before she's back where she belongs. With me.

"What's up Truck?" I go through the story again for Blade and Peg. Thereafter it seems to spread around the clubhouse.

Swinging around, I spy Mouse and Mariana. His arm is around her, holding her close. *Now why couldn't we be like them? They've decided to wait on kids, and are just enjoying each other. They haven't had any accidents.* Nah, it was just me and Allie who pulled the short straw.

By the time I go across the room to them, they've already heard the news.

"So sorry, Truck. It must be fuckin' hard comin' back alone."

I shrug. Hate leaving her there, but if they can help her feel better, she's in the best place. *It would be better if she wasn't pregnant at all.*

Now I'm talking to him, though, I'll seize the opportunity. "Wanted a word, Mouse."

"Whatcha need?" He jerks his chin toward Mariana who, smiling, takes the hint and wanders off in the direction of Sophie and Marcia.

I pull up a chair, and sit, leaning forward so my hands are clasped between my knees. "Allie's mom."

"Want me to find her?"

"Yeah. I, er, don't want to ask Allie for information."

Mouse looks at me. "Whatever it takes?"

I shrug, not knowing what he's talking about.

I realise in two seconds as Mouse puts his fingers in his mouth and whistles loudly. Peg reaches over the bar and turns the music off.

"Allie. Anyone got any info about her? Where she came from? Where she lived?" Mouse calls out.

I realise instantly he's thinking she might have let information drop over the years that she's been here. So worried about her, I don't care where the information comes from, even if it was pillow talk. Got over my jealousy weeks ago. If anyone knows anything, it just might help.

It's actually Dollar who steps forward. He draws up another chair, but doesn't sit. Instead he places one foot on it and leans over. "She's from Phoenix. Came to Tucson on the first Greyhound out of town." His brow creases for a moment. Then he brightens and comes up with the name of a street. "I'd had family there myself, wanted to see whether there was any connection."

"Good enough for me." Mouse drinks his soda, then, after blowing a kiss across the room to Mariana, gets up. "I'll have her full name and current address in moments."

"He will, too." The treasurer nods admiringly after Mouse as he walks off. "Truck, I—"

I hold up my hands to stop him. "Got over that a long time ago, Brother. Don't care about history or how you know what you do. Got enough to deal with, with what's ahead. I'm just glad everyone here loves her, you know? She's going to need everyone's support."

"As are you, Truck. You're not having it easy, either." He straightens, then moves around the table, taking Mouse's seat on the couch. "You planning on contacting her mother? Don't know if Allie would thank you for that. Mind you," he adds quickly, "you know her better than anyone else."

"Her condition might be hereditary," I explain. "Just want to find out if her mother suffered it to, and if she did, whether she found anything that helped."

He's thoughtful for a moment, then says, "You want company when you have that address? Count me in."

Of course I'd like someone along. Since that morning when Allie first got ill, I've only had a few short rides on my bike. Sometimes just to clear my head, sometimes as it was a way to get from A to B quickly. A two-hour ride to Phoenix, if that's where her mom still lives, would be a bit of a stretch.

I raise my chin to acknowledge his offer, then warn, "I don't want Allie to know. You're right, she's left that part of her past behind, and she's got enough to deal with as it is."

Dollar nods. Then changes the subject. "You alright, financially?"

I shake my head. "She's got no social security number, so she can't register for Medicaid. I added her to my health insurance, but there's the co-pay."

"You qualify for Medicaid, Truck?"

I shake my head. "Not while I'm getting full disability from being a firefighter."

"So, you're screwed."

"That's about it."

Dollar stares at me, his lips thin. "Let's hope Allie improves soon."

"The only good news is that she's getting more help because she's pregnant. If she was dying of cancer, there'd be nothing at all."

The treasurer shakes his head, acknowledging my point.

They kept Allie in for three days. I was pleased to have her home, noticing immediate signs of improvement, more colour in her face for one thing. But it soon became obvious what they'd done was only a temporary fix, not a permanent solution. She has medication, yes, but as soon as she swallows it, it comes back up. Anything by mouth and her body rejects it.

At the back of my mind is the niggling thought that if Allie's mom experienced it, maybe she found something to help.

Even though I'm loath to leave Allie for a day, something drives me to get all the information I can without delay, and I can rely on Sam and the other women to make sure she wants for nothing while I'm gone. So two days later, Dollar and I set out for Phoenix and the address Mouse had found. Allie accepts the excuse of club business without question.

I'm guilty as I realise I'm enjoying the ride, appreciating the fresh air wafting past. It seems all I smell recently is sickness, all I feel is helplessness that I can do nothing to help my wife, and a burning rage that bad luck has caused this.

We stop to remove our cuts once out of our territory, and store them in our saddle bags.

"You doing okay, Truck?"

"I'm doing fine," I reply, absently.

"Look, I may be speaking out of line, but you've got to look after yourself too, Brother."

I look at him sharply. "What do you mean?"

"Your whole focus is Allie and what she needs. This trip out today, even that's for her. You've done nothing for you since you found out she was pregnant."

It's true. But, what else can I do? I'm responsible for getting her into this mess, least I can do is live it with her.

Dollar leans back against his bike and folds his arms. "Truck, I understand that you don't like us pointing this out, but Allie's been in the club a long time. That woman's got a heart of gold, you think she doesn't feel guilty she's tying you down? You think she doesn't look at Marcia and Becca, and see them laughing with their men? That's what pregnancy should look like, getting ready to welcome a little one into the fold, not looking like death and being confined to bed."

Now it's my turn to stare at him. "Allie's not letting me down. My fuckin' fault she's like she is."

Dollar shrugs. "Far as I'm concerned, even if the pregnancy was planned, no one could have predicted this shit. But I bet it's playing on her mind."

He could be right. Allie hates being a burden, but I don't think that's what she is. Suddenly I round on him. Being away from the club, away from Allie, it's like a dam has burst inside me. "For fuck's sake, Dollar. The only person who might hold a clue to what's going on is the person I'm hoping to see today. Allie's innocent. If her fuckin' mom held back information she should have known, we could have…" I slap my fist into my other hand, but don't have a chance to complete my thoughts.

"Could have… what, Truck? Not fallen in love? Not fucked? You couldn't have done any more than what you had. I rely on condoms, so do all the others. You don't need me to tell you what the odds were against what happened to you. As for her mom? You gonna be able to hold it together? 'Cause looking at you now, you look like you want to kill someone, and I didn't come equipped to deal with a body today."

I swing around, looking away from him, trying to analyse exactly what I want.

His voice continues from behind me. "Even if her mom had known, she might not have thought it was something she could pass on. And if she didn't suffer in the same way, you going to try find a grandma or someone else to fuckin' blame?"

"No one's to blame," I say, tightly.

"Hallelujah. At fuckin' last." He's still talking to my back. "No one. Not you, not Allie, and not her mom."

My voice is more controlled when eventually I reply, "That's what's so frustrating, Dollar. There's no enemy I can take down. I can't fuckin' stand it."

His hand slaps my back, and then again more lightly as a gesture of understanding and support. Then, after I stretch to get the kinks out of muscles that haven't been used for riding this far in such a long time, I raise my chin to show I'm ready, and we get back on our bikes to continue the ride.

When we arrive at our destination, I check out the house Mouse has told us is where Allie grew up. It's a nice enough home, though looks like it could do with some work, and a clean-up of the front yard. I try to picture her as a little girl, playing with friends in the neighbourhood, skipping down the path to go to school. Then, remembering her childhood wasn't all happiness and light, feel a scowl appear on my face as I approach the front door.

I rap on it. It's opened by a youth, who quickly tries to slam it shut. *Yeah, a big angry man with a scarred face? He's probably wise.* But, anticipating such a reaction, my steel-toe capped boot is already in the door.

"Who are you? What do you want? We've got nothing to steal."

"Not here to rob ya. Just want a word with your mom. Jason, isn't it?"

He doesn't seem any more relaxed that I know his name. "Yeah. What do you want with mom?"

"Who is it, Jase?" A woman comes up behind him. She's leaning on a stick and frowns when she sees Dollar and me.

"Mrs Martins?" I'm sure it is without her confirmation. She's got a look of Allie in her eyes. "I've come about your daughter."

She shrugs. "I haven't got a daughter."

Bitch.

"Mom?" Jason swings around to her, a surprising look of condemnation on his face, then turns back to me. "You know my sister? You know where she is?" His questions sound eager.

Allie never mentioned much about her brother, or how she'd got on with him. But I decide to give it to him straight. "Yeah, I know her. She's my wife."

Allie's mom snorts. "Figures." She waves at my tattooed arms. "You look like a thug."

I hear Dollar's sharp intake of breath. "I'm a retired fire-fighter and vet," I state.

"That how you got those scars?"

"Yes," I answer the young man.

Jason's eyes widen in something that's akin to respect. "So how's Alison? Where do you live?"

"Jase," his mom says warningly.

Ignoring Jason for a moment, my eyes fix on the woman whose eyes have gone icy. "Allie's sick. That's why I'm here. I was wondering whether it was hereditary."

"Sick, how?" To his credit, her brother sounds concerned.

"Pregnant and suffering from Hyperemesis Gravidarum." I watch for a hint of recognition in her mom's eyes.

Allie's mom looks at me incredulously, then she starts to

laugh. She laughs until tears are running down her face and she's bent double with her hands clasping her stomach.

All three of us gaze at her in surprise.

"Mom?" Jase asks, hesitantly. Then his voice firms. "We've just heard my sister is ill. Where's the joke in that?"

"Alison tried to kill me from the moment she was conceived. I hated her in the womb, still hate her now." She stops to chuckle again. "It's rich she's going through the same thing. Justice at last."

Christ. *Her mom blames Allie?* The reason why Allie's childhood was so hard is now easier to comprehend, though it's hard for me to take in. *Allie wouldn't hate her child, would she? Nah. If she did, she wouldn't be continuing the pregnancy.*

My eyes narrow with thinly disguised hatred for the woman in front of me. "You never thought to warn her?" I ask, grimly. "Never thought to say that if she had kids, the same thing might happen to her?"

"What? No. Why should I? Didn't happen with him." She points to Jason. "Jason I loved even before he was born."

I'm here, I have to try. "Did you find a remedy? Any treatment that helped you?"

"Of course not, the whole pregnancy was a battle between her and me." She pauses, and then thinks. "Tell her to do what I wished I'd done with her. Get rid of it."

Jason turns his back on her, pushes past us and steps outside the door. He paces the small front yard. Not trusting myself to say anything more to Allie's bitch of a mother, I, too, go outside, followed by Dollar.

It's clear Jason is processing what he just heard.

After a moment he turns to us. "Never knew that. Knew mom preferred me, thought that was just because she'd wanted a son, and I was getting good grades. I'm at the university now," he mentions, with justified pride. "I was eight when Alison left. I was a brat, I know that now. I was just a kid. I suppose I lapped up the attention she never had. Didn't know there was a reason for it." His mouth narrows. "Not like that." He looks concerned. "Is Alison going to be okay? Can I visit her? I'd like a chance to make up for how I ignored her when she was here. Would like to get to know my sister now."

I pinch the bridge of my nose. "I'm not sure," I admit. "She doesn't know I'm here. I wasn't going to tell her. Her doctor asked about her family history, I came to find out. Seems I didn't get the answer I was looking for." I'd got an explanation instead.

"Does *she* hate the kid she's carrying?"

I'm truthful in my response. "She hates how it's making her feel."

"Why her? Why didn't it happen with me?" he asks, thoughtfully.

"It's more likely to happen with girls," I explain. "Your mom took a risk getting pregnant again."

"I was a 'happy' accident," he explains, with a quick grin. "An unplanned reunion with my deadbeat dad. Of course, he just took off again immediately afterward."

"You in contact?"

"Nah. You've, er, seen my mom. If she knows where he is, she hasn't told me. Look, I'll give you my number. If Alison will see me, I'd like to visit with her, and get to know my niece when she's born."

"It could still be a nephew."

"Whatever." His shoulders rise up and down. "If she doesn't want to know me, I'll understand. We weren't close when she was here."

I nod, then indicate to Dollar I'm ready to leave.

During the ride back to Tucson, I think about what I've found out today. Could there be a chance Allie would turn out like her mom, and hate the baby?

Heaven forbid, but it's just one more thing to worry about.

CHAPTER TWENTY-NINE

---

*A*llie…

Pussy sniffs disdainfully as she walks into the suite. "Smells like a fucking hospital in here."

Yeah, it does. Disinfectant everywhere. I'm so weak, and the bouts of sickness come on so fast, I sleep with a bowl beside me.

"You doing okay, Puss?"

She perches on the end of the bed. "Better than you for sure. Is it worth it?" She waves at my swollen stomach. I've lost so much weight everywhere else it makes it noticeable.

Is it worth it? I ask myself that question so many times every day. Truck, I know, would rather I halt this now while I still can, but he's not the one carrying a new life inside. I've had more thoughts about killing myself, than killing my baby. I'm convinced I won't survive this pregnancy, so why not just hasten the inevitable myself?

I never wanted a family, never saw myself with kids. Not even sure I'd make anything approximating a good mom. I certainly didn't have a good example. All my life I've had to fight for myself, addressing any challenge put in front of me. Deep down I suspect I'm continuing with this because I've always been a fighter, and this is just one more obstacle placed in front of me.

A flutter in my stomach, I put my hand on the spot, wondering if it's the baby moving, but this early, it's probably just gas.

"You're having a girl?"

"Yeah, it was confirmed last week. Statistics show it was always most likely. This condition occurs more often with girls."

"Thought of any names?"

I shake my head. The idea I'll survive the full nine months is so unlikely, I can't imagine ever holding a baby in my arms. Naming her seems overly optimistic.

"Pussy, it's good to see you, but you've got something on your mind." I hadn't lived in the same house as her so long to be unable to read her.

Ignoring my question, she picks up a magazine that someone brought me. "What's this?" she asks, distracted by something falling out. A transparent tinted piece of plastic.

"It helps me read," I tell her. "With that on the page the words stay put and don't move around. Mouse found the idea on the internet, and it works." It's actually one of the many different coloured overlays Mouse has tried, we've finally found the one which seems best. "He's going to get tinted glasses to help me."

I can't express how much difference it makes. Without it, the words shimmer making it hard for me to read. Still doesn't mean I can easily make out the words yet, painfully trying to put the letters together and work out the sounds, but it gives me hope that one day I might be able to learn properly. At the back of my mind is the thought I'd like to be able to read to my baby. If we both survive.

She throws down the magazine, losing interest. Then looks at me. "You know, bikers have prison benefits?"

Of course I do. Not that it's ever been used in the Tucson club that I'm aware of. Mind you, we haven't had men locked up for years. Prison benefits are where other members see to the physical needs of the old lady when her man goes inside. My eyes narrow as I've a suspicion where she's going with this.

"You," she indicates me and my swollen belly, "obviously can't see to Truck. Me and the other girls wondered if we should take care of his needs for you."

My initial reaction is complete horror. It's true. I'm so sick and weak, Truck and I haven't been intimate since we found out I was pregnant. He hasn't asked, hasn't indicated he wants to have sex, but what man would? He wouldn't risk starting some action only for me to puke before we'd even got going. What a turn off.

I open my mouth to dismiss it, not wanting to think of my man with anyone else, only to suddenly wonder whether he should have the choice or not. Am I being selfish? *What if I die?* It's only a matter of time before Truck goes with someone else, and no one knows better than I that with the whores, there'd be no emotional involvement. That's what they, and previously I, were there for.

Or is she asking because she thinks she might have a chance with a man who can put the knowledge his woman was a sweet butt behind him?

Pussy notices I'm not jumping at the idea, and shakes her head. "Oh, well, just something for you to think about. If you want to let your man off the leash, we'll be happy to take over for you."

Have I got Truck on a leash? Possibly. He's tied to a woman who's more than half dead. Not what he signed up for.

My few minutes of peace are up as my stomach revolts. Knowing I can't make the bathroom in time, I pick up the bowl placed next to me.

Pussy's eyes widen at the sound of me retching, and all but runs out the door, slamming it behind her.

It's opened seconds later, and my man is there.

Truck pulls back my hair, and strokes my head as I bring up bile and the few sips of water I'd managed to drink. Then, when I've finished, he takes the bowl into the bathroom. He's back in moments, the bowl now clean, he replaces it beside me.

I lean back on the pillows, exhausted.

"You didn't sign up for this, Truck."

He stares at me intensely. "Al, darlin'. You're my old lady. I signed up for all the shit, good and bad, sickness and health. Okay, so this isn't quite where we saw things going, but I'll be by your side whatever happens. I love you, Al. What I hate is seeing you this way."

"I'm getting worse, not better."

He stands, paces, rakes his hands over his bald head. "There's still time to end this, Allie. No, don't say no. I'm fuckin' scared I'm going to lose you. Think about it, please? You could be done with all this in a moment."

"Come here." I beckon him over. Then, with what little strength I have, wrench his hand toward me and place it on my stomach. "That's your daughter in there."

For a moment his eyes soften, then they harden again. "And you're my wife. Fuck, woman. Yeah, I'd love a daughter, love to hold her in my arms. But if losing you is the cost, I don't want to pay it."

"You'd be a good father, Truck, if I was here or not." That's one thing I don't need to worry about. If I give my life to save hers, Truck wouldn't turn his back on her.

"You can't say that, Allie. Remember Heart? He deserted Amy without a backward glance when Crystal was killed."

"She was loved, Truck, by the club. Drummer and Sam took care of the kid until he came back to his senses." Maybe if we were somewhere else, with no family to support him, I'd be more worried. But this baby will have cousins, uncles and aunts, not related by blood, but who will love her. I'm sure of that.

"She's killing you, Al."

"I'm still here."

I know what he wants. Oh, the thought of being normal again is tantalising. Just one word from me, and the doctor would perform the procedure. That she's indicated she would have no hesitation in recommending it, shows how ill I am. But that fighter inside me tells me not to give up.

"What did Pussy want?" His eyes narrow as he changes the subject.

I sigh, knowing I've got to give him the option. "She reminded me about prison rights, and drew comparisons about your lack of action."

"What the fuck?" he rears back.

I harden my soul. "Truck, you have needs…"

"And I'll handle them myself or wait until you're well again. Fuck, Al. You think I'd go with a club girl when you're lying so sick?"

"This isn't what you expected, Truck."

"Expectations? Nah, I wanted an old lady riding behind me. Instead, I got her pregnant. Instead, I put her life at risk. The last thing I fuckin' want, Al, is more sex with anyone."

"You wouldn't want sex with me?" Now my eyes go wide.

"Of course that's what I fuckin' want. But you, like this? You're too weak and I'm not a selfish bastard. You're growing my baby, Allie. If that means I go without, that's the sacrifice I'll be making. And I'll be having words with that whore. How dare she upset you?"

"If I die…"

"You're not fuckin' going to die, Al." His working eye blazes with emotion.

"Promise me, Truck. If I do, and she's born alive, you'll take care of her." Again I grab hold of his hand and hold it tightly, which, for me, is weakly.

"I won't let it get to that point," he insists. "If she's born alive, you'll be there to look after her."

"It wouldn't matter, Truck, I doubt I'll make a good mother."

"What the ever loving fuck?" I've shocked him again. His brow furrows. "Do you hate her, for putting you through this?"

The question surprises me. I take a moment to consider. "No, it's not her fault. I'm more worried I'm not providing everything she needs."

"Allie, you're giving her your fuckin' all."

"What if it's not enough?" I whisper, voicing my fear that arises in the dead of the night. *What if I'm going through all this, and she's also suffering?*

"Look at you, Allie. You're little more than a skeleton. You couldn't give more of you if you tried. The doctor is monitoring her carefully, she's a little small, but everything seems to be in the right place."

Low birthweight, early delivery, that's in the cards, but indications show she shouldn't be permanently damaged. But there are no guarantees, in anything.

"I don't hate her, Truck." I may not love her yet, but not because she's hurting me. I'm keeping deliberately detached in case she doesn't come to be. She didn't ask for this, just like I hadn't. He stands and paces again. There's something on his mind, I recognise the symptoms. "Spit it out, Truck."

"If I tell you something, promise not to hate me?"

That's easy. "Nothing you could do would upset me, Truck." Unless he asks me for the one thing he wants, for me to abort my baby.

"A few weeks back, I went to see your mother."

I'm stunned, shocked. "You didn't tell me."

"I didn't want to upset you."

"So why tell me now?"

He sighs deeply. "She had this HG thing when she was pregnant with you."

Dr Cassidy had suggested it ran in families. I close my eyes, thinking of our previous conversation, and this new revelation. "Is that the reason she hated me so much," I say, at last.

"Yeah, she blamed you."

"I don't remember much about Jason, whether she…"

"She didn't have it with him, or not so badly," Truck interrupts.

I lay my hand on my stomach and reaffirm. "I don't hate her."

He knows I'm referring to the baby I'm carrying. "Would be easier if you did, darlin'. Then, maybe, you wouldn't carry on."

I give a weak smile. "I feel like we're in this together."

"I met your brother too. Jason wants to visit you. He knows he was only a kid when you were at home, and just lapped up his mom's attention without noticing you weren't getting any. He'd like to get to know his big sister properly."

"Not now," I reply fast. It's not that I don't want to see my brother. It could be good to reconnect, or at least get to know the young man he's grown into, but it takes all my energy to take air into my lungs. Dealing with an awkward situation would be beyond me.

Truck nods, showing he understands.

Suddenly the smell of disinfectant gets too much. "Can you take me out for some fresh air, please?"

"Of course, babe."

We go through the motions that are practiced now. Truck pushes Sophie's old wheelchair that's yet again been called into use, closer to the bed for me. Then, he picks me up. He might be weaker than before his accident, but I weigh hardly anything now, so he has little difficulty lifting me, and placing me in it. Then, he hands me that inevitable bowl.

He drapes a cardigan around my shoulders, and wheels me outside onto the balcony where I watch the afternoon sun setting over the mountains. The temperature is currently pleasantly warm, but will drop as the sun disappears. When my emaciated body shivers, he wheels me back inside, then lifts me into bed.

My eyes close, completely zapped of any energy, I fall asleep.

~

TWENTY YEARS IN THE FUTURE – *Drummer*

I CHECK MY PHONE, *though I've lived here long enough for the disappearing sun to be sufficient indication, and the device only offers confirmation. It's almost time.*

"Lot of changes," Peg observes. "People come, people go."

"Some before they should."

"Viper?"

I nod. "Like Viper." I confirm, then briefly close my eyes. When I reopen them, the sun's almost disappeared completely, going about its business, uncaring about the humans it shines down on, or those that are no longer around to feel its warmth. "I miss Viper. So does Sam."

"We all do, Drummer. But hell, if there was a chance to choose how to go, what better way is there for a biker? Last thing he knew was he was riding his bike."

My lips press together. The news had been a shock, Viper's bike had flown over the side of Mount Lemmon. Until the coroner had made his assessment, we'd been trying to work out why the fuck Viper would have committed suicide. Turns out he'd had a heart attack which had killed him outright. He'd have been dead before he'd gone over the edge.

A good way to go? Well, Peg's right. If Satan had decided to call in his number, there were worse ways for it to happen.

"I miss the fucker," I tell him. Being Sam's father, Viper had oddly become my father-in-law. Not that I'd ever made it official and put a ring on her finger, but in our world, giving her my property patch was just as significant.

"Do you ever worry?" When I cock my eyebrow at him, Peg continues, "We're getting older, and it seems nature's thinning our numbers."

I shrug. "If it happens, it happens, Peg. Not much we can do about it. Life is fatal, there's no other outcome. Long as I can keep riding, I don't give a damn. Time marches on, and yeah, we're losing older brothers. The club's cycle's continuing, prospects keep coming along, those who make the grade get patched in."

"You're right." Peg muses, "Alba, Cast, and Toady are all new blood."

"Hound and Roadkill too, as well as the kids."

Yeah. Sharp, Bolt, Hawk, Throttle, Speed, Rev and Wizard.

Club is moving on and that isn't a bad thing. "Satan's Devils will still be here long after we're gone, Peg."

"That's our legacy, isn't it, Drum? What we'll leave behind."

We both pause a moment to think about that, then Peg suddenly chuckles. "Do you think one of those would qualify us for being able to ride a bike?"

When I see him pointing at Tommy's mobility scooter with the Harley trimming, I almost choke when I laugh.

CHAPTER THIRTY

*T*ruck...

I walk into church and take my place, thoughts churning through my head, and not ones about the meeting ahead.

"How's Allie?"

That Drummer's kicked off the meeting with that question both comes as a surprise, and, in a contradiction, is unsurprising. A rare occasion saw me wheeling Allie into the clubhouse last night, a chance for her to see the Christmas tree and join in with festivities, and then she'd fainted in front of everyone.

One moment she was sitting upright in the chair, the next she was slumped over, head lolling. She hadn't come around for a few minutes, and I'd been beside myself. An emergency call and paramedics had had to be summoned to the compound.

"In the right place." She's in the hospital. Again. I think this is the sixth time so far. She'll be in a few days, this time they're trying a feeding tube in her nose.

"The baby doing okay?" Heart asks.

Why does everyone always ask about the fucking baby? It's Allie who concerns me. "Looks that way," I try to reply without snapping. "She's in this for the long haul, now."

"They going to deliver the baby early?"

"Probably won't have a choice." I raise my chin toward Wraith. "That's one of the complications." *Early can't be soon enough for me.*

"Are they keeping her in for longer this time?"

"Nah, Prez. Only for a few days." I hate her being away from me, but am so scared when she's at home. She looks like a strong breeze would blow her away. "They want to try a concoction of various drugs. So far, some have made her worse, some improved her sickness but she was starting to have convulsions. She needs nutrition so they are trying different ways."

"How's the money holding up?" Dollar asks.

"Okay." I shrug.

"I'm worried about you, Truck."

Me?

My eyes meet those of the prez.

"Yeah. Six months you've been back with us, Truck. And in those six months, there's an anger within you which you work hard to conceal. It's burning you up from the inside out."

"I'm angry at the fuckin' world, Prez." Why not tell him how it is? "First I lost half my sight, my mobility and my job because of a fuckin' cat. Then I thought I'd found what I'd been searching for, an old lady of my own. But now, having to watch Allie fade away in front of my eyes? Fuckin' hurts more than when that fuckin' tree fell on that house with me inside it. I was trapped then, trapped now. Can't see a way out, and it's not even me who's sufferin'. Wish it was, Prez, fuckin' wish with everything I've got that I could go through this for her. Angry? Yeah, think I've got a right to be fuckin' irate." I thump my fist down on the table.

"Not sayin' you shouldn't get mad. But people are sick to death of walkin' on egg shells around you, Truck."

That brings me up. *Have they been?* I think of how I've been loving and calm with Allie, then storm down to the clubhouse to let all my frustration out. More than one person has probably been a victim of my barely concealed rage and short temper.

"Your woman's sick, Truck, not negating any of that. But you need an outlet, something to help you get your head back into the game. Despite your wishes, Allie's going to carry on until she gives birth. Ain't nothing you can do for her, except be there and give her support."

What the hell does he think I've been doing? "I'm doing that," I nearly shout.

In contrast, Drummer's voice is eerily calm. "Club needs you too, Brother."

His words stop me in my tracks. *Have I been neglecting the club?* My lips purse. *I come to church, work a bit at the auto-shop—when I'm not tending to Allie. I... I...* "I come to church."

"'Bout all you do."

Seems I have run out of any credit I might have had. Prez's observation and thinly veiled criticism has been like a slap around my face. He's right. I've been raging at the world, frustrated I could do nothing to change it.

"What do you need me to do, Prez?"

Drummer sighs. "Need you to get your head in the game." His attention switches from me, and looks around the rest of the members. "We've got a problem."

Each man sits up a little straighter. Problems affecting the club when introduced in the tone of voice Drummer's just used tend to be serious. He's captured my interest. As a firefighter, when prospecting I'd been far removed from all the goings on in the club, but mainly because I'd been trusted to turn a blind eye. You'd have to be stupid not to realise something was up when a man was brought to the compound, never to be seen or heard of again. Drummer may have had me cleaning blood from the storeroom, but as long as he didn't admit how it had got there and I hadn't asked questions, we could all ignore what was really going on.

One of the things that had attracted me to the club was when they had a problem, they dealt with it, dealing their own form of retribution. Since I'd returned and taken my seat around the table, things had been quiet. This is the first time I've been drawn into anything resembling one-percenter business. From the expression on Drummer's face, I've no doubt that's what the aforesaid problem is.

"Who do you want me to kill?" Blade asks, spinning his knife.

Drummer takes in a deep breath. When he lets it out, it's to pronounce, "Wretched Soulz need a favour."

The Wretched Soulz are the dominant club in Arizona as well as most of the US. Satan's Devils exist because they've given us a charter. A club who sets up without their permission, or who goes against their wishes are looking at a short lifespan with probably a painful end to it.

"What kind of favour?" Unlike Blade, who's perked up, the VP seems more cautious.

"Escorting a shipment of guns over the border."

A collective gasp goes around the table.

"We got out of that trade years ago," Bullet observes.

"At least the guns are going the right way, out of the US," Heart states. I know he's frowning as Amy, at just seven years old, has already taken part in active shooter drills at her school. He was complaining about it only yesterday that his poor kid had had nightmares.

I tend to agree with him. I might carry a gun, but I'd only use it as a last resort. Far too easy for an AK15 to get into the wrong hands, though fuck knows why anyone is driven to randomly shoot at people. Person like that is completely screwed up.

"Why don't they do it, Prez?" Peg looks confused. "They're set up for it, got the routes and everything.

"Because," Drummer's mouth twitches, "they've got an outbreak of the flu. Taken down most of the members."

"'Flu?" Rock snorts. "A MC brought down by a virus?"

"Appears that way. Chaz could hardly speak for coughing, and Bull isn't much better than Truck's old lady. As far as their members go, most of them are laid up, coming down with it, or recovering."

Joker starts laughing, Lady joins in. Soon everyone's doubled up. It's just the mental picture of big tough men all laid low.

Prez waits until the mirth begins to die. "Their road captain and most experienced riders are the worst. Transport will be passing through tomorrow, Chaz wants us to take care of it."

"Just an escort?" Joker's recovered fast. "Need me as Road Captain?"

"Yeah," Drummer looks his way. "Volunteers only."

"Count me in," Joker says without hesitation.

Dollar raises his hand. "Could do with some action. Been boring lately."

"I'll go." I jerk my chin toward Prez. It's about time I gave something back to the club who has given so much to me. Drummer raises his head in acknowledgement. Seems that's what he'd wanted.

Road, Shooter and Marvel are quick to offer too, quicker, I notice, than men with old ladies.

"Chaz assures me there's nothing to it. It's something they do on a regular basis. Escort the truck to the border and see them safely over it."

"You expect us to cross over into Mexico?"

"Nah." Prez shakes his head. "But you may need to create a diversion should ICE start looking too closely."

"They're crossing at a border point?"

"The truck will be full of agricultural equipment spares. Guns hidden under the false floorboard. They've used the same crossing point for a while, return with auto parts. They've found they're more likely to get searched on the return journey, so the fake floor gets removed."

"So the point of the escort…?"

Drummer shrugs. "Wretched Soulz protecting their business interest this side of the border. The cartel will pick up escort duties on the other side."

Sounds simple enough. I'd still put my hand up to it should there have been more danger involved, but there doesn't seem to be. Shouldn't take more than half a day, and I'll be back visiting Allie in the hospital before she even misses me.

I begin to perk up. A ride with a legit, well, in the club's eyes, purpose, and a chance to give back when all I've done is to take.

We go through the details. Joker's going to be checking the route provided, looking for any likely places that he could see being used for an ambush. He'll be liaising with his counterpart in the Wretched Soulz—by phone, don't want any germs brought back to the clubhouse—being a careful type, wants to make sure for himself.

I know the men around this table have a lot of respect for our road captain, so I am happy to put my safety into his hands. Can't see much problem, myself. Seems quite cut and dried.

Our meeting has been topsy-turvy today, we now get back to the business reports. I listen, the tattoo parlour has been up and running for a while, and Blade's reporting it's all going well. Rock takes a bit of joking that it's no thanks to him stealing the funds, he knows he'll never live that shit down, so doesn't try.

"You pleased with your back patch?"

"I am." Rock nods to Blade. "Feels fuckin' good to have my ink back. Fucker did a good job."

When it comes to any other business, Wraith waves his hand. "Sophie's come up with an idea," he starts. "This HG thing that Allie has, doesn't affect all pregnant women thank fuck. It tends to be dismissed as morning sickness by people who don't understand."

I nod. Allie and I had had our fair share of hearing every

woman goes through some form of what she is. Fact is, most don't suffer anywhere near as badly as her. Luckily, everyone here now understands.

"There's still a lot of questions about the best treatment, how to prevent it happening, long term effects and so on. Apparently it's affected a fuckin' princess in England, so it doesn't discriminate between rich and poor."

I wonder where he's going with this.

"Thought we could do something similar like we did for Dart's lad, Tyler. A charity run to raise funds and awareness. Donate it to an organisation doing research into HG." He leans forward and nods down the table at me. "Allie might be interested to get involved after the birth."

"I think once she's over it, she might prefer to forget about it."

"Doesn't always work that way though, does it, Brother? She's going through something traumatic. Doing something to bring it to the fore, help others understand it, might help her to know it was out of her control. Burying it and trying to move on and forget all about it might be worse." I suppose I'm looking unconvinced, as the VP adds, "It was just a thought."

"Fuckin' good thought too, Brother," Drummer says. "After this past year, first with Truck being hurt, then Allie suffering so bad, it would be something to bring us all together."

"Get Dart back from San D, and Beef and Pal from Pueblo," Peg suggests. "Bring the whole family together again."

Joker smashes his hand on the table. "Fuckin' good idea. I can start making plans…"

"Whoa." I hold up my hands. "We've got months to go until Allie's out of the woods. Let's not count our chickens too soon."

"Allie's going to be fine," Drummer says. "Know you're worried, Truck, as well you should be. But she's getting good medical attention. Whatever the outcome, I say this is a worthy cause, and we all know how long it takes to make plans. I say let Joker start getting on with what he needs to do."

"May would be a good time. Hot, but not too bad if we head for somewhere in the mountains." Joker clearly has put his thinking cap on. "It will be a push to plan, even if I start now."

"June will be too hot, then you've got the monsoons July to September. If we don't plan for then, we're looking at next autumn."

"Fuck," Drummer acknowledges what Rock is saying. "We haven't even got Christmas over with yet.

Apart from the Christmas tree having gone up in the clubroom, I haven't thought about the season at all. Can't even think of a gift to buy Allie. I frown. Christmas is only a week away now. Better hurry up if I'm going to get her anything at all.

Get this job that we're doing for the Wretched Soulz over with tomorrow, then I'll give her gift some thought. I won't go over the top as she won't have bought me anything, but something to show that I love her and appreciate what she's doing, even if I'd prefer she was not.

Hmm. Best get my thinking cap on. Go shopping on the way back from Nogales. Yeah, that's what I'll do.

CHAPTER THIRTY-ONE

*A*llie…

"How are you feeling, Allie?"

"Dr Cassidy. I didn't expect to see you." I press the button to raise the bed so I'm in a sitting position.

"Didn't want to drag you all the way to my office, and anyway, I'm making my rounds so thought I'd come see you." She pulls up a seat. "So, it rather looks like you're in it for the long haul."

"It's not going to ease off, is it?"

"You're coming up on six months now, so no. I think you're in the small percentage of unlucky ones."

"Do I need to do anything different?"

"Rest, like you've been doing. You'll have to keep coming in to be rehydrated. But we'll try and keep you at home for Christmas."

That they can't offer anything else isn't surprising. The season and whether I'm in the clubhouse or here means little to me. I've no gift to give Truck, haven't even had the energy to think about it. I do suspect keeping the hospital as empty as possible is more for the medical staff than for me.

While I haven't the energy to do anything, I have been thinking. "My mom suffered from HG with me."

"Yes, Truck told me."

I bite my lip. "Will my daughter get it too?"

"There's no way to tell. Her chances would be increased, yes. But medicine's moving on all the time, I'm confident we're heading toward knowing what causes it and how to treat it."

I've got a ton of questions, but don't know whether I can ask them. Her sympathetic smile encourages me. "Will I really feel okay after the birth?"

"Yes. Your sickness will disappear. We don't know exactly why, but the change in hormone levels has a drastic effect."

"Will I be able to breastfeed?"

"You should be able to. It depends on how you're feeling."

I don't even know if I want to. It always seemed a bit icky when the women fed their babies in the clubroom, however discreet they were about it. Then, I never expected to have a baby myself, and thought that my boobs were only there as something for men to play with. Not that I objected at all.

"Time to decide what to do when your milk comes in."

I can't imagine how my body would produce any sustenance to feed a baby. At the moment I don't feel inclined to feed her myself. I've been sustaining this growing baby inside me for so long, it feels like she's taken enough from me.

"Will you have help with the baby? I know you're not close to your mom."

I smile. "So much help," I tell her. "It's like a big daycare at the compound."

"That's good. You'll start to recover when the baby is born, but you should understand, it could take up to eighteen months to completely get back to your former self. Pregnancy takes it out of a woman anyway, but add in HG and the effects are much worse. You should be prepared and accept you won't be able to be a super mom and do everything by yourself."

No fear of that. I'll be handing off this baby as much as possible. I frown slightly. *Perhaps I'm more like my mom than I thought.*

She misunderstands my expression. "No harm asking for help when you need it." She stands. "Any other questions, just ask them, okay?" She pats the bed. "I'll see you again soon. Hang in there, Allie. You're getting closer."

Her visit, like everything else, has tired me. I doze.

A noise wakes me. My heightened senses breathe in an odour of leather, but it's not Truck. My eyes flick open to see the last person I expected. It's Drummer.

"Sorry to disturb you, sweetheart."

"No worries. It's hard to find me not asleep." I say the words, but inside me, a feeling of dread starts to settle. "Where's Truck?" It's visiting time, he should be here. The fact he's not is immediately concerning. And it's not every day an ex-sweet butt gets a visit in the hospital from the president of the MC. "Is Truck okay?"

"He's okay, Allie. But he can't come to see you."

I struggle to sit up. Drummer helps by balancing me against the pillows. "Where is he?"

Drummer sighs, and rubs his hand over his beard. My unease worsens. "He's been arrested, Al."

"What the hell? Truck? No, why? What's happening?" Words tumble out and I can't seem to stop them. "Why, Drummer? What…?"

"Calm yourself Allie. Wraith's gone to find out."

"What's Truck done? Where is he?" My man wouldn't do anything wrong. *Arrested?* It has to be a mistake.

"He's being held in Nogales."

At the border?

"Hush, Allie, calm yourself. Worry can't be good for you or the baby."

Reaching for the bowl at my side, I'm sick. Drummer looks concerned, but I'm used to it by now, habituated to the pain wracking through me as my stomach tries to expel everything it holds. My throat's rough and raw. Vomiting again makes my voice husky.

But right now I care little about myself. "Tell me everything, Drummer. Why the fuck was Truck at the border?"

"Club business."

My heart drops as I hear the words. I thought the club was out of anything illegal, that they were at the border, suggests I'm wrong. "That's not enough," I hiss. "Who was with him?"

He shakes his head. "No one else was arrested."

Truck. My man. In jail. Alone.

"We've got him a lawyer, Al. We'll get him out of there."

"What are the charges?"

"You're asking me things I can't tell you yet, Allie." Again Drummer's hands play with his beard, a sign I recognise as him being deep in thought, or searching for the right thing to say. "All I can say is, it seems unrelated to the club or what he went down there for."

"What was that Drummer?"

He knows what my eyes are accusing him of, but all he repeats is, "Club business. Allie, I came to tell you as I know you were expecting to see him today. When he didn't turn up, I knew you'd be worried."

"I'm fucking worried now," I rasp. Then my emotions do a one-eighty as anger gives way to sorrow. Tears start to fill my eyes as I realise how much of a rock Truck has been. "How can I do this alone?" I sob.

"Allie, Al." Drummer moves closer, taking my hand in his. "It may be nothing, hopefully he'll be released soon. Try not to worry yourself now, it can't be good for you or the baby."

The baby. The thing growing inside me, killing me slowly. If I'd known what was going to happen, I'd have taken the easy way out. It was Truck who'd kept me going. Knowing he'd like a family, I'd been doing this for him, despite his encouragement to have a termination. I know he'd be excited if it wasn't affecting me so badly.

Now the time that's past means that decision's been taken out of my hands, and I may be going through all this for nothing. If Truck goes away for a long time, I'll be on my own with a baby I never saw myself having. *I can't do this.*

"Drummer," I cry. "I can't, I just can't. I could put up with everything with Truck beside me. What am I going to do now?"

"You'll continue doing just what you're doing Allie. Fuck, woman, you've got the respect and admiration of the whole club for your determination to continue this pregnancy. You carry on as you are, doing this for you, for Truck, and for your daughter." He pauses and his eyes sharpen. "You are not going through this alone. You've got the whole of the MC who'd drop everything to help you."

"I'm supposed to be coming home tomorrow…" I wail, unable to keep the despair from my tone.

He anticipates my question. "If Truck can't be here, I will be, or one of the brothers. If it comes to it, while Truck's away, I'll assign a prospect to you. Your choice, Hound or Roadkill. They'll take you anywhere you need to go, get anything you need getting. We'll be doing everything to make your life easier."

I shake my head, not giving a damn who's assigned to watch over me. They won't be Truck, won't hold me at night, won't be there to soothe me when everything gets too much. I know this life, know what happens to brothers who go inside. If Truck's sent down, there's a chance he'll never be out again.

I can't do this alone.

I don't want to.

My tears fall. Sobs wrack my body.

Anguish such as I've never felt before sweeps through me. I'm vaguely aware of a hive of activity around me. A voice I recognise saying words I barely hear, Drummer explaining the little he knows of the situation.

"This isn't good for her or the baby. I'll change her prescription and get Mirtazapine added to the IV. It has an anti-depressant and sedative effect. It's lucky I was still here and hadn't left."

"Thank you, Doctor…"

"Cassidy."

I hear voices continuing to talk but fade into the distance.

I'm left alone with voices in my head. Memories of my mom berating me that I was the reason my father had left. Now history's repeating itself, maybe not for the same reason, but it seems I could end up on my own bringing up a baby who's tried to kill me. *Will I hate her too?*

Why has my gentle giant of a man been arrested? I don't understand what he could have done. *Had he been carrying drugs or weapons for the club?* I thought they were out of that business. But what do I know? I'm just an old lady.

Despite Drummer's optimism, Truck isn't released immediately.

The next day I almost don't want to go back to the club, but there's no reason for the hospital to keep me, though the nurse tried to joke she'd reserve the bed for next time. I didn't feel like laughing, knowing I will be back, as I've needed to do every two weeks since the first time.

She wasn't on shift last night, but the rumour mill must have started. I hear some of it as I'm getting dressed.

"Well, her husband's a biker, she must have known what she was getting into when she married him. Who knows what those Satan's Devils are up to? They're a criminal gang after all."

Anger rises, but I haven't the energy to do what I would have done before I got pregnant, so the nurses go without getting a piece of my mind. There's part of me that agrees with them, I did know what I was getting into. There was always a possibility that Truck's association with the club would come back to bite him. I just never expected it would actually happen. Not right here, not right now, when every fibre of my being needs him.

Though I've hoped, wished, looked up each time I hear footsteps, hoping to see my man walking toward me, I've been disappointed.

"Ready to go?"

It's not Truck, but Roadkill who walks in through the main doors to the ward. Good timing as I've just signed the discharge papers. He's a good looking man in his mid-twenties, and has a military bearing and short haircut which shouts his service. His eyes are always slightly haunted, as if he's seen things a young man should never see. He's a good choice if he's the one that's been assigned to me. Quiet, but thoughtful, and, to an ex sweet butt, respectful.

He helps me into a wheelchair, then takes me to the truck he'd brought. "Drummer sends his apologies. All the members are having an emergency church."

There's no point asking him what it's about, though I suspect the topic on the agenda is Truck. Roadkill's only a prospect and will know little more about club business than an old lady.

He's brought a bowl, which was thoughtful. The half-hour journey sees me being sick three times. He deals with it stoically, with sympathetic glances and grunts, but doesn't make a big deal about it. He drives slowly and carefully, but still the motion of the car upsets me.

Stopping at the clubhouse, he helps me out.

Sam is waiting for me, Sophie's wheelchair ready. My stomach hurts as it always does, my chest sore from retching. I wish I could walk, but my legs feel too weak to support both me and the baby growing inside.

"Allie." One word spoken conveying so much. A sad welcome home, commiseration that my man's not waiting for me. She must see my reddened eyes, but offers no words of compassion which, at the moment, would destroy me. She crouches down once I'm seated. "Wraith's back, he stayed in Nogales overnight. He's in with Drummer. They want to talk to you. You ready for that now, or want to rest?"

My eyes narrow. *Of course I'm ready.*

She nods. Then, without further delay she starts pushing me in through the doors of the clubhouse. It's busy for a weekday, every brother is here. *Looks like church has just let out.* It's a solemn atmosphere. Conversations already spoken in hushed voices die away when they see me coming in through the door.

I ignore the looks sent toward me, their sympathy would only make me break down, which I probably will do later. But now it's important I stay as strong as possible and find out what the hell's going on with my man.

Sam knocks on the door. Wraith opens it, and without a word comes around to take the handles of the wheelchair from her, and pushes me inside. Then he takes a chair to my left, and I raise my eyes to face Drummer sitting on the other side of the desk.

Wraith leans forward, clasping his hands between his spread legs. His gaze settles on me. "Some of the brothers took a ride to Nogales yesterday."

"Why?"

"Allie," Drummer says sharply. "What you don't know you can't tell. We'll give you the information you need, but you've been around the club long enough to know why there may be some things we hold back."

"Plausible deniability," I all but snarl.

The VP continues as though I hadn't interrupted. "The why doesn't matter, other than they had a hankering to go for a ride out."

There's more to it than that. Then I realise, it's my husband in jail. It's possible the police might want to speak to me. If I don't know more, I can't give anything away.

"Go on," I tell the VP.

"It was busy down at the border as it normally is."

I know that. It's one of the main crossing points between Mexico and the US.

"Truck saw something and went off on his own. Got into an altercation of some sort. Road said he hadn't seen exactly what happened, but suddenly Truck was surrounded by armed guards and taken off."

"Why? What the hell's going on?"

"We've just heard more details, Allie. Dart and Alex flew up to Tucson last night, and rode down to Nogales. As his lawyer, Alex was able to get in to see him."

Dart used to be a Tucson member. I knew him well, very well, or had until Alex, now his wife, had caught his eye. Dart's now the VP in San Diego, and the club paid for Alex to finish her schooling and get her law degree. To repay them, she acts as the club lawyer.

"What did Truck tell her?"

"There was a woman and her child. They'd come across the border. For some reason, a member of ICE wasn't happy with them, and called them back. Instead of turning, they'd started walking faster, the border guard ran after them. Truck saw him trying to stop them by yanking on the ponytail of the child, making her scream in pain and fright. She was about five years old, Truck said."

"He intervened?"

"Yeah, he got involved. His fist caught the border guard, hard. The woman and child got away in the confusion, and so ICE started on him instead. He started throwing more punches around…"

"Is he okay?" I don't give a damn about who he hit.

"Got bruising to his jaw, and his eye is black."

My hand covers my mouth. He can't risk his good eye.

"He's okay, Allie." Drummer says sharply, taking over the story. "But he's been charged with a Class A misdemeanour of assault."

"Which means?" That sounds serious.

"We don't know. Alex is talking to him about a plea. It's pretty clear he's guilty, but whether he should admit that or not, she'll discuss with him. There were enough border guards there witnessing it."

"He could just get a fine or probation," Wraith puts in.

"Or, serve time?" I hold my breath, waiting for the answer, hoping in vain to be contradicted.

"He could serve time." Drummer's stark declaration rings through the room.

~

TWENTY YEARS IN THE FUTURE – Drummer

"THE KNOCKS KEPT COMING that year, didn't they Drum? We'd have cancelled Christmas if it hadn't been for the kids."

I press my lips together as I think about the part I played in it. If I hadn't sent Truck to Nogales…

Peg glances at me. "Dark times, yes, but that wasn't the only one."

"We have had others," I admit.

Peg's jaw tightens. Showing he's on the same wavelength, his next question isn't unexpected. "Speaking of which, how's Ella doing?"

"She's doing okay, Faith too I think. Hit us all hard losing Slick."

"Another bad time for the club. Seeing a man brought so low."

It had been. Slick had given up cigarettes when Ella had gotten pregnant, trouble was, the damage had already been done. The lung cancer had spread before they caught it. He'd become a skeleton of a man. Slick kept riding as long as he could, but it beat him in the end.

"Ella proved her strength. She cared for that man right up to the day he took his last breath, and didn't break until the funeral."

I nod slowly. It was never good to lose a brother, but with Slick we had time to prepare, if you ever could for something so devastating. Ella had been welcome at the club, could even have moved back to the compound if that's what she wanted, but instead she and her daughter, Faith, had moved to Colorado to be close to Jayden and Paladin, and her nieces and nephews.

"Didn't think Pal would make sergeant-at-arms. The lad did good."

Lad? "That kid you're talking about is in his early forties now."

"I'll always remember him as the scrawny kid who prospected alongside Hank," Peg tells me with no apology.

"I did have my doubts he and Jayden would last, but they've still only got eyes for each other."

"They did it right. Waited a few years before starting a family."

I chuckle. *"Once they did, they didn't know when to stop. What is it now? Three boys and two girls?"*

"Think so, I lost count. Youngest was born last year, wasn't she? Think that was a girl."

"I think Pal should tie a knot in it," I observe. *"But if anyone can handle a big family, Jay can. We missed her babysitting when she left the club."*

"And now she's got Ella to help her. With that brood around, I expect it's a comfort now that she's not got her old man."

"Life moves on, doesn't it, Peg? We take it day by day, never expecting changes, but they happen just the same."

CHAPTER THIRTY-TWO

*A*llie...

"I want to go see him."

"Allie, you can't even walk. It's an hour and a half drive at least from here, you'd be sick as a fuckin' dog."

"I'll be sick sitting here doing nothing..."

"You can't help. You think it would help Truck if you struggled down to see him? He'll be worried enough about you as it is. He wouldn't thank me if I let you go to him."

"There's nothing you can do," Wraith supports his prez. "He was wearing his cut, so they know his affiliations, but luckily his gun was stashed in his bike which Road managed to get hidden out of sight. Prospects are already on their way to bring it back."

I don't give a damn about his bike. Only the implication that he won't be riding it home, as I say urgently, "No bail?"

"Bail denied."

A wave of sickness comes over me, I try to push it down. Wraith quickly passes me a waste paper bin. Ashamed, I use it. Drummer pushes a tissue across the desk and I wipe my mouth.

I get straight back to the matter in hand. "What's the worst-case scenario?"

Drummer shakes his head. "Alex says a twelve-month sentence could be in the cards."

The baby chooses that moment to kick, and I place my hand over where I felt the flutter. *Yeah, bad news for both of us, kid.* She could be nine months old by the time he comes out.

I can't. I just can't.

I thought I could hold off, break down when I was on my own later, but any strength I had seems to seep out, and I bend over, putting my head in my hands, unable to stop the sobs. Wraith's there, his strong arms around me. He doesn't seem to care my tears are dampening his cut.

"Let it out. Let it all out, Allie."

I grasp at his leather vest, but it's not the same as Truck's. He smells different, and it's not him I want holding me. When my tears start to dry up, I make an effort to pull myself together, and gently he eases away.

"It might not come to that, Allie. Let's hope he gets probation. Alex is going to be pushing his situation hard, that he's a vet, and was injured as a firefighter. She's hoping for leniency as it's a first offence. That's what you've got to do. Hope for the best, darlin'."

"But plan for the worst," I whisper.

I'm not stupid. Original members from Bastard's day had been in prison when I'd first arrived here. They had never come out. Rival clubs on the inside had got to them.

Truck's in danger if he does time.

Right now I want to be left alone, to try and process the implications of what I've heard today. To somehow come to terms with the idea I won't be seeing my man, or not for some time.

"When will we know something?" I twist in the chair, looking over the desk at Drummer.

"His initial appearance will happen this afternoon. That's when he'll enter his plea. Then he could be made a plea offer, or a court date will be set. Alex reckons if it goes to trial, it will just be in front of the judge as most misdemeanour defendants don't have the right to a jury trial in Arizona, especially in the case of assault."

"Is that a bad thing?"

The prez shrugs. "A jury could be swayed by Truck's good character. A judge might, but he's only one man. Depends how he feels about bikers."

"Will Alex represent him?"

"Yeah, she'll be his defence counsel."

I hadn't had much to do with Alex. When she'd lived at the compound I'd been a sweet butt, and, not knowing their embryonic relationship, had tried to get Dart into my bed. We'd steered well clear of each other after that incident. All I know of her is she's an attractive, curvaceous black woman. But if Prez trusts her, I'll need to as well.

"You can talk to her. Dart and his old lady will be staying at the compound for a while."

Yeah. Like she'll want anything to do with me. But I've no doubts she'll do her job and do it well. For the sake of Truck and the club.

Stepping forward, Drummer places his hand on my shoulder. "Try not to worry, darlin'. You've got to take care of yourself."

It's a simple enough saying, but one that hits me. How can I take care of myself? I can't eat or do anything that even involves standing as I'm liable to faint. All the things a pregnant woman is supposed to be doing, taking vitamins and shit like that is completely beyond me. I realise how much I'm going to miss Truck, and not just his company and support. It's the hundred ways he's taken over everything right down to the laundry, just getting on with what needs to be done without complaint, and without the need for recognition.

Now I'm reliant on friends.

As if to emphasise that, Drummer pushes me out of his office. His old lady is waiting outside.

"I'm sorry," my eyes go to Sam. "I'm going to be such a burden."

"Don't be stupid," she objects. "You'd step up for anyone else, wouldn't you? Lean on us for a while, we don't give a damn and are happy to help. After all, you're incubating a Satan's Devil."

"Told you before, woman," Drummer's hand curls around her neck, "not having women members of the MC."

Sam chuckles softly. "Marcia and I might have something to say about that. And when little ones like this are grown," she indicates my stomach, "things might have changed. You might have moved on from being a Neanderthal."

The prez barks a laugh. "That will probably be in Eli's time, not mine. Or so I fuckin' hope."

I highly doubt female members will be allowed even then. Eli's growing up to be the image of his old man.

Then, obviously, despite the brief interlude, my thoughts circle back around to Truck. I'm grateful when I at last reach the sanctity of my room, though it brings home that I'm really alone. There will be no Truck holding me as I sleep, no Truck rinsing the bowl after I'm sick, no Truck just doing the hundred and one things he does every day to show me how much I'm loved. No Truck. *He has to be released soon.*

I'm being selfish. Truck will be going out of his mind. As much as I'm missing him being here, he'll be feeling guilty for leaving me on my own.

What's he doing now? Are they certain he didn't hurt his remaining eye? I've watched far too much TV where prisoners are beaten in jail, *is that happening to him?* Is he scared, confused? Or angry and being difficult? *Don't make things worse, Truck. I need you here.*

My stomach growls with pains of hunger, digestive juices working though there's nothing inside. My oesophagus burns with the bile that's always close, my throat is sore, and my mouth dry. I'm uncomfortable, unable to find a good position to lie in, my back, legs, arms, head… everything hurts. I didn't realise how much the warmth of Truck's arms, his soothing touch as his hands massaged away my aches helped me to sleep, or that the low rumbling of his voice seems necessary to help me drop off.

I lie awake, worrying about my man. Praying that he'll come back to me safe, wondering how I'll manage to get through the next few hours, let alone days or weeks without him.

Don't let it be months.

I wouldn't survive.

"Try this." Sam lets herself in the next morning with an ice pop in her hand. "I've got several in different flavours. I know it isn't the same, but when I had morning sickness, I found these helped. The strawberry ones, in my case. You can try different ones to see if any work."

I've tried everything before, but it won't hurt to try it again. At least it's something to moisten my mouth.

"Any news?"

"None. Not yet."

Me asking for news and getting none in return sets the pattern for the next few days. Christmas comes and goes, I'm just pleased when it's over. Not that it made much difference to me, I stayed in the suite. I could see that Truck's absence had put a damper on everything, for the adults that is.

Each hour that passes I miss Truck more. I hadn't realised how much I'd depended on him for emotional as well as physical support. It's more than simply missing him being there, my heart is breaking at the thought of what he's going through. I know he'll think he's letting me down.

"I reckon Truck's pretty cut up about what's happened, Al," Sam explains in her reasonable way. "It's not that he doesn't want to talk to you, but that he can't. They're not allowing him calls. Alex says he talks about you, and is feeling so damn guilty he did something so stupid."

"He was trying to help," I justify his actions. "He wouldn't be Truck if he didn't stand up for someone weaker being abused."

Her lips press together.

"What is it, Sam? Tell me?"

She comes to sit beside me on the bed. "How was Truck with you?"

"Loving, kind, supportive," I list.

"He was different away from you. There was an anger inside him, like when he first came back. He hated that he couldn't control what was happening to you. Hated seeing you as you are. It tore him up. It was why Drummer sent him on the run, to give him something to do, and space to clear his head. No one predicted the outcome."

"What are you saying, Sam?"

She looks down, then back up. "That his anger got the better of him. There was a way to stop what was happening without using his fists."

It was my fault. I gaze at her while letting what she's told me sink in. That Truck's locked up is down to me. I finally speak, "If I'd had an abortion like he wanted, he wouldn't be where he is now."

"Don't think like that," she says sharply. "Truck wants that little girl with all that he is. What he doesn't want is you suffering all the time. That's what he found hard to cope with, and no one's blaming him at all. No one likes to see the person we love in pain."

Days go past. A week. Two. Then a month and still nothing's moved on. I've been back to the hospital twice, and when I'm on the compound, no one can do enough for me. Problem is, the only things I want that I've not got are my health and my man by my side.

Truck's still being held on remand with no bail, despite the various applications Alex has put in. All were turned down with some stupid excuse he was picked up close to the border, and could be a flight risk.

I'd had one phone call, which ended with both of us in tears.

"Allie, I'm doing everything I can to get back to you. I'm the model prisoner here. I take all the shit they dole out."

"How are you being treated?"

"Okay. I just want you."

"I want you," I whispered back.

"How you holding up, Allie?"

What do I say? Better would be a lie. Worse nearer the truth. But even saying 'the same' will cause him distress. "She's still growing, Truck. I had another scan last week."

"Can you get a picture next time? Get it to me via Alex."

"I can do that." With so many sonograms we've never bothered to take one home. Not even the first as most normal parents do. In the beginning it was because we weren't sure if the pregnancy would last.

"Fuck, Al. I can't stand speaking to you and not being able to hold you."

The call upset me, upset him. He didn't call again, but I don't know why, whether he couldn't, or because he didn't want to.

"Allie, there's someone here who wants to speak to you."

As Drummer pushes the door open, I get to my feet in surprise. My heart warming at the familiar face I see there, before a chill settles over me. There's only one reason Dart and Alex have come to see me.

They've got news.

"Allie." Dart walks straight in and over to me. He pulls me in close, but gently, as though I was made of china. He looks down at my bump, then critically into my face. "Damn, woman, never seen a pregnant skeleton before."

"Dart!" Alex admonishes loudly.

"Well? It's the truth." Dart isn't the slightest contrite.

I suppose what he's said is true. My gradual weight loss probably has less impact on people who see me every day.

"Have you heard anything." I turn to Alex.

"Sit down, Al," says Drummer. It's then that I know it's not going to be good news.

"Just tell me."

"ICE went pretty hard after Truck, Allie." Alex shakes her head. "I tried to list his good qualities, his service, how he got those scars and prosthetic eye. It wasn't enough. The judge saw his cut, and nothing beyond it."

"Tell me," I repeat, struggling to breathe.

Her eyes flick to Dart, then back to me. She takes in a breath. "Twelve months."

CHAPTER THIRTY-THREE

*F*ruck...

I stand, my hand on my pocket which holds the photograph of my unborn daughter. It's crumpled from the amount of times I've folded and unfolded it, staring at the image, trying to make out fingers and toes. My daughter. The baby who's robbing her mother of life.

It's too late now. Even if Allie changed her mind, she has to go ahead with the pregnancy. And I'm the fucking idiot who got himself incarcerated so I couldn't even be there to help.

It had happened in a blur. I saw that border guard yank back on the kid's hair, heard the child scream, and all my frustration and anger at the world welled up from inside. *How dare he hurt an innocent child?* Don't care what his excuse was, at her age, she probably didn't have a clue what country she was in.

They'd had papers, they'd crossed the border. It doesn't matter to me what their legal status was, or what reason he had for stopping them. Doesn't justify using force against a young kid.

My reaction though, had been extreme. I could simply have put myself between her and him, or have pulled him off. I hadn't. I'd punched him, then again. Surrounded by guards I'd continued hitting until I got a blow to my face which blurred my vision. Something from somewhere in the depths of my mind reminded me it was a very bad idea to risk my remaining sight and I'd returned to my senses. *A savage assault,* the judge had said.

Even at the time, part of me had realised the opportunity for violence had brought the last year to the fore. I hadn't so much been fighting the border guard, than trying to annihilate my demons. The fucking cat and the way I lost my life as I'd known it, then my helplessness over Allie.

I didn't kill him, nowhere close. He'd had my fist to his face and gut, bruising, but nothing broken. I came off worse, though nothing which caused any lasting damage. *Thank fuck.* It was a reminder that I need to be careful, the loss of my other eye would be horrific.

I'd been arrested and charged. The club sent me their lawyer, who was optimistic that with my background and being a first time offender, leniency would apply.

It all happened so fast. One minute Alex was talking me through what probation might mean, the next I was hearing the judge pronounce the maximum sentence for an assault crime. The judge threw the book at me, and then some. I'd not been expecting exoneration, but hadn't really thought I'd be locked up. Twelve months. At least the time I was held without bail gets taken into account. I've ten and a half months left to go.

Thoughts whirred around my head as I was led to the prison transport where I had my hands and feet cuffed.

I'll miss the birth of my baby. And I won't be there to support my wife during the last difficult months of her pregnancy.

I fucked up.

It's all I could think about as I was driven to the penitentiary as if I was a danger to society, instead of the man who'd spent his adult life serving the public and saving lives.

By the time I'd arrived, I was completely numb as I was processed, given orange to wear, and taken to a cell only to find

I'm sharing with an uncommunicative man called Hawker. Having placed my blanket and pillow on the lower bunk, Hawker having already appropriated the top, I sat with my head in my hands, trying to understand the change in my fortunes once again.

Allie. *Fuck.* How is she going to take me being locked up? Fucking good husband I'm turning out to be. Getting her pregnant when that's the last thing she wanted. Now I'm not going to be with her when she needs me most. Won't see my daughter enter the world. Won't be by my woman's side should any complications arise.

I shudder as a sob goes through me, my complete hand fisting on my thigh. *I didn't ask for any of this. Didn't asked for my injuries, didn't ask for my woman to be sick, didn't ask…*Or, did I? It was my temper that caused me to be locked up.

"You can cry. Doesn't mean you're not a man."

I glance up at the voice from the top bunk.

"Gets everyone when they first arrive."

I shouldn't be here. That's what I want to say. But I suppose everyone incarcerated feels the same way, that punishment is not what they deserve. That I was locked up is due to the cut that I wear, *wore* on my back. *Won't be feeling the weight of that for the next ten and a half months.*

Now Hawker's talking, I want some advice. "I need to call my wife." I want to hear her voice. Find out how she's doing.

"You sorted for that?"

They'd mentioned a ton of things when I was brought in. At the time I'd barely been listening. They may have gone through it, but it had gone right over my head.

"What do you mean?"

A sigh sounds from above me. "First time in the slammer?" When I answer yes, there's another drawn out exhale of air. I start to think he's not going to answer, when he asks, "She got a landline or a cell?"

"Cell."

"Okay, here it is in short. You make a list of ten people you may want to call. Have to say who they are, and their relationship to you. Any call you make has got to be made collect. To accept your calls on a cell, she'll have to register with a third party and set up a prepaid account. It's not hard to do."

If Allie can't do it, Drummer probably can help. But how to get her instructions? Would they allow me to set up Drummer as one of my contacts? He runs a one-percenter club after all, the one which made the judge give me the worst sentence he could. *Slade.* The name of my old captain comes to me. *They couldn't argue about him. He's an upstanding firefighter.* But do I give the station number or the cell? I doubt either would accept a collect call from the pen. I've hardly been communicable for the past year.

"How do I explain what she needs to do?" I wonder aloud.

Hawker answers. "Write her a letter."

A letter. Would she even be able to read it?

I'll have to get hold of paper and a pen first. I suppose I'll need to ask permission for that. Glancing up I see Hawker has opened a book and turned his back toward me. I take it as a sign he doesn't want to be bothered anymore.

That first night sleeping was hard. As days pass it hasn't gotten any easier. My mind circling through everything I've left behind. The what ifs overwhelming. *What if I'd never left to join the hotshot team? What if I'd asked for help earlier? What if I'd controlled my temper better, had never gone to that godforsaken place Nogales? What if Allie hadn't gotten pregnant? What if, what if, what if?*

The weight of how different my life could have turned out crushes me.

Until I realise my misfortune had led me to Allie. Would we have ever worked out had I returned as an able-bodied member? Or would I have been unable to get past seeing my brothers fucking her?

Would she have been equally upset seeing me with Pussy, Diva or Paige?

The what ifs and questions keep circling my head, and I don't come up with any answers, at least nothing that helps me adapt to my change in circumstances.

I find privileges need to be earned. Doesn't seem to matter what you're in for, or the length of your sentence, or what you might have been in the past. Here, you're little more than a number. Yes, I can make a list of contacts I can call, but unless I work, I won't be able to make them. That doesn't bother me at all, I'd rather be busy than have time on my hands. I suppose it was predictable, but learning my background, they put me on the maintenance crew, my job to check fire alarms and extinguishers. I don't mind how many hours I put in, if it means I'll be able to contact Allie.

It's the third day when I'm in the exercise yard, minding my own business, that I'm approached.

"You Truck?"

I turn fast. A man has come up on my left side and I hadn't been able to see him until he stepped in front of me.

"Yeah."

"Captain, or Cap." He grasps my arm and pulls me in for a back slap.

I return the greeting automatically, though I can't recall seeing him before in my life.

"Hey, Rat. Come introduce yourself."

Another man comes over and greets me in the same way.

Lines appear on my forehead. "I'm sorry, but...?"

"We're Wretched Soulz," Cap announces as though that should make everything clear. "There's a few of us around." When he sees my confusion, he grins. "You're new to all this, aren't you? Need someone to have your back in here, Brother. You were arrested whilst doing a job for the Arizona chapter, so you're one of us now."

"Yeah." Rat raises his chin. "You wouldn't last long in a place like this without backup."

A place like this is the penitentiary. Why I was sent to maximum security I have no idea. I presume it's the cut I wore on my back. I'd expected to go to the county lockup instead.

Rat is examining me carefully. "That a fake eye, man?"

Being bothered about someone noticing is the least of my worries now. "It is," I confirm.

"Fight?"

Shaking my head, I explain how I lost it. Then answer the questions which always follow. Well, why not? I've got all the time in the world for the next ten months. That I'd been a fire-fighter always impresses people, but fuck knows why. It's a job just like any other.

When I've satisfied their curiosity, Cap jerks his head in the direction of a corner of the exercise yard where no one else is. When we get there, he leans back against the wall, the sole of one boot resting against it. A few more men who Cap nods to form a barrier between us and the other prisoners. I take it these are more Soulz.

"First timer like you needs to know what you're up against." He breaks off, and nods to a group of bald headed and tatted men who are standing together. "They're the Aryan Brother-hood. White supremacists. They think Wretched Soulz are on their side, so they don't give us any trouble. They see you're with us? They'll leave you alone."

The men look ugly, not their facial features, their hard expressions and the sneering looks they're sending to a group of blacks on the other side of the yard. Not people I'd normally associate with, but if I've got to cosy up to them to stay safe inside, that's what I'll do. I've already let down Allie, not going to hurt her more by doing anything to risk me not going home.

"To stay on their right side, we don't mix with black or yellow." Rat adds an observation of his own.

"Some of the guards you need to watch out for. When they get bored, they'll try to get you riled."

"Won't work," I say, adamantly. As a result of losing my temper, I ended up inside. For the sake of my wife and unborn child, I've got to put a lid on that now. "I want out of here. Not going to do anything to fuck that up."

"Not always that easy. Guards can make shit up. Harder to do when you're in a group, so take the protection that's offered."

"You Soulz?"

One of the Aryans has broken away and stepped toward us, Cap's friends or brothers if my suspicion is right, have parted to let him through.

Cap answers for me. "Close. He's a Devil."

"Ah." The newcomer looks suspicious.

"Soulz speak for him." Rat puts himself between the man and me.

"Saw you limping. Cops do that?"

"Man's a fuckin' hero," Cap explains. "Lost his eye and fucked up his leg fighting a wildfire."

"Firefighter?"

I nod.

Luckily, he, too, seems impressed.

Suddenly an altercation breaks out on the other side of the yard. A Hispanic is surrounded by the Aryan crew. His friends have backed off, leaving him heavily outnumbered. As the scuffle continues, my new *friend* walks away, presumably to join it.

"Don't get involved," Cap warns, speaking quietly out of the side of his mouth. "Keeping yourself to yourself is the best way to stay out of trouble."

"Why aren't the guards getting involved?" The man's now on the ground, and I wince as I see a foot hit his side hard.

Rat shrugs. "It's their entertainment. They will, eventually."

They do. But not before the man's taken some punishment.

This life on the inside is going to take some getting used to.

CHAPTER THIRTY-FOUR

---

*A*llie...

"Allie, you listening to me?"

I nod. My mind as usual imagining all sorts of evil happening to Truck. "Sorry Drummer."

"I know you want to visit him. But there's the car journey, and you're so weak. Do you really think you're up to it?"

Whether I am or not, I can't stay away. "I've got to see him, Drummer."

He stares at me for a moment, hearing the need in my voice, then nods without further argument. "I'll get us both on the visitation list, and I'll come with you."

I'm so grateful to him that I won't be walking into the penitentiary alone. "Thank you, and thank you for everything else. I'm sure Truck will appreciate it too." I hope I'm saying the right words. I seem to be doing everything on autopilot, unable to accept Truck's not coming home.

Drummer's lips thin. "Not my first rodeo. Had men go inside before. Sort of got a mental checklist of things to do. Set up prison accounts so they've access to money inside. Arrange for old ladies to be able to accept collect calls."

"Will he be alright in there, Drummer?" There's more

309

emotion in my voice now, as I realise the danger an unprotected biker on the inside could be in.

"I've arranged protection for him, Al. Got the Wretched Soulz on his side. He'll be fine." He tries to inject certainty into his voice, but he can't hide the risk that my man's facing.

"Thank you," I repeat, inadequately. Pleased Truck's got backup, but terrified because he needs it.

"I'll get Hound to take you back to your suite." He stands, goes behind my wheelchair, and pushes me out into the clubroom.

I feel so damn useless and helpless.

There's a disbelieving air of quiet about the club. Brothers milling around, looks of sympathy sent my way, a shared misery that one of their own won't be coming home for a long time. Truck's incarceration being a stark reminder of what could happen to any of them just because they belong to an MC. If Truck with his good record behind him didn't get clemency, it doesn't bode well for any of them. The women, their faces are full of horror, and of understanding of how I must be feeling.

Hound takes over from Drummer. "You want to stay here, or…"

"Just take me back, Hound." My voice sounds like I'm choking. I just want to be on my own, to wallow in my misery.

He pushes me inside my door, and I dismiss him. Gingerly I pull myself up and stand. When they'd brought back Truck's bike, they'd brought back his saddlebags. I'd just left them in the corner, waiting for him to come home and put them back in their rightful place on his bike. Now, my eyes land on them, and I have the urge to open them up, to see what's inside, to touch articles that belonged to him.

With one hand to my stomach I get down on the floor and kneel beside them, my hands caressing the black studded and fringed leather. No plastic paniers for Truck, the traditional looking bags more the look he liked for his bike.

The contents of the first one are mundane, a tee shirt, his old riding gloves and a spare pair of safety glasses. I feel a piece of paper at the bottom, and after pulling it out and unfolding it, I have to smile. It's a selfie of he and I that I remember him taking, just before I got sick. We're lying in bed—suitably decent—both smiling widely, our eyes creased. *What was it he'd said?* I can't for the life of me remember, but it was something that had made me laugh. *Happy. We look happy.*

I raise my eyes and stare at the bare wall. *I can't remember what happiness is.* All I've been focused on for the last few months is the misery I've felt. *I didn't even send him off with happy memories.*

What can he be feeling now?

I open the second saddle bag, and here's where I find it. His gun. I pull it out, it's weight feeling heavy in my hands, but settles there all too easily. *Had I unconsciously been searching for it?*

I can't do this.

Not alone. When I thought Truck would go to court and then come home, I had something to hold onto, the thought I wouldn't be giving birth on my own. It's not only him that's been given a sentence, it's me as well. Only mine seems insurmountable. I've been condemned to continuing the rest of this terrible pregnancy without my man's support. I've been penalized with the promise of giving birth without my partner beside me. My penalty to raise my baby during those first nine months alone.

Truck had been right. I should have had an abortion. How could I do this to me or to her? With Truck beside me I thought I could be strong, put up with the needles and poking and hospital stays while they rehydrate and supplement my wrecked body. Now? It's too late. I've no desire to help myself, yet alone the life growing inside me.

What kind of mother would I be on my own?

But I've no choice. I have to go on. Or…

The gun twists in my hands as if someone else is holding it.

Placing it on my lap for a moment, I search the bag for

ammunition, find it, and load the weapon. I've not been around bikers without learning how to do that, even practiced shooting at targets, though I've not felt the need to own a gun myself.

"Allie?" A voice calls and there's a knock on the door.

I don't answer aloud, but mentally I'm screaming, *Go away.*

"Allie?"

My desire to be left to take the only option I feel I have remaining is taken from me when the door opens. *Should have locked it.*

"Allie!" This time my name isn't a question, but an exclamation. Sam drops to her knees beside me, and gently takes the gun from my hands.

"Give it back," I round on her. "It's Truck's."

"So it should be stored in a gun safe while he's away. What the fuck are you thinking, Al?"

"That I can't do this. Not without Truck. It's too hard Sam, I just can't."

Placing the weapon well out of my reach, she takes out her phone and taps on it. Then she comes back and hugs me to her. After a moment she puts a supportive arm around me. "Let's get you up."

I snort. I'm so fucking useless, I can't do anything without help. But I accept her assistance to get onto the bed.

Sam glances at me, taking in the sorry sight of what I've become. Sadly she shakes her head. "I can't begin to know what you're going through, not in so many ways. Sure, I can sympathise with being sick, I had morning sickness a bit, more with Zane than Eli. But nothing compares to this. Drummer was there for the birth, helped when the babies were young. I know what you're thinking, Al, and if I was in your place, I'd probably be at my lowest point too, but it will get better."

"Will it?"

"I know three months sounds like a long time, especially knowing you'll suffer every day. But it will pass, Allie. I'll be your birthing partner if you like, hell, any of the old ladies will be there to help you. And when your daughter is born? You certainly won't need to feel alone. Everyone will pitch in and help you."

"You make it sound easy," I scoff.

"It's not easy," she contradicts. "This is the hardest thing you'll ever do. Was hard before, but without Truck? Can't even imagine that for you. You've just got to take it one day at a time."

"Every day is so hard, Sam."

"I know, hon, I know. But it will turn out right. You just have to have faith. Hope in you and faith in your man."

She looks around my room. "I'll tell you the first thing we're going to do. Drummer and I are moving you into our spare room up at the house. We're not leaving you alone, Allie. You need help, and I'm going to make sure you get it."

I shake my head, not wanting to impose. I know what's behind her offer. "I'll be alright. I promise I won't…

There's a knock at the door. When it opens, it's Drummer. He's walking in with a deep frown on his face. "Got your text," he confirms to his old lady.

She nods toward the gun. He picks it up and puts it in his belt. Then, surprisingly, with a soft look he usually reserves for his woman, addresses me, saying, "Let's go get you settled."

Even I know you don't argue with the prez when he's set on what he's going to do. But the implications of his statement don't really sink in until he's wheeling me up past the suites, and to the top of the compound where his house was built. I can remember it going up, three houses being erected at the same time. Viper and Bullet using it to practice their fledgling skills on —skills now being used to build a shopping mall in town. Drummer's house, the sweet butts' and the one now occupied by Joker, Lady, and their adopted daughter, Maya which had originally been reserved for visiting officers. There's quite a village here now, with Peg's house, Rock's and Heart's, and I can see foundations being laid which will become Blade's.

Sam's in the lead. "You'll stay in the third bedroom, Allie.

Zane and Eli are sharing for now." When she opens the front door, Drummer pushes the wheelchair inside.

I haven't been in this house for a few years, but I have been here before. Well, not since Sam came along. I think it's best not to mention that to her, and of course, I'd not been given a tour. Drummer's bedroom, the kitchen table, and the living room wall is all I really remember.

The spare room I've not been in before. It's pleasant enough, I think as I look around.

"I'll get your clothes brought up, and your bits and pieces from your bathroom. You've got an en suite here. Feel free to use the kitchen, or come and join us in the lounge. This place is your home now, for as long as you need it."

It's happening so fast. "I don't need this, Sam. I'll be fine…"

"Al, you do. It's a choice between staying here with us, or having a prospect in the suite next to yours. You need support, and help around if you want it, as well as company." And no time to eat a bullet or look for some other way out is what she's saying.

"We'll leave you to get settled. If you want anything, just call out, okay? I'll be around."

"Sam, don't put yourself out for me."

She shrugs off my concern.

A little later I hear the opening and closing of doors, and then the excited voices of children. I listen to her sorting them out, admiring how natural she is being a mom. *Did she have a good example to follow? How does a woman know what to do?*

Far from being annoying, the sounds of a normal household going about their day is comforting. After another predictable bout of sickness, I snuggle back against the pillows and look at the positives instead of the negatives. How lucky I am to have people who care about me.

Sam had told me I had to have hope and faith it will all work out.

I have to have hope.

Hope in me that I can carry on and faith that my man will stay safe. Hope that he will return to me. Hope that my baby will be okay. So much to have faith in.

My daughter kicks and I smile. *Hope.*

If we all get through this and come out the other side, perhaps that should be her name. Hope. My lips form the words as I try it out.

TWENTY YEARS IN THE FUTURE – *Drummer*

"OF COURSE, the worst was to come."

"Truck, being sent down?"

"Yeah. There we were, Allie, a woman we all respected, and damn it, loved, so ill she looked close to death at times. It wasn't only Truck who thought she should have an abortion. I thought she should too."

"She looked so poorly. I honestly didn't think she'd survive, Drum. No one would have questioned it if she hadn't have carried on."

"She couldn't have. Not without the club."

"Club's family, Drum. No two ways about it. When one of us needs help, we all rally around. Allie wasn't just an old lady, she had been club for years prior."

"Club's loyal." I raise my chin toward him. "Someone goes against us, we hit them hard. Someone does us a favour, we owe them back."

He looks at me sharply. "You thinking of Ella again?"

Sometimes I think he can read my mind. "Yeah. At the beginning. She helped us out, paid a heavy price for it. Such a cost, we didn't know at the time."

"Slick thought she'd walked out on him," Peg muses. "Damn near broke him when he found out what had really gone on."

"Women are strong, aren't they, Peg? We treat them as delicate flowers that need nourishing, but hell, what Ella went through would have broken any man."

Peg gives a low chuckle. "Slick didn't want anything to do with her, but you insisted."

"She'd gotten hurt and more so than we knew then, doing something for the club. Whatever she needed help for, we were going to be there for her. Whether Slick wanted to or not."

"That trouble was Jayden, and the child grooming ring she'd gotten involved with. Fuck, even now it kills me to think of it. Fourteen-year-old kid should never be subjected to that."

"It started the war with the Herreras," I point out. "But even if I'd been able to see into the future, I wouldn't have done things different."

"Couldn't have walked away, Prez. Not from that."

Now Slick's gone, and Ella's proving how strong she is all over again. Building a life for herself in Pueblo.

"Club rallied around Dart's woman too."

"For her son, Tyler. We organised that run for him to raise funds."

CHAPTER THIRTY-FIVE

_T_ruck…

"D'you play chess?"

Hawker has continued to remain mostly silent. If I ask him anything, he's likely to answer with a grunt, if he makes any attempt to reply at all. So his question takes me by surprise.

"I used to." For a moment a wave of sadness passes over me. Hammer and I used to play from time to time at the station house, a way of passing time between calls, part of what's lost to me now, even if I wasn't locked up. I bring myself back to the present. "Can't say I'm a master."

Hawker chuckles. "Then you'll be easy to beat." He swings his legs off the top of his bunk, then takes a chess set down from a shelf. He picks up one black and one white pawn, and places his hands behind his back. Then, when he brings them to the fore, I pick his left. It's black.

He slides his white pawn to e4 in a typical opening move. At first, I'm not paying attention, and all too fast I find I'm at checkmate. The next time we play, I take it more seriously, using more minutes to decide my next move. When this time it's me who eventually is able to pronounce that I've blocked him completely,

I realise my head has been on the game, and for a while at least, not worrying myself sick about Allie.

"Thanks," I tell him gratefully as he puts the chess set away, having declared there's no time for another match tonight.

He shrugs. "You're good. We'll play again."

Anything. Anything, to stop what I have no control over going around and around my head.

Apart from the evening chess matches and the work I throw myself into during the day, another distraction to stop me thinking all the time, I find myself bored. I'd spent months willingly cooped up in my apartment, but now that someone else holds the keys to my freedom, I find it difficult.

That I'd been in the Army helps accept the routine, but I long to be out on my bike, breathing fresh air. A sentiment I share with Cap and Rat, and a few other Wretched Soulz I've now been introduced to.

When visiting day comes around, it's a break in the monotony to find someone has come to see me. Drummer.

I stand as he enters the room, my hand starting to rise, then realise I'm not allowed to shake his. *In case he palms something and hands it to me.*

As we sit, he examines me carefully.

"You doing okay?"

I shrug, then ask what's on my mind. "How's Allie?"

"She wanted to come with me, but she's taken bad again. She's back in the hospital." At my look of increased concern, he hurriedly adds, "Nothing other than what she's normally in for. Just topping her up as she says."

"Drum, I wish I was there for her."

"Know you do, Brother. Must be fuckin' hard. But it is what it is, and we have to deal with it. You can rest a bit easier though, Sam and I have moved her in with us."

That's good to hear, but I wonder why he thought it was necessary. *Is there something he's not telling me? Is she worse than he's said?* "Anything happen?"

"No," he answers fast. "Just thought it was best. She's sick and miserable with it, and giving her time to brood won't do her any good. Got a few numbers to give you, by the way. Mine, Alex's if you don't know it already, and Allie's. I've set Allie up with a pre-paid account so you'll have to use that number. At least you'll be able to talk to her yourself."

That's great news he's sorted that out. I feel relief I'll be able to hear her voice, but my spirits immediately fall, knowing speaking to her for ten minutes at a time isn't going to be long enough to say what we need to. "Tell her I love her, Prez. Tell her I think of her all the time."

"You think she doesn't know that, Truck? Guess what, that was her exact message to you."

"Prez, she needs money, needs to get prepared with baby shit…"

"Got that in hand, Brother. Paying her your share. Knew that would be okay with you."

"I'm so fuckin' sorry, Drummer…" There's a wealth of emotion in my words.

"Know that too. What's done is done, Brother. All you can do is keep your nose clean in here."

I nod. I'm trying. I've been attempting to stay out of the fights that break out in the exercise yard and keeping my distance from trouble. I don't want to be in here any longer than my sentence. That's long enough.

I ask about what else is going on back at the compound to be polite. I don't really care. All I'm concerned about is my wife, and how much I wish I was there for her.

Drummer seems to know that it doesn't matter what he's actually saying. His voice alone reminds me there's a world outside these walls, a world I'll get back to one day, however far away that might seem.

Visiting time over, I go back to my cell. I lose at chess that night, something I don't find surprising.

Two days later I get my chance to call Allie.

"How are you doing?"

As she tells me a little better as she normally does when she comes out of the hospital, something that doesn't last long as she soon slides back down that hill, the sound of her voice makes me close my eyes and gently put my fist to the wall in frustration. *I want to be with her.*

"Truck?" she asks cautiously.

"Yeah, babe?"

"I've thought of a name for the baby."

Well, that's a start. If she's thinking positively, maybe she's a little less uncertain about the future.

"What are you thinkin'?"

"Well," she chuckles softly, "Sam told me I had to have hope everything would turn out right. I had to have hope. So…Hope."

Hope. I try it out in my head, picturing a miniature Allie and calling her by that name. "I like it."

My time's up. My brief contact with my wife over. She says she'll come visiting next week, even though I try to dissuade her, knowing how much the journey will take out of her. Selfishly, I want to see her, to see with my own two eyes she's not gotten worse, but it's her I have to be strong for.

Forgot who I was dealing with as she insists she'll be there.

I find I'm looking forward to it.

Carrying my dinner tray through the dining hall, I'm distracted when I hear a man mention his wife just had a baby. Another man stuck on the wrong side of these walls as his woman went through labour. *That will be me,* I think to myself, as I make my way over to Cap and Rat. It's all my own fucking fault.

A man knocks into me. My drink spills and goes all over him. It's only soda so he's wet, not burned, and he'd approached on my left hand side.

"Sorry, man. Didn't see you."

"You fuckin' blind?" he snarls.

"On that side, yeah," I reply, unthinking. It draws his attention to my false eye. Swearing and muttering, showing me his middle finger, he stalks off.

Such an insignificant interaction, I think no more of it.

Next morning in the exercise yard, I notice the man who'd been the victim of the accidentally spilled drink staring at me, but think little of it. Okay, if I hadn't been distracted maybe I'd have been looking around more carefully, scanning left and right to make sure I stayed clear of everyone. But my mind hadn't been on what I was doing. No damage had been done though, just an affront to his dignity.

What I hadn't yet learned was dignity is everything.

Suddenly, I find myself surrounded.

"Gonna teach you a lesson so you'll have to be more careful where you're going." He's in front of me, surrounded by a group of men, making sure we're out of sight of the guards. In his hand is an implement which makes me shudder. It's a razor blade attached to a handle of a toothbrush. "Gonna make you match. You're going to need another glass eye."

"Might make him look where he's going," another man jokes, encouragingly.

Oh fuck, no.

Mentally thanking Peg for teaching me how to fight using the strength in my right hand side, I throw the first punch and put up a struggle.

Hands start clutching me, and while I kick, punch, do everything I can, I'm outnumbered and gradually they're overpowering me.

That razor blade is getting closer and closer to my one remaining eye. The fleeting thought goes through my head that I don't know these men, and apart from the spilled drink, I've done no wrong to them. Why are they targeting me?

I wasn't this scared while that house was burning down around me. Wasn't this terrified when I felt my own flesh burning. Then, I'd had hope, and didn't know how badly injured I'd been. Now I'm only too well aware of what that blade could take away from me. *The rest of my sight. I might never see my baby.*

Suddenly there are shouts. Fists causing the air to brush by my face much like the wind on my motorcycle. Hands holding me relax then release me entirely.

Cap's standing next to me, kicking and shouting, and members of the Aryan brotherhood are circling me too. The man and his gang are being beaten back.

Finally, when it's clear there are winners, the guards appear wearing masks, the reason for which becomes apparent when canisters are thrown and we all start stumbling around, just trying to evade the tear gas which makes us choke and blinds us. My eyes sting so badly I begin to wonder if the guards have done what my enemies failed to.

It's while I'm completely disorientated, I feel hands once again take hold of me. I flail automatically, with blurred vision, I can't see who's got hold of me. In my panic I imagine that razor blade is heading for my face and get my arm free to put it up defensively.

In doing so I hit someone, and get knocked so hard on the back of the head the blow stuns me and I fall to the ground. My last conscious thought is ironic. When I served, the military was banned from using tear gas in warfare, yet it's still allowed on domestic soil.

Tear gassed for a fight I didn't start was bad enough. After I came to and as I was hauled to my feet and led away, realising by that time it was by the guards, I wasn't taken to a hospital room, nor back to my cell, but instead to a six foot by nine foot room, with a window too high on the wall to look out of.

At first I was concerned with nothing more than splashing water onto my face and trying to wash all residual gas out of my eye, removing my prosthetic and washing the socket behind it. I continue until the stinging begins to fade, then, when I blinked rapidly and my vision began to clear, my initial panic starts to subside as my sight regains clarity. I'd been terrified I'd damaged the sight in my remaining eye. Bemoaning that I don't have a saline solution to clean it properly, I replace the prosthetic.

Then, once my breathing starts to slow, I look around me and wonder what the fuck had happened to me now.

There's a concrete slab that serves as a bed, covered only by a thin mattress. I sit down, putting my head in my hands as the realisation hits. *I've been put in solitary.*

Why? Did they lock up everyone who'd been in the brawl? And why me? I was the one who'd been attacked, not the instigator in any way at all. Any punch I'd thrown had been in self-defence.

It must be a mistake. I'll be back in the general population soon. I try to focus on playing my next game of chess with Hawker, thinking of new moves I could perhaps call into play, rather than worrying someone has locked me up and thrown away the key.

I'm a big man, this cell is small. I can't see out. It's not long until I feel there's no air in the room, and I'm beginning to suffocate. My vision blurs, my hands are covered in sweat. *I'm trapped. What if there was a fire?*

Realistically I know there are procedures for that, and that I wouldn't be left to burn to death. But my irrational mind sends me back to being trapped in the house with the world on fire around me.

Smoke. All I can feel is smoke burning inside my chest.

That's the aftermath of the tear gas, fool.

But even as I tell myself that, my body's already going into fight or flight mode, adrenaline rising with no release. I attack the only object I can, the door, flailing on it with my fists and yelling.

I'm successful. It brings two guards.

"Shut up in there."

"Where am I? Why am I here?"

"You're in solitary."

That answers one question. Not the other. "Why? And for how long?"

"You were fighting."

"I was defending myself. They threatened my eye." When they appear unsympathetic, I try to protest. "Look, I was minding my own goddamn business."

"Yeah, yeah. Heard it all before. Bet you're innocent of the crime they put you in here for as well."

I am not getting through to them. "I want to talk to one of your superiors. I want to call my lawyer…"

But I'm addressing thin air. They've shut the viewing pane and I listen to their footsteps as they turn and walk off.

Something tells me they won't be returning any time soon, nor will they bring another officer to talk to me.

Fuck.

CHAPTER THIRTY-SIX

*A*llie...

I lived with the sweet butts for years, then moved in with Truck. Thinking back, there was never a time when I had a place to myself until Truck was arrested. In the circumstances, being alone hadn't helped. Living with Sam and Drummer is definitely better.

It's just little things, the sound of people moving around, hearing voices outside my door, hearing the excited shouts of the kids or the more unwelcome crying and tantrums—usually from Eli, Zane seems to be more easy going, taking after his mom—that reminds me I'm not on my own.

Sam's even adjusted her routine for me, though I told her I didn't mind. But the smell of coffee brewing is certain to turn my stomach, so she's avoiding making it in her kitchen, instead topping off her caffeine levels down in the clubhouse.

When I'd been a whore I'd observed Sam from a distance, viewing her with the same suspicion we'd afforded to all the old ladies who'd come in and stolen the best of our men. Now she's taken me under her wing I can assess for myself what a good counterbalance she is to Drum, and just how good she is at being the president's old lady.

She'd told me straight, I can cry, rant, rage in her presence, her back is strong she can take it. No matter how bad I'm feeling, I should not hold it back and try to act polite as a guest in their home, but to consider the space they've allotted me as my own. When it all gets too much, I can lean on her.

I've come to appreciate that more than when I'd just uttered a quick thank you in response. It wasn't just words, she really meant it.

It's not only Sam either. If she's not around, there's normally another old lady visiting. Sophie, I've become quite close to too. Ella as well, though I don't see her so much as she lives off the compound. Darcy's always been really friendly, though her second baby's just been born, a girl named Lisa, and I don't see so much of her. Marcia, ready to give birth any day now, is tired all the time with swollen ankles.

I have spent time assuring Mariana and Tash that my condition only affects one in a thousand pregnancies, and even of them, I'm one of the worst cases according to the doctor. Neither of them currently have children, and I'd hate that what I'm going through would put them off in the future. Of course, Mariana's got her hands full with Drew, her teenage brother who is intent on joining the Satan's Devils, while she saw a good education in his future.

I spend time trying to persuade her he can have both.

"That easy?" she questions one morning.

"If you keep butting heads, Mariana, then Drew's going to rebel. Tell him he'll have your complete backing if he gets a degree first."

"I still don't like the idea of him joining the club. Look at what's happened to Truck. We all know he wouldn't have been sent down were he not a member."

I can't argue with that. "If you make a deal with Drew, then he'll go out and explore the world. Might see something he likes better. It's obvious why he's so intent on joining the club."

She raises her eyebrows, so I continue.

"He thinks the club saved both you and him from your father. We all know he's no longer around to be a threat. In Drew's eyes, he wants to give something back."

"You think?"

So she's been thinking he just likes the idea of living free and riding bikes. Perhaps I, as a stranger, can provide an alternative view.

"Yeah, that's what I think. Why not get Mouse to have a word with him? Show him there's other ways of paying it back. Mouse's own trade is example enough of that."

"You may have a point."

I do, but I can't press it. Instead I have to rush out. *Christ, I wish this sickness would stop.*

Mariana has restarted her training to be a nurse. She might not have experienced pregnancy but is pragmatic. She competently follows to hold a damp cloth to my forehead, and pass me paper towels. I gave up any embarrassment at vomiting in front of others a long time ago, but her no nonsense support is welcome.

The day after I'd given Mariana something to think about, I hear raised voices from the direction of the kitchen. It's Sam, and her stepmother, but I can't distinguish what they're saying. I don't try to listen, it's none of my business.

I go back to flicking through a magazine, trying to make out the words. The coloured overlays are helping the letters stay put, and I'm practicing my reading, painfully and slowly, phonetically mouthing the words until they make sense. I've been thinking again, what kind of mom would I be for Hope if I couldn't read to her?

It's when Sam shouts out, "Sandy!" and I hear the clacking of heels approaching my room, that I pay more attention.

A knock, then, without waiting for permission, my door opens. There stands Viper's wife, Sam's stepmother.

We've successfully avoided each other since I became Truck's old lady. Easy enough to do as I rarely go to the clubhouse any more, the smells in there mean I can't stay for more than a moment, so what's the point?

"Sandy," I greet her, cautiously.

Her eyes crease as she views me. Then observes, "You're all baby."

I huff a quick laugh. Her observation is accurate. There's not much of me anymore, just this huge basketball shaped bulge in my stomach.

"Can I come in?"

"Sure." She seems pleasant enough. Behind the open door I see Sam hovering cautiously. I raise my chin, knowing she'll have my back if this turns nasty. She backs away, but leaves the door open a crack.

Sandy sits on the bed. "I always wanted a baby. A child of my own. I thought about how wonderful it would be to be a mom, never considered what a toll pregnancy might take. Looking at you, I might have had a lucky escape."

Could her opening gambit be an olive branch? I'll take it as one until there are signs it might not be.

"I'm just unlucky, Sandy. Most pregnances are fine."

"Yeah, so that's why Becca's puking up every five minutes."

"She's pregnant again? Rose must only be what, eight or nine months?"

Sandy chuckles. "Rock's quite proud of it. Oh, she's nothing like you, just a bad case of morning sickness."

"Tell her to be careful," I say fast.

"Yeah, they've been to the doctor." What she means is they got checked out because of what's happened to me.

We could sit here and discuss pregnances on the compound until the cows come home. But I'm already feeling tired, so look her in the eye. "What do you want, Sandy?"

She's quiet, studying her hands, then she says, "Wouldn't wish what you're going through on my worst enemy, Allie. Your sickness, your man being in the pen. No woman deserves that, however much I might hate them."

"Hate?" At least she's giving it to me straight.

"I didn't like what you did. Achieving what all the sweet butts aim for, getting a biker to themselves." That's not how it was. Truck's the man for me, I didn't set out to go after him. But I keep quiet, wondering where she's going with this. "Most men were single, Allie. They didn't have an old lady, they were free to do what they wanted, but my man was taken."

"Okay," I interrupt, sitting up fast, then have to wait a second until the dizziness leaves me. "Let's get some things straight here. First, I, and the other sweet butts, were given food and a roof over our heads to perform certain services. Those services being to make ourselves available to any man who wanted to use us, and, in most circumstances unless it was something outrageous, in whatever way he preferred." Dollar's demands sometimes veered in that direction, but didn't quite go over. "How would Drummer have taken it, if we'd refused a member? Wasn't our decision to make, Sandy."

It was all down to her man. But I don't add that, I'll let her fill in the gaps.

"He never fucked you, did he Allie?"

"Never." I give her the truth. "Nor any of the others. You know his predilection, it was, we suspected, what he didn't get at home. And now he's stopped."

"Because he was ashamed his daughter saw him for the first time with his cock down a sweet butt's throat."

I bark a laugh, and after a moment, she joins in too. "Yeah, it wasn't his finest moment."

Poor Viper, I muse. Hasn't had a blow job in three years or so. And he did so like them, I can attest to that.

"Why don't you... Sandy?"

She shudders. "I don't like the taste."

I think for a second. "Strawberry flavoured condoms."

"What?"

My shoulders rise then lower. "Use flavoured condoms, then

he gets his rocks off while you imagine you're sucking on a lollipop."

"My God, Al." She stares at me, then bends double with laughter.

Again, I just shrug.

"You know, I was wondering what to get him for his birthday."

Now I'm chuckling loudly as well.

Sam chooses that moment to appear at the door. She seems genuinely delighted not only to hear me laughing, but Sandy too. "What's the joke?" she asks.

Sandy and I freeze, look at each other, then we're back to helplessly laughing again.

When Sam throws up her hands and walks off, Sandy leans in. "Please don't ever tell my stepdaughter what we've just discussed."

"I won't," I promise, wondering if she'll ever report back that my idea worked.

Having mended the rift with Sandy, it's one more worry eased. Now I've just got to wait out Hope's arrival, and my old man's return. Then I can truly take my place as an old lady.

Marcia gives birth to her third baby—not another set of twins, so many lost money on their bets. They call her Alexis. She brings her to see me, and I stare at the bundle in her arms in wonder, wondering whether Hope will come out looking as plump and healthy as that, worried she probably won't as the odds are against it. It worries me slightly that the sight of a newborn baby doesn't make me feel maternal in any way. Then I forget my thought as I have to rush to the bathroom.

My chats continue with the two new mothers. One topic we discuss is labour. Apparently Darcy and Marcia said it was easier the second time, especially as Marcia hadn't been trapped on the compound in the middle of a raging wildfire. The first time, they told me, it had been more painful, and they'd talked me through what to expect. This pregnancy has been so difficult, I haven't been focused on the mechanics of what happens at the end of it, just want it over and done.

Pain. Something I've suffered all these last months. I'm not particularly frightened, just hanging onto the hope that after I go through that, I'll have a baby and feel well again.

All I've got to do is keep going until it's time to bring Hope into the world. I'll have to survive with the minimal contact I have with my man. Odd phone calls when he's allowed to make them are the only connection.

It's not enough. I need to see him.

I've planned for the journey, sick bowls and bags will be within easy reach. I've had yet another visit to the hospital to get rehydrated and my electrode level topped off. Tomorrow's a good time to attempt a trip off of the compound.

Drummer's prepared me. I won't be able to hug my man, but at least, I'll be able to see him and satisfy myself he's okay. I'm slightly concerned he hasn't rung over the last few days, but force myself not to worry, knowing phone calls are privileges which can easily be taken away.

It's the evening before that Drummer comes in. I'm sitting in their living room, having a chat with Sam, my enthusiasm that I'll be seeing Truck tomorrow, overflowing.

When Drummer starts talking, it takes a moment for his words to sink in.

"What the fuck do you mean, I can't go and see him?" I take a deep breath, trying to calm myself. Drummer has to be wrong. "I'll be fine, Drummer. I'll…"

"It's not you, it's him. No, he's okay, Allie," he adds the last quickly to dispel any worry I might have. "He's been put in solitary, and isn't allowed visitors."

My hand covers my mouth. "Why?" I rasp out from behind my fingers.

"Chaz, the president of the local Wretched Soulz?" It's a question to confirm that I know who he's talking about. I nod to show I've heard of him. "Well, he's got a couple of men in there, and has been having words. Truck pissed off one of the other prisoners, who decided to retaliate by taking a razor to Truck's good eye."

I feel blood draining from my face, but again, Drummer continues fast. "He's good, Al. Got enough protection and nothing happened, but there was a fight."

Truck in solitary for fighting?

"How long is he going to be there for?" A week or two delay, that I can cope with.

Drummer sighs. "It's hard to tell, Al. Word is that it's not punishment, but for his own safety. The gang he is up against may not give up. But that could be bullshit. These prisons are a law unto themselves, and they can do whatever they fuckin' want. Alex, even in her official capacity, can't get an answer."

Someone's taken hold of my hand. It's Sam. "At least he's out of the general population. He won't be able to get hurt if he's confined."

But I see the look in Drummer's eyes. "He won't do well, will he, Prez? To be confined in a small cell, not able to see anyone." We've had men inside before, I've heard what solitary is like, and it's not pretty. Men who join a biker club are the type who love freedom. "Will he be able to call?"

Prez shrugs. "He might. They did allow him to speak to Alex."

So he might not. As Drummer had said, prisons seem to be a law unto themselves.

How much more will we have to bear? Truck's injuries, my disastrous pregnancy, him getting locked up in the first place, and now he's in solitary for God knows how long. Not only am I preparing for a baby alone, I won't even be able to see him, perhaps not even talk to him.

I miss him.

"Allie," Drummer crouches in front of me, taking both of my hands, "I know this is fuckin' hard for you, and for him too. Fuck knows I wish there was more that could be done to take this burden from you. I know it's no help at all to remind you, time marches on. You will both come out the other side."

"It's so hard, Drummer. I feel it's me, you know? That I'm being punished for being born, and Truck's suffering because he aligned his stars with mine. What if it hadn't been me that night, before he left for California?"

"Nothing to do with you, Al. Truck's cards would still have fallen the way that they have. Without you, he may not have come back to the club."

"Without me, he'd still have his freedom."

"Nah," Drummer shakes his head. "Where Truck was at before you went around calling? I suspect he might well be dead."

"You could equally say Truck's been bad for you," Sam interjects from my side. "If you hadn't fallen for each other, you wouldn't be in the state that you are. You wouldn't be fighting as much as you are to keep this baby alive inside you. Do you really want to wish your relationship with Truck away? And Hope too?"

"Of course, I don't," I cry out.

"Then why do you think Truck would be wishing he'd never jumped into bed with you?" Drummer raises his chin at his woman as he takes over. "What doesn't kill us, Al, makes us stronger. Reckon that's the thought you've got to keep in your head."

It's a good thought, but, as I run my hand over my swollen stomach, I wonder if Hope will be the death of me after all. Truck being in solitary is just one more obstacle I have to face, and worrying about how my man is coping, along with everything else, might be the death of me yet.

CHAPTER THIRTY-SEVEN

*A*llie…

"A month, Drummer. This is getting ridiculous."

Prez sighs, sweeping his hands back through his hair. "Alex is trying, Allie, but the harder we push on the legal side, the more they're digging in their heels."

"It's affecting him badly." I think back to the all too short phone call I had with him last night. Even Truck's voice sounds weaker, as if he's half the man he'd been before. "This good time credit is bullshit as well." I don't need to see Drummer's reaction. Alex has explained if Truck had been sentenced for a year and a day he'd be liable for a reduction in time served for good behaviour. As he's been sentenced for exactly twelve months, he'll have to serve the full time, though that does include time already served when he was denied bail.

"The right to appeal has been denied as well," Drummer reminds me.

Alex had tried to get his sentence commuted on the grounds the judge allowed Truck's affiliation with the club to overly influence him, but he'd sentenced the maximum he could give him and no more, so hadn't overstepped the bounds. My man is still inside, and will be for another nine months and two weeks.

Everything is one blow after another. At some point I expect to be knocked down.

Thinking about Truck takes some of my mind off my own misery. My back is aching, my feet swollen and sore. I'm still being sick tens of times every day, still going into the hospital regularly. In fact, that's where I'm going today.

Drummer stands. "I'm worried about you, Allie. You look very pale."

I must look bad if I appear worse than normal. As I go to stand, I wobble, my weight, front heavy, overbalancing me.

Sam's there to help me, her worried eyes meeting Drummer's for a second, before coming back to me. "You take care of yourself, Allie. When you're back from the hospital, we'll look through the things you need and get ordering." Sam sounds eager. She's been encouraging me to get stuff ready for the baby, but not wanting to risk tempting fate, I haven't wanted to buy anything. I've also delayed a baby shower, though the old ladies wanted to arrange one for me. Enough shit has gone wrong over the past few months for me to have no confidence in any outcome.

"I'm coming with you today," Drummer announces, as he settles me in the wheelchair.

That surprises me, normally a prospect would drive me to the hospital, then come and collect me when I was discharged. The prez is a busy man.

"There's no need, Drummer."

"Every need," he contradicts, as he starts wheeling me down the track. "I couldn't look Truck in the eye if we didn't take care of you, Allie, and your time's getting close."

One month to go. One more month of being sick and poorly.

"How are you feeling today, Allie?"

Tired, sore, nauseous as usual. Faint. A normal day.

I'm sick, of course, on the journey, but Drummer takes it all in his stride. He appropriates a hospital wheelchair for me, and we go directly to the ward and the bed that indeed seems to have been reserved for me.

I'm prodded, poked, hooked up to an IV, then Drummer leaves with promises to pick me up the next day. The same routine that I've become used to.

It's the next morning things take a turn for the worst. I can't feel the baby moving. When I guiltily realise I haven't felt her for a few hours, I call a nurse over in consternation.

"How long, Allie?"

"Since last night," I realise belatedly. I'd been relieved she'd been sleeping a few hours. Now I feel mortified. Should I have said something earlier? What if I've been through this for eight months, and it's all been for nothing?

"I'll get your doctor."

Luckily the doctor's office is only in the next building, and she's here quickly. I examine her face to see whether she's worried, but can't read anything. She's friendly, calm and business-like.

But she wastes no time. They bring in a handheld sonogram, then follow that up with the portable machine. There is a heartbeat, but even to me, it sounds different.

"Baby's in a little distress," the kindly doctor informs me. "Think we need to prepare you for an emergency C-section."

What? "You said it was better to carry her as long as I could."

"Allie," she starts while turning and issuing a few instructions before looking back to me. I know almost all the medical staff she's talking to from the number of times I've been admitted. I think this makes it close to thirty. "Allie, you've done what you can. You've given her the best start you could, now we can care for her better if we deliver her."

Deliver her? Today? *I'm not ready.* More importantly, is she? "Will she be okay?"

"We'll do our best."

I read between the lines. There's a chance she won't. A chance she won't have developed sufficiently to survive on her own. That despite the care they've given to me and her, something could have gone wrong.

The hurry they are in worries the hell out of me. Things move so fast they are soon giving me a general anaesthetic. Then I know nothing at all.

When I come around it's like trying to reach the top of a pool having dived in too deeply, but the water is as thick as molasses. My head pounds, as I try to distinguish voices talking around me.

What's happened?

My baby. It suddenly hits me.

"Sir, you can't be in here."

"Try to get rid of me." I hear Drummer's voice challenge. "She needs someone with her."

"She's in recovery," a female voice says soothingly. "She'll be waking any time now. You can see her as soon as she's come around."

"Why the fuck is she getting blood?"

"She haemorrhaged. It's not unusual with HG."

"She going to be okay?"

"She's going to be fine."

She manages to make a sound, nothing more than a groan, but it gets their attention. Despite the nurse's futile efforts to shoo him out of the room, Drummer steps forward and takes hold of my hand.

"Hope?" I stutter out weakly, staring into his eyes. If anyone's got bad news, I want him to be the one to tell me. My boss. My friend. "The baby?"

"Baby's doing as well as can be expected." The nurse comes to my other side. She glances up at the machine beeping beside me. "She's in an incubator in neonatal care. She's a little underweight and needs help with her breathing."

"Can I see her?"

"As soon as you're recovered from the anaesthesia, yes."

"Will, will she be okay?"

"I'll take this." Dr Cassidy steps into the room. "You've done well, Allie. You've got a lovely baby girl."

"Is she okay?" I repeat, anxiously. "Tell me straight, Doctor."

"She's got a condition called Apnoea. She doesn't breathe so well at the moment as her brain's respiratory centre isn't developed as much as it would have been if she had gone full term. It's not uncommon, but she will need to be in an incubator until she can breathe on her own. She's undersized, but that's what we expected."

"Will it affect her long term?"

"The long-term prognosis, I can't give you. But we'll be monitoring her closely over the first few months."

The nurse is putting a blood pressure cuff around my arm.

The doctor looks at the results, then says, "I know you're anxious to see her, Allie, but you need to let the anaesthesia wear off a bit first. We need to get your strength back up as well. Sir, she needs rest."

Drummer looks up from the chair by the side of the bed where he's been perusing his phone. "And I'm here to make sure she gets it," he replies in a tone broking no argument.

"But…"

"If I was her husband, would you make me leave?"

"No, but…"

"I'm here in his place as his proxy. Not going to let a brother down."

There are some battles you win, some you don't. I would smile if my head wasn't aching so much and a myriad of concerns weren't on my mind, but Drummer's not going anywhere.

"Rest," he tells me sternly, as the medical staff at last leave me alone.

I close my eyes, anxious for the time to pass so I can see my baby for the first time out of the womb, wondering how I will feel when I meet her at last. I no longer feel pregnant, and the nausea seems to have already faded. I feel strangely empty, the movements I'd become accustomed to, gone. My abdomen hurts, but I don't feel like I've given birth. Where were all the contractions and pushing Darcy and Marcia had told me about? My baby was taken from me with no effort on my part. One minute she was there, the next, she was not.

Surreal.

I'm a mother.

I don't feel anything like it.

When I next wake I can feel a change in myself. My head's no longer pounding, there's just a dull ache, and, for the first time in seven months, I don't feel the need to be sick. Drummer's place has been taken by Sam.

She smiles when she sees me awake. "Drummer's gone back to the club for a while," she explains. "He's going to try to get a message to Truck."

Truck's a dad.

"Do you think they'll allow a visit now that he's got a baby? Surely he's entitled to meet her?" They can't keep me from visiting, can they?

Sam looks at me sadly. "I don't know, Allie. He's in the pen, not in jail, and still in solitary. They make the rules, not us. Now," she brightens, "if I get a wheelchair, think you're up to visiting your daughter?"

I should be delighted, happy. Instead there's a dread deep inside me as I ask myself a serious question. *Am I going to be like my mom? Am I going to blame Hope for all she's put me through over the past eight months? Am I going to blame her for being the reason my husband is languishing in prison?*

I'm scared of my reaction once I see her. *Will love bubble out of me? Will I feel a need to hold and protect her, and keep her safe? Or will I feel nothing at all?*

As Sam takes me down to the neonatal unit, I'm terrified of what I might find. I've been warned she's wired up to machinery and I won't be able to hold her right now, so I'm sure I know what to physically expect, but it's my emotional reaction I'm most concerned about.

I expected a small baby. She's tiny, looking more like a doll.

"She's absolutely beautiful, Allie." Sam sighs, her eyes glistening.

Is she? She looks wrinkled. Her eyes are scrunched shut, and her fists are clenched tightly. A machine quietly beeps regularly by her side.

She's mine. Truck and I made her.

"I can't, I don't..."

Sam takes my hand in hers and squeezes it tightly. "It's a shock. You weren't expecting to meet her for another four weeks. You weren't awake for the birth. No wonder you're having trouble adjusting. Don't beat yourself up over it."

"I can't believe she's mine."

"That she is, Allie. She's your daughter."

I feel nothing. No connection at all. I try and appear interested as the nurse talks me through her condition, but she could have been speaking to someone else for all the attention I paid.

When she finishes, I turn back to Sam. "Can you take me back to the ward?"

"Are you sure?"

I nod, swallowing down a huge sob. My fears about going through everything that I have, and then not to want the result at the end have come true. I've never been overly fussed by the babies in the clubhouse, never oohed and aahed with everyone else. Never wanted one of my own, and now that she's here, it just emphasises how wrong it is for me to go through this alone.

If Truck was here, maybe it would be different. I might feel his joy and share it. As it is, I'm terrified. How the hell do I look after something so small when I feel nothing for it?

Sam's reluctant to leave me, but I just want her to go.

When, at last, she gives me space, I dissolve into tears.

I should never be a mother. I just don't have it inside me.

My phone rings. I grab it. My eyes widening as my voice rapidly accepts the call.

"Al? How are you? How's the baby?"

"Truck," I sob. "I'm sorry. She came early."

"You with her? How is she doing? She going to be okay?"

"I'm not with her. I can't, I don't know, Truck. They say she'll be fine. She's got tubes all over her, helping her breathe. She's so tiny, Truck." *Focus on the baby. That's what he wants to know about.* "You're a dad, now, Truck."

It's the wrong thing to say. "How can I be a fuckin' dad when I can't even see her? Can't hold her. Fuck, Al, it's killing me."

"Truck…" But what can I say?

There's silence for a moment, then he asks. "How are you, Al? Now she's here, are you still feeling rough?"

"Rough from the anaesthesia, but already, in other ways, I'm feeling better." I must be. I fancy a coffee.

"You gonna feed her yourself?"

It's something I hadn't thought about. The idea fills me with horror. She's already taken so much from me, how can I give her more? Having missed the birth, I don't even think she's mine. And, anyway, how will I be able to while she's hooked up to those machines? "I don't know."

Something in my voice must have worried him. "All this has been so fuckin' hard on you, Al. Hate that I haven't been there with you. Blame myself so fuckin' much. But you ask for help. What you've been through has been traumatic, then to have the baby while you were knocked out. One thing after another, isn't it, babe? But reach out, there are those that can help—my brothers, their old ladies, and the professionals. If you're feeling low and don't immediately take to her, from what the doctor warned me, it's quite normal and natural."

Is it normal? To not immediately fall in love with my daughter?

"Listen, Al. Don't hold it inside. Don't feel guilty over something you have no control over. Ask for help."

I hear another voice in the background, the words that I hate. *Time's up.*

"I love you Allie, so fuckin' much. So fuckin' proud of you for giving our baby life."

"I love you, too, Truck."

"Kiss our daughter for me."

Then he's gone. Kiss her for him? I haven't even touched her for me yet.

CHAPTER THIRTY-EIGHT

*A*llie...

I spend five days in the hospital after the birth. Three, I'm told is normal after a c-section, but they also wanted to get my eating under control. After months of living on nothing but sips of liquid, my stomach has shrunk. Well, on the inside that is. On the outside it surprises me I'm still carrying much of my baby bump as well as stretch marks.

Luckily I'm no longer a sweet butt. I'm hardly desirable.

Hope is doing well, her episodes of apnoea are decreasing, already she's stronger, breathing on her own. The hypoglycaemia she suffered from at birth has been controlled and her sugar levels have risen due to the intravenous feeding.

My body, wasted and wan, still tries to follow the rules of mother nature, and my milk comes in on schedule, but despite the nurses trying to encourage me, I just didn't want to attempt to feed her or even express milk. Deep inside, I worried I'd produce an insufficient quantity or quality to feed her. At least with formula you know you've got it right.

I don't trust myself to do anything for her. When they put her in my arms, I hold her loosely, waiting for the magical bonding to start.

It doesn't.

If it wasn't for Truck, I would consider having her adopted.

When I return to the compound, life hasn't changed much. My operation and need for healing means I still have to take it easy for another six weeks. Drummer, of course, assigns Hound back to me, and he drives me daily to the hospital to see Hope. Personally, I could have gone without the visits, the nurses seem to be taking care of her well enough, but they seem to be expected of me.

Hope is ready to come home before I'm prepared. The women have rallied around. I've been loaned a crib and all the accessories. A bottle steriliser and new bottles have appeared. Clothing, so much clothing, and a lot for a pre-term baby that she'll hopefully not need for long. Things that would have been given at the baby shower, they assured me, though I'd waited too long to have one.

Two weeks after she arrived in the world, she comes home.

The club, naturally, throws a party.

Though I'm still tired and sore, in many ways it's welcomed. Hope is cooed over, cuddled by all the women who call them-selves Auntie, and quite a few of her many uncles get in on the act too, while I look on, just happy I don't have to start trying to be a mom right away. I'm worried enough that I won't be able to do it.

Except—I'm surrounded by people who all know me. Men who I look on as friends, most of whom I've known intimately. Women who know what it's like to give birth, and how to look after a baby.

So why do I feel scared and alone? My sense of detachment increases.

Food is handed to me, after looking at it, seeing it moving, I put it aside. The voices seem overly loud, men who are just being jovial appear threatening.

My fingers curl into my palms, my head feels light, my

breathing speeds up. There's only one thought in my mind, to get out of here. Out into the open away from these people.

I stand, wobbling as I feel faint, and almost launch myself toward the door.

Suddenly, strong arms are around me, lifting me and carrying me out. Gently he lets me down to stand on my own feet and supports me as I struggle to get breaths of fresh air into my lungs.

"Steady, Allie. Deep breaths. In, out, in out. That's it." All the while a hand is stroking my back. "You're okay, Al. It's a panic attack. Frightening, I know. Just concentrate on your breathing."

"Is she alright?" Sam asks sounding anxious.

"Yeah, I'll take her back to the house."

"Okay, Drum. Al, I'll bring Hope up with me in a minute. Give you a chance to rest."

Rest. Like I want more of that. "I'm alright now," I lie. Stupidly, as anyone could see I'm still shaking.

"Come on." Drummer obviously is intent on me not going back into the clubhouse. His arm around me, he leads me up the track slowly with regard to my still healing stomach muscles and my residual weakness.

Instead of taking me into my room, he sits me on one of the sofas, then places his ass next to mine.

"How you feeling now?"

"Better." And embarrassed. "I'm sorry, Drummer."

"Nah. It was probably overwhelming."

But it shouldn't have been. This is my life. My home. My adopted family around me.

"You know what triggered it, Allie?"

"This is going to sound crazy. The food, it looked like it was moving."

"Truck warned me what to expect." He's surprised me, and my eyes open wide. "What do you mean, Truck warned you?"

"What you went through was traumatic, Allie. And trauma

leaves aftereffects. Hallucinations and panic attacks? Classic symptoms. You getting flashbacks, too?"

"Only every time I see food and when Hope cries. It makes me feel sick, though there's no need any more."

"Classic PTSD as I said."

"But that's what soldiers get, or people who've been raped, or abused." I scoff. "It doesn't happen to someone who's had a difficult pregnancy."

"Difficult? Fuckin' *difficult?* Darlin', watching what you've been through these past months, seeing you fight as hard as any soldier in a war, seeing you battle against your body every day of the past two-thirds of a year, no one could doubt what you've been through isn't trauma. Now you're coming down, learning to live again without the constant worry, of course it's hitting you hard. Add in lookin' after a baby? Fuckin' impossible to do by yourself."

They'd told me my symptoms would go when the baby was born. Not that it would continue to affect me.

Drummer half turns, his hand comes under my chin, and tilts my head to face him. "We're going to get you help, Allie. And don't doubt for one fuckin' moment, everyone here understands. You need help with Hope? You don't even need to ask."

"My mom hated me."

"You don't hate Hope. You're scared you can't be a good mom, but darlin', that's perfectly natural. Ask Sam or Sophie, hell, Becca, Ella anyone. It's always hard, but in your case, with her being so small and fragile, more difficult than most. You feel guilty as your sickness didn't give her the best start in life."

"I hate Truck for not being here, Drummer. He should be here with me." There, I've voiced it aloud. "I hate Hope for leaving me in this state, and I hate myself for hating."

"Some of that's on me, Al. I didn't realise Truck was dealing with it too. Thought sending him out on a ride would help and focus his mind on something else. Didn't expect his anger to bubble over."

"Not your fault, Drummer."

"Maybe, maybe not. But I owe it to him to make sure you're cared for in the same way you'd be if he was here with you."

I feel so messed up, it's hard to see how anyone can help. But slowly, gradually, with the aid of the therapist Drummer arranged, I begin to come to terms with my new world. Because I'm not breastfeeding, I'm given medication that takes the worst of my anxiety away. I sleep better, and begin to eat again, slowly regaining my weight. Sam cares for Hope as she would if she was her own, encouraging me to be involved, but not forcing me. As I get rest and am able to switch off, gradually I begin to do more things for her myself.

But I still go through the motions mechanically, doing the things I believe I should do, but don't take any pleasure in.

One day, I'm changing her. One moment feeling like this is all I'm reduced to, a feeding and cleaning machine, when I look down at her face to see her smiling. Smiling. *At me.*

"Hey," I try, my face cracking a smile back, the first in months. "You happy, baby?"

At the sound of my voice, her eyes try to focus on my face. I lean closer, "Hey, baby girl." The smile reappears and widens as my hands tickle her sides.

For the first time, voluntarily and not to feed or change her, I pick her up, move her to the chair I use to sit and give her a bottle, and just hold her in my arms. A sudden wave of emotion comes over me. So unexpected, so strong and overwhelming that for a moment I feel the symptoms resemble the beginnings of a panic attack.

Oh my God. I love my baby.

I love Hope.

"Allie, you there?"

"Yeah, Roadkill. In here."

When the prospect appears at the door to the bedroom, I cock my eyebrow at him.

"Can you spare a moment? Drummer wants to see you."

"Yeah. Give me a minute." I don't want to move right now, but if Drummer's got news, I want to hear it.

I quickly rummage through the stuff the women had given me for Hope, and come up with a baby sling. I figure out how to use it, and soon am entering the living room where the prospect is waiting.

"Oh? You taking her with you? I was going to stay." Roadkill has actually proved to be a good babysitter, it's because he comes from a big family he's said.

But today, I don't want to be parted from her.

Instead, he accompanies me down the track, pausing outside the suite one down from the one I used to live in before Truck went inside. He indicates with a nod of his head. "Drummer's in there."

"What?" Then I shrug. Perhaps Sam and he have gotten fed up with having a third child in the house. But if he wanted me to move back, I'd have appreciated a warning to get my stuff packed. And he's in the wrong bloc for that.

I walk inside the main entrance to find him waiting just inside. For once, Drummer seems less sure of himself.

"Al," he starts, then stops, his eyes going from Hope to me. "Al," he tries again. "Don't read anything into this. You can stay with Sam and me as long as you want to. Just did this for when your man comes home. You can decide with him what you want to do, but if you want to have a house built alongside the others, that will take time. Thought this would do for you in the meantime."

"What do you mean, Drummer? This is Peg's old suite."

"Exactly," he confirms. "Thought it would make a home for you and the kid when you're ready." He opens the door with a flare to the room that has been converted to a sitting room, the bathroom off to one side becoming a kitchenette. It's been freshly painted and so clean you could probably eat food off the floor. Best of all, a comfortable sofa and chairs have been arranged facing a brand new flat screen TV, and there's even a small dining table that could be pulled out. Though she's far too young to use it yet, a highchair is placed against the wall.

I glance around, then walk back through the door and take the step that leads to the bedroom. This has been newly decorated as well, and is laid out just the same as Truck's, but with a big space in the middle where a bed would be, though a brand-new crib has been set up by the wall . Both rooms have balconies looking out over the mountains.

I turn around slowly, balancing Hope in the sling. "You did this for Truck and me?"

"It's to tide you over, until you settle on your own place. Or, you can stay here indefinitely."

The idea of having a house built with a bedroom for Hope and a small enclosed yard similar to the ones the other houses have sounds amazing. But this would certainly do for now.

Drummer sees the small smile on my face, but doesn't mention it. He does appear pleased by my reaction and presses his point. "Viper and Bullet will construct the house to your specification. I can get them to show you some plans so you can get some ideas if you like?"

But it's not just me who'll be moving in. "I'd better wait for Truck for that."

He laughs. "As long as it's got a place to watch TV, a fridge to keep beer and a garage for bikes, that's all a man's interested in. Whatever you come up with Al, Truck will just be pleased to live in it with you."

I flash him a quick grin as I'm expected to.

"As I said, Allie. Don't think we're chucking you out. You want to move in here? Do. You find it's too much? Come back to us."

I glance down at Hope, fluffy down covering her head. Then back to him. "It's time I tried to cope on my own, isn't it?"

"You've come on leaps and bounds. But only you know if it's too soon. You say the word and I'll get the prospects to move Truck's bed and your stuff in."

I sigh heavily. "I just miss Truck, Drummer. Seems we had no time together before he was sent down. Now I can't even visit. He can't meet his baby."

Drummer's mouth hardens. "Darlin', no, you can't. He's still in fuckin' solitary."

"They can't keep him there for another six months, can they?"

"Who knows, Al? Who knows what the fuck they can do."

Having found a connection with Hope, I decide Drummer's timing had been perfect. I move into what's more like an apartment rather than two adjacent suites, and start settling in and making a home for myself and my daughter, always aware of the third in my family that's missing. I try to push my worry for him to the back of my mind. Selfishly, while I know Truck must be going crazy, I tell myself, at least in solitary, no one can physically hurt him. If I'm going to tackle being a mother alone, it's me and Hope I have to focus on, and try not to drive myself mad worrying about him.

It's about a week since I first left Drummer's and Sam's, and I'm getting myself and Hope ready for the outing I'm not looking forward to, when a knock comes on the door.

Hope's fussing and I'm trying to soothe her, so I just call out for whoever it is to come in.

"Oh, hi, Sandy." I'm still slightly nervous around her, though she's been nothing but pleasant over the past few months.

"What's the matter?" she asks, nodding her head at the crying baby. I notice there's concern but no censure, nothing to suggest I'm an incompetent mother.

"I don't know."

"Want me to take her while you finish getting ready?"

I'd rather use the excuse I've got a fussing baby and not go, but should put in an appearance. I accept her offer, and return to the bedroom. I haven't worn makeup in months, but I put a little on to make myself presentable. The sounds from the other room lessen, and when I return, Hope's asleep in a triumphant looking Sandy's arms.

I mouth a heartfelt thank you.

"You look nice."

I don't, but I'll take the compliment.

"This is an important day for Heart. I'm glad you're going to support him and Marcia."

I shrug. If I could get out of it I would, but Sandy is right. Heart's doing something he'd said he'd never do, making it official and marrying Marcia. It's a year later than planned though, as she wanted to give birth before walking down the aisle. The time's come now as Marcia's regained her figure. Unlike myself, I don't think mine is ever going to come back.

We were all surprised that Heart popped the question, he'd always been so adamant he'd only ever have one wife. But he'd changed his mind after visiting Crystal's grave for the first time three years after her death. It had given him closure.

He'd asked, and apparently Marcia had told him she was pregnant with yet another miracle baby at the same time.

Today's the day they're tying the knot, and all the club members are going to be there for him. It will only be a reminder that my husband is not.

"I thought you could come with me. I'm hardly dressed to go on the back of Viper's bike."

"You look lovely," I remark, sincerely. She does. "I was going to go with a prospect…"

"Come with me," she says quickly. "I know you'll be missing Truck. Stick with me and Viper, we'll keep you company."

I'm not certain, we're not exactly bosom buddies.

She suddenly grins widely. "We owe you."

What?

"For your advice. I've found I like mint."

She's totally lost me. My brow furrows, then, I howl with laughter remembering the advice I'd given her. *Guess Viper's getting his blow jobs now.* That would explain why he's grateful.

The wedding goes smoothly for a bunch of raucous bikers. Amy looks beautiful as a bridesmaid, and little Isabel takes her role as a flower girl seriously. Jacob's a ringbearer and Sam, as matron of honour, stands to the side holding Alexis. Marcia looks so happy and beautiful it makes me tearful, but as Sandy sniffs too and hands me a tissue, I realise everyone will think I'm just being sentimental, while the truth is I'm missing my man so much I'm hurting.

~

TWENTY YEARS IN THE FUTURE – *Drummer*

"YOU SAY Truck and Allie were the darkest days, Drum. I think you're wrong."

"Dragged the club down for well over a year, Peg. Lived everyday seeing that girl go through shit that would drag anyone down. As for Truck, we didn't know what the fuck was going on, it was hard to get word in or out of that prison."

"I hear you, but what about Heart?"

I think back for a moment. Heart's ended up with four good kids and a wife he adores, and who makes a fucking good old lady. Tend to forget she was once a cop, and that we weren't always as fond of her as we are now.

"You're right," I tell him, after a moment, as I dredge up memories of Heart not always being as happy as he is today. "Crystal, his first wife, was killed. He'd been in a coma himself and missed the funeral."

"We were planning his at the time."

Again, I nod. That he'd come around was the best fucking news we'd heard. Trouble was, he'd come back a different man. A man who hadn't wanted to live.

"He'd tried to get us to take him out."

He had. Done something so bad we couldn't have him in the club. "I sent him out on the road for six months."

"He nearly didn't return."

"Marcia was his lifeline."

"I worried about him all the time, Drum. We'd had no contact for months until Marcia told us he was in danger. Do you remember going to LA to rescue him?"

Do I. Fuck. I bark a laugh. *"Marcia shouldn't have come with us, but remember that rat bike she had?"*

Peg snorts. *"Fuckin' bike looked like something dragged out of a scrapyard. But it went like a bomb, I'll give it that."*

"Marcia brought Heart back to us."

"Remember the wedding? Took three years for him to get his head out of his ass and marry her."

"Yeah."

CHAPTER THIRTY-NINE

*F*ruck...

There's barely enough room in my cell to stretch, but I do push ups, well, mainly using my right arm, but taking the opportunity to keep building up the strength in my left. *Won't be any help to my baby if I can't hold her.* I do sit ups, a hundred and more at a time. I exercise until my body is screaming and I'm exhausted.

I try to tune out the sound of people crying out from other cells around me, repeating the mantra in my head. *My woman and baby need me. I can't give up.*

I've always been a man of action, playing any sport where I was invited onto a team, shooting balls if there was no one around but myself, joining the Army, then the fire service. Until I was injured, I'd never sat around and been lazy.

Maybe if I hadn't met Allie, if she hadn't drawn me back to the club, if I hadn't had rediscovered the delights of riding, I'd be better placed to handle this shit. But she had. If she hadn't, I'd probably not be in prison at all. *If she hadn't, I wouldn't have her and a baby.*

Solitary is bad. A small cell, and hour out each day, that's all, and even then with only uncommunicative guards around me. I use my free time to exercise my legs, my goal not to lose any of my hard-fought-for mobility.

It would have been dreadful enough were I not haunted by the fact I'd failed the woman I'd promised to be there for, knowing how ill she was, and all because she was growing my baby inside her.

As the days pass and the weeks go by, hope fades that I'll ever get out of this cell. I hadn't wanted to come to prison at all, but the thought of being in the general population now is far more welcome than I'd ever have thought. Playing chess with Hawker or talking bikes with Cap, those seem like freedoms far beyond me.

A guard let slip something one day when he sneered at me about being a hero firefighter. Seems they don't like a public servant gone bad, I'd crossed a line and become a criminal. That, as well as the protection of my remaining sight, a reason to keep me incarcerated within a prison.

There's always a light on. Always guards checking you've not managed to slit your own throat, days and nights pale into insignificance. It would be hard to count days even if I was inclined to. At first I try, scratching marks on a wall, but even then, losing count.

My gut feel it was far too long, but also, far too soon, before Allie had the baby, the girl she'd decided to call Hope. Yeah, well, she has faith, where I've got nothing.

The prison got the news to me, and I was allowed the privilege of a phone call. They'd been scant after that. One I'd used to call Drummer and warn him to watch out for her.

I've nothing to do but sit here and ruminate on what's going on in the outside world, a place I can barely imagine any more. My whole existence is these four walls which seem to close in more every day.

My mind conjures up images to haunt me. Allie being unable to cope with Hope, or of her feeling like her mother and resenting her. I don't even know if she's breastfeeding or not, whether she's taking care of herself, let alone the baby. Worst of all, I wonder whether now she's not pregnant any longer, whether her past needs have returned to her, and, unable to wait for me, she's warming someone else's bed. I'm only too well aware of prison rights. No one at the compound would probably think any the worse of her…

"Stop that!"

The command roared as the door opens and guards enter. I hadn't been aware I've been beating my head against the wall until they pull me away and I see the bloody imprint left by my forehead. For that I've earned four hours in a straitjacket *until I come back to my senses.* As if being unable to move will help me do that.

I'm going slowly mad, I know it. Even if the guards speak to me, I'm no longer able to respond in anything other than grunts.

Some sense of self-preservation, the knowledge I'll eventually get out, even though my brain can't process the notion, keeps me going. Keeps me putting that insufficient and tasteless food into my mouth, and drinking the water given to me even though I feel my humanity has been lost.

Days pass, though I barely notice, spending my time curled on the mattress or huddled in the corner with my knees drawn up and my head bowed. My will to exercise gone.

Punishment within punishment without reprieve and no contact with the outside world. My head-banging attack had lost me that privilege, and they refused to give it back. *Speaking to my wife had apparently upset me.*

It's not talking to her that's doing that.

Days turn into weeks and weeks into months, the monotony driving me crazy. The thoughts in my head, envisioning Allie or Hope dying or dead. *Surely they would have told me?*

All I can picture is the last time I saw her, life leeching out of her as she struggled with a pregnancy I wish she'd ended. I wouldn't be here if she had.

She's had my baby. I'm a father.

But here, in this cell, I don't feel like a dad. A true father wouldn't have abandoned the mother of his baby and left her to face everything alone. A real dad wouldn't have lost his temper and ended up here. A man who deserved a wife and child wouldn't slowly be going mad, wouldn't dread picking up those responsibilities, when he's lost the will to live.

When they eventually come to get me, I walk like an automaton out of that hell called solitary.

The noises of prison life startle me. The sounds of inmates calling out and rattling the bars of their cells, doors clanging loudly overwhelm me.

I've learned to hide what's inside me, so when my body shakes I make an effort to control it.

The elation I should be feeling is missing, fear of what's waiting outside the prison gates terrifies me.

The sunlight's so bright it hurts my eyes. I stand, blinking, feeling a warm breeze blowing around me, fresh air that doesn't carry the stale sweat of men and the scent of disinfectant. I breathe in deeply, and then again.

I'm free, but I don't know what to make of it.

"Truck."

I startle at the sound of my name and at the voice, and turn my head to the left. I hadn't seen the men and bikes waiting.

I don't move toward him, I let him come to me, unsure of my reaction. Pleasure at seeing my brothers? I grasp inside trying to come up with the right emotion. Back in my cell I'd seriously thought I'd made the decision to leave the club. If I hadn't been flying their colours that day, I wouldn't have been incarcerated the way that I had. It was my association with them that had made the judge look at me so unfavourably and sent me to the penitentiary rather than the county lock up.

But they're my family. They're all I've got.

If I left, I'd have to make a home for me and Allie.

How the fuck would I do that? For a start, who would employ an ex-felon? If I'd had access to a computer inside I could at least have tried to set myself up with a job, but I hadn't. Now, it seems, the club is the only option I've got.

Doesn't have to be forever. Treat it as a place to lay my head until I can set up somewhere else.

Drummer is in front of me. "Brother."

I reply with a nod, and when he pulls me in for a man hug, slapping my back, I can do nothing but accept it though I stiffen.

He pulls back, and hands me the item he's holding. *My cut.*

It looks strange, alien and unfamiliar. A memory seeps in of how I used to yearn to feel its weight again, now it seems more like it's a trap that's going to snap its jaws shut on me.

We both stand, the sun blazing down on us. Drummer holding out the leather, me looking at it like a snake that's going to strike.

I look into his eyes and see them brimming with sympathy. *Don't need your pity.*

What does wearing a garment matter? I all but snatch it from his hands and slip it on. It sits heavy on my shoulders, feeling foreign.

"Come, Truck," he says gently.

I remember belatedly to ask, "How's Allie doing? How's Hope?" My wife and my kid, though I feel nothing like husband or father.

"Good brother, time to see for yourself."

Time? I suppose it is. But the thought terrifies me. How can I pick up and become a husband again, much less a dad? How can I be anything to anyone when I have to remind myself to keep breathing?

I follow Drummer to my bike, the one that had been modified with an electric gear change, idly noting they must have brought it in the crash truck which is still waiting by the dozen bikes that are there. I keep my head down, not wanting to acknowledge anyone as they might try and engage me in conversation.

I pause before mounting it, half fearing I've forgotten how to ride, but when I swing my leg over the saddle, my hands auto-matically go to the handlebars, and I get the bike upright and kick the stand up without it being a conscious thought in my head.

Drummer's murmuring to Peg, then he comes up to me.

"You ride alongside me, Truck. At the head of the pack."

I shrug. His unusual offer strikes me as odd, but I'm glad I won't be in the middle of the bikes, I'm not sure how well I'll handle the ride after all this time.

He gets on his own Harley, then circles his hand above his head. The thunderous roar of all the bikes firing up goes right through me, causing a pain behind my eyelids. But I add to the noise when I start mine as well.

Then we're off, Drummer positioning himself on my right side where I can see him.

The vibration seems strange yet familiar. My gear changes are automatic as if my hands are controlled by an auto-pilot in my brain. Likewise my balance as I lean when cornering, not having to consciously remember how to ride as we travel roads I recognise.

Until, finally but all too soon, we arrive at the compound.

Where I'm expected to greet my wife.

Wife? She feels more like a stranger. We've been parted longer than we were together, and I'm no longer the man she married.

TWENTY YEARS IN THE FUTURE – Drummer

"FUCK, Peg. Do you remember when Truck left the penitentiary?"

"Do I? Prez. Who could forget that."

I gaze into the sunset, watching the golden orb slowly disappearing behind the mountains. "He was about as broken as any man I've ever seen."

"You got that right." Peg's also staring into the distance. "We'd taken his bike with us, but when he walked out, I had doubts he'd be able to ride it."

"Hunched over, a shadow of his former self."

"He'd let his hair grow, and he had a beard. They either didn't allow razors in solitary, or he'd given up caring."

I grin slightly at the memory. "Trouble was, he had so many bald patches, his hair was all tufts."

Peg lifts his chin. "Allie shaved it right off. She left the beard though."

I notice him finger his own, now so mottled with grey, it's hard to remember what colour his hair originally was.

My hands brush through the scruff covering my own chin. "Girls like beards." Well, Sam certainly does.

"Girls?" he huffs. "No longer that. They've grown old alongside us, Drum."

"Time's aged us all, Peg."

"It moves on whether we want it to or not, and that's what Truck needed. Time to remember how to live again."

I slam my hand down on the side of my chair. "What they did to him was barbaric." I don't need to tell the sergeant-at-arms, he already knows, but I do anyway. "They gave him the maximum sentence for a first offence, and then kept him caged as if he was an animal. That's what they turned him into when he came out."

"When you handed him his cut, he didn't know what to do with it."

llie...

I thought this day would never come. Now it has, I'm filled with a mixture of dread and excitement. My man is coming home, and I'm terrified. What if I'm not the woman he left? Certainly I'm not physically. I've regained my weight and added more on top, my stomach has not gone back to being flat, and it's criss-crossed with silvery stretch marks.

Mentally? I've been through hell and back, but with the support of my therapist and the Devil's—both men and women—I've come out the other side. I'll always need to be wary. Some things come out of the blue to trigger a panic attack, but at least I know the signs and how to deal with it.

And I've got Hope, my... our... baby, who's yet to meet her dad.

I've gone through all manner of feelings over the past months, from sadness Truck hasn't yet seen her, to resentment he'd left me to deal with everything alone.

What's it going to be like when he meets Hope? I'm worried about her reaction. She's going through a phase where she doesn't like strangers. *Is she going to cry?*

Christ, I hope not. That would upset him, wouldn't it? But he can't be expecting her to greet him as her father, not when she sees him for the first time. She has to learn to trust him. *Will he resent me for the relationship I have built with her?*

For months I'd anticipated this day with longing, thinking I'd feel nothing but happiness I was going to see my man, but now all I can think about are the problems which lie in wait for me. To pretend everything will be rosy will just be putting my head in the sand.

My dream is that Truck will walk in, throw his arms around me, tell me he's never going to leave me again. We'll play with Hope, put her to bed, then make love. I've almost forgotten the feeling of him inside me.

I've got the implant now, and will make him wear a condom, at least until he has that promised vasectomy. No more kids for me, I shudder. Never again. The thought of falling pregnant is enough to trigger a panic attack, the trauma too great for me to ever put myself through that again.

My dream won't come true, I already know that. It's not just Truck who has things he needs to work through. *What if Truck wants it too soon?*

I look at Hope, playing with a toy that makes sounds when she presses the buttons. My little girl is so precious to me. I don't need her to have a sibling. After all, she's got cousins all around. *My mom hated me.* I may have had those thoughts to start with, but now I can't understand how they can last a lifetime. Hope is a miracle to me—a beautiful, healthy baby, worth everything I went through. I just can't put myself through that again.

Yeah, I was thinking about Truck. My mind circles back to how I hope he'll greet me, but after last night's conversation with Drummer, I know I have to wind my expectations down.

"Drum." I'd gone into his office. "I want to come to the prison tomorrow. I'll go with Hound in the crash truck." I'm bouncing with excitement, so eager to see my man.

"Sit down, Al," he'd instructed, tiredly. "There are some things you need to consider."

I tilted my head to the side and waited.

"I've seen men come out of prison more times than I like to remember. Men who've kept up with the outside world through visits with friends and family. Even then they find they need a period of adjustment to get used to living on the outside again. Truck? He's been in solitary confinement for most of the time. Not allowed visits or phone calls. It's cruel what's been done to that man, and I'm worried about the effect on him."

"I realise that Drummer. I just thought he'll be excited to see me."

His steel eyes had that rare gentle look. "You've been through hell, Al, and have come out the other side. Truck might need to work through some shit too. Got no doubt he'll do that, 'specially with a strong woman like you by his side. But he may need time to return to being the man you married."

I bit my lip. Of course I knew being alone in a cell would be awful. To keep myself sane, I'd not been able to dwell on it. Truck was safe and alive, that's what I'd hung onto. I'd had enough to do getting myself well both mentally and physically, and learning how to care for a baby. I'd worried about Truck, but hid the worst of the details from myself. Now Drummer's making me face reality.

"You think seeing me would be too much?"

"Possibly. Too much, too soon. Let him adjust gradually, Al. Look, he might come out wanting nothing more than to see you and hold you, or he might need time. You've got a great excuse for not going to meet him. If he asks I can say Hope's fussing or something like that."

I considered his words carefully, then, after a moment, replied, "I've waited a year, Drum. I can wait a little bit longer."

"Fuckin' strong," he smiled, "that's what you are."

Strong?

The words spoken yesterday evening echo in my mind. Before my pregnancy I hadn't thought I was one thing or another, but being laid up while I was carrying Hope had put me at my lowest point. Strong? Nah, I was weak, had to have others do everything for me. *But I'd done it. Persevered and wouldn't give up, and have Hope to show for it.*

Well, there's no doubt I'll need all the strength I have now. I know I'll have to give Truck some leeway, he's not going to walk in and pick up where we left off. Too much water under the bridge now.

I just hope it's still me that he wants.

I pick up my phone to check the time. *Not long now.*

"Come on, baby girl. Let's go and meet your father."

Hope is dressed in denim shorts and has a pretty tee with *Daddy's Girl* written on it. A not so subtle message from me even if she doesn't understand it. I'm hoping it won't go unnoticed by Truck.

The brothers who haven't gone to the prison are all milling around in the clubroom. Voices are loud, well, it's something to celebrate after all, and bikers never need an excuse to party. Old ladies are laying a table with a feast suitable for a king. There's a Welcome Home banner stretched over the bar which Diva's standing behind.

She waves me over. "Oh, let me have a cuddle. She's looking so cute!"

Sweet butts don't normally mix with old ladies, but I'm not going to turn my back on them or deny my past. I've remained on friendly terms with the women, and Diva's taken a liking to Hope. She's getting heavy now, so I don't mind passing her over for a while.

"Drummer said he'd spoken to you," Sam says, having come to my side.

I know what she's talking about. "I'm ready for anything," I affirm, while wondering if that's really the truth.

A loud roar of bikes signals the time is here. They're back. And out there, somewhere, is my man. I take a deep breath. It's all I can do to stop myself from running out and straight into his arms. *What would I do if they don't open for me?* My worry keeps me rooted to the spot, and instead, I take Hope back from Diva, and position myself close to the entrance.

The room goes quiet.

When the door opens, Drummer steps in first, with Truck behind him. As soon as he enters, the room erupts with a roar.

Truck turns on his heels, knocks Peg who's close behind him out of the way and strides off. His familiar limp more pronounced now than when I last saw him, the sight tugs at my heartstrings.

I push Hope at Sam, who takes her for me without question, her mouth open and her eyes wide with concern.

I run out of the clubhouse and after my man.

"Truck!" I call out when I see him walking past what, for the last few months, has been my home. "Truck. Stop. You're going the wrong way."

He falters, looks at the blocs, then shakes his head and starts moving again.

His pause has allowed me to catch up. "We don't live up there nowadays. This is ours now." I point to the bloc we've come alongside.

"That was Peg's." His voice has changed. It sounds rusty as though he's not used to using it.

"Was," I echo. "It's ours now. Come inside."

He stands, undecided. His stare fixed on the mountains. Then he lowers his gaze, and his eyes look directly at me. "I don't even know if I can do this anymore."

What's he talking about?

He enlightens me. "You, me, the club. I don't know."

My heart sinks. His blunt statement chilling me. *Strong. Be strong.*

"Come inside, Truck. Come, sit down. Have a beer. Just relax. We don't need to talk if you don't want to."

"And if I want to be alone?"

Hasn't he spent enough time by himself? Too much, probably.

But I have an insight into why he walked out of his party. It was too much, too soon.

"Just come inside, Truck."

It may not have been my words. It might have been Blade and Peg heading in our direction that made up his mind. Whatever, I'll take it as he inclines his head toward Peg's, *our* suite.

I lead the way, bypassing the bedroom and opening the door into my, *our*, sitting room. I wave toward the couch and enter the kitchenette, taking two bottles of beer from the fridge. *If ever there was a time I needed a drink, this is it.*

Truck's at least sat down, his eyes fixed on the crib which I'd moved out of the bedroom, and the toys on the floor. The reality of having a baby probably hitting him.

He takes the bottle from me, his movements more jerky than smooth. He's far from the confident man I remember.

He takes a swallow, then another. His eyes closing briefly in what I take is pleasure. Maybe a drink, a taste he remembers, will bring something back of the man he was before.

Then his eyes fix on me. "I'm not the man who went into prison, Allie." He shakes his head. "I've dreamt of this moment for twelve months. Gone over all the things I wanted to say to you. Wanted to do to you. Thought everything would cycle back to how it was before. Now I'm here, I've got nothing to say. I feel numb inside. I don't even want to be here."

Don't let it get to you, I remind myself.

"Where would you prefer to be?" I ask him.

"I've no fuckin' idea."

"When I..." I notice then he's staring deliberately at the part of the room which isn't covered in reminders of Hope and change what I was going to say. "When I came out of the hospital, I thought it would feel like a magic wand waved over me. That everything would suddenly be right." I check that I have his attention. He appears to be listening, so I carry on. "It wasn't. It all seemed upside down and inside out, and I couldn't cope with... anything. It took time, Truck, time, love and support from the club and therapy. But I'm right again now. No one's expecting a miracle from you. It's hard to imagine what you've been through, but no one expects you to come out unscathed. You, we, have just got to take things slowly. I love you Truck, and I'll be here. However you need me."

He shrugs. "I don't even know if I love you anymore."

The old Truck would never have hurt me so bluntly. I remind myself that this is the after-effect of prison talking, and not my man. Neither of us should make decisions rashly. Though inside I'm trembling with fear that he might mean it, I suspect and hope, with time he'll come around to view things differently.

"How do you feel, Truck?" It's as though I'm back in therapy, this time in the opposite chair. Asking questions and prompting thoughtful answers.

He considers for a moment, before telling me. "I don't feel anything at all. No excitement, no commitment to anything. I feel empty."

"Time," I tell him again. "Just give it time." I reach out my hand to rest on his, he flinches and pulls it away. *Human contact must feel strange after all this time.*

His eyes fall on the crib again. He studies it for a while, then asks, "Where is she?"

"Do you want to meet her?" I counter with a question of my own.

Another rise and fall of his shoulders. "I should, shouldn't I?"

Luckily Hope's too young to realise if he rejects her as he's doing me. Telling him to stay where he is, having an expectation he might take the opportunity to escape while I'm gone, but knowing I've got to take the risk anyway, I leave the suite to go retrieve our daughter.

I don't take long, more time on his own won't help Truck any. I wave off Sam's concern, answer Drummer tersely with the briefest summary of Truck's state of mind—bad—then, with Hope in my arms, I make my way back to our home.

A baby that was in my slight swollen stomach when he had gone on that fateful ride to Nogales that day. A baby was something he'd asked about in the abstract before she came into existence. A baby was what he'd been told he had when she was born. It's totally different to see a ten-month-old wriggling bundle who already wants to exert her independence.

I stand, holding her in my arms, watching his expressionless face.

I don't know what he's going to do, or what I should do. Should I go over and hand her to him? He's her father after all.

Slowly he pulls himself to his feet. Then, with hesitant steps, approaches me.

Hope turns her head and stares at him with her big blue eyes. I'm wondering what she makes of the man whose face is so heavily scarred, with overlong hair flopping down into his eyes.

She gazes, curiously. Then, as though sensing he'll do her no harm, she reaches out her arms toward him.

For a second Truck's hands remain at his sides, then he raises his right, and gently touches the baby soft skin on her face. She grabs hold of his finger and pulls it to her mouth. Recently she's started teething, and will chew on anything. He grimaces slightly when she bites down with the one tooth she's got.

A strange expression comes over his face, making the decision easy for me. I hold her out.

"Want to take her?"

He hesitates, then his hands come around her waist, and I relinquish her to him, hovering making sure he's got her tight.

In that manner of firsts, first smile, first chuckle, first managing to roll over from her back to her stomach, Hope does something she's never done before. She kicks out her legs and says triumphantly, "Dada."

It's pure coincidence. It has to be. I always knew that was likely to be her first word, there's been enough babies on the compound. But the timing was impeccable.

"She knows me," Truck states, wonderingly. Now he's cradling her in his arms, rocking her gently.

As though she's accomplished a new trick, she says it again, "Dada, Dada, Dada."

"Yeah, I'm your Dada. And you're my clever girl."

The first emotion he's shown since he got here appears as tears start to run down his face.

"I'm your Dada," he repeats with a sob.

CHAPTER FORTY-ONE

*T*ruck...

I remember it was a standard joke around the club-house that all the babies say Dada first, before attempting Momma. The brothers used to mock the old ladies about it, so knew it was likely coincidence rather than the impossible, that Hope had sensed I was someone important to her.

But that she voiced it, then, at the point I was feeling so low, meant more to me than anything anyone else could have said.

So full of emotion, I hand Hope back to Allie and stumble into the bedroom where I lie on what seems an overly soft bed and curl up in a foetal position, tears running down my face and sobs coming one after another. It's as though a dam has broken. I'm hoping Allie has the sense to steer clear and not try to comfort me. Yes, these are tears of distress, but they're also cathartic. Stuck in that cell I'd locked all my feelings away to prevent myself going mad, or at least, as a weapon against being put in that straitjacket again. Feeling was too much when I couldn't do anything about it, and hurting myself seemed the only result, a physical pain to counteract the mental agony.

Now, like a black-and-white film that suddenly becomes colour, emotions hit me all at once as a kaleidoscope of images runs through my head. Allie, the first time I'd had her in my bed, Allie when she came to my apartment. Allie by my side when I had my eye fixed, Allie, Allie, Allie.

Then replaced by my brothers, one after one I mentally go around the table, realising I'd rebuffed them today. Allie's right, they once were my support during my physical recovery, they'll be there this time too.

I'm not going to return to normal in an hour, a day or a week. If I ever return to being the man I used to be at all. Prison has changed me irrevocably.

I recognise I'm not the only person who's different, Allie is too. I noticed a new hardness about her. Hardness? Perhaps the wrong word—strength, maybe. She's been challenged in ways she never expected, and that's all down to me. From getting her pregnant to leaving her to face her pregnancy, birth and first few months of bringing up Hope alone. I may have missed seeing my baby, but though she's been on the outside, she's had it just as difficult as me.

That she could greet me in the way that she did, that there was no blame, just understanding, blows me away.

I told her I didn't love her anymore.

Maybe my feelings have changed. Maybe the time we've spent apart means we have to get to know each other again, maybe we're both different people, shaped by our experiences and will have to grow together into our new personalities.

It's different what I feel for her, but also in many ways the same. She's my old lady, and nothing's going to change that. I married her for better or worse, and in time, I'll be the husband she deserves.

I'll hit bumps in the road along the way, setbacks which will make me retreat into myself, but I'll keep moving in the right direction. That's my promise to her.

We're parents. Fuck, that thought brings me to my knees. It's not just about us now. There's a third in our family, the most important member, who's just by chance or divine intervention called me by the right name.

Her dada, her dad, her father, her old man.

And she's mine. My daughter. Nothing is more important than making her happy.

I may only have known her for a couple of minutes, but already she's got me wrapped around her little finger.

A tentative knock sounds at the door. It has to be Allie. Straightening I roll over onto my back, and put my arm over my face.

"You can come in."

She does, but stands just inside the door, her arms folded. I watch from under my arm as she critically examines me.

"You like that hair?" she asks.

"Fuck no." It gets in my eye, and looks a mess.

"Come on then." She walks purposefully across to the bathroom as if expecting me to follow her.

For some reason, I find myself getting to my feet and doing just that.

"Sit," she instructs and points to a stool.

When she picks up the shaving foam and the razor, her intention is clear and I don't object. Soon I feel the coolness of the foam, then watch my hair falling to my feet.

"I'm leaving the beard," she tells me. "I like it on you, and it may have certain, er, possibilities."

I pick up on what she's not saying, and the thought makes my mouth quirk. Just a twitch. My cock though, he's not interested. *Time,* she'd said. *I need time.* I was only released from my nightmare this morning.

But I don't want to mislead her if she's got intentions. "Allie, I don't think…"

"I'm not ready yet," she says quickly. "Believe me, Truck, after everything I went through. I'm terrified about having sex again."

She's scared?

"Oh babe," I call her a pet name automatically. *And there I'd been worrying she'd jumped into someone else's bed.*

"I've got an implant. But I'm still worried."

"I'll never go ungloved, Allie, until I can get myself fixed." I still intend to do that. Even if she wanted another baby I couldn't see her go through that again.

"Let's just take everything slowly," she suggests.

Raising my eyes, I look into the mirror seeing a man I hadn't seen for such a long time, I barely recognise my reflection. A bald-headed man instead of a balding one, but now with a beard which hides some of my scars. I like what I see. I'll never be handsome, but I now look presentable.

As Allie wets and then uses a washcloth to remove the remainder of the foam, I grab her hand. "Allie, I…" I don't even know what I want to say.

But she understands. She covers my hand with her other and nods.

"Where's Hope?"

"Napping. I fed her and she's gone down."

"Do you… do you breastfeed her?"

"No, I never did. I was too low when she was born, Truck. I wasn't in a place where I could. Maybe I should have, but I didn't."

She might have, had I been there.

"It's what it is, Truck, like so many things. What ifs, and if I'd done that instead. No point dwelling on things we can't change now. You and I have both done things we regret. We can either let guilt drag us down, or move on and take what life offers us. We've got a beautiful baby girl."

"Who knows her dad," I can't resist saying.

"Hmm," Allie replies. "Typical." Then, her smile fades and she becomes serious. "She's not said a recognisable word before. That was a first, and you were here to hear it. You'll be here to see her take her first step and all the other firsts in her life."

"I didn't see her take her first breath."

"Neither did I," Allie reminds me.

"Tell me about it."

"One day, not now. We've got time, Truck. Don't have to get everything sorted right away."

She's probably right. Eventually I might let her in on what being locked up did to me, as she'll tell me what happened to her. Each of us will hurt for the other, and how did she put it? Shouldn't let the past drag us down when we've got a future to live.

I glance at myself again, still wearing the cut Drummer brought to the prison. Suddenly it feels right to wear it.

"You think the brothers will still be in the clubhouse?"

Her eyes widen. "Beer? Bikers? Just because the guest of honour didn't put in an appearance, you reckon they'll have ended the party?"

My mouth quirks again. Put like that, no.

I run my hand over the now smooth dome of my head. Just that one small thing has given me back a glimpse of the man I was before I went away. On the exterior anyway, I doubt inside I'll ever be the same again.

Prison's taken so much from me. Why should it take more?

"Allie. Will you come down to the clubhouse with me? Stay by my side?" Something tells me, if she's there, she'll be like a tether to where I want to get to. A man with a family.

She seems to understand. "You can lean on me Truck, however much you need to. I'll be there."

"Can we bring Hope?"

"Yes, she'll be stirring soon anyway. She never naps for long during the day."

"How's she sleeping at night?" Christ, there are so many things I don't know.

"She'll go down around ten and wake around five. She's good."

Hmm. *That's good?* Guess I better get used to early morning wake up calls.

As if on cue, I hear a baby's cry of complaint. Allie grins. I follow her as she crosses the hallway to our sitting room, shaking my head. Trust Drum to set Allie up in something that resembles a small apartment. He'd thought it through, obviously, that Allie needed a kitchen to heat bottles and wash up, even if there isn't space to cook a full roast or other big meal.

I stand, watching as Allie expertly changes Hope, noticing how my daughter finds the whole thing a joke and tries to wriggle away. I absorb the techniques my wife is using, determined to be a hands-on dad, not an asshole who leaves it all to his wife. I admire the way she's coping. From the little she's said, as the doctor had warned me, adjusting to having a baby was hard. At least she hasn't turned out like that bitch of her mother. Not that I'd had any real fear that she would.

When she's got Hope's fresh diaper on dressed her, I hold out my arms, and Allie puts Hope into them. First thing I learn is that kids don't hang on, they rely on the adult not to drop them. Hope has no fear as she squirms, leaning back and laughing.

Allie's face shows the concern of a mother. I suspect it's hard to relinquish control having come this far on her own. Making a note not to seem as though I'm taking over, or offering unwanted suggestions about things I know nothing about, I nod my head toward the door, then, taking a deep breath, follow her out.

Hope acts like my armour, giving me strength to walk into the busy and loud room. Noise, when I've mostly heard silence for the past months. Not that it was ever quiet in solitary, but I'd learned to tune out the cries from my fellow inmates.

"Truck! Here brother. There's a beer with your name on it somewhere."

There is. And Roadkill, clearly wanting to earn his patch, is offering it to me before I can look for it. I jerk my chin toward the table, unable to take it while my daughter is filling my arms.

"I got a new dirt bike." Instead of asking how I am, what it was like in there, how it feels to be out—the questions I'd been expecting to have to deflect, Road starts on his favourite subject.

"You still racing?"

"You bet. Not as often as I used to, but hey, I'm going after that title this year."

Road rides trial bikes. He practices up on the track that was built for him at the top of the compound. I ask him about it, he's soon giving me details. I make an odd comment here and there, but am more tied up with hanging onto Hope who seems to want to get down and play.

Allie notices, takes her from me, and plonks her down with Zane and Zoey who are playing on the floor under the watchful eye of Sophie. While Road mentions something about the power of his new engine, I watch my daughter, realising how much the club has to offer. Allie has returned to my side, able to relax knowing there will always be someone with their eyes on the babies.

"Good to see you, Brother."

I swing around to see Joker and Lady, acknowledging their comment. Maya, their daughter runs off as soon as they let go of her hand. I'm amused to see she's making a beeline for Eli who's playing with Olivia. All three kids appear to be about the same age.

With another beer soon inside me, I find myself beginning to relax.

"See you need some time in the gym," Peg greets me.

Yeah, I'd tried to keep myself fit inside, but over the past couple of months, I'd given up physically as well as mentally. I groan in anticipation, and Peg, the bastard, just laughs.

"VP," I raise my chin at Wraith, noticing while he was walking toward me, it wasn't without a sideways glance to check on his wife and kids.

Wraith doesn't speak, his hand just lands on the back of my cut, then after a piercing look into my eyes, he walks away.

Words weren't necessary for me to know I have his support, however I want it, in whatever way.

The room suddenly goes quiet as the music is switched off. Drummer neatly jumps up onto the bar.

"Brothers," he calls out, "I'll make this short. You all know why we've gotten together today. There's a fuckin' banner above my head and I know Truck can read, so I don't need to say the words.

"Those who have been inside know what it feels like. Others can imagine I'm sure. Gonna take Truck a minute to adjust to living free once more. For myself, I'm pleased as fuck Truck's back where he belongs, with us, his club, his ol' lady and kid."

His heartfelt words make me pull Allie into my side, my arm snaking around her with some sort of muscle memory, the familiar gesture, the willingness with which she trustingly leans into me, makes something loosen inside.

When Drummer raises his glass of what undoubtedly will be very expensive whisky, and the cries start around me, I loosen my hold on Allie so I too can thump my hand over my heart and join in as the cries comes out of every man's mouths.

"Satan's Devils ride together. Ride Satan's Devils."

My lips twitch when I realise no one's voice is louder or more enthusiastic than Tommy's.

May still have some way to go to fully accept it, but I am a Satan's Devil. Worked hard to earn it, not going to throw it away.

The club door shuts with a bang as someone goes out, and I flinch. Yeah, still got aways to go.

Twenty years in the future – Drummer

"Well look who it is."

I glance up with the corners of my mouth turning up. I've always had a lot of time for the nineteen-year-old who's approaching, who, like her mother, is a pretty girl. I might not have sired a daughter myself, but in some ways, Hope's been a surrogate. "Hey, Hope. How's it going?"

"Great, Uncle Drum, Uncle Peg."

I've told her many times now she's older, she can drop the title and just call me by my name, but Hope's called me uncle so long, I think it's stuck.

"What you up to?"

She shrugs, "Nothing much. Just wanted to see if Dad's around."

"I think he's in the clubhouse. You need anything?"

She looks down, and frowns, "Unfortunately, yeah, what any student wants. I need textbooks, Uncle Drum."

Hope's studying to be a nurse at the community college.

"If he'd let me work…"

"Your Dad doesn't want you working off the compound, Hope. We'll see you're set for anything you need, you know that."

"I don't like asking," *she explains quietly, in a way reminiscent of her mother.* "But I am really grateful Uncle Drum." *She moves around Peg, approaches me and, leaning over, gives me a hug. My arms automatically go around her, thinking of the many times over the years I've held her like this.*

"She's a good girl," *I tell Peg, when she's disappeared into the clubhouse.*

"Turned out well," *he agrees.* "But Truck's never going to let her do one of the seedy jobs students have to take."

I give a sigh. "Fuckin' glad I only had sons. And don't look like that, Peg. You're no better with Lisa."

"Daughters, huh?" *He laughs.* "At least I've only got one. No wonder Wraith's losing his hair."

"Heart's got three," *I remind him.*

"Remember his twins being born during the wildfire that nearly took out the compound?"

"That was a fight and a half, Peg." *My eyes automatically scan the* mountains in the distance, something that I do every day during the dry months. I've noticed I'm not the only one, none of us want to see flames heading toward us ever again.

"Things come in threes, Drummer. I'm always wondering when the third will strike."

I shrug. "Fire destroyed the original vacation resort that was here, Peg. We moved in, what, getting on forty years back? Only had that one fire threaten us since, and we beat it then."

"Darcy and her firefighting team did, you mean," he corrects me.

"How's Darcy doing now?"

"She's still lovin' her job. Done fuckin' well, Drummer. But I'm hoping she'll retire soon."

My mouth quirks. Ever since he married her way back in the day, her job's been a bone of contention between them. She has done well, is a captain herself now, only taking a little time off when she had their two children. My money is on her dying in harness, so to speak. She's giving no signs of slowing down.

But I don't speak my mind out loud. "I think the compound's safe now, Peg. We keep the firebreak well maintained and an eye out."

"Can't get complacent. Fires burn every summer. We're just lucky it hasn't decided to come for us again. But one day it will."

"Hopefully not in our lifetime."

"Fuckin' with you there, Prez."

Again I stare up, craning my neck so I can see the three mountain ranges that encircle us, but there's no smoke or flames. I shudder slightly, once was more than a-fuckin-nough.

"Not long after the fire, the Chaos Riders came into town," Peg reminds me. "You set Rock up."

"I did. And I had my reasons." My president's glare hasn't lessened with time.

It has no effect on him, he just shakes his head. "Wasn't a good time. We hated Rock then. Would have killed him on sight."

I ignore him. I did what had to be done, and Rock had volunteered when I'd asked him. "Remember the state Becca had been in?"

He's quiet as he thinks back. "Chained in a filthy basement. If Rock hadn't found her, she would have died."

"She's grown, hasn't she, Peg?" I chuckle softly. "She's not afraid of making decisions now."

"Okay," he remarks, suddenly. "I'll give you that. What you did saved the club and Becca. Back then, I'd never have expected Rock to settle down."

"That was when Beef 'died'," I put the word in air quotes. It hadn't been a bullet that had almost taken him, but the fuckin' infection that came from the wound. We'd all but read him the last rites, all said our final goodbyes to him, when the fucker had woken up.

"Satan hadn't wanted him."

"Clearly not." I bark a short laugh. "Then, of course, he went to Colorado."

"And another fucker went down." Peg glances at me. "Woman-wise, I'm talking."

CHAPTER FORTY-TWO

*A*llie…

It's been a difficult couple of weeks. I feel like I'm walking on eggshells around Truck, trying to keep noise down as I notice loud sounds make him jump. I'm wary of pushing Hope on him, but also don't want him to think I'm monopolising her.

He's learned to change her. He's been here when we put her in the highchair and gave her her first solid food. She seems to enjoy mashed-up bananas. His face lights up every time she calls him Dada, which seems to be quite a lot. But then she does get rewarded for it.

"Did you enjoy your ride?" I look around as Truck walks in the door.

"Fuckin' ace. Just what I needed." The smile on his face seems genuine and wide. "Had a chance to talk to Peg when we stopped for a break."

"Yeah?"

"Yeah." He goes over to the cot, sees Hope is sleeping and stares down at her for a moment. "She's fuckin' beautiful, Al. I can't believe we made that."

I know what he means. It still irks me that I missed the birth just like he had. Of course, I'd been there physically, but I hadn't been conscious to see her born. Sometimes I wonder if she really is mine. She seems so perfect. But if someone had passed me a different baby instead, I never would have known. Sometimes I wake up sweating and wondering whether she's a changeling, then realise how stupid I'm being. She showed every sign of being a premature underweight baby. No doubt about it, she's mine.

Truck's looking at me strangely.

"What?" I ask, hoping he can't read my mind. He'd think I was crazy.

"Come next door. I want to talk without disturbing her."

His words sound ominous. Has he decided I'm not what he wants now? Although we'd both agreed to take it slow, I'm concerned he hasn't made a move toward me since he returned home.

In the bedroom he settles himself on the bed, with the pillows propped behind him. The wave of his hand shows he expects me to join him. I settle myself down, careful to leave a gap between us.

When he doesn't start speaking immediately, I sneak a sideways glance at him, seeing him swallow a couple of times.

"I don't know how long what happened is going to affect me, Al. I haven't opened up to you, but I think I need to do so now. I'll be living with the effects forever, and it will help if you understand."

"Truck—"

"No, I'm not asking for sympathy. I've got to move on, accept the experience is a part of me. What I don't want is you forever tiptoeing around, frightened to say the wrong thing. That's not a relationship, babe. That's two people ignoring, rather than facing up to and trying to find ways to cope with things they can't change."

I have to ask. Don't want to draw this out if he's going to take a long time to get around to it. "Do you want to leave me?"

He sits up fast, turning to face me. His hand coming up to cradle my cheek. "Fuck, no, woman. The thought of you and Hope were the only things keeping me from going insane. Those months inside, you were my lifeline. Fuckin' killed me I couldn't be with you, couldn't see you or hear your voice, but the thought of you being here waiting? Couldn't have survived without that."

"The thought of you coming home, Truck. That's what I was holding onto."

"Tell me, Al. Tell me what you went through."

I shake my head. "It's water under the bridge now."

"Maybe, maybe not," he replies enigmatically. His thumb strokes my face gently. "You're my ol' lady, Al, and I'm your ol' man."

"Am I? Are you?" Suddenly my fears come tumbling out. "We were together such a short time before I fell pregnant. Then apart for a year. We haven't got a normal to return to, as we never had that to start with."

"Then," he begins with his gaze blazing, "let's build our new normal now. Our recent past has shaped us. Doesn't mean we're any worse than we were. Could be we're better for it." His stare intensifies. "Allie, I want to kiss you, now."

I'm not ready.

Will I ever be?

How can I love this man but still feel a physical detachment?

I open my mouth to tell him, but he takes advantage instead. His lips gently close on mine, and I automatically respond.

He's not demanding, there's no pressure to do more than simply move our mouths against one another. This close, his natural perfume seems to do something to me, and I find it's me taking the lead, with my tongue parting his lips and pushing inside.

He moves, keeping our faces melded together, leaning over me with one hand resting on the bed to my side.

Suddenly our kiss becomes more, it becomes full of emotion, an expression of our love for each other. In a rush, everything I've missed comes tearing back into my mind. My fears about intimacy taking a back seat when my body automatically begins to respond to my man.

Without my brain issuing a conscious instruction, my hands clutch at his tee, and I moan into his mouth.

"Tell me you want this, Al," he demands, as he pushes his pelvis toward mine. Any questions about whether I can still arouse him are answered when I feel his hard cock against my thigh.

"I…" My mind is still holding back, but my body presses against him.

"We'll go as fuckin' slow as you want, Al. You need me to stop? You just tell me. You don't have to offer anything you don't want." Another intense gaze wills me to believe and trust him. There's no doubt in my head about that. Being in prison might have changed Truck, but he's still the same honourable man inside.

He waits for my slight nod of agreement, then his hands go to the bottom of my tee. "Want to see you, Allie."

Instead I push at his.

"Al," he says warningly. "Don't think I haven't noticed you locking the door when you take a shower. How you change in the bathroom at night. I haven't feasted my eyes on my wife since I've been back, and I'm getting impatient."

"I've changed, Truck."

To my surprise, he rolls onto his back and starts laughing, chuckles booming up from deep down in his belly. When he's at last able to speak, he tells me, "Al, for fuck's sake. I returned with only one eye, my face scarred to hell and back. A withered arm, fingers missing, and an ankle that doesn't bend any more. What did you do?"

I shrug. *It's different.* But I answer anyway. "I saw you, not your body. It's not the same Truck, a woman wants a man to see her as something sexy."

He shifts again, this time leaning on his elbow and staring down at me. "You saying you don't find your man sexy?"

Scarred, broken… He's the sexiest man alive. "No, I'm not saying that, I…"

"Take off your shirt."

It's a command. I want to deny him, want to delay the moment when I see his cock deflate. I was a whore who made money because men were attracted to me. I'm far from the woman I once was. But eventually, this moment will happen, whatever reaction he'll have won't matter if it's a minute, a day or a year from now.

With sudden resolve I sit up and rip off my tee, then undo and drop my bra, letting the straps fall down my arms. Then, I stand, undo my shorts and let those to, descend to the floor. I'm standing in front of him in my plain white panties, conscious I've neglected grooming my pubes since Hope was born. What was the point when I had no man who was going to see?

Truck leans forward as though to get a better look, and something flares in his eye. I hold my breath, wondering what to say, or whether I should just put my clothes back on. I'm nothing like I was before.

"Jeez, Al."

He's disgusted. Disappointed his memory isn't reflected before him.

He holds out his hand. "Come here."

When I reach out mine, he grabs it and tugs so I tumble onto the bed, then once again he's looming over me, straddling my hips.

"These, Al, fuck. They're bigger."

My breasts are. "Not so firm now."

Lowering his head, he nuzzles first one nipple, then the other. Despite my expectation of rejection, they form peaks.

Then, he raises his head, and begins to smooth his hands over my belly, no longer flat and covered in stretch marks.

"Soft, feminine," he smiles in appreciation. "And these?" He traces the silvery lines with his tongue, making my skin erupt in goosebumps. "Each a sign of what you went through when you were carrying my baby."

"I've put on weight."

"Which you should have done, darlin'. You're healthy now and look it."

"I can't wear those dresses that you like so much, Truck. I've no waist…"

"Think I give a fuck about what packaging you come in, babe? Doesn't mean fuck all. You want to know what I see when I look at you?"

Do I?

But he doesn't give me the option of not finding out.

"When I look at you I see a woman who brings me to my fuckin' knees with her bravery. Who fought to give life to my baby, and nearly lost herself doing so. These scars on my face that I got from doing my job? Nothing to these marks on your body. I didn't want you to have Hope, Al. Didn't think it was fair on you, didn't think my desire to have a child was worth losing you in the process. But you fought on, anyway, didn't you? Like any fuckin' warrior facing adversity, you didn't run away and give up. You think I don't find you sexy? Feel my cock, babe. Can't remember it ever being harder than this."

As if to demonstrate he leaps off the bed and shrugs out of his cut and clothes as fast as humanly possible, then takes his cock in his hand, grimacing as his fingers stroke his shaft as though he's in some kind of agony. His head goes back and his eyes close, his jaw is clenched.

After a second, he looks back down. "Dreamed of tasting you, Allie. Fuckin' dreamed of seeing you like you are now. I knew you'd have changed, just couldn't have imagined how even more fuckin' beautiful you've become. Let me taste you?"

"I haven't…"

"Shaved? Happens I like you this way better, Al."

Although his expression conveys his urgency, his hands are gentle when he gets onto the bed and pulls my panties down, and his mouth kisses my feet when one by one he lifts them and pulls the plain garment completely off.

With his eyes on mine, checking for any sign of my discomfort, he pushes my knees up and apart, and then stares at me. It makes me uncomfortable, but I don't know why. It's not like he hasn't seen it before.

"Fuckin' beautiful."

When he lowers his mouth, I stop thinking. Allowing myself to switch off my overactive mind and simply feel, a luxury I hadn't experienced for some time. I'd forgotten how talented he is.

If he was a dying man in the desert tasting his first drink in weeks, he couldn't sound so enamoured of my taste as he moans while lapping up my cream, then as his tongue plays my clit like a maestro. And that beard. Wow, I was right when I said it had implications. The feeling of the hair moving over my sensitive spot is incredible. He notices and makes good use of it, adding the effect to his repertoire. He hasn't forgotten one thing about my body, nor how to get me to the point fast where my thighs tighten, trapping his head, and I open my mouth… at the last moment remembering I have a daughter in the next room, so stuff my fist between my lips to deaden my scream.

Truck looks up, his mouth and beard dripping wet, and he's grinning. "Glad you remembered. Rather she stayed asleep for a while." He pauses to fiddle with something in his mouth, and then pulls out a short curly hair.

I shudder, embarrassed. There were benefits to me being bare, but he doesn't object. In fact he grins wider.

Then he catches my eyes and holds them with his. "Are you ready, Al? We can stop now if you want."

"Condom," I gasp. I know I'm on the implant which should

be working by now, but I'm not taking any chances. If he tried to take me bare, I'd have to ask him to stop.

But of course he doesn't say anything, just holds up the condom he'd already got out of the packet. I watch, entranced as he smooths it on.

Then he's there, between my legs, pushing inside me. I'd wondered if it would feel different, if I'd be less tight having carried a baby. But I needn't have worried. Maybe it's the months of disuse, but I feel I'm tighter than I was before.

Truck works his way in, then stops, reverently lowering his forehead to mine, and gasping out, "Home, now I'm fuckin' home, Allie. Never leaving you again. You're mine, woman, you hear me?"

"I'm yours," I rasp my reply, unable to stop my body pushing against his.

He takes the hint and begins to move.

His hips twist as he gets that spot which makes me contract my muscles around him. Each thrust he makes count. He quickens his pace, and I doubt he'll last long, it having been such a long time for each of us.

"Fuck, Allie, I can't hold back."

He presses hard on my clit and it seems that I can't either. The dual sensations of his cock and fingers on both the right spots this time make me forget and my scream conjoins with his bellow of release.

We clutch and hold each other as our bodies quiver with his final pumps and my aftershocks.

Until a loud cry reaches us.

"Shit. Think Viper can soundproof our bedroom in the house?" Truck says as he pulls out with a firm grasp on the condom.

"He did say he'd build it to our specifications," I counter, reaching for my robe then putting it on, wondering how Truck is going to take the hindrance to our canoodling after sex that we used to engage in.

I needn't have worried. He's only a moment behind me when he comes in and takes Hope from me.

There's just something about a man wearing only jeans cuddling a baby.

This wasn't the way I'd expected this day to go. If asked I'd have said I hadn't been ready. My head had started to believe I never would be. I'm so glad Truck found a way to persuade me.

"Truck?"

"Yeah?" He looks up from where he's expertly changing Hope as if he'd done it every day for a year.

I smile coyly. "I don't know what Peg said to you, but thank him for me, will you?"

He chuckles. "I think that will stay between me and the sergeant-at-arms." Suddenly, he grows serious. He stands up, holding a fresh smelling baby to him. "Allie, I was a fool when I first came back. Needed a minute to get my head on straight. I felt numb, destroyed. You put me back together."

"Truck—"

"Nah, let me say this. I fuckin' love you, Al. Never stopped. That's what kept me going. Never doubt it. I love you."

I didn't know how much I needed the words until I heard them. I step forward, putting my arms around my man and my daughter as well as I can, hugging them both. "I love you, Truck."

Hope seems to look at me and then him, and then says loudly, "Dada."

Twenty years in the future – Drummer

"Okay, if we're discussing everyone. What about Joker and Lady?"

Another loud snort. "I called it, Drummer. Two men transferred in from Las Vegas, neither went with the whores. They hid that fuckin' relationship from everyone else, but I saw it."

"You did." Others, like me, might have had suspicions, but it had been Peg who'd voiced them, meaning I'd had to act on it.

"They'd lied to the club. Should have gotten a beatdown."

My head moves side to side. "Yeah, we could have done that. But they had their fucking reasons. Joker hadn't been accepted all his life, had lived a lie that would have destroyed him if he hadn't found a man like Lady to be by his side."

"Lady's Man," he offers the full handle I hadn't thought about in years. "Can't think when there was a more inaccurate moniker."

Once again, I stare ahead, this time not seeing the scenery, but a scene around the table instead. "I didn't know how everyone would take it. I hoped no one would be an asshole, but I couldn't be sure."

"You called them out on it." Peg's brow creases. "No warning to them or to us."

"Most were aware of it in a 'don't ask, don't tell' fashion."

"Some weren't," Peg grins. "But after finding out everyone was cool, Joker became a changed man."

He was. He'd stopped trying to pretend to be something he wasn't. Ended up with a lovely little girl too. Under sad circumstances, of course, following the death of his brother and his wife. But Maya had been young enough to adapt quickly, and fitted in well with the other toddlers in the club.

"We're a strange family, Peg."

"That we are. Mismatched and dysfunctional as I've always said. But the better for it."

That's what binds us together. We'd each give our lives for any of our brothers and their families.

"You should be proud," Peg announces, catching me off guard.

"Why?"

"Because of what you've built."

"I didn't start it, Peg, that was my old man, Bastard." He was the one who'd originally breathed life into the Satan's Devils Motorcycle Club.

"*He certainly deserves his moniker,*" *Peg snaps. "Yeah, Bastard started the club, but it was different. The brotherhood was there from the start, prospects having to earn their patch. But life was cheap and many lost it. When you took the helm, you started to build something different. A club where men who wanted to live outside the citizen world could feel safe doing it.*"

"*Wasn't safe for everyone, Peg. Lost a few good men along the line. Tongue, Adam and Hank for starters. And Raptor a few years back.*"

"*They died protecting family,*" *he reminds me.*

We're quiet for a moment, both lost in our thoughts of the brothers who have gone.

"*Even Mouse got us into some shit.*" *The memories are continuing to surface in my brain.*

"*Colombia, wasn't it? Where we had to go to rescue Mariana.*"

I raise my chin, then shake my head. "Fuck, that was some outing. Then she had to take on immigration."

"*She's a permanent resident now.*"

She is. As soon as that was confirmed, she and Mouse had started on their family. Got three kids now, had them all in quick succession.

Peg chuckles. "When she started having those babies, she came down less hard on Drew."

"*Didn't hurt him none that she insisted on him getting an education. Helped grow him as a man.*"

"*Then he patched in, anyway.*"

He did, and I've got one hell of a lot of respect for the member he's become. "He's solid, Peg." With Mouse's encouragement he got a degree in computer shit. Earned the handle Wizard and has proved more than once what a clever motherfucker he is. "He'll do right by the club."

"*He will,*" *the sergeant-at-arms confirms.*

We go quiet for a moment, each reminiscing in our own ways. The silence is broken when Peg suddenly announces, "Never expected Blade to find someone, and not that he'd find her scavenging for food."

My turn to snort. "None of us expected to find our old ladies in the way that we did, but maybe Blade's is the strangest."

"Or Hound. Didn't he run her down or something?"

"Or Cast."

Peg grins, "BDSM club, wasn't it?"

It was. With the result Peg's gym now has a partitioned off area which we all use from time to time. May have picked up a thing or two from one of our newer members.

CHAPTER FORTY-THREE

Truck…

"Come here you little rascal." I swing Hope up into my arms. She squirms, wanting to get down. Now that she can walk, she doesn't want to be confined, something I can fully understand. Why I baulked at Allie wanting to put reins on her —she's my daughter, not a dog to be put on a lead. Trouble is, we now need eyes in the back of our heads. Hope is likely to toddle off any chance she can.

I'm not surprised that today her eyes are open in wonder and awe, and she's itching to explore.

She loves bikes, the look and the sound, even the loudest engine roar doesn't get her fazed. I think she's attracted by the gleaming chrome and bright paint colours. I haven't told Allie, but I'm thinking of getting her one of those kid's electric motor-cycles as soon as she's old enough to ride it. Can't wait for that. 'Bike' was the first proper word she said.

"Momma. Momma."

Yup, here's Allie coming back now.

"You done?"

"Done."

I notice she looks tired. "You okay?"

She brightens immediately, "I'm fine, Truck. Just, talking about it, you know? It brings it all back. Thank fuck Sam was with me—I don't think they'd have believed how bad it was if she hadn't been there to back me up."

Allie's just given an interview to a local newspaper about the condition she'd suffered. It's her aim to get HG on everyone's radar so women like her aren't told to just put up and shut up when they're so ill during pregnancy.

What we're doing today will go a long way towards that. We're currently at the end point of a charity run. There has to be a few hundred bikers milling around, stalls and catering stands set up, auctions, raffles, and all manner of competitions and prize-giving going on. Bikers from all over are here rubbing shoulders together, including those from other Satan's Devils chapters, of course.

Our aim to raise money for research, and increase awareness of Hyperemesis Gravidarum. Allie's already been on a local radio show, part of the reason for the big turn out today, and now she's just been talking to the press. Other women have contacted her to share their stories, and in many ways, talking to people who have gone through the same thing has helped her.

Allie's still not completely recovered, still gets the occasional panic attack, and gets tired easily. For that reason, she didn't ride behind me today, but came in the truck with Hope. I'm constantly watching her as she tries to do too much.

"How's our monster been?"

"A monster," I confirm. Hope's a spoiled brat, I'll admit it. She's the family I never thought I'd have, and, surprisingly, Allie is as soft with her as I am. I know she regrets not being able to give her a brother or sister, but I wouldn't put her through that again for the world. It's no longer possible in any event. I only fire blanks now.

"I just saw Tommy. He's in his element."

"Yeah?" I ask with a grin. "Doing his job?"

"And loving the responsibility," she replies laughing.

Tommy's been put in charge of making sure no one touches our bikes. Something he's proving he's good at. Patient, doesn't mind staying in one place, and big enough no one is going to risk a fist they have no idea he'd never think to raise.

"I hear Hound's going to give him a break soon, and Roadkill is going to take him around the stalls."

As she's agreeing she's glad Tommy's not being left out, a voice comes from behind.

"Hey, Sis."

I swing around, putting out a hand to shake Jason's before he leans in and gives Allie a peck on the cheek.

She waited until I was out of prison before contacting him, wary, I think, of meeting a member of the family which held no happy memories for her. They've spent more years apart than they had together, and needed to learn about each other all over again, as adults, not children. I don't think they'll ever be close, but that he's here to support her today speaks volumes.

"This is what mom should have done." Her brother glances around before returning his attention to his sister. "Spoken up, faced it head on. But instead of thinking it was a medical condition, she put all the blame on you, Alison."

Allie shrugs. "At times I hated Hope when I was carrying her. Well, not so much her, as what she was doing to me. But not when she was born."

"You're not your mom, Al," I reassure her. "You could never be."

"And you're not our dad," Jason pronounces, nodding at me. Then continues at our twin looks of curiosity. "I found him, you know? Having reconnected with you, I wanted to meet him. He's not a deadbeat, as Mom always said, but he's nothing to admire, either. Unlike Truck, when mom was sick with you, he couldn't take it and walked out. Thought he'd try again when you were older, but when Mom got pregnant again, didn't want to take the risk of history repeating itself. He said he couldn't take someone being sick the whole time. So he fucked off, that time, for good." He raises his chin my way. "Truck stuck beside you. You've got a good man, Alison."

"I know," she tells him, sparing a smile for me.

"Momma. Dada." Hope's getting agitated. I immediately see why.

"Down you go then."

Putting her gently on the ground, she immediately runs off, and is launched into the air by Drummer. He's always had a soft spot for my daughter, reckon that's because he stepped in when she was born. He's patient with her, but then he's done the baby thing a couple of times himself.

"Doing okay, Allie? Not getting too tired?"

Her eye roll gives Prez a negative answer. But I mouth, yes.

"Things will be wrapping up here shortly, anyway. Have you seen Dart and Alex?"

"Yeah, we spent some time with them earlier. Lost too."

"Pal and Jay are around somewhere as well," Allie says. "I wasn't sure Jay was going to give Hope back."

"I told you." I lean in, nudging her arm, "We should have run away and left her with them. You were too slow."

Allie's laugh, well, I'll never get tired of hearing it. The way her face lights up makes me want to leave Hope with Drummer, and take her away and find a barn or something, fuck, a wall will do. I will my cock to behave, this is a family affair and not the place to be sporting a hard on.

But Al's got enough experience to glance down as she sees me widen my stance, and a knowing look comes into her eyes. Then, she winks. A promise for later? Fucking hope so.

I also don't appear to have hidden it from Prez. "Best get this one tired out so you can have time to yourselves when we get back," he suggests, smirking.

"Like you're not doing the same with Eli and Zane," I counter.

He barks a laugh, and doesn't try to contradict.

"Hey, what am I missing?"

"Beef!"

I don't feel the slightest bit jealous as Allie throws herself into Beef's arms. Instead, once he's free, I give him a hug myself. A manly one, of course.

"Missing us yet, Beef?"

"Not as much as I'm missing my ol' lady. You haven't seen her, have you?"

Drummer nods. "She's with Sam. Think Sam's trying to adopt Max."

"Well, she won't have much luck with that," Beef says bluntly. "Ah, there she is."

A woman is approaching holding onto the harness of a dog who's unerringly leading her through the crowd toward us. When she reaches us, Allie starts talking to Steph and the two move slightly away.

"Allie okay now?" Beef leans in and quietly asks. "She's looking good."

"Still getting there," I reply. "But she'll be right in time."

"And, my niece?" He reaches out and takes Hope from Drummer. "How you doing, kiddo?"

"Dada."

"No, I'm not your dada. I'm your Uncle. Can you say Uncle Beef?"

"Bee."

"That'll do." He snorts a laugh.

My daughter cracks me up. I give him a moment, then take her back from him, grinning.

"Club settling down now, Beef?"

At Drummer's question, Beef's smile fades. "Getting there, Drummer. Getting there. Going to take a long time to get over that. Fuckin' hurts." His face has darkened. "Never saw it coming, no one did. Never fuckin' suspected."

"Don't see how you could have, Beef."

"So, how's Tucson, Drum?" Beef clearly wants to change the

subject and I'm not surprised. He's here to enjoy himself today, not rehash the recent troubles at the Pueblo club.

As they wander off, him collecting his old lady in the process, Allie comes back to my side.

"I'm ready to go home, Truck."

If she's admitting she's tired, she really is. I immediately summon a prospect and soon have my wife and child safely installed in the crash truck, and have issued strict instructions to drive my precious cargo home carefully.

I stay a bit longer, then ride back with my brothers. I walk up to the top of the compound and enter our house, still smelling of fresh paint. I peek into Hope's room, but she's not in her crib. Next I try our bedroom.

There, in the middle of the bed, curled up around our sleeping daughter is Allie, lost in the land of deep slumber herself.

I stand quiet at the door, just watching them, feeling my heart beating with love for them both.

I'd thought I'd never find a woman who'd want a scarred man like me. Thought I'd never have my dream of a family. Thought that wildfire had ended any chance of finding happiness in my life.

I'd been wrong. What it had given back was way better than anything I'd had before.

It's not been without its ups and downs. Allie's still not completely fit, and I still have nightmares, but what we're building together makes the past pale into insignificance.

What doesn't beat you, makes you stronger. Prez has said that a time or two, and he's got it right.

We survived.

We came through.

I couldn't wish for anything more than I've got at this moment.

EPILOGUE

TWENTY YEARS IN THE FUTURE

*D*rummer…

In the way of old men, we come back around to the subject we started with.

"Okay, you win, Drum. That time with Truck and Allie took its toll on the club. But it all worked out in the end, didn't it?" Peg turns to look at me. "Wouldn't say they had it easy, both had to work through their demons, but they did it together."

Rolling my head on my shoulders, I hear my neck creak. Another sign age is creeping up on me. "Sure, they did." I shudder slightly. "Of course, it wasn't long before Truck got the snip and made sure they wouldn't be adding to their family."

"But they did." Peg roars with laughter. "Though Grunt's nose was put out of joint."

Yeah, it had surprised all of us. For understandable reasons, Allie didn't want any more kids, and it wasn't only Truck that hadn't wanted to see her suffer, none of us did. That period had been fucking difficult on the club as a whole. I gaze at the stars just starting to

399

appear, and chuckle along with Peg. Truck, so in love with Allie, wanted to give her everything she'd ever wanted.

As if on cue, Precious appears, from under the clubhouse with a mouse in her mouth. Can't deny she earns her living, even at her advanced age. An unbelievable eighteen years old and that cat's still a good mouser—when one walks close enough. Most time she spends sleeping wherever she wants. She's outlived Heart and Marcia's wolfhound mix by quite a few years.

The timely appearance of Precious has caught Peg's eye as well. I remind him, "Still remember the day Truck brought her as a kitten onto the compound. Presented her to Allie in the clubhouse. Thought Allie was going to faint."

Truck hated cats, with good reason. But in getting Allie a kitten, he'd proven he loved his wife more.

"Yet, in the end, I think Truck was as taken by her as she was."

He's right there. They treat that darn cat like a second kid.

Peg goes quiet for a moment, then chuckles again as Eli comes marching up to the clubhouse, Olivia close behind.

"Shit comes and goes, but some things never change," he remarks.

Nah, they don't. Ollie's been following my son around since they were both babies in the clubhouse.

Eli raises his chin toward us, and jerks his head toward the clubhouse, then walks on past. From the sounds coming out of the window behind us, all the members are making moves to go into church.

"Ready for this?" Peg gets to his feet, his bones cracking as he does.

I take a deep breath, then let it out while looking around me. Remembering old times with Peg has helped confirm the decisions that have already been made, reminding me time marches on. I follow my sergeant-at-arms into the clubhouse, making my way across the room that's now emptied, and walk into church.

I take my seat, then listen to the sound of the gavel banging against the wood. While conversations come to an end, I glance around the table. I'd wanted to build up the mother chapter, and I'd been successful at the job. Over the years, faces had come and gone. Road, well, he'd transferred early on. Slick, sad, but he'd succumbed to lung cancer.

Hyde had decided the club wasn't for him and Sarah, and we allowed him to go without even a beatdown. Viper, another man lost, turned out he had a weak heart. God's ways of thinning our numbers, to make way for the new guard I suspect. No one wants a club full of old men.

"Brothers," a voice full of emotion starts from the head of the table. "Tonight marks a new chapter in the history of the Satan's Devils. I thank you for giving me your trust and voting me into the top seat."

Drew, or Wizard as I should call him, new prez of the Satan's Devils is looking straight down the table at me. I raise my chin.

Mouse is beaming proudly. Mariana had been dead set against her brother even joining the club, and now he's got the top spot.

Wraith, sitting on his left, raises his hand. "Prez," he nods at Wizard, "and I have already had this conversation, so it will come as no surprise to him. It's time for Wizard to pick his own second-in-command, so like Drummer, I'm stepping down." He slides off his cut, and taking out his knife, slices the VP patch off. He hands it over to Prez ceremonially, then vacates his seat. He goes to stand at the back of the room with his arms folded across his chest, and a wealth of emotion on his face.

I hadn't known about this, but it's not unexpected, and I reckon Wizard's got something up his sleeve. It seems too orchestrated.

"Brothers, I need a VP."

Eyes come to me, I hold my hands up. "Taking a leaf out of Hellfire's book. I'm done and dusted with leadership of the club, that's why I'm stepping down. Done my time, brothers."

Wizard nods as though that's what he wanted, confirmed when he says, "I propose Hawk steps up."

I can't help the look of pride that I'm sure I'm wearing. Eli hadn't stepped into the VP's shoes because of any nepotism, he's done it all on his own merits. I had to smile when early on he'd developed a take no prisoners attitude, and a steely grey death stare to rival my own. He'll make a good VP, and I wouldn't be surprised if one day he's president of his own club. Too young now, of course, at just twenty-three.

Then Peg barks a laugh. "Suppose you want fresh blood, Prez. Who you got in mind for my seat?"

Wizard turns his intelligent eyes on the sergeant-at-arms. "Don't want to push you out of your post, Brother."

Peg, still chuckling, states, "I've done my time. More than ready to pass the baton over."

Wizard raises his chin at him, "In that case, well, Hound."

He's a good choice and I nod approvingly. Hound had left us for a while, joined the Marines and did a few tours. Returned to the club about eight years back having gained knowledge and skills which will serve him well in his new role.

Hound himself seems surprised by the turn of events, but vacates his chair and with a broad grin, goes to sit at the right hand of his prez.

Blade growls and spins his knife. "Still got men to scalp in my future."

Wizard's eyes soften when they land first on his face, then drop to look pointedly at the hand that resembles a claw on the knife. The enforcer has become crippled with arthritis.

Blade sees where he's looking, grins and shrugs. "Aw, shucks. I'll step down as long as I'm still allowed to have fun from time to time."

"You're moving your fuckin' seat, Blade, not leaving the club." But from the look of sadness in Wizard's eyes, we all know that time may come. It will come to all of us old-timers when we're no longer able to ride. Christ, I'm not looking forward to that.

Blade's not finished. "If you're looking for my replacement, I nominate Throttle."

Peg's son, Noah. I glance at him and see him grinning proudly, and giving a nod of encouragement to his boy. Young, of course, but he's got the right character to take on the enforcer role. Big too, taking after his father, with a serious demeanour and a strong sense of right and wrong, when it comes to club regs of course.

Wizard laughs, "Couldn't think of a better man for the job, Blade. Throttle, step up."

After Blade and the new enforcer change places, Wizard raises his chin toward him, then looks at the man sitting by Eli's side. "Dollar, don't you go thinking of retirement. Still need someone to cook the books."

"Goddammit," says the treasurer, but I think he looks relieved.

"Or you either, Heart. Or Mouse."

"Christ, he's as bad as you, Drummer. Gonna have us in fuckin' harness until we die."

Laughter greets Mouse's observation. Nothing will ever stop that man doing what he does best. Even now he has a gadget with the latest technology in front of him. I see Wizard's eyes catch sight of it and gleam with interest. 'New?' he mouths, getting a nod back, 'yes'.

His mind quickly returns to the meeting. "Got another announcement," Prez begins. "I'll let the VP tell you his news."

Hawk's grin is wide, and he doesn't keep us waiting. "I plan on taking an ol' lady, need the vote to put my patch on her."

"'Bout fuckin' time," Wraith growls, from the seat vacated by Throttle. "If you ever hurt her, Eli…"

Now my son applies that death stare. "Have I ever fuckin' hurt her, Wraith? In all these years, have I ever fuckin' looked at another woman?"

"You certainly don't take after your dad," someone quips. I think it was Toady, and I give him a glare just in case.

"Let's vote," Prez suggests. "Think we all saw this coming."

Yeah, we had. From the time Eli and Ollie were in their cribs.

I sit back, vote 'aye', when the time comes and consider, with not a little pride, how the Satan's Devils Tucson chapter has turned out. It may not have been planned, but those of us with old ladies have chosen wisely it would seem, and now it's time to hand over to the new generation.

I'm hoping it will be a while before I have to hang up my riding boots, and while I've handed over the gavel, I've still got something to give. Leaning back I interlock my hands behind my totally white hair, and think of the future that's now opened up. Long rides alongside my old lady riding one of her bikes. In fact, Peg and I already have a ride planned to visit the other chapters. Taking our time with stops in nice spots. Riding to Utah in one day, for example, is no longer quite as comfortable as it once was.

Having voted Hawk can put his patch on Olivia, Wizard bangs the gavel. "Now we've got the touchy feely shit out of the way, let's get on with the updates. Roadkill? How did you and Cast get on when you paid a call on that pimp?"

"Truck came with us. Took out his fuckin' eye as a joke in front of him and put it in his pocket…"

Eli's eyes gleam just like they had when he was a kid. Seeing it, I shake my head. Seems like he hasn't grown out of his morbid fascination with Truck's eye despite how otherwise he's matured.

Truck nods and takes over. "He saw it as a sign we were about to get down to business, and ran the fuck off."

"Yeah," Roadkill takes over again. "Got in his car and drove, and from what we can make out, never came fuckin' back."

"Right," says Wizard. "I want confirmation of that. Mouse, can you get onto tracking him down? Let me know if you want me to help."

Mouse seems unfazed by the offer of Wizard's assistance in what was previously his sole area of expertise.

"Movin' on," Prez looks at Bolt. "Need some info from you so we can decide what to do next."

Club business. I wink at Peg. As he raises his chin at me and grins, I take it he's not going to be missing being in the thick of things either.

Blade, seeing our interaction, catches both our eyes, and thumps his hand over his chest.

Copying his gesture, I too bang my hand over my heart, while Wizard continues to conduct business from the seat I so recently vacated.

I sit back and listen, I don't mind. I've given more than forty years to this club, thirty plus as president. I'm not going anywhere, I'll still pull my weight as a member, but no longer having the decision making on my shoulders, it means I can relax.

The club's in good hands, Wizard has chosen wisely.

The club isn't about any one individual, whoever's at the helm, Satan's Devils will ride on.

Melissa

I fought it, fought it hard. I wasn't the type of woman a biker would go for. I'm a homely type, not adventurous or bold.

But he dragged me into his world, and I found I liked it. Loved the family vibe, how everyone would gather around to protect what was theirs.

Until, he disappeared. Wiped off the face of the earth. He'd pulled me in, now he's gone. The only explanation for him not coming back is that he's dead.

Pyro

She wasn't mine, and never could be. She'd been claimed by someone else. The perfect woman who I could never have as my own.

I stepped up when she needed someone beside her. Held her when she needed a friend. That my brother was dead was something I'd help her accept.

The truth though, that hit the hardest. How could any of us deal with the knowledge that there was something worse than death?

READING ORDER

Satan's Devils MC	Satan's Devils MC Colorado Chapter
Turning Wheels	
Drummer's Beat	
Slick Running	
Targeting Dart	
Heart Broken	
Peg's Stand	
Rock Bottom	
Joker's Fool	
Mouse Trapped	
	Paladin's Hell
Blade's Edge	
	Demon's Angel
	Devil's Due
Truck Stopped	
	Devil's Dilemma

Note 1:

Each book can be read as a standalone, but to get the best reading experience for the Satan's Devils, read the books in the order above.

Note 2:

While the Blood Brothers series is completely separate to the Satan's Devils series, there is some crossover. Turning Wheels continues the story of a minor character who appears in Second Changes, and some characters appear in both series.

OTHER WORKS BY MANDA MELLETT

<u>*Blood Brothers – A series about sexy dominant sheikhs and their*</u>
<u>*bodyguards*</u>

Stolen Lives (#1) Nijad and Cara

Close Protection (#2) Jon and Mia

Second Chances (#3) Kadar and Zoe

Identity Crisis (#4) Sean and Vanessa

Dark Horses (#5) Jasim and Janna

Hard Choices (#6) Aiza

Satan's Devils MC - Arizona Chapter

Turning Wheels (Blood Brothers #3.5, Satan's Devils #1) Wraith and Sophie

Drummer's Beat (#2) Drummer and Sam

Slick Running (#3) Slick and Ella

Targeting Dart (#4) Dart and Alex

Heart Broken (#5) Heart and Marc

Peg's Stand (#6) Peg and Darcy

Rock Bottom (#7) Rock and Becca

Joker's Fool (#8) Joker and Lady

Mouse Trapped (#9) Mouse and Mariana

Blade's Edge (#10) Blade and Tash

Satan's Devils MC - Colorado Chapter

Paladin's Hell (#1) Paladin and Jayden

Demon's Angel (#2) Demon and Violet

Devil's Due (#3)

#Coming Soon: Devil's Dilemma (#4)

GLOSSARY

Motorcycle Club – An official motorcycle club in the U.S. is one which is sanctioned by the American Motorcyclist Association (AMA). The AMA has a set of rules its members must abide by. It is said that ninety-nine percent of motorcyclists in America belong to the AMA

Outlaw Motorcycle Club (MC) – The remaining one percent of motorcycling clubs are historically considered outlaws as they do not wish to be constrained by the rules of the AMA and have their own bylaws. There is no one formula followed by such clubs, but some not only reject the rulings of the AMA, but also that of society, forming tightly knit groups who fiercely protect their chosen ways of life. Outlaw MCs have a reputation for having a criminal element and supporting themselves by less than legal activities, dealing in drugs, gun running or prostitution. The one-percenter clubs are usually run under a strict hierarchy.

Brother – Typically members of the MC refer to themselves as brothers and regard the closely knit MC as their family.

Cage – The name bikers give to cars as they prefer riding their bikes.

Chapter – Some MCs have only one club based in one location. Other MCs have a number of clubs who follow the same bylaws and wear the same patch. Each club is known as a chapter and will normally carry the name of the area where they are based on their patch.

Church – Traditionally the name of the meeting where club business is discussed, either with all members present or with just those holding officer status.

Colours – When a member is wearing (or flying) his colours he will be wearing his cut proudly displaying his patch showing which club he is affiliated with.

Cut – The name given to the jacket or vest which has patches denoting the club that member belongs to.

Enforcer – The member who enforces the rules of the club.

Hang-around – This can apply to men wishing to join the club and who hang-around hoping to be become prospects. It is also used to women who are attracted by bikers and who are happy to make themselves available for sex at biker parties.

Mother Chapter – The founding chapter when a club has more than one chapter.

Nomad – In an outlaw MC a **nomad** is typically a member who's been given permission/instruction by the national president to enforce the laws of the club at other chapters.

Patch – The patch or patches on a cut will show the club that member belongs to and other information such as the particular chapter and any role that may be held in the club. There can be a number of other patches with various meanings, including a one-percenter patch. Prospects will not be allowed to wear the club patch until they have been patched-in, instead they will have patches which denote their probationary status.

Patched-in/Patching-in – The term used when a prospect completes his probationary status and becomes a full club member.

President (Prez) – The officer in charge of that particular club or chapter.

Prospect – Anyone wishing to join a club must serve time as a probationer. During this period they have to prove their loyalty to the club. A probationary period can last a year or more. At the end of this period, if they've proved themselves a prospect will be patched-in.

Old Lady – The term given to a woman who enters into a permanent relationship with a biker.

RICO – The Racketeer Influenced and Corrupt Organisations Act primarily deals with organised crime. Under this Act the officers of a club could be held responsible for activities they order members to do and a conviction carries a potential jail service of twenty years as well as a large fine and the seizure of assets.

Road Captain – The road captain is responsible for the safety of the club on a run. He will organise routes and normally ride at the end of the column.

Ronin – A biker who travels alone, sometimes wearing a patch denoting he's Ronin. Not affiliated to any club, but often bearing a token which will help ensure safe passage through territories of different clubs.

Secretary – MCs are run like businesses and this officer will perform the secretarial duties such as recording decisions at meetings.

Sergeant-at-Arms – The sergeant-at-arms is responsible for the safety of the club as a whole and for keeping order.

Sweet Butt – A woman who makes her sexual services available to any member at any time. She may well live on the club premises and be fully supported by the club.

Treasurer – The officer responsible for keeping an eye on the club's money.

Vice President (VP) – The vice president will support the president, stepping into his role in his absence. He may be responsible for making sure the club runs smoothly, overseeing prospects etc.

ACKNOWLEDGMENTS

When I was first persuaded to write Turning Wheels, I had no idea it would turn into an eleven book series and be the start of several other spin off series too.

I'd just written my third book in the Blood Brothers series, and had included a throwaway line that a minor character, who'd been put in a wheelchair, and had gone to an outlaw MC in Tucson for protection. What happened to her? Came the question from all quarters, including my editor and readers.

For a while I resisted taking it further, while the idea lurked at the back of my mind. I'd used the location of Tucson as it was a place I'd visited on more than one occasion, a place that I loved and could picture in my head. I knew what it was like to ride a bike, we'd owned a Harley for twenty-five years, but riding with the local Harley Owners Club did not qualify me for writing about an MC in the US.

But slowly Sophie and Wraith started living in my head, and the more I thought about them, the more they excited me. I could do this, perhaps, if it was a short novella, a one off.

What a joke! They had so much to tell me, and, as the characters in the Satan's Devils MC began to gain life, Turning Wheels turned into a full length book. Not only that, Drummer started asking, what about me? Don't I deserve a woman for myself? Then I wanted to write about Slick and Ella, and explain why he claimed someone who then disappeared. One by one the stories began to unfold.

I can't tell you how happy it makes me to know my boys have found places in so many people's hearts. To every reader who's taken the Satan's Devils MC journey with me, thank you so much.

The main series has to come to an end, but I've written this final chapter with a heavy heart. I don't want to leave my men behind. So I won't. They belong to the mother chapter and will pop up from time to time in other books. There'll be at least one more book about a character you've come to love.

I've already started the Satan's Devil's Colorado Chapter series, and the next book, Devil's Dilemma, will be the fourth. After that I intend to stay with Colorado for at least one more book.

Where after that? Well, there's that mysterious chapter in Utah which no one knows much about. Maybe Drummer should send someone there to investigate? How are Lost and Dart getting along with the San Diego club that suffered so much betrayal? Have they managed to hold it together?

I can't forget Red and the boys in Las Vegas. We learned a lot about them in Joker's Fool, and I know more than one of you want to know about Rope and Cuff.

There will be many more Satan's Devils coming along.

I hope you liked Truck Stopped. It could never be a feel good book due to the trials Truck and Allie went through. I hope you enjoyed the glimpses into the future of the club, and how the new generation has panned out. Will I ever write about them? My gut feeling is no. But then, I was proved wrong when I first started out with the Devils, so perhaps the answer should be 'maybe' instead.

Now to the thank yous.

Readers, I am in absolute awe of the messages I get sent, the comments on Facebook and the reviews. While I'm sitting at my lonely desk it's hard to imagine how each book will be received. I'm blown away how you love my bikers as much as I do. It's you buying, reviewing and letting me know you enjoy my books that keeps me ploughing on. So a massive thank you to each and every one of you.

I wasn't sure about Truck Stopped when I'd finished it. So uncertain I subjected only my editor and one beta reader to the first draft in case I had to tear it up and start again. I was amazed to receive the comment back that I had another winner on my hands. Wait, what? But the book's all doom and gloom, isn't it? So I sent it out to other beta readers, and got positive feedback back.

My wonderful team of beta readers – Danena, who read the first draft and who helped shape the final version and who is very good at picking up UK English terminology that sneaks in. We often have a laugh as I teach her the meaning of some words. Terra, Tami, Zoe, Nicole and Alex who also came back with amazing comments giving me the encouragement to press that publish button. I must give special thanks not only to Danena, but to Sheri who's eagle eyes spotted something not in this book, but in Blade's Edge.

A confession. I always had it in my head that Truck went with Allie the night before he left for California. Sheri pointed out that this was impossible for him to do, as she was manning the bar that night. One word change in Blade's Edge sorted that out. It's incredible that I have beta readers who go that extra mile, not just reading the current book, but having a better knowledge than I of what I wrote in a previous book.

Although it's my name on the cover of the book, it takes a team to bring the final version to you. One very important member of that team is my editor, Maggie Kern. Sometimes she has a hard job translating my UK English to the US version. I enjoy working with her so much. Her suggestions are excellent and help shape the book. Maggie, thank you.

This is the second time I've worked with proofreader Melanie Darrow. Thank you, Melanie, and I'm grateful for your positive words about this series and so glad you enjoy proofreading these books.

Once again Lia Rees has come up with an amazing cover. Thank you.

My life is definitely made easier by my PA Tracy Wood. By taking over a lot of my social media tasks, she allows me to concentrate on writing. She also does my graphics for the teasers, taking far less time than I would. My skill is getting words on the page, so the more time I have to do this, the faster I can bring you more books.

My success is growing, slowly, but surely. Part of that is down to you readers who, without hoping for thanks, promote my series on social media. I promise I see you, and appreciate every single mention. It helps immensely to grow my audience.

Reviews obviously help authors, and I'm grateful for each and every one written. I love hearing what you think about my books, and there's no denying, the more reviews a book gets, the more successful it becomes. So if you can see your way to leaving one, you'll make this – and any other author you review – very happy.

Apologies for the acknowledgements being so long this time around, but I felt it important as I feel it's the end of one thing, but the start of something new.

I do hope you'll continue to accompany me on the Satan's Devils' ride.

There'll be another Devil along very soon.

STAY IN TOUCH

Email: manda@mandamellet.com

Website: www.mandamellet.com

Sign up for my newsletter to hear about new releases in the Satan's Devils and Blood Brothers series.

Facebook reader group: https://www.facebook.com/groups/mandasbadboys/

facebook.com/mandamellet

twitter.com/manda_mellett

ABOUT THE AUTHOR

Manda's life's always seemed a bit weird, starting with a child-hood that even today she's still trying to make sense of, then losing her parents in the late teens. Going from the tragic to the bizarre, who else could be unlucky enough to have had two car accidents, neither her fault, one involving a nun, and another involving a police woman?

There isn't enough space to list everything that's happened to Manda, or what she's learned from it. But by using the rich fabric of her personal life, psychology degree, varied work experiences, and amazing characters she's met, Manda is able to populate her books with believable in-depth characters and enjoys pitting them against situations which challenge them. Her books are full of suspense, twists and turns and the unexpected.

Manda lives in the beautiful countryside of Essex in the UK, the area's claim to fame being the Wilkin's Jam Factory at nearby Tiptree. She can usually find jars of jam which remind her of home wherever she goes. As well as writing books and reading, Manda loves walking her dogs and keeping fit. She lives with her husband of over 30 years, who, along with her son, is her greatest fan and supporter.

Manda is thankful that one of the more unusual, and at the time unpleasant, turns her life took, now enables her to spend her time writing. Confirming, in her view, every cloud has a silver lining.

Photo by Carmel Jane Photography